THE
NAMES
OF
HEAVEN

Flavia Idà

Cover design by Niki Lenhart
nikilen-designs.com

Published by Paper Angel Press
paperangelpress.com

ISBN 978-1-944412-56-2 (Trade Paperback)

10 9 8 7 6 5 4 3 2 1

For more information about the author and her work visit:
flaviasvoice.com

Dedication

For my son Adam,
born in the New World to parents born in the Old.

With thanks to
Adnan Aydin, Daniel J. Langton and Steven Radecki
for their help and support.

N

Ecab

Mani

Xelha

Tulum

Canpech

Island
of
Cuzumil
(Cozumel)

PROVINCE
OF COCHUAH

Champoton

Xul Ha

Culùa
Mexica
(Mexico)

Chetemal
(Chetumal)

Cuautemallan
(Guatemala)

Ulùa

Honduras

"Here it was again, that most ancient of road forks. The choice of one course or the other had nothing to do with power, money, knowledge, love or age. It was a purely internal matter. Every child older than six knew the fork, and knew what the good guys did there and what the bad guys did there. The fork was a familiar one the world over, and the good guys and the bad guys, whether dressed in chaps, togas, overalls, ponchos, chain mail, crinoline, leopard skins or pinstripes, all separated there."

— *Kurt Vonnegut Jr.,* Player Piano

BOOK ONE

THE CASTAWAY AND THE SLAVE

ONE

A ll through the night the reef had waited for them, and now it had them. There was a sudden crack of planks splitting in half, the noise of the rock biting into the ship, then the wind rushing in through the broken ribs. The rigging snapped, chain links ground apart. The mainmast doubled up on itself and came down smashing onto the deck. Canvas ripped from one end to the other, and the topsail flew away in the night. The prow reared up, shook, stuck in the grip of the stone. The sea flooded into the hull.

They all heard them, the sounds that meant no hope. Crawling, pushing, wrestling the ropes and barrels that trapped them, the men reached out toward the only lifeboat left whole. They fought to be first.

Captain Valdivia's voice raged against the gale. "We can still float her, you bastards. I say we can!" He called the first mate. "Santiago, cut the mast loose. Send Felipe and two more below deck." But they all ignored him, as though their names didn't belong to them anymore.

1

Santiago Alvarado crossed himself, holding onto a spar. "No, Señor Don Capitán. We couldn't float her if she grew wings." He looked over his shoulders. "The boat, Señor Don Capitán!"

Captain Valdivia cursed, his hand welded to the wheel. "Stay back, damn you. Mind your places!"

The men heard only their own fear. They put their hands to the capstan and struggled against the rope to lower the boat. "Mother of God, deliver us from evil. Queen of the Sea, save our lives." But the sea had no ears and no heart, the sea had only a mouth.

The boat hit the water. The men held onto the rope until their hands bled. The keel cracked, timbers fell apart. Muskets and crossbows slid down the half-sunken deck. Like yellow hail the twenty thousand gold coins of King Ferdinand of Spain pelted the waves. Off plunged the fine steel breastplates, the letters and reports to His Honor the Governor of Hispaniola, and Juan de Córdoba with his good sword on, and Diego García with the name of his woman slurring in his mouth.

The ship groaned out loud beneath them. At last Captain Valdivia let go of the wheel and tumbled toward the gunwale.

"Find me the lookout," he begged. "Get the son of a whore into my hands." But the lookout lay crushed under the mast and had paid already for looking the other way when out of the water the Víboras had lashed out, true to their name of Viper Rocks.

The men fell, jumped, slipped into the boat—without sail, without oars and without food or water. The wounded screamed in pain, trampled.

Someone was crying out from the twisted shadows of the ship. "Don't leave me behind. For the love of God, help me!"

Gonzalo Guerrero reached out with both hands and felt the wet, desperate grip of Jerónimo de Aguilar. He pulled Jerónimo down, as their weight sank the boat further and the others fought and shoved to keep their places. Aguilar crouched in his sliver of space. In a frenzy he kissed the prayer book he'd salvaged from his hammock. The keel came apart. The night sounded like wood and iron.

The fallen sails had covered the stern, a shroud for the burial. Captain Valdivia looked up at the wheel that was spinning as if under a ghost's crazed hand. The pride and sweat of his whole life, his pretty *Esperanza* with the gilded figurehead was shuddering her last in the waves.

Slowly the laden boat drifted into the black nothing. It pitched and it scratched along the edges of the reef. The men threw out their hands blindly, feeling for the hard stone blades. Then the sea pulled them into its void.

Gonzalo Guerrero crossed his arms, his fingers clawing with cold and with fear at his sodden shirt; and like all his nineteen companions he thought, That's all I'm left with now, my life and my shirt.

Five days. The sea was smooth now and the wind was gentle, that tropical wind smelling of spice that drove them toward a point it alone knew. Five days they'd lived like steers packed in a slaughterhouse, close enough to hear the next man's thoughts knocking against one's skull. They'd laid the wounded on the bottom, on the others' feet. They wailed and begged continuously. The bilge water had turned brown with blood and vomit. During the night the wind froze them, during the day the sun scorched them. Those who could sleep woke up screaming, maddened by the endless rocking of the boat, their tongues cracked with thirst and their stomachs shrunk with hunger.

Once in a while someone started to rave and tried to walk out of the boat. "I'm going to Prudencio's tavern for some wine. Who wants to come with me?" Captain Valdivia raised his voice and quieted the man down. He could still keep some order among his men, who were no longer his men but the sea's. He'd threatened to throw overboard the next man who started a brawl: they all needed the extra room.

Most of the time they lay coiled against the sun, in attitudes of orphans helping one another to sleep. Then someone would burst into fevered talk, about how beautiful Castile looked at harvest time, about how they were all going to live and to remember. They would start trying to catch fish with their hands.

"Let's hope the currents take us eastward, into the sight of baptized eyes," Leon Sandoval kept saying.

Santiago Alvarado the first mate cursed him. He was a big, quarrelsome man with a thick beard.

"Damn your soul, boy, can't you even recognize the cardinal points anymore? We're drifting to the west, away from known land."

"And what is to the west, in God's sweet name," Leon broke out with a fit of cough. "The stars at night make no sense. No one's had time to name them yet."

Captain Valdivia was holding in his lap the head of the dying helmsman. He looked at nothing.

"Maya," he said through swollen lips. "I spoke to Don Cristóbal Colón seven years ago, when he returned from his fourth voyage." He seemed to smile. "He told so many lies he made me want to have a ship… To the west of Cuba, he said, is a land called Maya."

Leon lay back and moaned in his teeth. "Maya" was just a name, a single outcrop of syllables against an entire breadth of dread. They still belonged to the unknown.

Felipe del Castillo grumbled something to himself, his forehead matted with blood. "That old madman, talking about Paradise as though he'd seen with his own two eyes Adam and Eve running about naked!" His face twisted. "Lord God, we're here on account of a fool, we die because of an old man's delusions!"

Captain Valdivia forced him to go back to his corner. The sun pressed down on the bare heads, on the parched mouths. The boat stank like an open coffin.

"Paradise," Felipe murmured. "He called it Paradise."

Gonzalo Guerrero looked at the black fin that had been following them for two days and nights. He was a tall, well- proportioned young man with a handsome broad face and hair the color of dark copper. He'd always been content with his looks. Work had made him strong, and women found him pleasant. He watched the sea around him.

At the other end of that sea wide as the breath of God there was Palos de Moguer, where he was born and from where, when

Gonzalo was barely five, Christopher Columbus had sailed to search for the Indies. By now his uncle would be pulling the nets in by the cove. His sister would be sewing, with supper ready. By now his parents' grave would again be growing with poppies.

It was a tough sea, stingy old cheat. It called him in the nights; it told him to come, to come. He had listened for hours to the same tale, told and retold in Palos, the tale of the mad Italian who had nagged three ships from the sovereigns of Castile and had gone off to find another world.

The strange animals, the strange people old Don Cristóbal had brought back from that other world. The fever, the dreams he'd stirred. They had haunted Gonzalo's childhood, then his adolescence, then his manhood. He pulled in fish and he thought endlessly of, "some day, some day." He went to bed hungry and in his sleep the Queen of Cathay wanted to marry him.

In 1502, when the Admiral had set out on his fourth voyage, Gonzalo had begged his father to let him go with him. He was sixteen, and for his last expedition Don Cristóbal had enlisted boys, some as young as twelve. His father had refused. Gonzalo, mingled to the crowd that watched the Admiral walk down the pier for the last time, had thought of jumping after the ship.

Then his father had died, leaving him with nothing to keep him in Palos anymore. He had strained long enough at the bit, yearning to escape that hencoop of oppression and toil. Finally the day

he'd turned twenty, old enough for the law, he'd gone out of the house, bought a second-hand breastplate and signed up for the next caravel due to sail for the Caribe. His sister had cried while she sewed the image of the Virgin of Seville in his good coat. His uncle hadn't said anything, except that he wanted him back by next year's Easter, to help out with the herrings; and Gonzalo had promised.

So he had endured the four months at sea that it took to reach that other world. Four months of nightmares on a filthy hammock, of cockroaches and lashings and womanless misery, always with the vision of Eldorado burning the sense from his mind: to be fed gold in bowls at breakfast and supper, to be awash in gold like the sunset!

Not that he knew where this gold was to be found. No one knew. He thought of streams where he would pan under the natives' benign eyes, or of marketplaces where they would trade cloth and axes for the precious metal. He imagined the day he would return home with a hatful of nuggets the size of duck's eggs. "Uncle, buy a new boat. Sister, no more scrubbing laundry in the river for the Countess Moncada." He had stepped off the gangplank walking like a prince.

Then had come the brutal awakening. There was no gold in the Caribe, certainly not enough for a hatful. The bright yellow light had gone out for him as it had for countless others, beginning with Don Cristóbal himself. For three years he had followed ship after ship to island after island: to Hispaniola, to Darién, to Jamaica, to Cuba.

There was no gold anywhere, no silver and no gems, no palaces of the Queen of Cathay. There was nothing but mosquitoes, alligators and snakes—green hell.

The sole property that could be acquired was the islanders, a people as simple as the air that was their only clothing. They laughed and wondered at the newcomers, they brought them food and drink and women; and they could be driven to abject terror by the mere noise of the guns, by the mere sight of the horses. It had been the islanders who'd paid in full for everything that wasn't there.

What Gonzalo had seen in the Caribe had been enough to sadden him for the rest of his life. He'd always thought the Spaniards went to Mass every Sunday and paid their taxes to the king. Here, where there were no churches and the king was many thousand of miles away, the Spaniards did something else. They hunted the natives down, burned them alive, tortured them to make them say where they'd hidden the gold they didn't have; they raped little girls and they hanged old women.

On Hispaniola an adventurer named Hernando Cortez rounded up men and women with his dogs and worked them to death by the hundreds in his estates. Because the population of the islands had been almost wiped out in less than ten years since the New World had been found, black slaves now had to be shipped in from Africa, to be worked to death in their turn.

Left on their own, the petty governors sent from Spain with nothing more than a title on a piece of paper passed the time making war on one another, while the gallows kept sprouting everywhere now for this, now for this other "traitor to the Crown," rows of black gallows all along the coral shores of Paradise.

Gonzalo had felt caught in a trap, betrayed by everything he had ever held dear. He knew he didn't want to go home empty-handed; but he knew even more that he was sick at heart of having to bear daily witness to the nightmare that the New World had become. It seemedthat every evil from which he had tried to escape had been carried to the islands in the hold of the ships and was now flourishing tenfold.

Not knowing what to do, he'd kept risking his life on land and sea for nothing more than his sailor's pay, a pound of salt pork every week, and an allowance of hopes gone insane. When yet another war had broken out, this time between Diego Nicuesa and Vasco Nuñez de Balboa, he'd signed his name on Captain Valdivia's roll only because Captain Valdivia paid a few *maravedí* more than other captains.

All he wanted was to get away long enough to decide once and for all. Now he was drifting to his death, having found nothing, not even an answer.

He turned his head away from his companions. The sea was so close, and waiting with its terrifying smile.

Ten days. The ship's cook, whose ribs had been broken by a falling spar, was dead. They waited for the sharks to lag behind, then cast him overboard. During the night two more men died, simply gave up. There was more room now, but the empty places meant it all would soon be an empty place. Wounds festered. Their skin had begun to wrinkle and crack like that of old men.

Captain Valdivia had stopped shouting. He was a hard, graying man who now cursed himself under his breath for wanting to cry. But Leon Sandoval used his good eyesight to scan the endless water for signs of land. Once a cormorant flew over, making him cry out that the coast must be near. He was a boy of fifteen.

Hallucinations taunted their minds. On the ninth day the bosun flung himself into the sea, claiming he'd seen a vineyard full of ripe Málaga grapes. Before they could pull him back in, the sharks found him in an instant. But that day it rained, and they gathered the rain in their hands, in their boots, in anything they could get, sobbing at the wet bliss in their throats. They held up their faces with their mouths open, drinking until they retched.

Jerónimo de Aguilar spent his every waking minute reading from his prayer book and praying for the salvation of his soul.

Gonzalo could hear him whisper Latin in his teeth, hurrying to repent.

Jerónimo was a thin but not delicate man, with soft hands and the skittish manners of a schoolboy. To his parents, who kept a butcher shop in Écija, his religious vocation had come at first like a catastrophe, for he was the son who must follow in their footsteps.

When he had made his decision to sail for the Indies, they knew he lusted not merely for gold but also for heathen souls to convert to Christ. However, they had reasoned in giving him their blessing, if there was gold in the heathens' lands, a rich priest would be even better than a rich merchant.

So far, for Jerónimo the rewards of both profit and proselytizing had been slim. He had spent whatever money he had in preparing a lawsuit against a man who wanted to cheat him out of a piece of land on Hispaniola. The lawsuit was the reason for his voyage aboard the *Esperanza*. The documents he was bringing with him for this purpose had now been lost in the wreck.

As for the spreading of the Gospel that was so dear to his heart, all the islanders of the Caribe had already been converted, more often than not at sword point, and they now flocked to Mass, though some of the friars said it was only to get some respite from their labor. Even so, now that the Lord was calling him to His presence, Jerónimo had at least one good deed to bring before His judgment. With eloquent pleas he'd been able to persuade an old cacique to accept confession, before the man was burned at the stake for arguing that Mary could not be both a Virgin and the Mother of God.

Against the glare of the sun, Gonzalo eyed him closely. He'd never been fond of Jerónimo. There had been many times during their voyage when his piety had galled him. It had an answer for everything; it made Gonzalo wonder what was is that made some people so vulnerable to that sort of unblinking faith. Fear, certainly; of the elements, of illness, of all that could not be explained. Of all these things Gonzalo too was afraid, like all men. But he also loved whatever justice could be done on earth and now instead of somewhere else and later. For the sake of justice he could become fearless. Once he had protested the punishment of a shipmate whom everyone knew was innocent, and he had ended up sharing the man's appointed lashes.

After his father's death he had saved up what little money his uncle gave him and he had spent it to have a priest teach him to read and write. He had seen how easily those who handled a quill cheated those who didn't. If he could even the odds, it was worth going without bread and wine and everything else.

It was taking too long to die, he thought. Once God makes up His mind, He should at least be quick. A sound like a sob came from him. Jerónimo looked at him with a haunted look.

"Brother Guerrero," he said. "I pray for you too. Take heart, for soon we will all be in the glory of the Saints."

Thirteen days, and Christ's own passion had lasted only one. By now some were so dry they could not weep or urinate. One of the officers burned out in a single night. The helmsman and Luís Gallego lingered on, dwindling like candles.

During his last hours Luís begged Jerónimo to confess him and absolve him of his sins. Jerónimo looked terribly sad.

"I'm not a priest yet, brother Luís. I took holy orders when I was a boy, but I have not the power to absolve you." He helped Luís join his hands. "Confess to God and to Jesus. In His mercy He will hear you."

Luís' lips quivered. His eyes stared out with a grief beyond words. With that grief that no one could soothe, he went.

They didn't throw the three bodies overboard because the sharks were all around. They had to leave them where they lay, their faces covered with their shirts, horrible to feel at night when the flesh of the living turned as cold as the flesh of the dead. Death had become their only deity. Hurry up, they prayed, hurry up you old whore. And when the coast smiled, they felt almost as though they'd been cheated.

It was Leon the boy who sighted it. His mouth was too dry for him to shout. He started waving his arms with inarticulate sounds. From the water it looked truly like the piece of Paradise in old don Cristobal's tales: green and wild, tangled with trees and brush, skirted in pink beaches and humming with herons.

Captain Valdivia crossed himself. "O Blessed Mother of God, we thank Thee."

As if welcoming them, flamingos rose high, long red wings flapping. Gently then the current nudged the boat into the lagoon.

Gonzalo could not take his eyes off the shore. Relief as fierce as pain gripped him. He crawled over the gunwale and let himself fall into the water. It was clear as new glass and warm as milk. He floated, arms outstretched, his blunted senses savoring the rebirth.

They tumbled out of the boat and onto the sand. A few of the men had to be carried and put in the shade. Jerónimo sank to his knees and kissed the ground. Others joined him in whispered prayers to God's infinite and infinitely incomprehensible mercy. For a long time they just sat, pressing their hands on the comforting firmness of the earth. Then the well-known endeavors of survival flooded back into their minds, sent trickles of forgotten energy through their limbs.

Captain Valdivia began dividing the men to their tasks. "Felipe and Leon, you two seem strong enough to go searching for fresh water. I need others to make a grave for the dead. The rest of those who can walk will look for food."

Gonzalo reached into his boot, pulled out his good knife. "Who else has daggers?" he asked. "We can tie them to branches, use them as spears. If the savages can survive, by god so shall we."

"We'll build a raft, sail back to Hispaniola," said Ponce Noriega the gunner.

"Yes, but where are we?" wondered Pedro Mendez.

Captain Valdivia took off his soiled shirt. "That we will find out later. To your tasks, now. Stay within earshot if you can."

Up in the palm trees the brown jays chattered like gossips, curious about the strangers. The air was hot in the long afternoon of the Caribe. The men worked slowly. Each movement was painfully tiring, but they were held now by their new hope. They dug a shallow pit in the sand, placed the three dead bodies in it and covered them with more sand. With twigs and dry seaweed Jerónimo fashioned a cross and planted it on the grave.

In the shallows there were sea urchins, abalone and crabs; on the beach, turtle eggs and a dead bird. The men wobbled, fell, crawled back up, maddened by their hunger and their clumsiness. Then they gathered around with whatever they'd been able to find and started to scrape, cut, break and divide the food, their mouths open in anticipation.

"We look like old women making supper," Gonzalo said. "Old gypsy women in Granada."

Before sundown Felipe and Leon were back with the news of fresh water they'd found not too far away. The water was a bit brackish, but clear. They had gathered some in large waxy leaves, and the others fell onto it. Like a nurse Jerónimo fed small pieces of mussels to Alonso Carrera, who was too weak to sit up. They ate the turtle eggs with the soft shells and all. The seaweed provided the salt they all craved.

Then Rodrigo Gutierrez told the others to watch, for he was going to piss. They clapped their hands at the feat and bet on who'd be next. Life, wayward and drunken, had resumed its place among them.

The night came slowly, spreading long layers of blue over the ocean and raising clouds that looked like tall baroque ceilings. They lay down on the sand next to each other, and sleep took them quickly.

11

Now they could speak again the word that helps a man's heart to beat: *mañana*, tomorrow.

TWO

Gonzalo woke up in a sweat, his mind still plagued with demons. But there was sand under him, softer than any bed he'd ever lain upon. A toucan blinked his staring eye at him and flapped away. The dawn was fresh, soothed him like a linen handkerchief. So many things to do today that he'd come back from the dead, he thought.

Many were still asleep. He looked around, scavenging for leftovers. He couldn't wait to return to the reef, where yesterday he'd spotted a lobster's nest. If only they had a cooking pot, he thought, and some olives and some onions, they could made *pescado en escabeche* just like his mother used to make. He laughed softly to himself.

He saw that Captain Valdivia was awake. "What shall we do today, Señor Don Capitán?" he asked.

"We'll move to the other end of the beach," Captain Valdivia answered, "closer to where the drinking water is. We'll build some sort of shelter. We'll wait for our strength to come back. One thing at a time."

Gonzalo saluted. "Aye aye, Señor Don Capitán. One blessed thing at a time."

Leon pulled himself up on his elbow and eyed the jungle behind them. He looked like a baby, his pretty face still soft with sleep. "What about savages, Señor Don Capitán? They are bound to be somewhere in the land."

Captain Valdivia stood up. "So they are. What sort of savages, I don't know. I wish to God I had my pistols with me." He touched Santiago on the shoulder. "We move camp. Into that thicket of palm trees, here we're too exposed."

With the sun the parrots woke up. Alligators slid ponderously down their trails, oblivious to the ragged men walking in single file along the surf so that the waves would erase their footprints. They made a hole in the ground and lined it with mangrove leaves, to keep in it drinking water for those who couldn't go get it themselves. They found *sapota* fruit and scooped out with delight the sweet sticky flesh. Then again they spread out in search of food. When the morning grew ripe they returned with their catch.

They sat down to eat and to drink. Hummingbirds whirred by, shimmering like Venetian glass. The men were hungry, intent upon the vital motions of picking up and chewing food. They didn't notice the sudden silence that had congealed the air around them. Then a sound like the bellowing of a bull echoed across the beach, chased away the gulls. They froze, the unswallowed morsels turning woody in their mouths. Gonzalo bent down slowly over the knife he carried in his boot, then looked up. To be surrounded he expected, but never by so amazing a breed of natives.

They were a small race, like the islanders, and like the islanders they had eyes as black as obsidian. But the islanders were as plain as plucked birds, while not an inch of these people seemed to have been left to artlessness. Their foreheads were flattened and their hair bound with bright feathers.

Their faces were tattooed and their bodies painted red and black. They wore good cotton breechclouts and mantles.

Some were clad in jaguar skins draped over their shoulders. No less wealth and skill showed in their weapons—flint knives as painstakingly honed as Toledo swords, strong spears and spear- throwers, large three-pronged shells whittled to razor-sharp edges and looking like havoc. Any Spanish nobleman on his Sunday stroll would have admired such fierce finery.

Between the two crowds the astonishment hung heavy. Both groups stood hunched over, like hunters trying to guess the power of the unknown beasts they'd come upon. Felipe crossed himself.

"Holy Lord Jesus, we're dead," he whispered.

One of the painted warriors lifted to his mouth a conch shell, and again the deep bellowing sound reverberated in the air. Ponce tried to stand up, but didn't have time. With cries and clattering of weapons the natives fell onto the castaways, seized them two to a man and forced them out into the open.

Captain Valdivia struggled and shouted. Alonso Carrera had to be dragged, more dead than alive. It took three to subdue Alvarado the first mate. They grabbed hold of his hair and pulled him up from the ground. Another throng of warriors ran to the boat moored on the beach, looked inside, found nothing. They smashed stones through the bottom and sank it. A third group scattered the food and gathered up the two daggers that lay on the sand. They yelled like wildcats.

Not after all he'd been through, Gonzalo thought as he tossed in the hold of his captors. He was a good head taller than any of them, and if starvation hadn't taken the sinew out of him he could have thrown them back as they came. Stunned, drained of strength, he and the others let themselves be herded away from the beach and into the jungle.

"Tell them who we are, Señor Don Capitán," Leon begged. "Tell them we just want to go back to Hispaniola."

"Where are they taking us, what do they want with us," Pedro kept asking, limping on his right leg. The warriors shouted over their voices. They would not let them speak to each other.

"We're Spaniards, we're Castilians," Santiago roared. "Take your filthy heathen hands off me."

The trail they'd taken wound deeper into the bush. Clouds of butterflies swarmed around them like splinters of rainbow. Hot and humid as a huge cocoon, the jungle crackled with a thousand secret sounds and smells.

They hadn't looked in his boot, Gonzalo thought. But it was just one knife, and they were so many. How long had they been walking? The man who marched him on wore a strange bracelet, a full jaw with all the teeth in it. Gonzalo couldn't tell whether it was a human jaw, and he didn't want to tell.

"Filthy savages, shit eaters, "Santiago was cursing.

The trail was narrower now, forcing them to walk single-file. They stumbled through red knots of enormous cedar roots, then bent low under yokes of tough, tangles leaves. Petulant macaws scolded the intruders. Monkeys hung hidden and high like hairy acrobats, howling.

Then the jungle parted. They were before a large white road raised on a solid bed of stone, running straight and level between banks of cactus and lanky trees. Two stone markers covered with complicated signs stood at the point where the trail joined the causeway. The warriors drew their prisoners along, unmindful of their amazement. The last time they'd seen a road as handsome as this one they were still in Spain. What place was this? Where had God in His wisdom cast them?

The causeway was as smooth as if it had just been built, unmarred by wheel ruts or hoof prints. Small groups of men stopped to stare at the captives. They carried packs of some dried brown leaves, the bulky loads held by tumplines. Merchants, slaves? Gonzalo wondered. Both categories were unknown in the islands of the Caribe. The mystery of this land gnawed at his soul.

The road fanned into a glade. The jungle thinned out and another miracle appeared, a town. Strong houses with palm-thatched roofs gathered in wide circles. The ground was paved around enclosed in gardens. The shutterless doors were graced with brightly colored curtains and garlands of red pods drying in the sun. The smoke of cooking fires carried unknown aromas.

Women ground corn in their *metates* like in the islands, but dressed in the prettiest gowns, not naked and unkempt like the islanders. The children played with what looked like mice grown to the size of cats, leading the animals on leashes. To the strangers walking into the town everything looked the same and everything looked different.

Then they saw the temple, taller than the tallest tree, a massive pyramid cut across by a steep stairway. The cell on top looked small and stark, the singledoorway was ominous as hungry mouth. The thatched roofs below cringed in its shadow just as the narrow houses of Spanish towns stood humbled by the soaring mass of the cathedral. The prisoners couldn't help gawking, as if in a daydream. Those were the first stone buildings anyone had ever seen in the New World.

"Where are we, Señor Don Capitán?" Melchor Herrera asked. "Is this Egypt? Is this Cathay?" His guardians pulled him on, silenced him with their shouts.

"Could it be, Señor Don Capitán?" whispered Felipe. "Are these the people of the Khan, the ones Don Cristóbal couldn't find? Are we in the land of Cathay?"

Captain Valdivia shook his head, as if forcing himself out of a haze. "I don't know... Lord God, I don't know anything anymore."

The warriors prodded them toward the temple. Women gathered their children, people flocked to look. A stir of voices ran through the houses.

As the castaways neared the temple, the carvings that covered its walls stood out. They looked like the jungle turned to stone—a writhing mass without order or pause, a suffocating malignancy where jaguars, eagles and snakes tangled in every inch, bristling with fangs and feathers, painted in a brilliance of tremendous colors. No islander could have produced such demonic masterpieces. Jerónimo clutched his prayer book in his hands. What monstrous idols were hidden inside that hill of stone, challenging the one true God?

They were pushed into the courtyard. Here too sculptures swelled all over the walls like barnacles of nightmare. Smoke rose from great braziers of carved stone. Along with the incense there was a stronger smell, one that reminded Jerónimo of his father's butcher shop back home. It was a smell like rotting entrails that made one weak in the knees.

The crowd around them babbled in its unknown tongue, pressing forward to see. The children pointed in amazement.

Exhausted, the castaways dragged their feet, heads hanging. In a corner of the courtyard, in the sloping shadow of the temple, there was a wooden cage. The upright poles were planted in the ground. The painted warriors opened the door and pushed the prisoners in.

The floor of the cage was strewn with corncobs and potsherds.

They heaped up on the ground, their hearts pumping fear through their drained limbs. The crowd quieted into silence. Eyes behind the bars looked at them with sadness. The warriors ordered everybody out, and the courtyard was empty.

The afternoon was already waning. Shadows welled up among the stone snouts thrusting from the walls. Gonzalo pulled himself up and tried to make out the shapes around him. At the far end of the enclosure was a doorway cut through by a blade of light. Next to it was a basket full of stone knives, and fans made of iridescent blue feathers. Heaped under the fans was a pile of bones. He squinted, pressing his face against the bars of the cage. The bones were long and white. He couldn't tell to what they'd belonged. The pit of his stomach felt hollow with nausea. Yes, perhaps this was Cathay, he thought, but no bejeweled Queen from his dreams would come down those stairs and marry him.

"What will they do to us, what will they do to us," Melchor kept whining.

Santiago shoved him away. "Keep quiet, God curse you. Keep quiet I say!" Melchor fell back on all fours and began whining again.

"We're not dead yet," Captain Valdivia said. He sounded so different from the man who used to spew out orders aboard the *Esperanza*. "They didn't kill Marco Polo when he came to this land. These are not savages. But how in the name of Jesus will I talk to them? They don't speak any language I know."

There was silence. Jerónimo bent his head and joined his hands. "O Lord, look down upon your children. Do not leave them in the hands of their enemies."

As if to answer his prayer, a sound of soft footsteps came from the doorway. Two boys approached the cage. They brought food in clay plates and vessels that were long and narrow, made to fit through the bars. There was fowl meat, corn soup, flat corn cakes and a thick brownish liquid that smelled like strong vinegar. The boys bowed to the prisoners and left.

Gonzalo took one of the dishes, sniffed the delicious aroma of roasted fowl. "God bless you for being right, Señor Don Capitán." He handed him the dish and for no particular reason he said, "You're a good man, Señor Don Capitán."

They shared the meal, but there was enough to fill everyone. Only Alonso Carrera refused to eat. He was skin and bones, wasted past the point of return. The brown liquid turned out to be some sort of mead and it tasted awful. But it put warmth in the belly and it eased the mind, so they all drank some.

Rodrigo Gutierrez chewed noisily and in a hurry. "If this is Cathay, there must be gold. Think of it! Think of us going back to the world and saying, We found it, we have the bearings of Eldorado."

"And what would you trade?" Gonzalo scoffed. "Your underwear?"

Rodrigo broke another flat corn cake in two and stuffed it into his mouth. "For gold? I'd trade my head."

They were drinking the last of the mead when the door opened, making them start. Someone was coming, and what a delegation. It was led by a short, stocky man whose dress revealed him beyond all doubts a lord of the place. Sunbursts of green feathers fell from his headdress almost down to his knees. His chest was covered by a breastplate of jade and turquoise. His ears were pierced by topaz plugs. He carried a staff carved in the shape of intertwined snakes, and a small bunch of red flowers which he smelled from time to time.

Behind him walked attendants waving fans. Further behind were four old men whose stark appearance made the greatest contrast with the others'

19

colorful attire. They wore plain white robes hemmed with small seashells. Their hair, unkempt and unwashed, reached down to their waists. They were followed by two warriors carrying lances.

Beyond the walls of the courtyard the crowd buzzed.

Captain Valdivia stood up and wiped his mouth on his sleeve.

He wouldn't want to meet the Great Khan of Cathay with a greasy face. The feathers fluttered and the jewels flashed in the last of the light. It all looked like the stuff of dreams.

The four old men resembled hermit monks, lean with fasting. Their cheeks were crisscrossed with cuts, their lips torn, their earlobes frayed. Their old leathery skin was all a maze of scars, unexplainable and unpleasant to look at, and their eyes had an almost frantic look, as though they lived under a constant threat of doom.

The lord stopped before the cage and peered at the captives. He had a hard, mask-like face plowed with tattoos. His mouth curved haughtily downward as if passing forever a final judgment. Inside the cage no one dared breathe too loud.

The lord kept his flowers under his nose. "*Baax u kabaob?*" His voice was deep, and he spoke without curiosity. "*Tuux cahal a ex?*"

Captain Valdivia put his hand on his heart, as though he were standing in front of His Honor the Governor of Hispaniola. Not knowing what he'd been asked, his voice was weak and uncertain.

"We are Castilians, subjects of the Christian king Ferdinand of Spain. We come from—"

"*Baax u kabaob?*" the lord thundered.

Valdivia pointed at his men. "Spaniards," he said. "Castilians." The lord's retainers started a brisk parley among themselves. "*Matàn c'ubah thaan. Baaxi Castilàn? Tuux Castilàn?*"

"Castilian, yes. Castilian," Captain Valdivia repeated, nodding.

They were all no less confused than before, no less alien to one another. The lord tossed away his flowers. He put his arm through the bars of the cage and fingered Valdivia's beard. He marveled at the hairy growth on the stranger's face, uttering his surprise for the ones behind him. But when he tried to touch José's curly hair, José stood back, insulted.

The lord motioned the four old men to come forward. The old men answered him at length. Stubborn and resolute, they held their own against him in as if they, though dressed so humbly, wielded a power even greater than the lord's. Over and over they spoke with great reverence a word sounding like "*chaac.*" They seemed to use the word almost as a weapon to convince him. Their tongues wagged like myna birds', pressing and warning, until the lord could oppose them no more. Inside the cage the captives were taut with impatience.

Santiago swore under his breath.

At long last one of the four old men stepped closer, squeezing his eyes at the strangers. He pointed at Captain Valdivia. "Halach uinic?" he asked.

Captain Valdivia motioned he didn't understand. The old man pointed at Santiago, at José, at Jerónimo, at Gonzalo. "*Halach uinic? Halach uinic?*" He had a wide mouth with only a few teeth in it, and a scraggly beard that gave him the good-natured look of a goat. He pointed at each man and asked each man the same question.

Gonzalo drew his breath in. "I think he's trying to find out which one of us is the leader, Señor Don Capitán."

Captain Valdivia blinked. "Yes..." He pointed at himself. "*Halash... unic.* I'm the one."

Pleased, the old man nodded. He touched Captain Valdivia on the shoulder, then he touched at random Santiago, Martín, Rodrigo and Melchor. He turned to the other priests and indicated the five captives, nodding each time to mean that the priests must remember well each of the ones he had chosen.

"Why does he want us?" Melchor said. "Ask him why, Señor Don Capitán."

"Quiet down, Melchor. Maybe they just want to talk to us. They seem to have no ill intentions."

The lord had a few more words with his retainers, then walked away with his procession. The old man tarried by the cage. He pointed first at the food left in the platters, then at his own mouth, inviting the captives to finish their meal. He looked like an innkeeper plying his customers with his fare, and that made them smile. Captain Valdivia bowed his head as he joined the others on their way out. Only the two warriors remained, hunkered down at some distance from the cage.

Inside the cage the men sat back around the dishes, relaxing their strained souls.

"It's as I said," Captain Valdivia reassured them. "They seem to have no ill intentions. We'll have to be patient... We'll have to behave properly with these people. They will understand. They must see we're no threat to them."

"But why did that old bastard point at us?" Melchor wanted to know. "You I understand, Señor Don Capitán. But us, uh? What about the four of us?"

Santiago grabbed Melchor by the shirt. "Stop asking your damn questions," he growled. "Stop sounding as though we've been picked out for a hanging."

"I guess we'll know soon enough," Gonzalo said. "In the meantime, I see no harm in putting some flesh back on our bones."

They finished their meal. Clearly they would spend the night in the cage, so they set about looking for a better way to share the littered space.

"Alonso needs water," Jerónimo said. He glanced at the guards, mustering his courage. "We need water," he called. The two guards craned their necks.

"Look, he's dry," Jerónimo said. "We all need to drink." He mimicked picking up a glass and drinking. "Water. *Agua.*"

"*Haa?*" one of the guards echoed. He moved his hands up and down.

"*Haa, haa,*" and he walked to the doorway.

Jerónimo was struck by the similarity between the two words. "I wonder whether these people might be descendants of the Romans," he said, "whether they might speak some corrupt dialect of the ancient."

Melchor shook his head. "I say they're Egyptians." He pointed at the temple. "I've seen buildings just like these in the northern parts of Africa."

The guard returned with a stone vat and a ladle made from a hollowed-out gourd. Like the dishes, the vat also fit perfectly through the bars of the cage.

"*Haa*," he said, his tattooed face betraying no emotion.

Jerónimo cleared his throat. "*Gratias agimus*," he thanked the guard. But the man showed no signs of understanding his Latin, and walked back to his companion. The water was mixed with ground cornmeal, which made it cloudy and sweetish. The dry gourd added its own papery taste. They all drank their fill.

Night was falling. Even its texture of silence was different.

Gonzalo curled up on the ground. There was nothing else he could do but sleep. The strength he gained now would pay off when he'd need it. But sleep would not come, and in its place a hundred ghosts tormented him. He forced himself to listen to a distant bird call. It was regular as a belltower's clock, as a heartbeat; and because it stayed the same, he needed it now that nothing familiar was left except fear.

Four long days passed, so uneventful that their nerves itched with peace. Romans, Egyptians or God knew what else, the natives seemed to have forgotten about the captives in the cage. Even the guards got bored, walking around with nothing to do. The only distractions came with the meals—good meals of meat and fish, *cassava* bread, fruit, and always the liquor. They wondered at their treatment. They could see the two guards munching simply on flat corn cakes and pod-like vegetables.

"Say what you will about these people," Captain Valdivia praised, "except that they let their prisoners starve."

Often during those four days the guards looked up at the sky, then hung their heads in disappointment. It became irksome not to be able to do anything except sit and think. Perhaps a king of these people was expected to come and see the strangers. Perhaps a council was debating their fate. Perhaps they would spend the rest of their lives penned up inside that cage.

"I would mind my doings with that *cacique*," Pedro warned. "He looks like a real son of a whore."

"And the four old buzzards," Santiago said. "They don't smell any sweeter to me."

Some voiced what they wished would happen, others what they feared would happen. Gonzalo hardly listened. He sat looking at the sculptured walls around him with the same concentration with which he'd stared at his first alphabet letters. Most of the time he slept, tamed by the heat and the fatigue, and dreamt he was somewhere else.

At sundown on the fourth day everything changed. The gate opened, and the four old men came in, now followed by attendants who carried bowls full of some blue paste. The guards opened the cage. Captain Valdivia stood up first, tidying up his torn clothes. The old men motioned him out first, then the other four they'd chosen four days before. They mimed the gestures of daubing the strangers' faces and bodies with the blue paint.

Captain Valdivia didn't understand, but nodded to show goodwill. Melchor began asking again his testy questions, addressing directly the four old men.

"What do you want from me? Where are you taking me? Tell me, bones of Saint Peter!" The old men bobbed their heads, took Melchor by the hand and led him out.

Santiago was the most hostile. "I'm not going. I don't follow savages around."

Captain Valdivia glared at him. "Santiago, you only have one life to worry about. Don't play games with God."

The old men marched them on with their frail motions. "*Yan c'bin, yan c'bin.*"

They filed out of the cage. Gonzalo watched them go with his heart in his mouth. If they let them go, he swore, if they let them free, he would never set foot out of blessed Spain again.

The guards closed the cage. Captain Valdivia held himself straight. The small procession disappeared into the distant doorway. At the same time the crowd was let in, men, women and children. The women wore white shawls and carried their smaller children astride their hips. The children were naked and plump and beautiful. They all stood as quiet as the faithful in church.

Gonzalo sat back in his corner, pressing his hands together.

He kept his eyes on the doorway.

"What in the name of the Virgin are they doing in there?" Ponce snapped.

A breeze was rising from the jungle, moving gently the treetops. The temple above them squared its blind bulk against the pink sky. Then lights flickered in the courtyard. Young men holding torches emerged from the doorway and began to climb the staircase, stopping in pairs at each side on each step until the staircase was a dark river between two banks of light. The prisoners in the cage pressed against one another to see.

Out of the doorway came the four old men with Captain Valdivia and the others. They'd been stripped of coats and shirts, and they'd been painted with the blue paste. They walked as if drunk or drugged, their arms hanging at their sides. Melchor was held by two attendants.

As they passed before the cage Gonzalo called softly. "Señor Don Capitán?" Captain Valdivia walked on, a strangely vacant smile in his glazed eyes. At that sight something broke inside Gonzalo. He started to shake.

"What in hell are they doing?" Pedro cried out.

Gonzalo looked desperately for something to climb on. He yelled away the spectators who stood in front of the cage, making them jump aside as though he were a dangerous animal.

They looked small atop the temple. The four old men were white and sinister. There was a stone altar on the high platform. Why hadn't anyone noticed it before? Gonzalo climbed on the poles of the cage, rattling them like a captive ape.

"Can you see?" Leon begged. "Can you tell?"

It was a round stone altar, he could see it well now, shaped like a mound. Next to it was the statue of an old man with a long nose curving upwards and cheeks pocked with stone tears. The four old men grasped Captain Valdivia by wrists and ankles and forced him down spread-eagled on the altar. Out of the dark cell a fifth man appeared, dressed in a wide dark mantle that made him look like a monstrous death's-head moth. He held a flint knife high for all to see.

Gonzalo began to shout savage sounds without meaning.

Captain Valdivia's body lay arched and taut, the blue paint hideous in the torchlight. With a motion so swift it only seemed thought of, the knife plunged in and across, cutting a wide furrow through his chest. The living heart inside stood out naked and whole as an almond in the shell. They could almost hear it beat across the distance. While it was still beating, the mantled executioner thrust his hand into the wound and tore it out warm and bleeding.

Gonzalo reeled back from the bars, his mouth flecked with vomit.

The four old men swung the body off the altar and tossed it down the staircase. It tumbled down with a sound of cracking bones. At the foot of the stairs two attendants armed with flint axes cut off the head, the arms and the legs and put them in baskets. They cupped the blood in their hands and smeared the walls of the temple with it. Inside the cage the captives had become strangers to their own voices. Pedro crouched motionless, in shock, and Ponce wasn't even aware that he had soiled his breeches.

On top of the pyramid Santiago Alvarado was howling and twisting. They had to call two more men to hold him down. He was still howling and twisting when the executioner lifted his heart out of his chest and placed it before the stone idol. Gonzalo had turned his back, battling the heaving inside his belly.

By the time Melchor was laid on the altar he was already gasping his last breath. Rodrigo took hold of the executioner's mantle and wouldn't let go. Martín called out curses until the very end. The axes kept chopping with dull repeated sounds. The base of the pyramid had become a red pool reflecting the light of the torches.

Back and forth the attendants went, plastering the walls with blood. The crowd stood watching in silence. The children looked bored.

Once the baskets were full, the celebration moved down to the courtyard. The mantled executioner disappeared back inside the cell. The four old men remained kneeling before the idol. Fires were lit. The crowd came to life as if at the end of High Mass, began to walk around or to settle in groups. The sound of musical instruments could be heard. Dancers carrying drums stepped in with nimble motions, their bodies painted and their faces covered by masks resembling the face of the idol.

Leon hung onto Gonzalo's arm with his eyes wide, his voice hoarse.

"Please let me out of here. Gonzalo, please let me go home."

The drums began a heavy dialogue with the night. The children scampered around the cage, peeking at the captives and giggling. Some of them while running and playing knocked down one of the baskets. Rodrigo's head rolled out. The attendants chased it and picked it up by the hair. Jerónimo gave up trying to put together the words of the Hail Mary.

Then the feast began. Vats of liquor were passed around, the voices rose, a woman laughed. The braziers began to smoke with the rich roasted smell. The hands and feet were collected and carried up to the four old men.

"Mother, let me go home. Mother, mother," Leon whispered in his lonely hell.

Gonzalo stumbled here and there in the cage like a blind man.

He felt the body of Alonso Carrera under his feet.

"He's dead," Jerónimo said. "We must not let them know... He's dead," he said again. "Alonso is dead."

Women turned around to spy on the captives. Their black eyes were full of a wet, lustrous beauty. The men walked closer, growing free with the liquor. A small girl had fallen asleep against her mother's back, a half-chewed morsel in her bowl. The dancers beat their drums and stamped their feet, shaking the copper bells tied around their ankles. Bats came flapping above the courtyard. The fat spattered and colored the flames.

Gonzalo put his hand into his boot and felt for his knife. The coldness of the blade gave him a shudder of lucidity. He breathed in, shutting his ears to the noise and his soul to the horror. Rage came inside him. God was asking too much of him, and he would not be abused.

"By the blessed womb of the Virgin," he said, "I will not be a savage's supper."

In the dark Jerónimo grasped him by the arm. "How can the Lord hear my prayers while you foul the holy name of His Mother? Kneel down, Brother Guerrero, and die like a martyr of the true faith."

Gonzalo pushed him away. "I'm not going to die. I'm going to leave this place. I'm going to live to ninety-nine years of age." He turned toward the crowd, banged his fist on the poles of the cage. "Heathens, pigs, filthy demons," he shouted. In the drone of the feast his voice carried no threat.

He returned to his corner of the cage. He sat down and made himself into stone. His mind began to roll thoughts of escape—when, where, how. Kill the guards, take the four old men hostage. Then a shout, a strain of music, a whiff of the ghastly smell would bring him back to reality. It was a long night.

Intoxicated with liquor, the dancers stumbled. Their gestures mimicked water falling from the sky and an abject prayer. They wanted rain, Gonzalo thought; they would not stop until it rained. He sank his head in his arms and didn't look up anymore. After a while, exhausted beyond all endurance, he drifted off to sleep.

He dreamt that thunder woke him up, and that he was wet with rain. He opened his eyes with a start. It was almost dawn. The courtyard was empty, except for the two sleeping guards. Wisps of smoke coiled up from the braziers, embers still glowed. For too short a moment it all hung like a bad dream in his mind.

Jerónimo was sitting up next to Alonso's body. He'd put his prayer book in his lap and his face was at peace, as though he'd finally given up his desperate monologue with God. Felipe crawled over to Gonzalo with a cooked ear of corn in his hand.

"They left more food for us," he whispered with a short high laugh. "I guess they want to fatten us for their next meal, uh?" He chewed absently on the corncob, rocking his head.

Gonzalo looked away. He damned himself for falling asleep.

Now there was too much light for an escape. He motioned his companions to come closer. "Listen to me. Tonight we get out of here."

"Tonight we will be spitted and roasted like the lambs of the Basques," Ponce said.

Leon the boy got up feverishly. "How will we get out? What do you have in mind?"

Gonzalo touched his boot. "I have my knife. We'll cut the thongs off those two bars there. We'll climb the courtyard wall." He pointed to his left. "That side of the wall. There are no houses behind it, remember? There's just a sort of square leading out to the jungle."

Jerónimo shook his head. "This is madness, Gonzalo. They're bound to find us, and you know it."

"Madness is waiting here to be butchered," Gonzalo replied. "If you wish to stay, Brother Aguilar, believe that no one will force you out."

Leon took Jerónimo by the arm. "You will please come. We will all try together." Jerónimo didn't answer, but he looked resigned to following the others.

Gonzalo turned to Ponce, to Felipe, to José. "Are you all with me?"

Ponce shrugged. José said, "If you ask me, I'd rather die running than sitting down." Felipe saluted smartly. "Are you our new captain, Gonzalo? Aye aye, Señor Don Capitán Gonzalo."

"It's settled, then," Gonzalo said. "José, I want you to hide the food they'll bring us today. We'll need to take it with us." He touched Pedro, who seemed deaf and dumb to everything around him.

"He's cold. Give him Alonso's shirt. Talk to him, tell him that if he doesn't wake up we'll have to leave him here."

Finally he went back to his corner and sat down, twisting his hands together. He looked up at the temple and breathed in deeply.

"Keep your eyes and ears open," he said, "for by the grace of God we'll be out of here yet."

Everybody in town must be drunk. The guards walked around unsteadily, laughing once in a while. The stones emanated waves of heat like those of an oven. The blood on the walls dried and cracked, merging with the paint, attracting flies. Time had never moved so slowly. Gonzalo was a patient man, but nothing came easily anymore. Nothing he was doing now he'd ever surmised he would have to do. It was like watching someone else do what he did.

"We'll take the road due south," he said, "the one we came here on."

He studied how the sculptures went up row after row all along the courtyard. "Look, it's like a staircase. All we have to do is climb it."

"But once we're out?" José asked. "Why due south?"

"I don't know why due south" Gonzalo snapped. "I like the way it sounds. Do you have a better idea?"

José looked at him, lost. For a while nobody spoke.

"Maybe we should try for the inland instead," Ponce ventured. "The road will lead to other towns, there will be more people who can find us."

"But there are snakes and tigers in the jungle," Leon countered. "I'd rather stay close to the sea. We need to find a boat if we want to sail back to Hispaniola."

Gonzalo ran his hand on his face. "It doesn't really matter which way we go. We have no choice."

The air was hot and sticky. From the top of the pyramid the long-nosed idol sneered down at them silently. In the afternoon two of the old men came to the cage. They checked the bowls and dishes.

They looked pleased to see them empty, though none of the captives had touched the liquor. They noticed Alonso's body, and opened the door to take it out. As they stepped in, Gonzalo felt the urge to put his knife to their throat and drive it in as they had driven theirs into Captain Valdivia's baptized flesh.

Jerónimo looked in grief at the body being dragged out by the feet. He began to explain to the old men that it must be put in the ground and covered, his hands frantically shaping the grave. The old men shook their head in annoyance; their attendants kept him away from the door. Anguished, Jerónimo's eyes followed the body as it trailed like a rag on the pavement, toward an unknown fate.

The afternoon spread out golden and wide as a silk sheet. The muted buzz of the town beyond the walls of the courtyard was almost like the one that used to lull them to sleep on feast days back home.

José sat with his back hiding the bundle of food he had hoarded in his shirt: ears of corn, flat bread and pear-like fruits with green leathery skin.

Gonzalo looked at the sky, where soon, soon the first stars would come out. Here, the sun dipped to the west and slowly disappeared; here, shadows woke up like long-winged butterflies.

Leon was holding Pedro by the arm. "Yes, I can walk," Pedro was whispering, white-faced. "I'm all right now."

By the doorway the two guards shook the dust off the feather fans and spoke in their tongue full of unpronounceable sounds.

Gonzalo could no longer sit still. His every limb tingled painfully. He told the others to eat some of the food for strength, but he himself could hardly swallow. The green fruits had a soft pulp with a bland, buttery taste. Then it was finally night, it was finally time.

The two guards went to get the mantles they would sleep in. They shouted something to the captives, who pretended to be tired. After some time the two rolled themselves up on the ground next to one of the braziers and fell asleep.

"Start walking ahead," Gonzalo whispered. "Ponce, you stay with me. We'll have to mind the guards."

The thongs were tough, made of some dried vine steadier than leather. But in the end the good steel knife was even tougher. To think he'd almost refused to buy it from that Arab seller because the man asked too much. Without a sound the cage's door opened. He motioned the others out. In his sleep one of the guards called the same word twice.

Five filed out silently, Leon helping Pedro along, José with the food bundle. Ponce and Gonzalo came last, their eyes on the guards, the knife ready. Suddenly Jerónimo turned around and motioned Gonzalo to look: the courtyard's main gate was wide open and clear.

Gonzalo stopped, considering that unexpected exit. Because he didn't trust God, he'd have preferred to think it was a trap. His heartbeat rose so loud inside him that he feared it would smother every other sound he needed to hear. He stole up to the gate and peeked out in every direction. To his astonishment, he saw that ahead of him lay the safest and quickest way out. God too must be drunk asleep, he thought.

He signaled the others to come. Bent low, close together, they slipped out of the courtyard. Behind them were only a few lights, which like fear's own compass told them to walk in the opposite direction.

Gonzalo led them as though by the flash of his dagger. He fled stone and sought bush, light-footed as a thief. The town was very quiet. No dogs barked, no watch bells rang at regular intervals as in Spain. Every time their boots cracked on a twig their breath thickened with panic. They cut a large half-circle between the last distant houses and the rim of palm trees that surrounded the houses, then plunged into the vast blackness of the jungle.

"We're out... My God, we're truly out," Gonzalo whispered. The rush of his blood carried new waves of clarity to his mind.

Neither his arms nor his legs felt weak anymore. Furiously he opened up a path for the others with his knife and with his body, slapping away at low branches that scratched his face, pulling up loose vines that grabbed at his ankles. Behind him he could hear Ponce gurgling a strange broken laugh.

The night was warm and wet as a woman. They were surrounded by screeches, hisses, cries, sighs. Startled eyes glared at them, green as phosphorus, red as coals. Wings brushed their hair, flapping drowsily above them. A shuddering thickness of living creatures glided and crawled in the night to their endless pursuits, with the two-legged ones only one more species on the run.

They sped on; bent on tricking death more than once if that could be done. Gasping for breath they quickened their pace through the easier bush, then halted before some impassable curtain of leaves, then went on all fours across fallen tree trunks spongy with rot and swarming with insects, then again trudged and hobbled and pulled one another along. Chandeliers of huge fireflies floated under the roof of the forest. The moon weaved in and out of the dark tangle, dappling it with light.

Then the ground became smoother and clearer of vegetation, breaking into loose rubble that crunched under their steps. Gonzalo knew they must be deep enough in the wilderness. He stopped. They let themselves fall to the ground, their limbs aching, their faces and arms burning with cuts and mosquito bites.

"Can we stay here... till it's light," Leon panted. "We must be far enough now."

Gonzalo fingered his knife as if it were a good-luck charm. "We may have been walking in circles," he said. "I'll climb that rock, see if I can find out where we are."

"I'll come with you," Ponce said. He was no longer the listless and resigned man in the cage. He sounded as though now he would follow Gonzalo straight down to the pits of hell.

The rock felt like a mountain under the two men's tired legs. Ponce pulled Gonzalo up on top. The land for miles all around them was a dark, unbroken pelt of trees, so uniformly high it looked as if it had been topped with scissors. They couldn't make out any clusters of lights from towns or villages. They sat down to catch their breath.

"We're safe... for now," Ponce said. He lay down with his arms outstretched, looking as haggard as Christ about to be nailed to the cross. "O Lord," he moaned. "I thought I would not live another night." His voice cracked. "I have a wife... She was pregnant when I left. By now I figure I'm a father... I wonder of what, boy or girl. I wonder if I'll ever see that baby."

Gonzalo wiped the sweat off his neck and kept silent. It was only worse with a family, he thought. A man ended up suffering twice, three, four times as much, and all for nothing in the end. Nothing sold for the fair price, not bread, not love.

He breathed in deeply. From the jungle came a primal, savage scent like jasmine and carrion that overwhelmed his lungs. He'd never seen so many stars, big and furious as bonfires. It occurred to him that at least one maudlin notion of homesick sailors didn't hold true anymore: those were not the same stars that shone on his faraway homeland. He felt crushingly alone, left to his own deadly devices. For the first time in his life the world was truly a philosopher's mystery.

Ponce was falling asleep on the naked stone. He touched him gently. "Let's go back. I guess we can rest until dawn."

Ponce held his head as if he were drunk, broken with fatigue and grief. "And then?" he asked.

"God knows," Gonzalo said. "But He won't tell, as always."

THREE

He'd always taken the dawn for granted, and he'd always thought it should be so for all men. But now every dawn returned like a canny trader offering him the expensive merchandise of a new day and told him to start the haggling.

A great *ceiba* tree had stood watch over them with its clusters of velvety red flowers while they slept through the last of the night. Without a word, knowing like all hunted beasts what they must do, they set out again.

It was a flat, endlessly uniform land of living rock, with only a meager dusting of earth to soften its surface. In the daylight they were able to see where they were going and to choose the easier trail.

Because the trees kept the sunlight from reaching the ground, not much grew there to hamper their way; but there was not a rock of different height, a shrub of different branches, anything they could use as a beacon. They kept wandering around, losing as much ground as they gained.

"It's like being at sea," Gonzalo cursed. "We could go on like this forever."

And there was not a drop of water to be drunk. Not a river, a pond, a stream, a trickle. It was like the sea and like the desert.

Snakes cut swift wakes before them and rustled away. Attracted by the sweat, clouds of ticks stuck to their flesh like a hundred hot needles. They walked all morning, wild with thirst and heat. Even the food they ate while plodding on was only one more torture, pasting their dry mouths like bark.

Once Gonzalo struck by accident with his knife a thick thorny plant, and noticed the moisture that oozed out. He made more cuts, and they all sucked the liquid stored in the fleshy blue leaves. For some time they lay exhausted on the ground. The heat was a coat they couldn't cast off; the canopy of trees trapped the air as if under a glass bell.

Only Gonzalo seemed to have enough strength left to talk. "We'll have much to tell in Hispaniola," he said, to encourage the others. "Jerónimo, you might even have to write a formal *relación* for the governor." Jerónimo tried to smile.

"You still haven't told us how we're going to go back to Hispaniola," said Pedro, whose wounded leg bothered him a great deal and made him ill-tempered.

"I'll tell you when I know, believe me," Gonzalo said flatly. Ponce leaned in belligerently. "He took us out of that cage,

Pedro, and don't you forget it." Pedro looked the other way. Felipe laughed his short hysterical laugh. Before the shipwreck Felipe had been a silent, hard-working man; now he was fraying at the edges like an old piece of cloth.

The afternoon was waning. It was time to find a place where they could spend the night. They gathered up whatever food was left and started to move toward a jutting ledge of limestone they could see in the distance. Again they didn't seem to feel the miles as they went, with the ghost of deliverance walking among them. Clumps of purple orchids growing from the trunks of trees lined their way with beauty.

The limestone ledge opened up like a roof over a hollow in the rock, a niche softened with matted moss. They piled up in it, the molded walls soothing their bodies. From the roof Gonzalo surveyed the surrounding area and found nothing dangerous. On his way down he spotted some swallow nests and sacked them of the eggs.

Pedro kept complaining about his leg. "This thing is killing me. How can I walk again tomorrow?" He looked at Gonzalo. "Why don't you just say it? We're lost, God curse the day I left home!"

Gonzalo's patience toward Pedro was wearing thin. "So we're lost," he said. "Would you rather be back there?"

In the morning when they set out again, Pedro begged the others to hold him as he walked, promising to reward them with a keg of good wine from his father's vineyards. José grumbled that he slowed them all down. An argument started that echoed through the jungle like a meeting of quarrelsome monkeys.

They were going south, or so they reasoned, but in senseless zigzagging paths that led nowhere. Soon walking became almost impossible. Their feet sank into a watery, swampy undergrowth. They would alight on some spread of roots, only to fall back in fear at the glimpse of a scaly snout cleaving through the slime. They were lost inside a rank, smothering tangle. They struggled on in a panic, as if the jungle were taking roots on them.

Gonzalo pushed on, but soon the others were clamoring for rest. "We cannot stop here," he warned them. "We must find an open place. We still have enough daylight." They kept walking as if in a daze, unable to see the deadly fer-de-lance brushing past them, the bushmaster coiled around the same trunk they'd leaned on for a moment's respite.

They decided to return to the limestone ledge they'd left that morning, but their wanderings had taken them much too far from it. While they still desperately tried to find that shelter, the jungle began to clear and to break, the grass before their boots to flatten, the signs

of human passage to show. Instantly, but too late, they realized they'd strayed too close back to men.

Strange noises and rustles made them stop in their tracks. They could feel eyes spying on them, feet following them. Then the jungle grew arms and legs, and they were snared.

It was a party of about a dozen men and boys, hunters returning home. Some were armed with spears, and carried in nets the deer they'd killed; others shouldered blowguns, and their catch was a flock of live parrots. Their rope sandals were old and worn, as those of people who walk much. They wore plain breechcloths, and amulets made of deer bones.

Gonzalo leant away from the spear leveled at his throat. In the eyes of his captors he could read an almost comical surprise. What were those unexpected, preposterous quarries with bodies as hairy as apes', white skin and round skulls, so tall and with such large hands and feet? Surely some trickster spirit must be playing a prank on these tired hunters!

In despair Pedro bent over, his leg burning him up with pain.

Ponce let his arms fall to his sides, defeated. One of the hunters, perhaps the head of the party, motioned his companions to be brave. He himself just rattled on. He swaggered forward, and with a sudden move snatched the knife from Gonzalo's hand. Gonzalo lunged for his dagger. He hunters surrounded him, pulled out their snares and pinioned him to the ground.

Ponce threw himself to Gonzalo's defense. One of the hunters hit him on the head with the shaft of his spear. The others cowered all in a body. Made bolder, even the boys now helped to tie the quarries' arms. In a few instants the seven were subdued. Pedro, who could no longer move a step, had to be trussed up in one of the nets and lifted up just like the dead deer.

The hunters' leader examined the dagger. Marveling, he felt the edge, fingered the unknown metal. He raised it high for all to see and tucked it proudly into his belt, an aggrandized man. He had a coarse face and a round thatch of greasy hair. At his signal, the ragged group of strangers was made to follow its captors.

How many times had he hoped he could fool them? Gonzalo thought, looking at the knife tucked in the hunter's belt. He had to fight the fear that was welling up again inside him. The ropes around his wrists chafed. The dryness in his throat was unbearable.

"I'm thirsty," he shouted. His captors pushed him on and barked their gibberish at him.

"I said I want to drink," he demanded again. "*Haa*," he cried out. He nodded toward a water-skin carried by one of the boys.

"Haa!"

Startled, the hunters looked at one another. The stranger spoke their tongue! This was a request they could not ignore. Keeping good watch, they had the skin taken to him so he could drink. The water tasted foul, made him choke. He jerked his head toward the other captives. "*Haa*," he shouted again. One by one the hunters made them all drink. Pedro growled an oath and Leon wept quietly.

On they walked. From the swamps rose an odor of dense teeming water, a smell as thick as that of afterbirth. The eyes couldn't unravel root from branch in that network of quagmires. The air was enmeshed in vines that hung like huge tentacles. How could anybody live in such a land, Gonzalo wondered, and build cities in it, temples even.

Yet sure enough here was a road—straight as a surgeon's cut, precise as a number, its solid logic of stone taming the green chaos.

Who knows to what other wonders and to what other horrors would this road lead.

The hunters quickened their pace. The nets swung and the deer dripped blood. Travelers appeared, some laden with cargoes. As they saw the captives they stopped; some came closer to look. A woman carrying a stack of painted pottery circled slowly around them, her small black eyes prying. The hunters explained, pointed, certainly bragged like all hunters, and then pushed their prey on. A small crowd of onlookers had formed. Some who had no particular business to attend to followed them all the way to the city.

It was a marvel of a city, as handsome as any fortified Spanish seaport. It stood atop a high cliff lashed by the waves of the open sea and covered with thorny cactus. A stout wall ran parallel to the coast, then reached toward the edge of the cliff. The top of a temple painted entirely in red could be seen towering above the wall, with a plume of smoke trailing from it across the salty air.

The captives stared at the stronghold with their mouths open.

By now they were willing to believe every fairytale they'd ever heard about the golden bells of Cipango. If only they knew about this city back in the islands! Gonzalo thought. He thought of the Spaniards' muskets and cannons, of the mounted cavalrymen in their steel armor whom the naked islanders believed to be giant armadillos. God knew how many, noblemen and stable boys, would have lusted after this prize.

The road became a ramp, on which the crowd hastened toward one of the narrow gateways. They were surrounded by a low hum of voices. Children clustered around Pedro being carried in his net. Through the gate and into the city they went, down a street lined with massive obelisks carved in cobwebs of strange figures. Some of the monuments, Gonzalo noticed in amazement, bore large ornaments of gold, pure beaten gold shining in the ancient weathered stone.

Toward the southwest was a temple decorated with idols diving from the sky like plummeting hawks. Incense burned before the images; the scent wafted above the rooftops. Gonzalo felt as though he'd stumbled into the world beyond. He'd never thought the human eye could be greeted by so many colors at once. The people, the houses, the sculptures, everything was alive and pulsing with red and blue and yellow and green. Green especially, from turquoise and jade, the color of the jungle itself solidified into shimmering stone. The harsh tropical light seemed to strike sparks from everything it touched.

They crossed a paved plaza bordered by colonnaded halls. From the surrounding streets, from patios and walkways the crowd thickened. As they approached the great temple, Gonzalo felt his legs turn to lead. He could see old men dressed in white bending down to look. The memory of Captain

Valdivia and the others returned to stop his blood. He began to tug back. The hunters pulled him on. He started to shout. The steep stairway came closer and closer and the crowd babbled its meaningless sounds. But his captors kept walking. Now the temple was behind him and he could breathe in. It wasn't the temple they were headed for. It was a marketplace.

The sights, the sounds and the smells of a diversity unimagined in all of Christendom were spread under the cotton canopies. For every piece of merchandise the captives could name, there were countless other that seemed to have been thrown in only to make them doubt their senses.On one side sat the sellers of meat, among cages full of rabbits, small hairless dogs, armadillos, brown quail and some fat birds with feathers the color of green iron and tails like those of peacocks. On another side waited the sellers of the sea, surrounded by fish and conch shells, turtles and alligators and salt packed in pottery dishes.

Under a sun-dappled roof old women guarded mounds of corn speckled with purple and blue kernels. The feather-sellers' corner was a small forest of plumes that had all the colors God had forgotten when he'd made the rainbow. Vendors called, buyers haggled. Porters jostled their way through, bent under loads of coiled straw mats that made them look like giant yellow snails.

The news of the hunters coming with their outlandish catch had already made the round of the walls. They were closed in by a throng that floated them toward an expected destination. Gonzalo peered ahead. Amidst the many unfamiliar sights, an all-too-familiar one struck him with the abrupt pain of a knife. It was a sorry crowd of men, women and children tied together by their necks to wooden poles, just like the Africans that the Portuguese brought in from

Guinea. A surge of repulsion swept through him. Not a slave, he thought. God, not a slave!

By now the hunters were struggling to reach a place where they could display their prey undisturbed. Waving his arms, the head of the party called on an armed guard who managed to have some room made around the newcomers. Leon stumbled and lay on the ground. Pedro had fainted in his net. The walking came at last to an end.

The man who'd taken Gonzalo's dagger spoke loudly. He pointed toward a certain direction and repeated the same word. After a great deal of such expounding, the guard was impressed enough to start moving. The midday sun bore down stubbornly; the air was thick with dust.

Gonzalo forced himself to look again at the ragged group of slaves. In all that milling crowd they alone could not move. One woman carried a baby astride her hip, and around the baby's neck, too, was a rope.

Ponce looked up. "What do you think they'll do to us this time?" he whispered.

Gonzalo shook his head wearily. "Ponce, make up your own nightmares."

The guard was back, his spear waving above the crowd. The hunters caught sight of someone approaching with him, and immediately pushed all their prisoners down on their knees. They themselves hastened to touch the ground, picking up handfuls of dirt and putting it on their heads. Men took off their mantles and laid them on the ground to make a carpet. The sandals Gonzalo saw stepping on that carpet were entirely covered with sheets of gold.

A middle-aged man, hairless and fat around the middle like an infant, stopped before them. The profusion of jewelry he wore gave an impression of self-indulgent gaudiness. He was cross-eyed; his face was not intelligent, and not too familiar with humor. Stripped of all his finery, he would have commanded no more attention than a cautious and content shopkeeper. Silence fell.

The leader of the hunters couldn't wait for the lord to give him permission to speak. Gonzalo gave up trying to figure out what was being said between the two of them. The hunter made his prisoners show their faces, then pointed breathlessly at each special feature of his human wares. Look, Exalted One, what prizes I bring you! *Slaves, yes, but bizarre enough to make every other noble peer jealous of you. Put them on a leash like your pet beasts and make me a rich man, Exalted One!* He spoke as though he smelled gold beyond his most shameless dreams, Gonzalo thought. He sounded the way Gonzalo had sounded when he'd left home.

An air of mild curiosity appeared on the lord's face. The hunters reached out to take off Felipe's tattered shirt. Yes, the stranger was covered with matted red hair! The crowd sounded very much gratified by that tidbit. Felipe looked down at his own chest and grinned wide. The lord motioned the hunters to take off Felipe's breeches as well. Felipe didn't mind. The women in the crowd turned their backs. Red hair, red hair all over!

The lord laughed. He fingered one of the jade bracelets he wore around his wrist, feeling its weight, its value.

The leader of the hunters was groveling in the dust. "*Nohoch ahau!*" he called. "*Ten c'in ziik ppentacob tech.*"

The lord's eyes became slits. "*Ziik?*" he said.

His hand left the bracelet, and the smile left the hunter's face. Whatever the seller had said in his hurry to turn his life around, it had been the wrong thing to say. The lord motioned the guard to take custody of his new slaves.

The hunter was holding out his hand in a wretched plea. "*Nohoch ahau,*" he called again. "*Nohoch ahau!*"

Too late. With some satisfaction, Gonzalo realized the man would receive no payment for his merchandise. The hunters were still berating the gods when the guard marched him and the others after the litter of the lord, out of the marketplace.

The house stood within a grove of palmetto trees, borrowing the city's wall for protection on one side. The fret massing on the entrance spread all around the building into a rampage of dressed and painted stone, with figures of birds repeated in rows. A large sculptured basin reflected the intense green of the trees. Cloths of embroidered cotton fluttered at the windows. Despite the fluster of people coming out to greet their master, the house gave an impression of comfort and peace.

The lord came down from the litter and went into house. The prisoners were herded toward a squat and unadorned hut with a steep thatched roof that had begun to rot here and there. The whitewashed front was punctuated only by an entranceway that had no shutters.

The most amazing thing about what were clearly slave quarters was the fact that only a few yards separated it from the low curtain wall. Above the edge of the wall Gonzalo could sea the far point where the sea became the sky, and he could hear the waves rushing toward the base of the cliff. Even as he was being prodded into the hut he was dizzy with that sound. The sea meant freedom, and the sea was so close.

Exhausted, the prisoners tumbled in. The inside of the hut was nothing more than rows of pallets made of ragged blankets and mats heaped on the earthen floor, and a few bowls and baskets. The guard let his prisoners lie on the ground. Pedro had regained consciousness, but he was in pain and screamed from time to time.

Felipe crushed an insect between his thumbnails and wiped it on the sooty wall. "Gonzalo, what do we do now?" he asked playfully, like someone whose existence is no longer his own concern.

Gonzalo hugged his knees. "At least it's not a temple," he said. Some time went by. Inside the hut it was dim and stifling.

Then the guard stood aside and the lord came in. He had doffed his jewels and he looked much more at ease in just a breechclout wrapped around his portly waist. He was accompanied by a woman who must be his wife, and by a man whose appearance and dress seemed different from those of anybody the prisoners had seen so far: his forehead was not flattened and he wore a small stick of jade through the septum of his nose.

The man was indeed no less a foreigner in this land than were the new slaves. Under the lord's annoyed gaze, he addressed the prisoners in what sounded like three or four different languages, trying to find out where these unusual white-skinned people came from. At last he gave up, bowing to beg for the lord's understanding. The woman was pretty and contemptuous. She looked affronted at having to stand in her slaves' quarters, and she held up with both hands her beautiful gown.

Nothing Gonzalo would say would make any difference. Had he had any way at all of communicating with his captors, he would have told them with his heart's outrage that he was the head of Spanish sailors and of free men. He would have heaped on these half- naked cannibals the number of muskets and lead balls that stood piled high in Hispaniola's arsenals, just a few miles away from whatever this appalling land was called. Instead he could only sit with his back to the wall, staring at his befuddled owners.

When he was a boy he'd often caught some small fish and put it to swim in a bucket. As he watched it he'd wondered how the fish must feel, torn from everything it knew, made to live at the whim of alien creatures, to eat their unnatural breadcrumbs, to knock its head against the wooden sides of its narrow new sea. Now he knew how it felt.

The attention of the two lords was now on Pedro. They looked at his wounded leg and they shook their heads. They summoned the guard from the door and told him to take Pedro away.

Suddenly Jerónimo jumped to his knees, shaking with desperate courage. "Don't kill him. He'll heal, he'll be all right. Don't you have anything human in your hearts at all?" He tried to take the lord's hand. The guard cuffed him hard.

The lord said something in a very loud voice. Screaming and moaning, Pedro was forced out of the hut, God only knew where to. Gonzalo's eyes were filmed with a darkness he'd never thought possible. The world had begun to flicker around him like a distant horizon on a hot day. The lord peered closely at him. In his cross-eyed stare there was nothing Gonzalo could translate.

Again there was an unintelligible rattle between the two men. The foreign lord with the nose stick motioned the captives to take off their clothes. José answered him with an obscene gesture. To be sure, no one else liked the idea, not because of modesty but because they remembered the naked bodies of their captain and shipmates rolling down the steps of the temple. Jerónimo had shrunk against the wall, trying to hide the prayer book tucked inside his belt. Only Felipe, who'd stood happily unclothed in the marketplace, unfastened his coat again without complaints.

Too tired to think, Gonzalo propped himself up and removed his shirt, his boots, his breeches. Right away he felt better without the sweat-encrusted homespun clinging to his raw skin. He pushed the heap away and he thought of his sister bent at the loom for hours in the twilight of Palos. He felt as though by taking off the clothes that she had made for him he had betrayed her. I'm sorry, he thought. I'm so sorry.

Everyone else followed his example. The woman didn't flinch or affect squeamishness. The clothes to her seemed much more foreign than the bodies they covered. Arms, legs and groins: children of the gods. What troubled her more was the condition of filth these particular children of the gods had let themselves fall into. She went to the doorway and called someone.

The two lords were trying to pry a mysterious object away from the fever-eyed stranger who'd spoken so boldly before. With the same ferocious determination Jerónimo kept one hand cupped over his privates, the other over his prayer book.

"It's only a book!" he cried. "What harm can a book do?"

The cross-eyed lord kicked him with his golden sandal and got hold of the book. He leafed through it, voicing his amused comment for the other man. Then he tossed the book back to Jerónimo, who threw up both hands to catch it, mindless of decency for a second.

The woman came back, followed by a female servant who carried a stack of folded cotton loincloths. The girl shut her eyes at the sight of the naked captives, and had to be prodded in. She made small whimpering sounds as she stood there stiffly, her arms stretched out to hand over the cloths. Despite himself, Gonzalo could not but see that she was beautiful. She had a soft face and a full soft mouth and thick black hair coiled on her bare shoulders. On her forehead the faint tendrils of tattoos crowned her like a permanent garland.

The lady of the house was manhandling the girl's arm to make her open her eyes, much irritated by her bashfulness. "*Kanalsin!*" she called. "*Kanalsin!*" Because the word sounded too pretty to be an insult, Gonzalo fancied that it was the girl's name. Naked and shaking, he remembered the last time he'd been gathered into the perfect shelter of a woman's body—truly the last time, he thought, if his life was about to end now in this godless land.

The girl opened her eyes. They were wide, almond-shaped eyes of a black without depth. How very young she must be, he thought, fifteen at most. She took a few more steps forward and bent slightly to offer him one of the cloths. Hunched over, he reached out to take it. Might God strike him if he knew why, but the last thing he wanted to do at that moment was frighten her.

She would not look at him, at any of them. As soon as each man got his piece of cloth she dashed out. Then she rushed back in to gather up the alien clothes of leather and wool and carry them away.

The long strips of plain white cotton, no wider than an Arab's turban, dropped instantly undone in the captives' clumsy hands. Ponce gave a sound of contempt, and José tossed his loincloth away. The two lords said something to them, but José for one preferred his nakedness to that travesty of a garment. Only Jerónimo, in his hurry to cover himself with any means available, and also to show gratitude for having been allowed to keep his prayer book, began to wrap his cloth around his hips and between his pale legs as best as he knew how. The lord smiled with condescension. Then, since all his concerns in the slaves' quarters were over, he left. It seemed enough to him that these barbarians could be persuaded to wear clean clothes; the rest could wait.

Only the foreign lord with the nose stick remained. He studied the captives one last time, then raised his hand.

"*A ex ppentacob ahau ah kin cutz*," he said solemnly, warning them to fix his words well in their minds. "*Yetel le uluum Maya.*"

Gonzalo clutched his piece of cloth and remembered. To the west of Cuba is a land called Maya. So that was the name for the belly of the beast.

FOUR

He didn't know how long he'd slept. For all he knew it could have been a hundred years.

He'd curled up on the bare earth and he'd fallen into a pit of blankness. Once he thought he'd heard Felipe's hysterical laughter. Then another voice that resembled Ponce's had made the laughter go away, and he'd heard nothing else. He awoke to the sound of rain splashing down the palm leaves. In a moment everything came back to him; where he was, who he was with, and why. But none of this mattered to him as much as the rain. He leaped to the doorway, where only a rope strung across kept the slaves from venturing out.

He felt a hand on his shoulder. "Gonzalo, are you all right?" He turned around and reached for Ponce's arm. "It's raining!" he said out of breath.

He stood leaning over the rope, letting the rain stroke his face. "We're going to live, Ponce," he said in a happy mutter. "This is what they wanted, don't you see? It's here now, it's raining. What day is today?"

Jerónimo had his prayer book open to a page bearing a gilded cross. "It's the Day of the Cross," he answered, and kissed the book. "It's a sign from God. It has begun to rain on the Day of the Cross."

The sky was blotted out from view. It wasn't the grey sky of rainy days in Spain. It was more like being underwater, drenched in a thick green light, as though the rain made the color of the palm trees run and drip down. Steam rose up from the ground, and it was just as hot as before, hot and steamy as a cauldron.

Ponce nudged Gonzalo back in, and together they sat down next to a scooped-out gourd in which rain from a hole in the roof was collecting. Felipe was scampering around, fearing the roof would collapse. José lay alone in a corner, naked; the loincloth he would not wear was still on the ground next to his mat. Leon was asleep.

Ponce told Gonzalo what had happened during the past days; rather, what had not happened. They'd been left to themselves in the hut. Nobody had come to see them except the boy who brought their food. The food itself was not the lavish fare they'd been fed in the cage. Most of the time it was flat corn bread, green pods as fiery as hell flames, and fish. Ponce had saved those of Gonzalo's rations that would not spoil. Now he offered them to him.

Gonzalo was moved by Ponce's devotion. Ponce seemed to have appointed himself as his special protector. He had watched over him while Gonzalo slept, and he had been doing the work Gonzalo should have been doing: shelling corn.

Large baskets full of corncobs were scattered all over the hut, together with smaller baskets for the grains. "Yes," Ponce said. "We're going to live. We're going to live and we're going to shell corn until our fingers drop."

Gonzalo touched him with a gesture of impatient affection. "If you intend to be my guardian angel, Ponce," he chided him gently, "you must begin to think differently around me." Ponce tried to smile, then hung his head.

Leon woke up. He went to join the others, listening to the rain as it if were utter magic. He tagged along the older men like a puppy, dreading to be left alone. His ribs didn't show so much anymore; even so, he seemed to have added ten years to his fifteen. Gonzalo looked at the boy and wondered how the nightmare had made *him* look. He thought of his sister and then, incongruously, of the girl who'd come to bring the loincloths.

The natives had been burning the jungle in those past days, Ponce told him. He'd seen the smoke, and smelled the green fuel. He had observed the coming and going of other slaves to and from the house. They must be clearing patches for the planting of the corn, the corn they were shelling now. Gonzalo listened, taking up his own work with clumsy hands. The hard blue and purple kernels danced steadily down into the baskets.

"What's wrong with José?" he asked under his breath.

Leon shook his head. "He won't work, he won't talk, he won't do anything he's told to. He's looking for trouble," he worried. "Felipe, too. I think he's gone mad. What are we going to do with the two of them when we try to escape?"

Gonzalo shelled corn and tossed cobs, shelled and tossed, shelled and tossed. "When we try to escape..." he said with a tired grin. "Eat now, Leon. You're still skin and bones. Your mother will never forgive me if I bring you back to her in those conditions."

Leon's eyes welled up with tears. He stopped his work and began to sob. Gonzalo put his hand on the boy's head. Leon sobbed hard, and the rain fell with the same hard sound.

It rained as though it were the flood without Noah's ark. Soon there weren't enough pots and scooped-out gourds in which to hold the rain that kept coming down through the roof.

Felipe had become a source of constant vexation. He would sidle up to them and talk endless nonsense. José beat him to make him shut up and Leon tried to calm José down. Everybody was being driven insane by the very closeness of each other. The water hissed as it steamed up from the ground and the monkeys shrieked, sometimes thumping on a tree and sending down pieces of sodden thatch that crawled with millipedes. Nothing to do but shell corn all day. Twice a day the boy with the food came. Other slaves brought in and took out the baskets as they emptied and filled. Leon wept, Jerónimo prayed, José sulked and Felipe rocked his head.

Gonzalo couldn't stand it anymore. He felt ready to risk any punishment if only it would end the feeling of impotence that ate away at his heart. Back into his life had returned regular food and regular sleep. But the food was often impossible to name, and the sleep was crowded with the strangest dreams he'd ever dreamed.

He spent most of his time watching from the doorway. The courtyard was a lively place. As in any Spanish mansion, it was the domain of household servants shuttling busily from the water basin to the trash heap, from the storage rooms to the butchering block.

Servants were all he could learn from. The master could be seen only toward the end of the day, when he returned home in full feathered regalia, and his wife avoided the new slaves as if they were lepers. Only the young girl who'd brought the loincloths came often to draw water from the basin or to see to some other errand. There were times when Gonzalo caught himself waiting for her to show up, with that heavy clay jar of hers. When she did come, he watched her with a sort of bland curiosity, the way a prisoner might become fascinated with a bird that keeps its nest under his barred window.

It was when he thought he could no longer endure to be cooped up inside that dank, sweltering hut, that he was let out. Early one morning one of their guardians came to wake them up and motioned them to get out. In the past days Gonzalo had figured out who this man must be, some majordomo or head of the household slaves whom the master kept constantly busy as his mouthpiece and right-hand man. He thought he even knew what the man's name was, because he'd often heard the same word spoken by the other slaves when in the man's presence: Ahktam, perhaps Ah Citam, most often simply Citam.

Towering above all his household subordinates but not above any of his white-skinned charges, Citam was a sturdy middle-aged man with a big top-knot of black hair hanging from the back of his flattened skull. He had harsh manners, and the look of someone who under no circumstance would suffer to be made a fool of, especially if the master was watching.

The rain that morning had dwindled to a light drizzle. It felt wonderful to let it wash all over one's body, if one could forget what it was doing to the floor of the hut where they would have to sleep again that night. There, in the floor, Jerónimo had found a small dry spot where he hid his prayer book. Jerónimo's attachment to that little book had become an obsession. It was as if he could not keep intact the very sinews of his soul unless he kept intact those dog-eared pages.

Jerónimo wasn't alone in his obsession. Everyone had found something to hold on to for the sake of sanity and pride, with the exception of Felipe whose sanity and pride had left without saying goodbye.

For Leon it was the memory of his mother; for José, his hatred of his captors; for Ponce, his loyalty to Gonzalo; and for Gonzalo the relentless thought of escape. In between shelling corn and lying idle with plenty of time on his hands, he had nothing else in mind but to return to the islands and once there change the face of history. Yes, because if this was not Cathay or Cipango or Eldorado or whatever else, one thing was sure: fate had chosen Captain Valdivia's castaways to be the first discoverers of the land that all the king's men starting with Columbus himself had searched for and died for in vain.

The islands of the Caribe were trinkets compared to this land. Here there were palaces, temples, marketplaces—and gold at last, the gold he'd seen with his own eyes on the monuments in the town's main street. If he did make it back among his countrymen, the whole of Christendom would owe to him that staggering find. He would go to don Diego Colón, who was now Governor of Hispaniola, and he would tell him that to the west of Cuba, where his father the Admiral had never thought of looking, was a vast heathen empire ready for the plucking. He would be given a title, troops, claims to this land. He would return to it no longer as a castaway but as a true Conquistador. Day and night his head buzzed with such thoughts. It was worse than before he'd left Spain, it was unendurable. This time he had seen what his dreams looked like, he had been sucked right into them.

For days he'd been waiting for a chance to be let out of the hut, if nothing else just to see what he was up against. The morning Citam signaled him and the others to start moving, all of him became alert to the opportunity. But there was José, whose hostility put them all at risk of reprisal. First it was Citam who tried to convince José to come out or else. The "or else" was conveyed by means of grim gestures and by the showing of a quirt made of what looked like a particularly vicious sort of animal hide.

José had never been one to respond to threats. Gonzalo had to go to him and plead with him for what seemed like an eternity. "Humor them for now. There must be a way out, we'll find it sooner or later."

José grumbled and spat on the ground.

"For the love of God," Gonzalo insisted, "don't give us any trouble. Let's all stay in one piece until we can break free." It was the mention of freedom that finally moved José to stand up, put on the loincloth he'd so far refused to wear, and file out of the hut with the others.

Keeping his head bent as though to protect his face from the rain, Gonzalo took in that side of the master's house that up to now had been hidden from his eyes. The wall wasn't higher than ten or twelve feet. It must seem like a good obstacle to people as short as his captors, but it was much less of a challenge for the strapping boy from Palos who could climb over the truly respectable walls of the count Moncada to steal his big black figs.

To make things even better, the six captives had been handed, together with bags full of corn kernels for the planting, long sticks whose fire-hardened tips looked sharp enough to go through a man's chest as properly as any spear. Gonzalo traded glances with Ponce and with José, to make them understand that something could be done if they all kept their wits about them. Only Ponce nodded back.

The town seemed deserted that morning. There was no plume of smoke to be seen atop the temples, and the guards at the gate looked glum as scarecrows, feathers all wet. They made their way out of the wall and down toward the countryside, with their sticks on their shoulders, José grumbling all the way.

It was quite clear that Citam didn't like having to go out in the rain. He was a house servant, not a menial laborer who must share the demeaning work of field hands. It was clear also that he was well on the alert. It would take some doing to evade his surveillance, Gonzalo thought. Not only had Citam kept his quirt, but he carried also the flint knife he customarily plied on the necks of the wild fowls of which the master was particularly fond.

Citam didn't want the white ones to mix with the rest of the farmers and slaves who were doing the planting. These had reached the cornfields long before the small bedraggled group arrived. Once there, two men joined Citam as overseers. These two were not armed, Gonzalo noticed, in fact they looked small enough to be disposed of easily.

What they remembered as lush green jungle had been turned first by fire and then by rain, as if by twin biblical disasters, into a scorched and soaked welter of dead vegetable matter. Trees had been felled and burned, their torn branches still smoldering. In their places large clearings gaped under a layer of choking smoke. Armed with stone axes, a group of half-naked, top-knotted workers was slashing away at anything that had survived. It was in that mess of ashes and mud that the corn was being planted, in holes punched with the digging sticks.

The overseers prodded the six into the fields and showed them how the sticks must be used and the kernels dropped. José made a threatening gesture, to which Citam put his hand to his quirt.

Once again Gonzalo had to intervene. "José, listen to me, you'll ruin everything like this." Citam hated it when they began to talk among themselves in their tongue. He shouted something at Gonzalo to silence him. Gonzalo stepped in the mud, poked his stick at random and dropped a few kernels of corn.

"Come on, José," he coaxed. José kept shaking his stick threateningly. Gonzalo was desperate. "Yes, that is what we'll do, kill them with their own damn sticks, but for God's sake, not now!"

Citam took a step closer. Gonzalo made a tortured effort to be silent. He poked another hole and dropped a few more kernels. Before anybody could stop him, José lurched at Citam with his stick, unable to utter his hatred in words and giving instead a sort of bark from the depth of his belly.

The two overseers piled up on top of him, struggling to keep him away from Citam. Gonzalo fell down on all fours, damning José in his mind for the stupid thing he'd done. While he crawled away he felt the quirt crackle on his bare back and he screamed out his outrage. Ponce helped him up, put himself between him and Citam; but Citam's attention was all on José, whom the overseers could barely hold down as he thrashed in the mud.

What happened next was quick and simple. Citam pressed his knee on José's chest, took out his knife and cut José's throat from ear to ear. It was as if there had been all the time an understanding between him and the slave, a predictable way to deal with a predictable rebellion. This wasn't the first time Citam dealt with insubordinate slaves. No wonder the master trusted him so.

Gonzalo looked at José sprawled on the soggy ash and red from the chin down. That's each and every one of us, he thought, until not one of us is left. After that he could do nothing but dig holes and drop corn all day in the rain, while the two overseers took José's body and tossed it out in the jungle for the jaguars to find.

Hole after hole and kernel after kernel, he learned that hated labor of slave in no time, as though he'd planted corn all his life. He became nothing but hands, hands doing what they had to do all by themselves. It was like back in Palos, when he sat hunched over the broken nets that had to be mended until the whole world became one broken net; like back aboard the *Esperanza* and the other ships, when they made him splice bits of old rope for hours on end while the officers' arrogant footsteps beat a knell in his brain.

No dreams left. They were slipping away from him the way the corn kernels slipped from his hands into the ground. No telling the Spanish governor to send ships to the west of Cuba. No titles, no claims, nothing. Even the humblest dream of all seemed lost now—to go home, no matter how. No matter if that meant returning poor and powerless as he'd left, to face the ridicule of kin and neighbors. So many among them considered don Cristobal

Colón just a foreign charlatan, a teller of tall sea tales whose empty promises had led many a fool to ruin. If they only knew instead, Gonzalo thought. Don Cristobal was right, there were rich lands waiting beyond the edge of nothing; but from those lands Gonzalo would never return alive.

The thought of a lifetime of slavery tore him apart. He'd never imagined there could be anything worse than the brutal discipline of a sailor's life. But when he was a sailor he could still juggle choices with the blessed frenzy that came simply from being twenty years old and in good health. Now he knew there was no way out. Not in Spain, not here, not in God's own hell. For people like him who didn't have the good sense to be born with money and power, there was nothing but the whip and the grave.

FIVE

If not for his bond with Ponce, those first times would have been simply despair and the sort of shrugging madness that was making Felipe smaller and lighter every day.

Jerónimo with his ever-present prayer book vexed him beyond endurance, and Leon kept pestering him to try to escape, even though Citam now kept one of his men posted day and night in front of the hut. Ponce instead with his gentle, plodding soul, knew how to simply sit next to him when not only plans but mere words became impossible. This was often enough after a day spent in the cornfields, bare feet bleeding and everything else too sore to lie down.

It was as though the planting would never end. From dawn to dusk they had to trudge in that damnable expanse of scorched brush, going constantly back on their own steps since they were unable to tell where they'd punched holes already and where they hadn't yet. They got very little help from the overseers and none from Citam, who was there just to carry his knife and glare at them, since he loathed this job as much as they hated theirs.

To Gonzalo it seemed like the deadliest sin that his life, the life God had given him, should be used for nothing better than raising crops that fed a race of murdering cannibals.

"How's that now, Jerónimo?" he would taunt. "How is it that God wants us to plant corn for the unbaptized? Couldn't he have made us prisoners of the Portuguese, of the French, of the Dutch?

With so many enemies that Spain has, surely he could have picked some fellow Christians to be our jailers."

At first Jerónimo took it upon himself to answer those blasphemous questions. "It's not for us to demand explanations. God can't be so easily persuaded to yield His mysteries. Or else He'd be no better than a heathen idol that yields rain only because some crazy old men feed him human hearts in a basket."

But this was the sort of sparring that only exacerbated their wounds like the salt water splashed on a sailor's back after a lashing. After a while Jerónimo decided to turn a deaf ear to Gonzalo's baiting. It was just for trying times, he said, that the Devil waited to poison a soul with doubt, and he would not invite a challenge.

The glimpses of that world that had so amazingly revealed itself before were now reduced to what they could observe during their daily walk to and from the cornfields—the same piece of street bordered by the same houses, the same piece of field rimmed by the same jungle. That daily walk, however, was hardly an uneventful occurrence. Unlike their master, who after putting the strangers to good use hadn't gone once to see whether they were still alive, the people of the town remained curious.

They still crowded in the street when the slaves were let out, they still pointed. They never looked at them with contempt, but always with surprise, as if at a magician's trick. Certainly among these people there must be some-one he could talk to as to any Christian, Gonzalo thought. They could not all be bloodthirsty savages. Every time he wanted to run to them, desperate to find out what they were saying, and every time he was held back by Citam, that detested watchdog.

Once, when they were close to the gate through which they left the town every morning, a woman rushed toward them holding a small idol painted red and yellow, which she waved in the air while frantically indicating the strangers, especially the strangers' beards.

From what they could see, it seemed that the idol too wore a beard. It took Citam a lot of shouting to drive the woman away. This incident puzzled Gonzalo for days. His ignorance of the natives' tongue kept him more of a captive than did the rope strung across the doorway of the hut.

Then, for reasons that couldn't be fathomed, all work in the cornfields stopped for nearly a whole week, though it was far from over, and the food rationed to all workers, slaves and freemen alike, dwindled to the bare mini-mum. It was during those days that Felipe surrendered to his madness. He became convinced that the master wanted to starve his slaves to death, and no way was found to persuade him that the master couldn't possibly want to kill all his property, including the indispensable Citam. Where Felipe had gone nobody could reach him anymore. One morning they found him swing-ing from the rafters of the hut; he'd hanged himself with his own loincloth.

The usual allowances of food resumed that same day, along with the planting of the farthest clearings. In the rain the corn was pushing out at an astonishing speed. It fattened as if by the very eye of the gods, curling and unsheathing like those tendrils of stone that enveloped the walls of the tem-ples.

But it wasn't just the rain that produced that uncanny burgeoning. One day the master himself went to the fields, followed by his wife, his retainers, a priest and an old woman who carried in her arms a newborn baby boy cov-ered with blue paint. The farmers, including the four surviving whites, were made to gather round. There in the middle of the field the priest cut open the baby's chest and offered his tiny heart to the corn.

The sight of that little body lying among the new sprouts stayed with the four prisoners for a very long time. Jerónimo was sick for two days and even forgot to say his prayers. Truly no captivity among fellow Europeans would ever compare with the horrors they had witnessed among these worshippers of Satan.

Once the planting was done, the weeding started. This had to be done no longer standing up and poking with the digging stick but with bent backs, or rather on all fours, for that was the only way for the new slaves to tell weed from sprout in the confusion of the charred fields; and since the rain fell on both crops and bad grasses, the latter shot up at the same lush pace as did the corn.

In the hut it was as it had been in the boat after the wreck, more and more room left now that José and Felipe were dead. Leon wandered around saying he was next to die, as though he'd looked into God's own ledgers. Ponce was becoming impatient with Gonzalo, who seemed to have abandoned all plans of escape for no better reason except it was too dangerous. Had it been less dangerous to break free from that cage? Ponce reminded him; had death ever been closer than out there in the jungle, with no water, no direction, nothing but sheer desperation?

Gonzalo replied that it was neither the right time nor the right way. There had to be a plan saner than sheer desperation. Maybe he could learn enough of the heathens' tongue to persuade the master that for someone like him owning four less slaves was like owning four less of the clay pots in which he relieved himself.

That was a time-consuming plan, Ponce objected, and they had not a day to spare. He muttered that if Gonzalo intended to remain forever a slave, he would try to escape on his own.

Gonzalo knew well his plan was an improbable one. Having fallen as close to the bottom as any man can, he didn't know where he could find a soul willing to address him with something else beside the orders Citam and the others barked at him. There was only the girl of the loincloths. Lately, either because she was so ordered or of her own will, she had begun to linger around the hut more and more, in a way Gonzalo found encouraging, especially since he remembered how terrified she'd been the first time she'd seen the new slaves.

He convinced himself that she was actually looking for a chance to see him. It was a preposterous thought; but he stuck to it, because it was only with that preposterous thought in mind that he could bring himself, one afternoon when no one was watching, to stand in the doorway and beckon to her.

She responded to that wordless call by bending her head in such a sweet and unaffected way that Gonzalo felt touched in his heart, ready to absolve her of every sin her cannibal countrymen might have committed. Ponce asked him what he was doing. When Gonzalo silenced him, he kept his peace, no doubt thinking Gonzalo was finally up to something that would help them break out.

Instead when the girl stood by the doorway on the other side of the rope, all that Gonzalo could do was stand there and motion her not to leave, as he tried to think of something to say. Yet clearly, for one of those absurd miracles between men and women that he could never gauge, she was no longer terrified of him. She would not run from this very tall, big-boned, blue-eyed, copper-haired, pale-skinned man who looked like no one she'd ever seen and came from no place she'd ever heard of.

Whether she'd always been a slave or had only recently become one, she knew enough about dignity to have kept a great deal of it. She was spotlessly clean in her short cotton gown that flushed with red embroidery around the neck. She was no taller than his heart, and slight as a foal. The only thing he couldn't find appealing was the way her forehead became one with her nose, with that bizarre flattening of the skull that all these natives seemed to possess. She didn't gape at him, she didn't fidget or giggle. She simply looked him in the eyes.

"*Baax u kaba?*" she asked him quietly.

Gonzalo shook his head. "Me? Nothing, nothing. I just wanted to talk to you."

She covered her mouth to hide her smile. Gonzalo shifted his weight. Ponce squinted at the two of them. Gonzalo waved him away.

"*Kaba*," the girl said again, carefully. She put her hand on her chest. "*Kaba... Kanalsin.*"

"*Kanalsin!*" he cried out. Yes, he did remember that word. The first time he'd heard it he'd thought it was her name. So then, *kaba* was "name." He pointed at himself.

"*Kaba...* Gonzalo," he said eagerly. "Say it, say my name."

The first consonant proved to be much more of an obstacle for her than any foreign novelty might be for him. All that came out, though she tried earnestly, was an odd mutilated sound. He shook his head, giving up. This was foolish, he thought, utterly useless. How could he make her understand if he didn't even know where to start?

She lifted her hand to his mouth, and kept it there until he realized he must be silent and pay attention. She pointed at the rope between them.

"*Taab*," she said. She motioned him to repeat the word, making the rope sway gently. "*Taab.*"

Gonzalo opened his mouth and repeated, "*Taab.*"

Then the girl pointed at the doorway. "*Hol na*," she said.

Gonzalo was beginning to understand. She was teaching him her tongue before he'd even asked her to. "*Hol na, hol na*," he almost shouted, like a little boy at Sunday school.

She broke into the widest grin he'd ever seen on anybody's face. Then she pointed at her own mouth. "*Hol.*" She pointed at the hut. "*Na.*" Again she made him put the two words together.

"*Hol na...* Mouth, house... Mouth of the house?" he ventured. "The door! The door is the mouth of the house! O blessed God!" He grasped her hand. "Please tell me more," he begged.

From behind the water basin Citam was coming to see what was going on. The girl said something Gonzalo couldn't catch. He thought she meant she would be back, because there was nothing in the world he wanted more. He indicated first her, then the threshold. "I want you here again, do you understand me? Here!"

She nodded over and over. "*Halach than, halach than.*"

"*Halach*... yes?" he asked. "Yes you'll be back?" But she could wait no longer, and she ran from him before Citam could find out who she was talking to. Gonzalo slapped his thigh in frustration.

When he went back into the hut, he saw that Ponce and the others were looking at him as though he'd lost his mind. But he didn't care. All night in his sleep he kept hearing the first precious sounds Kanalsin had taught him. All night he kept thinking of nothing but the moment she would come back and help him pry open, one word at a time, his way back to freedom.

SIX

She would come toward the end of the day, when Citam and the young man who stayed posted by the hut went to have their supper. She would sit against the wall, always with some work to be done, cotton skeins to be braided or pod-like vegetables to be strung together. Gonzalo had no idea whether she was in danger of being punished. He imagined her comings and goings were of no great importance to anyone. Probably nobody would even notice if some day she'd simply vanish, like those yellow butterflies that alighted on the wall and then fluttered back into the jungle. He would sit facing her, forgetting the rain, the filth and the mosquitoes, ready to drink in everything she brought him. She didn't come every day, and he didn't grasp everything she said; but even so he was grateful.

First came the words that had to do with the all-important staple to which he'd been indentured: *ixim,* the sunbeams of the gods, corn. He learned the name of the cornfield, of the stick for planting corn, of the granary in which the corn was kept, of the cornmeal he ate while working, of the corn soup he had for breakfast.

Then came the words that had to do with the second most important thing in the world: *haa,* the teardrops of the gods, water; and the places where water was found, stored, used. All life as these people conceived of came from corn and from water, the father and mother of their race. Everything revolved daily, monthly, yearly and eternally around them.

It wasn't quite the same thing that fish and the sea meant to his father, or wheat and the rain to the Castilian peasants who paraded the statue of the Virgin across their fields scarred by the drought.

There was deep reverence in the way she spoke of the two things that made the crops, as though both were as real as any living, breathing human being.

To explain what a corn sprout was, Kanalsin made the gesture of cradling a baby with the utmost tenderness, as if nothing were more precious than those pale shoots arching from the seedling. As he watched her rock in her arms that ghostly baby, Gonzalo saw again in his mind the newborn slaughtered by the priest after the planting. He understood very well what she meant.

Such worship of soulless objects and such disregard for human life was monstrous, he thought. Then he remembered that when the Virgin didn't listen and the drought turned Castile as hot as the hooves of Satan, the first ones to die were the newly-born, starved and dried like the crops starved and dried in the fields. The monstrous thing, he realized, was not that human life should be regarded as less important than crops, but that everywhere he knew, no crops meant no life.

Whatever understanding of his captors he gained from those first sounds exchanged across the doorway split him from his companions in a most confusing way. Leon and Jerónimo sometimes came to sit with him. Leon stared at the girl as though she couldn't be for real. Jerónimo instead bristled at her presence even as he couldn't resist his own curiosity. What he was most anxious to find out was whether anybody in this land had ever heard of Our Lord Jesus Christ. Gonzalo dismissed that question with a laugh.

Ponce was the one who resented her most, pained that Gonzalo could forsake him for someone like her. Gonzalo replied that he was taking advantage of Kanalsin for a purpose, that there was no harm in trying to fathom the minds of these people. But he felt awkward sitting between her and the three men, like the needle between the arms of scales.

Nothing like the heart of a woman, he thought when he saw her slip out of the master's house. It took so little to move them to compassion. Once in a while she even smuggled to him food left over from the master's table. The day she managed to bring him a brand- new cotton mantle he felt quite clever. Not only was he making good use of Kanalsin's good heart, but he was also leaving Citam none the wiser.

Soon after she left, and the young man who guarded the door came back from his evening meal, Gonzalo grew bold enough to test on him one of the young man's favorite words. "*Maatan!*" he cried. "No! I will not move from the door. Try and make me." The young man could only glower and shrug.

Gonzalo's gloating was short-lived. A while later Kanalsin was back, this time with the same old woman who'd carried to the cornfield the newborn sacrificed to the new crops, Brand-new cotton mantles were given to the remaining three slaves as well.

"And we thought the young lady had a soft spot for you, Brother Guerrero," Ponce scoffed.

Gonzalo ignored him. He bowed his thank you to the two women, making Kanalsin step back delighted. Then the old woman went to Leon without hesitation, as though she'd known him since birth. She was a good-looking, ample woman who carried her years graciously. Smiling, she lifted a hand to Leon's face.

"*Chin in al,*" she said, stroking his cheek and cooing what sounded un-mistakably like words of endearment. Leon blushed from head to toe.

"*Chin in al,*" the old woman blessed him.

Gonzalo had to avert his eyes. It had been so long since a touch like that, a touch like a mother's. When both women left, the four men scattered to their corners in a painful silence.

Gonzalo stayed awake a long time. The only sounds he could hear in the twilight were the distant growl of the thunder and Leon's heartbreaking sobs. Leon cried himself to sleep every night now. It was a strangely comforting sound, Gonzalo thought. He wished he could weep as openly as Leon did. He himself wasn't much older, much farther from that release that was allowed to boys but denied to men, as least according to men's wisdom. It was as though Leon cried for all of them, sorrowing without shame for everything they had lost.

Some sort of festivity was in the offing. They left the cornfields earlier now, and the house resounded with a happy bustle. Jerónimo consulted his well-thumbed prayer book. It was almost mid-July, but the heathens' activi-ties resembled those that in Christendom took place at the end of December, when people celebrated the New Year by discarding old objects and replacing them with new ones.

The slaves were busy scrubbing and cleaning and sweeping out worn mats and broken stools. Citam, looking more imposing than ever in his new livery, carried away from the kitchen stacks of chipped pottery. The trash heap at the farthest end of the courtyard kept growing like the pile of wood under a heretic before the *auto de fé*.

There must be thousands of frogs wheezing all over. The courtyard was full of them, some lined up along the rim of the water basin like musicians in a church choir. Yet none of the natives did so much as nudge one away. In-stead everybody seemed delighted by the endless croaking. Gonzalo couldn't stand them, fat and bug-eyed. He jumped up shouting when he found one under the folds of his mantle.

Kanalsin had almost no time to stop by the hut now. She looked very pretty in her new yellow wrap that started barely above her breasts and ended barely below her knees, showing her smooth cinnamon skin. With a smile on his lips, Gonzalo spied on her from the doorway. For a moment he imagined he was back in Palos, when he went sneaking on María del Pilar and she pretended not to see him wile she dunked her bedsheets into the river and her girlfriends almost fell in laughing. Not even Ponce's grumbling could make him feel guilty in those moments.

During one of those days of preparations for the festival Leon was taken away. Citam walked into the hut at an unholy hour before dawn, just like the envoy of the Inquisition did in Spain, and laid his hands on the boy, ordering him to get out.

Everybody was torn from sleep in utter confusion. Gonzalo put himself in front of the boy and searched desperately his brain for the simplest and the most hopeless question he'd learned to ask in the heathens' tongue. "*Baax a kati?*" he stammered to Citam. "What do you want?"

Citam didn't appear much impressed by whatever knowledge of the language the slave might have culled. He looked at him superciliously, as though admitting that the white-skinned one wasn't as dumb as he looked after all. Then he laid his hands on Leon again and began to tug him toward the doorway.

More and more unnerved, Gonzalo kept asking his one question. Ponce and Jerónimo joined him in Spanish. Leon could not move for terror. The commotion attracted the man posted outside, who called two more for good measure. In a babble of tongues, with everybody cursing and threatening, the boy was plucked from the hut like a chick from the henhouse, leaving behind outrage and noise.

While Leon's pleas became faint in the wet dawn, no one could speak. No one could deceive himself. They'd seen it happen before, in the cage, when the four old men had come to take away Captain Valdivia and the others. If they had thought they could start burying their fear, fear had now returned to addle their souls.

"He said it," Ponce whispered. "He said he was going to be next... He knew it, God strike us all. And we let them take him!" He turned to Gonzalo. "It's all your fault for not wanting to escape, for wasting time with that little heathen whore!"

That was more than Gonzalo could bear, even from Ponce. He pushed him against the wall so hard that Ponce staggered and fell. Ponce tried to strike back, then collapsed to the ground like an empty sack.

Gonzalo struggled to regain his right mind. He paced back and forth.

"I'm going to talk to them," he said without thinking. Ponce laughed. "Talk to them? Why not preach to them,

Brother Guerrero? Just go out there and make them listen to the word of the Holy Spirit!"

Gonzalo could feel Ponce's resentment like a whiff of poison.

If anything happened to Leon, he would never again have Ponce on his side, and Ponce was all he had left on his side. He banged his fist on the wall until it went numb.

Nothing happened to Leon, not for the next few days. One afternoon in desperation Gonzalo stepped out of the hut, grabbed hold of Kanalsin and forced her to tell him what she knew about Leon, jumbling words in her tongue and his own. She made him go back to the hut before Citam could find out. There she managed to convey to him that Leon was not only alive and well, but that he had become both *chin*, beloved, as the old woman had called him, and kuyan, holy.

Gonzalo's mind was in a fog of desperation. What was she talking about? Had Leon been consecrated a priest, monk?

"*Yan in,* I must... What is the bloody word? *ilah,* yes.... *yan in ilah.* I must see him," he begged her.

Kanalsin's eyes saddened. Clearly he had asked for the impossible. Head bent, she left. He didn't see her again that day.

The worst was having to face Ponce, who he knew would never forgive him. He wanted to tell Ponce that they must stick together now more than ever, but pride stopped him. It was Jerónimo who approached him.

"Leon's alive," Gonzalo answered brusquely.

"But what about that... consecration you spoke of?" Jerónimo insisted.

"I don't know what that means."

Jerónimo joined his hands. "I tremble to think of it.

Consecrated to the devil, for their hellish worship! Leon's so young, and so pure... He told me he's never known a woman. He's untouched as the day he was born."

Ponce twisted his mouth. "That must be why they chose him," he said. "If I were a savage, I'd prefer untouched meat myself."

Jerónimo looked at him in horror. "May God have mercy," he whispered.

The next time they saw Leon was on the day of the festival, the sixteenth of July. All the members of the master's household, from the master himself down to the last kitchen helper, walked out in procession to the temple that rose closest to the sea, the tallest one of all. The three white slaves formed as usual a group apart, guarded by Citam and his minions. That morning they had been ordered to wash up for the occasion, and to wear their new mantles. Not a word had been spoken among them.

A great crowd had gathered at the temple. It wasn't out of spite, or in order to punish them, that the master had made his three foreign slaves join him. In fact, Gonzalo realized, inviting them to such a glorious ceremony must mean that he intended to treat them with the same familiarity as he treated every other slave of his own race. Even more so, Gonzalo found out, since at this particular ceremony no women were present. Witnessing the rite that was about to be performed was clearly an honor not female could share, not even the master's wife.

Gonzalo felt like a child dragged to a public execution. Full of anger and fear, he moaned to himself. Jerónimo whispered instead over and over the prayers to Our Lady. Ponce alone, with a strength he'd never shown before, kept his head high and his body straight as a curse.

In the middle of the temple's courtyard was the image of an idol, half snaggle-toothed man half lizard. The lord first, then minor dignitaries handed the priests gifts of food and liquor, of new clothes and new bowls. Much music went with the offerings, and much chanting of prayers and burning of incense.

When Leon appeared, carried in a litter like a princeling, Gonzalo started: he was so decked out with feathers and gold and jade that he resembled one of those mummies of saints kept under the altars of Spanish cathedrals. He lay resting on his elbow, a vacant smile on his face. It was the same smile Gonzalo had seen on Captain Valdivia's face. At least the heathens were charitable enough to drug their victims before butchering them. Thank God, Gonzalo thought, thank God.

It was almost as though the boy had become too holy even to be handled like a common mortal. Clearly he'd been treated well in the past days. He looked well-fed and spotlessly clean. The priests only motioned him out of the litter and toward a pole that rose near the statue of the idol.

Leon went to the pole with a step like a dancer's. There he stripped himself naked with such grace that the priests couldn't hide their pleasure. His heart was marked by a spot of white paint. Now he appeared for what he was, a stripling on the brink of manhood, still untainted by lust, slim and white.

The priests cleansed themselves with the smoke from the incense. Then they tied Leon to the pole with ropes that were braided with flowers. One of them with a knife wounded the boy slightly at the point where his member grew out of downy hair, and with that blood smeared the face of the idol. Ten archers filed in, their pace one with the thumping of the drums and the shaking of the rattles. Leon's head was tilted to one side as though resting on a pillow, hearing and feeling nothing.

The archers began to circle around the pole in perfect cadence, bows cocked, limbs writhing like those of lizards to please their lizard god. At the priests' signal, the first archer shot the first arrow straight into the white spot painted on Leon's chest. Leon fell forward, held only by the ropes. Mercifully, the first blow had been enough.

Then the second archer struck, again within the spot; and so did the third and the fourth and all ten, until Leon's chest became a sunburst of arrows all growing from the same root that had been his heart.

Jerónimo lifted his hands to the heavens and cried out, "Take him among your angels, O Lord, for he was as innocent as they. Wipe these savages from the face of the earth!"

For once Gonzalo could only be grateful to Jerónimo for uttering what he himself was too horrified to say. He remembered how he had promised Leon to bring him back to his mother, and how Leon had promised never to leave her again.

"How much longer, O Lord?" Jerónimo begged. "How much longer must we endure?"

The archers left. The priests lifted a flagstone at the feet of the idol, making sure the blood that was pouring from the boy ran into the grave they'd dug below. The lord was being congratulated by his peers for offering such a handsome sacrifice. The boy was laid to rest together with the jade and gold and feathers that had adorned him.

The flagstone was sealed and strewn with flowers. Finally the priests lit a fire on the grave, and as the flames began to rise they handed food and drink to all present.

Gonzalo watched the first cups of liquor being passed from man to man. He'd never gotten drunk in his life; then again he'd never been a guest in hell before. If such were the celebrations to be had there, he might as well revel with the rest of the damned. Under Ponce's and Jerónimo's appalled eyes, he seized the cup that Citam was offering him.

"*Baax u kaba?*" he asked Citam with grim merriment. "What do you spawn of the devil call this stinking brew?"

Citam seemed in high spirits. "*Balchè,*" he replied.

"*Balchè,*" Gonzalo repeated, smiling. He took a sip, retched, then swallowed down hard. If this was poison, he thought, bless their kind hearts. In a flash, making violence to every nerve in his body, he emptied the cup.

Everything began to blur. He could feel an obscene glee rising from the depths of his soul, a thing as vile as the last dregs in a battered cask. Citam handed him another cup, and he sloshed it all over himself, barely aware of Jerónimo's pleas, of Ponce's disgust, of the laughter that grew louder at his every reeling gesture.

"Give me more," he begged, even as his belly was roiling with the liquor and he couldn't stop retching. Anything to forget Leon, to forget this place, to forget himself.

Citam was patting his shoulder, saying God knew what.

Gonzalo could barely sit up now. The world went like a top.

He lifted the cup. "*Salúd!*" he toasted one and all. "May you all rot for a thousand years," he gaily slurred, his eyes stinging with tears and with the liquor. "And may your wives give birth to a thousand snaggle-toothed lizards!" He elbowed Citam in the ribs. "Do you have a wife, huh?" Citam bobbed his head and laughed. Gonzalo wiped his eyes. "Well, if you do, I'd love to give it to your flat-headed, flat- breasted, flat-assed wife!"

Every one of the natives was rolling with laughter. Gonzalo had become the happiest of New Year celebrants. What did anything matter anymore? One step further and he'd finally touch bottom, he'd finally be left with nothing more to lose.

When he regained himself, many miserable hours later, Jerónimo was bringing a wet rag from the water vessel. His hands felt good as he brushed back Gonzalo's hair.

The hut reeked of vomit. The *balchè* had gone through him like fire through kindling, leaving him perfectly limp. With all the strength he could muster he lifted himself up on his elbow. He squinted toward Ponce's corner. It was empty; the sleeping mat was rolled up against the wall.

"How long ago did he leave?" he asked.

Jerónimo tried to make him stand still so he wouldn't start vomiting again. "Last night," he answered. "I was asleep and you were... sick. He's taken nothing with him." He laid the wet rag on Gonzalo's forehead. "I guess he made it at least out of the town walls... or else by now they would have found him."

Another wave of nausea ripped Gonzalo's insides. Ponce was gone, as he had promised he would. He grappled with the thought before doubling over in pain. Ponce would never be found. He knew it as he knew the pain that was cutting him in two. The jungle would find Ponce, find him and bury him on the same day.

SEVEN

The days that followed were for Gonzalo the most dismal ones of all. He blamed himself for Leon's death and for Ponce's disappearance, and he could find no comfort. Once after the New Year ceremony Kanalsin stole to the hut and asked him if he wanted to talk. Gonzalo told her to go away, even shouted at her when she still stood there with a great sadness in her eyes. After that, whenever she was in the courtyard she went about in a hurry, avoiding his gaze.

After the corn got under way, they started to plant other crops, crops they couldn't even name, fruits and vegetables they'd never seen before. When work in the fields was not required, they had to carry water or chop wood or weave baskets. At day's end all Gonzalo could do was grope to his mat and pray for sleep.

Now that only he and Jerónimo were left, he couldn't help but wonder why of all people that pale man full of the fear and fervor of the Gospel should have been chosen to be his only surviving companion. Certainly God meant to punish him for his sins, because Jerónimo was the very last person with whom he was willing to share his captivity. Should he die before Jerónimo, he joked with himself, at least he could be sure to receive plenty of religious comfort in his final days. Who knows, Jerónimo might even make a proper Christian out of him.

It was as though when God had made the two men he'd been looking at two different blueprints without even knowing it. There was not one thing Gonzalo did that Jerónimo wouldn't do some other way. Even Jerónimo's way of rolling up his mat was enough to anger him. Why would anyone in the middle of such desolation insist on keeping everything as neat as possible? he ranted. Jerónimo looked up at him like a small boy confronting a bully. He smoothed the mat with his hand and answered that it was in the middle of desolation that a man was supposed to show his mettle.

What infuriated Gonzalo the most was Jerónimo's conviction that they would not remain slaves of the savages forever. Jerónimo was sure that someone would be sent for them sooner or later. After all, the *Esperanza* was freighted with twenty thousand gold ducats from the coffers of don Diego Colón. Certainly the Admiral's son would want to know what had happened to his money, or his career as governor wouldn't last much longer.

"Don Diego Colón has no time for the likes of us," Gonzalo replied. "As for the money, this isn't the first time the bottom of the Caribe becomes a Spanish bank. No one is coming. No one would even know *where* to come for us."

Jerónimo's faith was unshakable. All they had to do was endure their misfortunes with fortitude, like Joseph among the Egyptian idolaters. The Lord would help His lost children.

"The Lord helps those who help themselves, when he does help anybody at all," Gonzalo retorted. "We can't just sit here and wait for heavenly deliverance."

Jerónimo lost his patience. "Well, Brother Guerrero, I don't see *you* helping yourself much. All you do is mock the Almighty with your every breath."

Much as Gonzalo hated to admit it, Jerónimo was right. Out of spite, to prove him wrong, he forced himself to overcome his own despondency. The next time he saw Kanalsin he gave her the signal that meant he wanted to talk. Kanalsin pretended not notice, and for a moment he feared he'd lost her just as he'd lost Ponce. Then instead she headed toward him, trying to hide her joy.

Before she could open her mouth Jerónimo was at the door, his arm raised to keep her at bay. "Don't you dare consort with that woman again. She is a child of sin. She must not be allowed to come near us!"

Frightened by the wrath in Jerónimo's voice, Kanalsin stepped back from the doorway with a cry. Gonzalo gestured her to stay, then turned around with equal rage.

"Brother Aguilar, I will consort with whomever I please. I will consort with the devil himself if he can make me a free man again. If you don't want to be near her, all you have to do is move to the farthest corner of this hut."

For a moment Jerónimo was so outraged he couldn't speak: Gonzalo looked ready to use his fists. "You would actually turn against a fellow Spaniard at a time like this," he said. "How can one sane man fight against so much darkness?"

Then he walked away from the door. He gathered up his mat, his mantle, his bowl and his prayer book and he put them where Gonzalo had told him, in the farthest corner of the hut. He sat down with his back turned and he began to pray with passion and grief, asking God for strength to fight the evil that stood at the door in her indecent yellow wrap and bare cinnamon skin.

Gonzalo averted his eyes and faced Kanalsin. As always, having her so near threw him into a quandary. He loathed the thought of her belonging to such a race of people, yet he couldn't help himself but smile to someone as gentle and pretty as she was. Perhaps he'd better make up his mind, he thought. He'd better decide whether he wanted to abominate her the way Jerónimo did or else make her once and for all as human as himself.

She knew his pain. He could tell by the way she was looking at him. She remembered the boy who'd been chosen for the New Year sacrifice. She was about Leon's age; perhaps next year she would die in the temple the same terrible death.

Gonzalo lifted a finger to her face and traced the faint lines tattooed on her forehead. "What do you know," he said. "It wasn't you who invented all this. Who knows how long ago one of your great-grandfathers got it into his mind to carve a snaggle-toothed lizard and offer him a living heart instead of a candle."

She bent her head, understanding nothing of his words but everything of his touch. In the courtyard two other slaves were staring at them. Everybody in the master's household would soon know. So be it, Gonzalo thought. Let them go tell that son of a whore who thought he owned him that he'd touched one of his women. Kanalsin was almost on tiptoe with expectation. In the first evening breeze the leaves of the palmetto trees scraped against one another like long green blades.

It seemed to Gonzalo that he was facing two equally dreary choices—giving everything up or giving everything back to hope almost by habit, as though hope, like breath, were something that went on without anybody's consent. Kanalsin was motioning him to sit down, to start that sort of game they had, when he'd point at something and she'd tell him the name of the thing. She was straining toward him with her whole being, as if to reach his bitterness and tear it away.

He hesitated. From the bottom of the hut he could hear Jerónimo's whispered prayers: secretive, conspiratorial, spoken in a language only Jerónimo and God understood. For a moment the sound of those words made him shiver. What if they were really powerful? he wondered. What if Jerónimo could really wrest freedom for himself with nothing more than his own faith?

He blinked. Kanalsin was nudging him to sit down with the imploring manners of a child.

"*Ten c'in cambezik tech,*" she begged him, with the phrase they exchanged almost as a password. "I will be teaching you now."

He sat down across from her, "Yes, teach me," he said softly. "I have a conspiracy of my own."

From a distance, unseen, Citam and the young man who guarded the hut were watching. The young man started to walk toward the hut, but Citam stopped him. He squinted at the two figures in the doorway, then motioned to let them be.

❖　　　❖　　　❖

Jerónimo's move to the farthest corner of the hut was final. When it became clear that he would never return from it, Gonzalo christened that corner "the chapel" and resumed his merciless taunting.

"If the evening mass is over down there in the chapel, I would quite gratefully go to sleep now, Brother Aguilar."

Jerónimo put his prayer book away. "I've seen men die among torments for smaller blasphemies than yours."

Gonzalo folded his mantle to be his pillow. "So have I, yes, back home and back in the islands. Thank be to God that here at least, no matter what other horrors we might have, we're still free from the Holy Inquisition."

Jerónimo took a step forward and faced with him rage. "Brother Guerrero, listen. We were both born in the same country, we both speak the same language and we both want to come out of this place alive. Other than that, you and I have not one thing in common. If you will kindly leave me in peace, I shall do you the same favor with the greatest pleasure."

Gonzalo rolled over. "Amen to every word."

All through August the rain poured on. It fell in sudden afternoon squalls, forcing everyone to return home early, including the lord of the house who repaired to his mansion grumbling about the blessed wrath of the gods upon his person.

Kanalsin now came and went with Citam's knowledge.

Gonzalo almost felt sorry for Jerónimo, who had no one to talk to, while he now had not only Kanalsin but also the young man who guarded the hut. The latter was a friendly fellow who liked to join their in their evening conversations, showing his teeth in a good-natured laugh whenever Gonzalo mauled a new word more imaginatively than ever.

The name of the language was *Mayathàn*. It was punctuated by certain doubled sounds he found a bit startling, yet it was also as strangely pleasant as the sound of a musical instrument he'd never heard before. It managed to do without some important consonants, most notably Gs and Rs. For this reason Gonzalo's first and last name, which in Spain were as common as dirt, here had become unutterable.

After it became obvious that neither Kanalsin nor the young man would ever master those two sounds, he resigned himself to being called Zalo, the closest they could get to what he'd been given on the day of his baptism. It wasn't long before Citam, too, began to address him with that half name. Half a name was better than no name; soon enough Kanalsin's lovely way of shaping her mouth when she said it made him forget that smallest among the outrages inflicted upon him.

Perhaps because of Gonzalo's success with Kanalsin, Citam now seemed much more curious about his resourceful new slave than he'd ever let on. Once Gonzalo caught him spying on him, his thick neck craned in the direction of the hut's door. Good, Gonzalo thought. He was glad to see his captors paying attention to him. He would not blend in with the rest of the slaves or shrink into a corner like Jerónimo; and he would not be destroyed like Felipe or Ponce or José.

But the work in the cornfields in the rain, dressed only in a loincloth, was beginning to take its toll even on him who'd known hard work in all weather. A few more years of this life, and he knew he would be buried long before his time. Jerónimo, who wasn't used to toil, had it even worse. On the day of the week that he reckoned to be Friday, he not only abstained from eating whatever scrap of meat happened to be in his bowl but fasted altogether in penance. His body, weakened already by so many hardships, had reached a point of almost cadaverous thinness.

Gonzalo couldn't stand the sight of the food left untouched. That waste in the face of their need to survive seemed sheer idiocy. But the two of them spoke to one another only when absolutely necessary, like an old married couple that has long lost the pleasure of each other's company. So every Friday the leftover food was given to the dogs, while Gonzalo shook his head in contempt and Jerónimo retreated stiff-shouldered to his mat.

In September the rain was followed by the *huracàn*, the winds that in the islands lifted men, trees and roofs and scattered them to the four directions like straw. The first of those storms caught them in the open fields. That week they'd been bending downwards the ears of corn; it seemed the bent ears ripened faster like that.

The sea that morning boiled like a pot, stirred by lightning as though by the devil's own ladle. Everything moved in the wind, topknots and mantle flaps and palm trees bowing as if to sweep the earth with their green mops. Corn stalks went to and fro, ripping from their vines the beans and squashes planted next to them.

Gonzalo eyed the darkening sky and Jerónimo shook from head to toe, seemingly about to topple over. Citam's calls came in broken gusts as he debated with the overseers. At last a fellow worker told Gonzalo they were going back to town. By the time they were outside the gate it had become hard to hold one's own against the wind, and the noise of the sea below the cliff resembled a pounding of cannon. Jerónimo could not walk on, propped up against Gonzalo, struggling to catch his breath. Gonzalo had to help him through the gate that, narrow as it was, sucked the wind in like a funnel.

Pieces of thatch flew through the air. Fishermen laden with nets and harpoons hurried up from the beach, women with water jugs hastened from the underground well. The guards were trying to herd everyone in so they could shutter up the gates. In the confusion Gonzalo became separated from the rest of the slaves. As he wrapped his mantle around his head against the rain, he suddenly thought how easy it would be to race past the guards with his face hidden and head toward the beach, toward one of those canoes he'd glimpsed so often on his way out.

He was already turning around when he saw Jerónimo collapse, white-faced as a dead man. Not knowing what to do, he looked left and right to see if someone else came to Jerónimo's help. But people were running around helter-skelter, and no one was paying any attention to the two slaves. Almost unconsciously, as though the sight of a human being fallen to the ground could not produce in him any other reaction, he lifted Jerónimo up and out of the rush of the crowd. A moment later Citam found them and led them home.

He had to half drag, half carry Jerónimo to the hut. He laid him on his mat and covered him with his blanket. Jerónimo was running a fever and kept asking for water. Gonzalo drew some from the basin. The other slaves were going in every direction, fastening doors and windows. The courtyard emptied. He remained alone with Jerónimo, in the hut plunged in darkness and creaking in the advance of the hurricane like a tree about to be felled.

He brought the water to Jerónimo's lips. Jerónimo was shaking with chills, overcome by fits of cough. Gonzalo watched him without moving. Right at this moment he could be out there, if only he hadn't heeded a different call and stopped to help instead. What a foolish gesture, he chided himself; as if Jerónimo would ever do the same for him, for a man with whom he shared nothing.

Outside the hurricane broke out with a dreadful howl, rattling the walls, beating on the roof, whirling rain and torn leaves.

"I'm cold," Jerónimo said. "Don't let me die."

The overhang that sheltered the water basin was ripped off and came crashing against the hut with a banging of wooden poles. The wind keened like a woman at a fresh grave. Gonzalo was shivering. He thought about Kanalsin, hoping she was safe.

Jerónimo's pleas became louder. "Don't let me die in this place..."

Gonzalo gave a frightened shout. "Stop saying that! There's nothing I can do for you!"

A feeling of desolation took him. Watching Jerónimo was like watching himself die there on that miserable straw mat, thousands of miles away from home and forgotten by all. At least Jerónimo still had a companion in that last hour; when *his* turn would come, there would be no one. It seemed like the ultimate malice that Jerónimo had decided to die first. The wind became the hiss of a huge scythe, mixed with the thudding of tree branches.

"All right," Gonzalo said. He took off his mantle and wrapped it around the ragged blanket already soaked with Jerónimo's cold sweat. He had no other cover to add to that. He could only hold his hands on Jerónimo's chest to keep the mantle more snugly around him. Jerónimo was grateful, quieting down.

"All right. I won't let you die, Brother Aguilar."

He lay down next to him with his face against the damp ground, one arm wrapped around his own head and the other around Jerónimo's chest. Perhaps that was how the souls at the Last Judgment threw themselves at the mercy of the Judge, he thought.

The gods kept the town from the hurricane, and Gonzalo kept Jerónimo from dying. Through Kanalsin, when the storm passed, he managed to obtain first another blanket, then better food and permission to stay with Jerónimo and tend him back to health.

Jerónimo was very sick for several days; but with rest and with whatever care Gonzalo could give him, he eventually healed.

One day Citam came to the hut with by the young man who guarded it. "Zalo," he called. "You and you will no longer work in the cornfields. You will go to market for me now."

He pointed at the young man. "Ah Yax Ceh will go with you."

Gonzalo couldn't have been more relieved. He knew he owed that small victory not to Citam's sympathy but to Citam's loathing of his job as overseer. After the hurricane Citam must have pleaded hard with the master to be exempted from that undignified duty.

Nevertheless, it seemed like the sort of news that required a show of gratitude, and he chose the most slavish show. He crouched down, picked up a handful of dirt and scattered it on his own head. It was the gesture he'd seen performed by Citam himself when he saluted his noble master. Citam looked down at him with half-closed eyes. The faint trace of a smile revealed that he was pleased but not deceived by that slyly exorbitant homage. Without a word, he left.

Gonzalo returned to his evening meal. "Good news," he told Jerónimo. "We've been assigned to market. We're through breaking our backs in the cornfields."

Equally happy, Jerónimo smiled. "I thank the Lord for this." Gonzalo looked quietly at him. "Thank Him for me too,

Jerónimo," he said.

EIGHT

T he first time he went to market it was almost a holiday, shore leave. One morning Ah Yax Ceh put a net bag in his hands and told him to come along. Jerónimo, who was still too weak, was exempted for now. When they were about to leave the house Kanalsin joined them. The sight of her and the thought of being let loose in the town made Gonzalo as happy as he hadn't been in a long time.

If only he closed his eyes, the smell of the air that morning could have sailed him home on just a plank of memory. All towns at the edge of the sea had the same air, he thought. Beyond the rim of the walls he could see stretches of beaches that reached north and south, and what he couldn't see he could guess and guess forever. No wonder those born near the sea felt always the need to go somewhere.

Ah Yax Ceh was humming some barbarian love song of his. A few grubby children tagged along. Some darted forward to pinch Gonzalo's leg, then backward to boast about it with the others.

Kanalsin tried to send them away, but the children had really nothing they'd rather do than giggle at the stranger on his way to market.

"What is the name of this..." he asked Kanalsin, moving his arm around to mean the town.

"Xamanzanà," she answered. "It means The Place of Dawn."

Gonzalo breathed the word in eagerly, as if the name alone would bring him some long-awaited revelation. He attempted to say it, with the only result of laughter from both Kanalsin and Ah Yax Ceh. Kanalsin lifted a hand to stop him. "Some have begun to call it Tulum, because of the wall."

Gonzalo repeated, "Tulum, Tulum. Funniest name I've ever heard."

Now that he was at leisure to look around, he could see that the town was far from the other-worldly place that had so stunned him at first. After the nakedness of the islands, it commanded attention indeed; but the stucco crumbled from houses and temples, and the streets had been baked by the sun and scourged by the rain over pitiless cycles of years.

Heaps of rubble overgrown with weeds and left for the monkeys to play on could be either the first nubs of buildings that had never been built or the last remnants of many a better century. The scars of time, of war and of all the hardships common to the human race were as unmistakably visible within the walls of Tulum as they were in the ruined hovels that had once been Rome's imperial palaces.

The people of Tulum, though dressed in different clothes, also didn't appear much different now from what he himself had become—practiced survivors of misfortunes, determined to make the gods take notice that they were, despite the gods' neglect, still alive. The market had its appointed share of beggars, warriors maimed by their craft, old people who had outlived their families, orphans well acquainted with hunger.

Not much worth remarking after all, Gonzalo thought. But to be moving freely among this market-day crowd, to be able to wander and stop as he pleased, that was a most remarkable thing. In a sudden rush of hope he took Kanalsin's hand, as if the feel of someone else's flesh would help him see that his own was still solid with promises.

With her by the hand like a lover, he started to lope from vendor to vendor, curious about everything and everyone.

Kanalsin couldn't keep up with his questions. "What's the name of this? And the name of that? And of that over there?"

Ah Yax Ceh tried to impress on him that they were there on business. After some tugging he managed to direct him to a stall where a woman who was nursing a baby tied to her by a shawl was calling attention to her ducks. It was the wild ducks the lord was fond of, Gonzalo noticed; but with what currency would they be paid for?

Ah Yax Ceh knew all the tricks, from complimenting the mother on the baby's appetite to puckering his mouth in studied contempt for the plump, fresh fowl. This surely wasn't the first time the woman gave in to such a persuasive buyer. The bargain concluded and the price agreed upon, Ah Yax Ceh took out of the knot in his loincloth what looked like a wrinkled old hazelnut and put it in the woman's hand. Very pleased, the woman thanked him over and over.

Gonzalo could only ask one more time his favorite question. "*Baax u kaba?* What is this thing's name?"

Ah Yax Ceh got hold of the ducks by their limp necks and stuffed them into his net bag. "*U kaba, u kaba,*" he snickered. *Your* name should be U Kaba."

Kanalsin scolded the young man, then answered Gonzalo's question. The strange-looking hazelnut was called *cacau*. It was the currency he'd been wondering about. With enough of it they could buy not just wild ducks but half the marketplace.

"With those... peach stones?" he marveled. "How can anything so ugly be worth so much?"

He shook his head, looking at the woman who was hiding her money inside her shawl.

"That's like asking to be cheated," he said. "With gold instead," and he repeated the word for the benefit of his companions, "with gold you know what you have."

Or did one? he asked himself then. He remembered the time a customer in the fish market had palmed off on him some fake *maravedí*, and even his father at first couldn't tell them for the painted alloy they were. One more thing he'd always understood began now to look different. It didn't matter after all that one man paid in yellow metal and another in *cacau* stones. The way he saw it now, they could all use the leaves of trees, with apple worth a piece of ten and fig a piece of twenty. What was this land doing to him, he panicked, that he should start to see through the minds of savages?

Lost in thought as he was, he let Ah Yax Ceh lead him on to the rest of their errands. One man cut for them the hind leg of an animal that resembled a boar but had the fleshy snout of an elephant; very tender to eat, the man said. Another vendor sold them one of those birds with feathers the color of green iron and tails fanning like peacocks'. They were called *cutz,* which was also the master's name and the name of the sculptured birds that adorned his house. Indeed, Gonzalo thought, the master did look like one of those pompous prancing turkeys.

Ahuacatl was one of the names for the pear-shaped fruits with the leathery skin whose taste he remembered. He looked at them, heaped at the feet of the girl who sold them, and thought disconsolately of the corn mush that awaited him in the hut. Without a word Kanalsin undid the embroidered sash she wore and offered it to the girl in exchange for four of the fruits. Then she offered them to Gonzalo.

He realized he still didn't even know how to say Thank You. As always, however, she understood. Cheerfully she told Gonzalo to eat one of the *ahuacatl;* and as he shared the velvety fruit with her, Gonzalo wondered whether it had been by the same beguiling simplicity that Adam had been tempted into forgetting who he was. She had made the sash with a snippet of cloth left over from the gowns she cut for the master's wife, she told him, so it was hers to do with as she pleased.

Cloth and all that had to do with clothes was the reason why Kanalsin had come to market. Once the two men were done with their errands, she led them to the covered arcade where the luxury items were sold. Separated from the noisy core of the market, this shady place was the preserve of well-fed, well-groomed traders who showed their wares only to buyers who could prove their means. Some of them were burning incense to an idol painted in black, surely the patron saint of such a distinguished caste.

The cloth merchants, who knew Kanalsin by sight, let her choose from their most expensive cottons and their best dyeing pastes without quibbling. They knew well to whom those items were destined. While he stood by to help her, one of the merchants eyed Gonzalo suspiciously.

"Who are you?" he asked.

"*Ppentac*," Gonzalo replied with a tone almost of challenge. "A slave."

"And where do you come from, slave?" the merchant insisted.

Gonzalo pointed at the sea. "The east," he answered in Spanish.

The merchant had Kanalsin confirm the answer in Mayathan, then told her to wait. He returned with a book whose pages of thin bark folded like the pleats of a fan and were covered with rows of intricate-looking characters. The merchant opened the book to display a map with four gods placed at the four cardinal points. He put his finger on the east and showed Gonzalo where the town was.

"This is Tulum, and this is the east. Which one of the islands is your home?"

Gonzalo had to ask for help from Kanalsin. "No island is my home," he answered then.

He indicated further to the east, beyond the red god who guarded the sunrise, beyond the edge of the page. "My home is here. Out here, very far."

The merchant knitted his eyebrows. "There is nothing out there. Nothing lies beyond the islands."

"That's how much a landlubber like you knows," Gonzalo shot back. "There are thousands of people who live beyond the islands."

He touched his beard. "Thousands of people who look like me. They are called Castilians, and I will go back to them, and I will no longer be a slave."

The merchant made him repeat what he'd said. Like Kanalsin and like Ah Yax Ceh, the man stood hunched over to catch the import of this news. It was the same stance in which the people of Palos had heard from the sailors of the Niña, the Pinta and the Santa María that the world was much, much larger than their minds.

The merchant called two of his peers and passed the news on to them.

Discussions started, more men joined in. Ah Yax Ceh, worried about trouble, didn't know how to regain control of the situation, and Kanalsin kept asking, "Is it true, Zalo? Is it true?"

A few of the merchants dismissed the matter and returned to their business. But the majority was willing to believe. In an instant the word *"Castilàn"* bounced from one corner of the arcade to the other. Now taut with excitement, Gonzalo imagined the word being carried wherever the traders went, and the news of the bearded stranger being wafted all the way to the islands.

And look how close the islands were, he noticed, bent on the map that the merchant had left open. He could recognize each island by its shape; if the distances were even remotely correct, he couldn't be more than six or seven days away from the western tip of Cuba, especially with a good pair of oars. God, he thought, if only he could take that map!

Ah Yax Ceh had had enough of the attention being paid to the man he was in charge of. The last thing he needed was for the master to find out about all this fuss. He took Gonzalo by the arm and pulled him away, even as the merchants tried to keep him.

"This isn't the last you've heard of me!" Gonzalo shouted. "It won't be long before you'll have a whole army of *Castilàn* at your door!"

On his way home he quieted down. He turned to Kanalsin. "Please come with me again?" She nodded, took the basket he'd carried for her and reluctantly went into the house.

Jerónimo, as usual, had his nose in his prayer book. Gonzalo had already decided not to tell him anything—not about the merchants, the map, or the fact that he now knew where they were, only a few days away from deliverance. In his mind he envisioned without qualms the day he would steal a canoe and start rowing toward Cuba alone. He had already saved Jerónimo's life more than once. Let divine providence take care of Jerónimo from now on.

Jerónimo eyed the two remaining pear-like fruits in Gonzalo's hands.

"Here, take one," Gonzalo said. "They're called avocado or something like that."

NINE

By the end of the first week of his daily trips to the market, Gonzalo had stocked up together with turkeys and avocados a good deal of useful information about the layout of the town and the easiest way to get to the beach.

Ah Yax Ceh even took him outside the town walls, to show him where his father lived: Cuzumil, the Island of the Swallows, just a few miles off the coast. It was inhabited only by the priests of a goddess named Our Lady of the Rainbow, who kept there a famous shrine. Kanalsin added she'd once made a pilgrimage to the shrine, since the goddess was the patroness of weaving women.

Gonzalo carefully kept from asking questions. He knew that Ah Yax Ceh reported to Citam everything he did. One misplaced word could alert both to his plans. He squinted at the tip of land barely visible across the sea and he thought the island of Cuzumil made a perfect stepping stone to Cuba. When he then asked Ah Yax Ceh to walk further on, the young man pointed at a stone marker broken in two and choked with creeping vegetation.

"You may not go beyond this point. The master wants so."

The bitterest anger overcame him. To be standing at the very edge of the land and not to be able to take one more step, like a dog on a leash! He threw down his load of firewood, cursing loudly. He thought he would lunge at Ah Yax Ceh, bang the young man's head against the stone marker, then jump off the cliff and put an end to his misery.

Kanalsin stopped the madness. She reached out to keep him away from Ah Yax Ceh, who already had his hand on his knife. Don't, don't, she begged him with her eyes. Let this pass.

Gonzalo breathed in hard. Indeed he had nothing to gain from a gesture like that, he thought. Even desperation had become a luxury he couldn't afford. He picked up his bundle of firewood. As he glanced one last time at the island, in his mind he saw a fleet of Spanish ships, sails unfurled and cannons primed, plowing straight through toward him.

But no matter at what price he tried to keep the scales from tipping the wrong way, his presence within the town couldn't pass quietly. As soon as Jerónimo began to go out as well, new clashes arose.

From two sticks of wicker Jerónimo had made a cross, which he wore around his neck hanging from some rope. Armed with that and with the indispensable prayer book, he ventured into the crowds of the marketplace like Daniel into the lions' den.

The first confrontation happened when they were approached by an elderly man who must be a temple attendant. He carried a bundle of paper masks, wooden images and other items used in ceremonies. On seeing the two slaves, the man came closer to look at the cross hanging from Jerónimo's neck.

"We have forgotten everything," he harangued Jerónimo, pulling at the cross. "We have forgotten most wickedly!"

Ah Yax Ceh tried to send the man away, but Jerónimo stood his ground. "What ails you, old man?" he asked in Spanish.

The old man sorted out of his bundle what looked like a staff of a wand. It was carved in the shape of a cross, with tendrils curving from both ends of the horizontal beam. Jerónimo put down his jugs of water with a look of triumph.

"Do you see now, Brother Guerrero? I knew the Lord had found a way to reach even this forsaken land, for His might knows no bounds. Please," he begged him, "tell me what this man is saying."

Intrigued himself, Gonzalo translated the man's words.

Jerónimo's voice rose louder. "You say you have forgotten? It is the Gospel you have forgotten, turning to the worship of false idols like the ancient Hebrews with the golden calf!"

The old man was too upset to listen. "Who made this for you?" he asked, pointing at the tendrils missing from the arms of Jerónimo's cross. "How can you wear this mockery of the true shape?"

Having grasped what no one around him seemed able to grasp, Gonzalo watched the scene in disbelief. The old man and Jerónimo were blasting each other for sins neither one could name, in an absurd pantomime of righteousness that must have both halves of heaven rolling with laughter.

It became clear that Jerónimo had allowed his eyes to see what they wanted to see. As Kanalsin explained, while Ah Yax Ceh persuaded the old man to leave, the staff was the image of something these people called The Great Tree That Holds Up The Sky. It had a straight trunk, two straight branches, and tendrils of foliage curving out from the branches. Only too happy to dispel the confusion, Gonzalo conveyed the explanation to Jerónimo.

"The Cross is indeed the Tree of Life," Jerónimo insisted, as people began to gather. "It's the tree that bore the fruit of Christ's body offered in sacrifice for your redemption. Your own graven images are wiser than your hearts!"

Gonzalo started to walk away. "Brother Aguilar," he punned, "you're talking at cross-purpose."

From that day on, the bickering that divided the two of them in the hut spilled into the streets of the town, as each man pursued aims of his own. Jerónimo's aim was to single-handedly convert to Christ the entire population of Tulum. To his surprise, Gonzalo found out that Jerónimo too had also learned Mayathan well enough, although so far he'd refused to speak it. Jerónimo's vocabulary, however, took quite a different slant, with the words for 'good' and 'bad' used strictly according to the speaker's own judgment.

While Gonzalo contented himself with learning the name of each thing, Jerónimo went around assigning those things to one or the other category with unyielding conviction. Bad were the temples that rose above the marketplace, the dog meat that the butchers cut up for their customers, the nakedness of the little boys and girls playing in the streets. Bad was just about everything the people of Tulum did, said or believed in. When it came to preaching the Word, Jerónimo's shyness blew away like a lace scarf in the wind. Give him two or three loiterers who came to market only to pass the time, and Jerónimo vociferously began to denounce the work of the devil upon their souls, while Gonzalo ran out of saints to curse.

To escape this vexation, whenever he could Gonzalo begged Ah Yax Ceh to be sent on his errands without Jerónimo, even if that meant waking up at the worst hours or carrying a load twice as heavy. When begging wasn't enough, he resorted to bribery. From a woman in the market he stole three *cacau* seeds, and with that money he bought the privilege not to be confined to the hut during the day.

Now he could move freely around the master's house.

The house was much larger than he'd imagined. Only the central dwelling inhabited by the master was forbidden to him. Around the lesser courtyards were the rooms where the slaves lived together, with a few partitioned spaces for those who were thought loosely form a family.

Kanalsin and the other young women slept in the room where the looms were kept. When she showed him the place, Gonzalo's appearance caused a stir. After some arguing, the women whose curiosity was stronger than modesty pulled him in so they could finally look at him at their leisure.

Flustered, he stood there not knowing what to do with himself. Some women lay with their small children on hammocks and beds; others were weaving, their bare breasts rising and falling with each motion of the looms held by straps tied around the women's backs. Their brown bodies glistened with sweat and rippled with whorls of delicate tattoos. One woman was rubbing a pebble against another's teeth, filing them to a sharpness that went well with the girl's olive-dark features. Under a clay image of Our Lady of the Rainbow, herself half naked like the women, two girls were braiding each other's hair, smoothing it with a cake of scented grease.

Even if he closed his eyes the air alone in there would have unsteadied him, the smell of dyeing herbs mixed with the smell of the women. They talked thickly among themselves, not daring to touch him yet pressing around him like a flock of birds ready to alight all at once. When the ones who'd tried to keep him out renewed their protests and shamed Kanalsin almost to tears for bringing the stranger there, he was all too glad to leave.

For nights afterwards the memory of that room full of women made him hard. There was something about the women of the islands, too, which he knew well from his sailing days. It was a frankness of manners that not even years of daily masses could disguise, to the grief of the friars. It must be the weather, he reasoned, for there wasn't much a human being could wear in these hot places except his own skin.

He remembered the layers of wool and linen he'd stripped away in Palos, the buttons and strings he'd grappled with before he could bring flesh to light like a midwife at a childbirth. In the islands all it took were two fingers to untie a belt worn at the hips just because it looked pretty. He lay on his mat in the dark and stroked himself to pleasure thinking about Kanalsin asleep only a few walls away.

Once or twice he considered stealing up to the women's room.

But of all the things that moved him, lust was the most treacherous. This wasn't the sort of need that could be satisfied by whispering under a window like in Spain. Over there the only danger came from an overzealous father threatening to call the constable.

To arouse himself he sometimes imagined that he was the master and could take his pick of the women anytime he wished. With so much female property living under his roof, it seemed that there was nothing to stop the master from turning the weaving room into a harem.

That was the question he asked Kanalsin while the two of them sat on a slab of ruined limestone eating their midday meal between chores.

Yes, she answered, the master took to his bed the best-looking women in his household. Most of the children Gonzalo had seen in the weaving room were of his blood, though they were destined to become slaves like their mothers.

"The bastard," Gonzalo muttered, spitting out the seeds of a custard apple.

A few moments passed before he asked the next question. "And you? Has the master ever taken you?"

She shrugged "No. Perhaps I'm not among the best-looking ones."

He wanted to laugh. "Perhaps he's blind," he said. The air seemed to have grown thicker between them.

"I'm glad he doesn't want me," she said then, with that unsettling way she had of putting her soul squarely before him. She touched him lightly on the shoulder with a gesture full of gravity and sweetness.

"You could be the first, Zalo."

Something caught in his throat. All those past nights alone on his mat there had been nothing he'd wanted more—to press his body against hers, to feel her yield like the flesh of that custard apple, sheathing him in a warm husk of cinnamon skin.

He felt sick at the thought of that fat savage old enough to be her father forcing himself on her, using her for a while and then leaving her to raise one more slave. But this was also the man who for a trespass could send them both to be butchered on the sacrificial stone. He asked himself if he could risk so much for a few instants of happiness, and he decided he wasn't. He finished eating in silence, thinking that nothing in the world tasted worse than a custard apple.

The freedom to go about the house was in time granted to Jerónimo as well. It wasn't long before Jerónimo too found out about the weaving room and the double service to which the women were bound. For him too it was a most trying discovery. Nothing he'd ever railed against seemed to anguish him more than the thought of living in a whorehouse, amidst adultery, fornication, illegitimacy and every other carnal sin he could name. He muttered endlessly to himself about it, until Gonzalo lost his patience and another squabble began.

"Does it matter anything to you that those women are slaves, that they have no choice just as we have no choice?" Gonzalo argued. "Even so," Jerónimo countered vehemently. "It's in the very nature of women to bring about corruption, as the Serpent knew well. Their mere presence is enough, the mere closeness of them."

"Your poor mother should hear what you think about her," Gonzalo said, breaking up some wicker for a basket he was making.

Jerónimo hardly paid attention. "There is no greater obstacle than the flesh for those who want to give their thoughts to God," he murmured, pressing his hand against the wall as if afraid he'd fall down.

Gonzalo stopped. For those who want to give their thoughts to God and to just about everything else, he thought, remembering the effect that the weaving room kept having on him. He looked at Jerónimo, and for the first time in a long time he felt bonded to him by compassion. He realized that one thing at least the two of them were doing much in the same way these days and nights, fighting their own bodies against the hunger that howled to be either satisfied or mastered; and how much harder it must be for Jerónimo, who had nowhere to hide from the Almighty.

"Women have little to do with it, Brother Aguilar," he said. "The Serpent went to talk to Eve because her husband was still asleep."

After the first shock, Jerónimo not only stopped pretending the weaving room didn't exist but sought to be near it as much as Gonzalo did—for reasons that turned out, of course, to be the opposite. What Jerónimo wanted was to put himself to the test, convinced he would win against temptation even though temptation was barking around him like the hound from hell.

Clothed in his armor of faith, he sallied forth with gritted teeth, like Saint Anthony confronting the naked maiden in the desert. Sometimes at night Gonzalo, halfway through sleep, heard strange noises coming from the corner of the hut where Jerónimo kept his mat. With a length of knotted rope Jerónimo flogged himself to drive out the lust that kept him from his demanding God.

Jerónimo's best weapon against what he considered his worst enemies was his own contempt for them. Even if he were ever smitten by a woman, he claimed, he would never yield to desire for native women, those bestial creatures who lived outside the bounds of civilized society.

This was an argument Gonzalo had heard often while he was still among Spaniards in the islands. Tirelessly the friars met to determine whether the natives should be considered beasts or else possessed of a soul, with many fine points taken from theology in support of the first argument. In the islands, after years of oppression, the natives themselves seemed to have come to believe that they deserved to be treated like beasts; but in here the master's house, where the two white captives were the ones reduced to packhorses, whenever Jerónimo spoke like that Gonzalo expected him to be torn apart on the spot.

Instead, perhaps because Jerónimo's use of native words resulted often in unintended puns and bizarre turns of phrases, the reaction was one of unending hilarity. Not only did his fellow slaves shrug off his attempts at evangelization, but sometimes they baited him into delivering his ranting sermons, turning the would-be preacher into an unwitting buffoon.

Once an old woman, skinny and wrinkled like one of those *cacau* nuts, taunted him with a mimicry of seductive gestures that made Jerónimo blush from top to bottom and the whole courtyard burst with laughter. Eventually even Citam stopped trying to silence him, and Kanalsin learned not to cringe in his presence. Only to Gonzalo

Jerónimo's presence remained a source of annoyance, and he damned himself for not being able to ignore Jerónimo like everyone else did.

Fed up with Jerónimo's antics, Gonzalo now spent more and more time out in the streets, where the phantom of escape gave him relief from every sorrow. Sometimes his wanderings took him close to the great temple that rose near the cliff. What interested him was that it doubled as a watchtower. Guards were stationed on the roof, armed with conch shells to sound the alarm, and at night a signal fire turned it into a lighthouse.

He surmised that the coast must be visited by seafaring marauders who might try to land and scale the cliff. There was something else under guard, however, something that lay on the coast itself, toward the north. The idea of going into the temple gave him nightmares, but he must find out what it was.

The occasion came one day when he was paired to a slave he'd never seen before, a listless man who just slouched along willingly. Gonzalo was able to walk with him all the way to the temple without objections.

"Why there?" the man asked simply.

"Do you remember the New Year sacrifice?" Gonzalo improvised.

"Yes, I remember. One of you Castilàn was offered up." "I just want to see the grave of my friend in the temple."

The slave nodded. "It's a good thing to visit the grave of a sacrifice."

On their way, as they passed by the stone markers that lined the main street, Gonzalo asked the slave if he knew the place of origin of those yellow disks that decorated the monuments. The slave replied that the gold had been there since before anybody could remember.

Besides, why would anybody bother with the stuff? What made a man rich was jade, those green stones that merchants kept from the eyes of common buyers by covering them with cloth. But wherever it was that the gold came from, the slave concluded, it must be a very distant place indeed, because there certainly wasn't any in the province of Tulum.

So much for delusions of wealth, Gonzalo thought. One more white fool asking for directions to Eldorado and getting a shrug for an answer.

Nobody stopped them as they went into the temple's courtyard. His legs growing numb with fear, Gonzalo reached the covered steps that led to the watchtower. His companion warned him that they were allowed only in the courtyard, and certainly nowhere near the roof. With a conciliatory gesture,

Gonzalo went down a step but kept his eyes fixed on the beach below, where a convoy of canoes had just left.

"Where do they go?" he asked the slave.

"To the salt beds," the man answered. "Let's go now."

So that was the precious stretch of land being watched day and night, he thought. All along the flat coast he could see more watchtowers and beacons, just like the chains of Moorish towers that dotted the coast back home. He must be sent to work in the salt beds, he thought. It was the only way he could safely be near the ocean.

In his excitement he'd almost forgotten the reason he'd given his companion for coming to the temple. It was the man who pointed him to Leon's grave. The stone was surrounded with incense burners and covered with starbursts of red hibiscus flowers. Gonzalo hunkered down and picked a blossom that had wilted. It felt good to stroke the stone, his back warmed by the winter sunshine. Barefoot and silent, a woman smiled to him as she arranged the flowers in a pretty pattern.

He closed his eyes and imagined he was back at his parents' grave, in the old cemetery by the river, with the leaves of the chestnut trees falling softly on the Day of All Souls. Homesickness took him at the throat, savagely. He couldn't even begin to say how much he yearned to be back among people and things he knew.

Everything seemed so easy back home. His father had been falsely accused of stealing, had confessed under torture to something he hadn't done, and had died in jail a week later. His mother couldn't live with her pain for more than a year after that. Simple, black and white like the robes of the judges in their high seats. Here in this land nothing was simple anymore. Everything had to be renamed, rethought, reshaped day after day.

He looked at the woman who was praying a few paces away from him. How could these people first kill Leon and then honor him with their memory and their love? It was almost as if they didn't see the difference between the horror of Leon's death and the beauty of those flowers strewn on the grave. Who knows, he wondered, perhaps there was no difference—no black and no white. Truly the world was no longer flat for him, no longer had just two sides. It was round as awheel, and spinning without up or down.

TEN

With the return of the dry weather the master began to administer his duties in the front porch of his own home instead of the common house that was the meeting place of the town elders. To Gonzalo, whom his busy guardians left more and more to himself, it was as if all of Tulum came to the house for him to look at.

The plainest thing to see was the power that lord Ah Kin Cutz wielded. One word from him and a thief became a slave along with all his family, an adulteress was stoned to death, a murderer had his intestines drawn out through his navel on the public plaza. Judges argued each case, sitting cross-legged on the mats that were their symbol of office, but the sentence belonged to the master.

Lord Ah Kin Cutz seemed to find pleasure in personally humiliating the culprits by tearing away their loincloths and leaving them to cower in dishonor on the ground. There was nothing more demeaning for these people than to be naked in public. For those sentenced to slavery the first shame was instead the cutting of the hair. Gonzalo and Jerónimo had their hair regularly cropped. It was the easiest way to identify a slave, since all native men took great pride in their long, elaborately braided queues. It was the equivalent of branding cattle.

Toward the end of the afternoon lord Ah Kin Cutz let in the vassals who'd been waiting to bring him their tribute, full baskets and net bags which Citam waved into the kitchen or the storage rooms. From those vassals who hadn't brought enough, lord Ah Kin Cutz took a son or a daughter destined to remain hostages until their fathers came up with the proper amount.

For some days then Gonzalo watched the master rule the province of Tulum and all the lives therein, as he waited for the moment he could ask him to be sent to work in the salt beds. Finally something happened that helped him make his move. Early one morning all visitors were turned away from the house, with the exception of a group of warriors whose appearance caused an uproar in the town. Even as they were being led into the courtyard of the house, men and women protested their coming in loud voices.

Gonzalo stood by the water basin to glimpse at the newcomers, and what he saw almost made him let go of the stone ax he was using to chop wood. Over their armor made of stiff quilted cotton, the warriors wore as a sort of heraldic emblem the image of intertwined snakes. He couldn't have forgotten that emblem. The lord who had had Captain Valdivia sacrificed carried a staff carved like those intertwined snakes.

His hands shook so hard he couldn't get the ax to land on a single piece of wood. Had they come for him, and how did they know he was there? While the warriors were forced to surrender their weapons before entering the house, he sought Ah Yax Ceh and asked him about the unwelcome visitors.

"Enemies," answered the young man, spitting in contempt. They came from the province of Ecab, which lay to the north and bordered with the lands of Tulum, and they hoped to arrange another truce—another swindle, rather—between their overlord and lord Ah Kin Cutz. For years the two provinces had been at war, because the ruler of Ecab claimed the salt beds belonged to him, that bastard born of monkeys under the bushes. And for a while lord Ah Kin Cutz had let him have the salt for a price; but now he threatened force again, parading his canoes along the coast with the drums sounding.

All day long the envoys from Ecab, secreted in the house, debated their quarrel. Finally before sundown they were escorted to one of the gates, surrounded by a mob of people who heaped insults upon them and upon the man who'd sent them. When they were barely out of the wall, the guards discharged their arrows. When they lay dead the mob rushed out and did things to their bodies that had never been done even to the bodies of sacrificial victims. The heads were impaled on spears and left to rot at the entrance to town for as long as it took.

The following day lord Ah Kin Cutz let everyone knew that his patience with the people of Ecab had run out. Let them come and try to cheat him again, with as many canoes as the dogs could afford. The order went out for more men to be sent to protect the salt beds. All Gonzalo had to do was ask Citam to let him join them, and his request was granted. Jerónimo remained in town, so he was at once rid of his nemesis and assigned to the place where he'd wanted to be for such a long time.

The salt beds could be reached by taking first the trail fishermen used to go to the beach, then by trudging along the steep cliff. The farthest ones, tucked in the coves and marshes that dotted the coast, were accessible only by canoe. Every morning the slaves climbed aboard huge dugouts made of red cedar and rowed to destination, past the southern tip of the island of Cuzumil.

Gonzalo was put to man the third oar from stern. Before him curved the bare backs and cropped heads of some thirty fellow rowers, capped by the slave master at the far bow. Behind the slave master rose a wooden standard carved in the shape of a wild turkey, lord Ah Kin Cutz's namesake. Smaller boats full of armed warriors followed each canoe. The warriors were under orders to aim their spears not only at the enemy but at the slaves, should they attempt to row in a suspicious direction.

During the rainy season the salt settled within the water of the marshes in big white chunks. The younger workers pried the chunks loose and carried them away to dry; the older ones pounded the salt in mortars and then packed it in clay dishes. The only women allowed in the salt beds were those who delivered the dishes, scrambling up and down the cliff.

The prying and carrying to which Gonzalo's sturdy back appointed him was as hard as anything he'd had to do in the cornfields before. Worse, he had to stand for hours in a briny slime that ate into the skin and caused painful sores. The guards kept on the lookout for alligators, but they could do nothing against the snakes that came underwater at the men's feet and legs. The first week alone two of the slaves died of their bites.

Food was always *posol,* a mixture of water and corn sourdough carried along in gourds. Sometimes the guards caught fish and cooked them on the spot. By the time he rowed back to town Gonzalo was so hungry he had to forage for scraps in the kitchen if they let him and steal if they didn't see him. His overseer was even stricter than Citam, and the other slaves were so inured to their brutal life that the mere notion of freedom seemed to have been scourged from them. Since raiders from Ecab were expected any time, the warriors kept constantly on the alert.

It didn't take Gonzalo long to realize that he'd put himself in an even worse trap. The sea was close now, yes, maddeningly close all day, and the island of Cuzumil, his stepping stone to Cuba, seemed to be just within reach of his hand. Yet an escape had never been more impossible.

Sometimes, when the warriors sat in the shade to doze off, he walked quietly into the thicket of mangroves that banked the lagoon, scouting for a place to hide. Other times, when they were allowed to bathe in the ocean, he waded toward some secluded corner where a cave might be. But sooner or later someone came looking for him, threatening punishment. One time he replied he was doing nothing wrong, and that time he wasn't allowed to eat all day. Soon his captors would have him fight like a dog for a bigger handful of *posol* or a smaller load to carry, and then he would become truly and forever their slave.

There was nothing left to keep him from going under except Kanalsin. It was as though she'd pledged to stand by him through every trial, making him wonder what good deed he'd ever chalked up in heaven's books to deserve such devotion. Some days after he was sent to the salt beds, he saw her coming down the cliff with the women who brought the jars and dishes for the salt. How long she must have walked to get there, he couldn't tell; but the guards found nothing strange when she joined him for the brief rest they granted the men at midday.

The other women didn't understand. They came to the salt beds to be with their men, but the white-skinned one was just a stranger washed ashore from nowhere.

"Why do you do this?" Gonzalo asked her in despair. "Can't you see I'm done for? Why do you even bother with me?"

Kanalsin was looking at the sores in his legs. "I can get you something for those. Ix Chebel, the old woman in the weaving room, knows about healing herbs." Then she handed him the corn bread she'd brought, still almost warm from the griddle. But by now everything he ate tasted of salt, like tears.

After that day she started to come to the salt beds whenever she could, stealing time between her chores. When she was late, he found himself waiting almost frantically. When he returned to town the thought of her made him walk faster toward the master's house, the very place to which he was shackled like chattel. Even as he dreamt of the day he would leave this land, his plight drove him to seek her blindly, as a small child seeks the only source of warmth he knows.

Toward the end of February, because the sea was so bad that the canoes couldn't be put out, the slaves were allowed to remain in town. Jerónimo was sent to Xelha for the usual supply of the tree bark used to flavor the *balché* liquor. Almost beyond his fondest wish, Gonzalo was granted a few days of rest and the run of the hut. The first thing he did was beg Kanalsin to come stay with him for a while. She took her loom to the hut, and there the two of them sat all day, forgotten by the world.

While she plied her thread he listened to her with joy, thankful simply to be near her. Ix Chebel, the old woman who supervised her in the weaving room, had rebuked her for going to the hut, calling her immodest and heedless. But Kanalsin had no one she must answer to; her parents had died when she was small, and since then she had learned to fend for herself.

The one thing that saddened her about having no family was that there would be no one to make the *emku* ceremony for her. Now that the month drew to a close, every other girl her age was getting ready for that solemn day when mothers took their daughters before the priests so they could become women in the eyes of the world and allowed to marry.

"Tell me about this ceremony," Gonzalo asked.

It was a most joyous and honorable day, she answered. Within a sacred space marked by a rope that the priests drew to keep out evil, boys and girls about to leave childhood were sprinkled with virgin water collected from the hollows of the oldest trees in the jungle, then were given flowers to smell and a pipe to suck, that their new life as adults might be as sweet and pleasant.

The boys came of age when the priests cut the jade bead they wore fastened to their hair; the girls when their mothers removed the seashell that had covered their private parts since the day of their birth. No man could take the shell from a girl before the *emku* ceremony had been performed, she finished saying as her voice became a whisper; but there would be no such day for her.

Twilight had come. They could hear the sea beyond the wall, beyond the palm trees. Her hands stopped, and she turned her head with a look full of desire and regret, asking him with her eyes once again to be the one.

A hush grew inside him, a silence that made everything clear.

Gently he reached out and found the hardness of the shell tucked between her legs. He felt her open them slowly, so he could follow its ridged contour all around.

"You be the priest and the mother and the father," she whispered. "You take the shell from me, Zalo."

If they both had to die for this, it no longer mattered. She slid back from the loom and lay on the mat. He almost couldn't move, as though after so much time he'd forgotten what it was like to be happy. To think that he should be the one to make her into a woman, he told himself, he who was just another orphan for whom no blessings would be chanted.

He loosened the yellow wrap and let it fall on the mat.

Underneath it she wore only a thin cord tied around her hips from which the white seashell hung, cupping her snugly. She was smooth as a pebble, her tiny nipples turned up with cold. He searched for the knot of the cord, molded with the long wearing against the small of her back. Then with infinite care, as though he were really kneeling in the temple, he removed the shell and put it in the folds of his mantle.

Even under the shell she was as hairless as a small girl, tight as the bud of the plumeria flower and of the same moist pink. Trembling he kissed her there, nuzzling her softness. He'd never felt so clumsy, so big, reluctant to put his hands on her who'd never been touched before. If she hadn't pulled him down, he thought he would never lie on her for fear of smothering her.

He wondered how each old gesture could bring him such new joy, as if the first time had come around all over again for him too.

Even the same hard throbbing in his flesh had turned into a patient bliss, as he would not go into her before she signified readiness.

First her fingers ran the length of his body, learning not just the feel of a man but that of a man unlike any she knew—the shape of muscle and bone differently knit, the growth on chest and belly of the hair that brushed against her skin like down on a young bird. And it was only when she arched closer under him that he began to push gently, ready to stop if she so much as winced.

But she only sighed, pressing her hands on his back to make him rest his weight, because she would not cry out, she was there for him. So finally wrapped in her and in the merciful night that gathered around them, with the sounds of her pleasure in his ears he took the last plunge, as grief and despair poured from him in burst after shuddering burst to perfect peace.

Breathing hard, happy, she settled beside him on the mat and stroked his eyes shut. Once before drifting off he touched his mouth to her hair and smiled to himself, hardly believing that she was really there, warm as all life. Then he slept.

Toward dawn, in the pale blue light that entered from the doorway, he became aware of someone stepping over the threshold of the hut. It must be a dream: the man looked like Jerónimo, only Jerónimo couldn't be standing so perfectly still, his shoulders rising and falling with a single shiver. He pulled Kanalsin closer to him, wishing the ghost would disappear. But Jerónimo seemed made of pale blue stone, his eyes riveted to the two naked bodies lying together on the mat.

"Go away," Gonzalo said. "Go and take your angry God with you."

Silently Jerónimo reeled back from the door and vanished.

Upon waking up they were summoned by Citam, to whom they went in terror. Jerónimo had told Citam what he'd seen in the hut; he'd also asked to be given a place with the slaves who slept on the floor of the thatched lodge behind the kitchen, and if not the lodge the kennel, or anywhere Gonzalo and Kanalsin were not.

Hunched before Citam, they waited to be cast out like Adam and Eve betrayed under the tree. But to Citam, who'd spent his life herding people, the couplings of the men and women in his charge were as simple as those of birds in the fields.

"Do you want her?" he asked Gonzalo. "Yes," Gonzalo answered.

Citam shrugged. "Then take her." And with that blunt, unhallowed wedding they were joined together for the better and the worse that lay ahead.

ELEVEN

It was as if someone had taken an ax to his life, splitting it into the most of misery and the most of bliss. From sunup to sundown it was the numbing toil of the salt beds; from sundown to sunup it was the healing comfort of Kanalsin. She found, smoothed, borrowed and begged anything he might nod at. In the midst of things he could neither control nor comprehend she was always, unconditionally, his.

Of native women he'd had his share in the islands, from the servants in the mission on Hispaniola to the proud beauty who claimed to be the daughter of a Kuna chief in Darién. But those were sailor's women, easily found upon each arrival and easily left upon each departure. With Kanalsin instead it was nothing less than a matter of survival, for body and mind.

After Citam's summary sanction, and with Jerónimo removed to the lodge, the hut became their home. Ix Chebel went once to check on Kanalsin's weaving, and at Kanalsin's request she stayed. For all her previous scolding, the old woman was of the kindest disposition, discreet and helpful. She brought in also two boys, recent purchases from the slave market, to help her with her chores.

Sometimes when he hurried back to the hut at nightfall, Gonzalo drifted into strange musings. There he was, sitting at his supper like any husband, with Kanalsin fussing around him like any wife, Ix Chebel busy at her spindle like any mother-in-law, the two boys asleep side by side like any sons. Everything seemed so oddly normal, even though it was only fortune playing at making a family out of outcasts.

Because there was so much Kanalsin gave him and so little he could give her, he had begun to feel the weight of a gratitude that was almost too painful to bear. His old plans of escape were becoming more difficult to hold on to with each passing day. He couldn't see himself just tossing her aside at the first chance, perhaps swimming away to freedom even as she struggled down the cliff to bring him his midday meal.

Torn between the heaven and the hell that his life had become, he found it easier to resent her love. He'd never asked for it, he reasoned, or done anything to cause it. In fact, it was ruining him as much as it was saving him. And he didn't love her, no matter how strong was the tie that kept him by her. All day, bent at the command of the master's watchdogs, he chastised himself for his own lethargy; and all night, in Kanalsin's arms, he found yet another excuse to push deliverance away.

Even the one thing Gonzalo hated the most in Jerónimo he could overlook in Kanalsin—that faith in powers unseen, in gods and ghosts forever prodding at one's soul like hungry creditors. With her loom and her cotton, Kanalsin had brought from the weaving room the small clay image of Our Lady of the Rainbow. True, she'd done so at Ix Chebel's bidding, and the old woman was much more devout than she was; still, she kept the idol in a place of honor, and offered it *copal* incense and flowers every day.

Yet Gonzalo didn't mind her devotion. The whisperings of the two women before the image of the goddess sounded just like Jerónimo's prayers, those prayers he'd mocked with such satisfaction. The language was equally mysterious, words that thousands had repeated for centuries with blind trust. But because the prayers came from the mouth of someone else, he did listen, more or less attentively, to Scriptures of another kind.

The name of the goddess was Ix Chel. She governed the cycles of the moon and the wheeling of the morning star. She'd taught mankind the art of weaving; she was also the patroness of medicine, and helped pregnant women bring forth new life. There was an image of the Virgin that Gonzalo's mother kept under a glass bell by her bed: a plaster lady dressed in white, with twelve stars strung on a crown around her head and a half-moon curving under her feet. His mother put flowers and candles every day before the image. She'd called on the Virgin when she was in childbed, and when other women were, and she had woven a beautiful cloth for her convent. As for the idol's bare breasts, the church in Palos had a painting of Mary holding her breast to Jesus' mouth like any peasant woman in the market. He wished he were Jerónimo, so he could tell what made Our Lady of the Rainbow different from Our Lady of Seville.

And some of the tales he heard from Kanalsin were as lovely as the ones he'd heard as a child. One day while she was weaving, Ix Chel the Moon was seized from her father by the Sun, who was in love with her. Angry, the old man shot Sun with his blowgun. Moon fell into the sea and shattered. Tiny fish came to her help and patched her with their silvery scales. Then, each holding in its mouth the tail of another, they made themselves into a net and tried to lift the girl to Sun, but in vain. So they had to leave Moon in the sky, where she still runs after her lover. It didn't matter to Gonzalo that Kanalsin spoke of these tales as if they were true. The sound of her voice was truth enough for him.

Besides Ix Chel, these people worshipped an array of gods and goddesses, minor deities and daily demons. It was a bewildering crowd, far more complicated than any Christian calendar of patron saints. There were protectors of hunters, fishermen, farmers, traders, warriors and lovers. There was even an elegant matron shown hanging from a noose; her name was Ix Tab, Our Lady of the Rope, and she had in her keeping the souls of those who took their own lives.

Very near the top of this multitude towered someone named Kukulcan, half man half feathered serpent. When Kanalsin told Gonzalo about this god, he was jolted like someone forced out of sleep. Kukulcan, whom these people called the Creator of their race, after bestowing upon them every gift they would ever be grateful for had vanished on the sea in the direction of the east, and from the east he would return, no one knew in what disguise, to pass a last judgment on how his gifts had been used.

Tulum, Kanalsin added, lived under the very shadow of the Feathered Serpent. Poised as it was at the edge of the eastern sea, it would be the first to learn of the god's return and to spread the news to the rest of the world. But how would the people of Tulum know it was him? Gonzalo asked. There could be no mistake, she replied, because Kukulcan looked like no one else: white skin and a full beard.

Gonzalo froze. Immediately he remembered the way everybody kept marveling at the white-skinned strangers, at their beards. He remembered the woman who'd once showed that idol painted red and yellow, the idol with the beard. Was that why Kanalsin had given herself to him? Did she think herself blessed among women, chosen to announce the return of the god?

She had treated him differently almost from the start, and for reasons that now seemed to make sense in a completely unexpected way. Gods, and the Sons of God, had a habit of appearing without worldly notice, scorned, forced to live among the lowly. Did she think perhaps he was testing her faith to see if she was worthy?

He looked at her. There was nothing in her behavior that could be read as awe, fear, or hysteria. She was too smart for that, he reasoned. At most she would have asked him outright, the way she did everything else, if he was indeed a god in disguise. But perhaps it was good to have her believe, to make the most of her devotion. Who knows to what it might lead? Perhaps Ix

Chebel could be persuaded, too, pious old women looked so easily to miracles.

He blinked. This was true blasphemy, he told himself. It was such a sickening old trick, too. In the islands, to frighten into submission those natives who'd never seen a white man before, they fired cannons and muskets, made the horses rear up, set fire to alcohol claiming they could turn water into fire. Would he really stoop now to such pitiful witchcraft?

He tugged at Kanalsin's dress. "Do you think that when this Feathered Creator comes back he'll be hungry enough to eat all the corn bread he can find, even the one that's burning right now?"

Kanalsin turned toward the griddle, gasping at the smoke that was rising from it. She ran to pluck out the flat loaf, singed her fingers and gave a wail of dismay.

Gonzalo laughed. But she didn't want to be forgiven so easily, and she sulked for some time.

❖ ❖ ❖

The attack from Ecab came on one of the last days of the salt harvest, and at a time of day when everybody was most tired, as the slaves rowed with the last of their strength and the warriors leaned on their spears thinking of home and supper.

They had barely passed the navigation marker on the headland of Tulsayab when the slave master in the canoe that brought up the rear of the convoy sounded the alarm. Right behind them had sprung out of nowhere another fleet of canoes carried with murderous speed by warriors waving the banner of the intertwined snakes. Instantly the slave master gave the order to double the rowing time. With his heart in his mouth, Gonzalo doubled down on his oar. The thought of being captured by the people who'd killed Captain Valdivia and his shipmates was enough to make him row with a frenzy he didn't know he could still exact from his body. Around the canoes the sea begun to turn white, whipped by dozens of paddles.

Seeing that the convoy wasn't gaining enough distance from the pursuers, the smaller and swifter craft full of warriors that escorted it quickly put themselves between it and the attackers. Standing up in the pitching hulls the men postured at the enemy, shaking their spears and raising a hellish noise. Faster and faster the cedar keels dashed toward the beacon of the great temple that rose like a fortress above the beach of Tulum.

The last canoe in the convoy listed violently, scraping against the reef with a sound like a shudder, the oars knocking against one another. Most of the rowers were thrown overboard, then the canoe capsized and was smashed on the rocks. Gonzalo saw the men who could still swim being scooped up by the enemy like small fish into a bucket.

While the pursuers slowed down to gather that fortuitous human catch, lord Ah Kin Cutz's warriors put their spears in their spear-throwers and released a volley that found its target without fail. The closest of the enemy craft was instantly half empty, and the banner of Ecab went bobbing on the sea in a red foam. The cries of the warriors covered the pounding of the oars.

At last the great temple came into view. Knowing the attackers would not dare follow so close to the town, the slave masters directed the convoy toward the first safe cove, and there the rowers were allowed to rest. Two men in Gonzalo's craft fainted. Gonzalo thought he would never be able to breathe freely again.

Up on the cliff the alarm had been given. But now the attackers hung back desperately. They were starting to turn their canoes when lord Ah Kin Cutz's warriors fell on them with the assurance afforded them by their closeness to their town. Atop the walls of Tulum the people shouted and blew the conch shells. Of the battle that followed Gonzalo saw nothing, as he lay exhausted on his bench. But it was a predictably short one; and when the canoes were finally beached, after the line of slaves going up to the gate came naked captives whose hearts would nourish the gods for many days to come.

Gonzalo dragged himself homeward among the singing, dancing crowd. Before reaching the master's house he nearly collapsed in Kanalsin's arms. She'd been looking for him everywhere. With her he sought the comfort of their sleeping mat, and there he became aware of how his body seemed to have been battered in every fiber by a leisurely torturer. Even hunger had been wiped out, and he could eat only a few spoonfuls of the bean soup he usually devoured.

Out in the courtyard, there was great rejoicing among the master's household. The women cried out and the men clapped their spears together. Above it all, from the temple, came the savage heartbeat of the drums. Gonzalo stretched out on his mat and tried to blot everything out. All he wanted to hear was the rustling of Kanalsin's feet, the whispering of her voice that lulled him back to peace.

"Merciful are the Gods, the Makers, Begetters," she was praying. She drew across the doorway the cloth that hid them from the eyes of all outside, then sat down beside him, while he turned his head to find her lap. If he'd been captured, he thought, he would have never seen her again. Slowly darkness fell. That night Ix Chebel would stay in the weaving room, getting drunk on *balché* like everyone else; the boys too had gone to hear the drums.

Kanalsin kept one hand on Gonzalo's hair, the other pressed against her own body. Now that some of the terror and fatigue had gone, he noticed the way she was looking at him. She placed his hand on hers, on the hand she kept on her lap. "Zalo, listen," she whispered. "Listen in here, where your child is."

He sat up, a jumble of feelings pulling at him. His first thought wasthat if he could not leave her before, now it would be a despicable thing to do. On this he had no doubts. He knew his heart; it seemed to have become his greatest hurdle.

She saw how he'd winced. "If you don't want it, there are ways."

"No," he said quickly. How could he not want it? Though he did want to know why now of all times, and here of all places, and her of all people.

"No," he smiled. Then he lay down again in her lap, close to her flesh and to what was inside her flesh.

How easy it would be to resent her for this too, he thought, to cry out that he'd been trapped. Easy and perfectly useless. Why not, he asked himself then. Why not? With all the things he'd been denied, he had not been denied this wonderful and terrifying thing that was the making of another life. In this at least even the lowest of men could fancy himself as bountiful as God.

He thought of Jerónimo, of how Jerónimo would rail against this latest blasphemy; and it made him almost vain to imagine himself a father, even if among the heathen, while Jerónimo with his sanctimonious chastity would let his seed dry up inside him and never even know what could be born of it.

Gently he motioned Kanalsin to lie down beside him. "I cannot wait," he said, with his mouth against her hair.

He stroked her belly, narrow as a little girl's. "No matter what else happens, for this I cannot wait."

TWELVE

With the salt harvest done, Gonzalo hoped to be returned to his old chores in the market, which he would have welcomed back as nothing less than pleasant. Instead the slave master who'd been in charge of his canoe borrowed him and a dozen other slaves from lord Ah Kin Cutz and put him to build more canoes, starting with a replacement for the one lost in the battle with Ecab. The only requirement was again a back sturdy enough to carry the cedar logs down to the beach. A mule would have been borrowed in much the same way, if these people had any beasts of burden.

There had never been a better time to attempt an escape than the time he now spent shaping a log into a boat while the slave master snored under a palm tree. It would take nothing, one of those afternoons when even the macaws drooped with heat, to slip the canoe into the surf and start making his way back to the world of the living. Instead the days went by, and then the weeks and the months, while under his hands the logs grew more and more hollow and Kanalsin's belly grew more and more round.

At first she came every day to the beach as she'd come to the salt beds. But soon she had to give up the trek up and down the steep path. Ix Chebel, who awaited the birth of the child as though she were the grandmother, lavished help and advice on her. The image of Our Lady of the Rainbow was cared for more than ever, as the two women offered food and incense to ask for protection.

Jerónimo had been granted his wish to live as far away as possible from his one white companion, for which Gonzalo was only too grateful. However, they still saw each other often enough; and when Jerónimo finally grasped Kanalsin's pregnancy, he threw them a look of blistering condemnation, making her grieve that so much hatred would bring evil to her and the child. But Gonzalo looked back defiantly, putting his hand on her belly with a gesture of proprietary swagger, to which Jerónimo hastened to leave.

From Ix Chebel Gonzalo found out that Jerónimo had asked the master to become one of the carefully chosen men who guarded the weaving room, after he'd volunteered to give proof of his trustworthiness around women, although by now this was a staple of town gossip. To Gonzalo that request seemed most appropriate. Only Jerónimo would try to advance his career by means of his virtue, thus serving profitably both Caesar and God.

While soaking corn for the next day's meal, Ix Chebel commented on Jerónimo's celibacy. To her, as to all natives who knew him, it was the sign of a haughty and unresponsive nature. Gonzalo, who was setting the three stones that formed the hearth, explained that Jerónimo thought himself holy enough to become a priest among his people.

Ix Chebel still didn't understand. As she explained in her turn, the holy priests of her people could marry and father children, like all men worth the weight they carried between their legs. True, before a festival they were to sleep apart from their wives, as was everyone who wished to please the Gods; but it seemed most curious to her that someone who would be called upon to counsel men and women throughout their lives should have to shun half of his flock.

What was even more noticeable about Jerónimo was how humble he'd become with the passing of the time spent in captivity. Whatever he was told to do he did quickly and precisely. If anybody ordered him to perform a task he saw to it immediately, as if his life depended on besting the other slaves at slavery itself. On one occasion it nearly did.

As rumors of a military expedition soon to be launched against Ecab kept Tulum on the alert, some of lord Ah Kin Cutz's warriors started coming to the palmetto grove outside the house to practice. They balanced their arrows, honed the tips of black obsidian, then set their target high on a tree and urged each other on with wagers and boasts. The target they used were small dogs tied up by the forelegs; most often the warriors aimed at the eyes, muzzle or other such difficult marks.

To Gonzalo the yelping of the dogs was hard enough to put up with, and Kanalsin prayed to herself that the men would go elsewhere to do their shooting. But to Jerónimo the sight of the small animals writhing helplessly as the arrows whistled past was torture.

More than once he walked over to the warriors and begged to find some other sort of target. Finally one of the men, tired of the slave's interfering, took Jerónimo by the arm and dragged him under the tree to which the dog was tied.

"What if *you* were the target?" he taunted him.

He poked an arrow at Jerónimo's groin. "Do you think we would miss if we hung you up for our practice?"

From where he was watching, Gonzalo held his breath. The warriors were laughing and hooting, but on the face of the man who held Jerónimo under the tree there was no hint of jest.

Jerónimo spread his arms. "Do with me as you wish," he answered meekly. "But you are a good man, and I am a good slave."

The warrior grunted some oath, they let him go. Shaking, Jerónimo walked away with his head bent. After that incident, when the warriors came he just went about his business as if neither they nor their target were there. His fellow slaves had taken to calling him Ah Ac, the Turtle, because he kept his soul impenetrably hidden as if inside a shell.

The expedition against Ecab ceased to be a rumor in the last of the dry months, at a most ill-advised time. Lord Ah Kin Cutz was so eager to strike that he was going to empty the cornfields of men right before the planting season. For five days the warriors kept a vigil in the temple with the priests. On the last day they went to the house of the war captain and carried him out on a litter, a startling figure heaped with fetishes of destruction, his head topped by a swirling mass of feathers.

Almost lifted out of their bodies by the relentless, hypnotic beating of the great drums, the men danced around him, lunging at each other with their weapons; still dancing and shouting they streamed out of the wall. Among them was Ah Yax Ceh, who had joined in only at the last minute, as he was young and untried in battle.

With the war resumed and the rain late again in coming, fear of the drought and of a bad harvest turned Tulum into a quiet town. When the time came to prepare the clearings for the corn, every man who could be spared was sent to the fields, including Jerónimo and Gonzalo, reassigned to their work as farm hands. The men gathered around holding their stone axes, and Gonzalo heard them speak the prayer whose meaning he could now understand.

"Here before you I stand, Lords of the Earth, Lords of the Forest and Trees, that you may hear my worship and forgive my offenses. Now I offer you words, that you may know I am about to burn you, destroy you, for I am in need of food. Let no creature attack me. Permit neither scorpion nor snake to bite me. For with my hands and with my heart I must now work you."

Then the trees were cut, the brush fired. The sun was darkened by smoke, and at night flames surrounded the town. The priests, bent over their books of divination with their unkempt black hair sweeping the ground, singled out those days that were best for the dropping of the seeds. They offered the Gods their own blood, slashing their bodies with the razor-sharp tails of the sting ray.

Still the rain would not come, and the earth in the clearings cracked like a brick under the blows of a hammer. So lord Ah Kin Cutz promised he would choose a sacrifice from among his slaves, and a hush of dread fell on his house, as the men and women whose lives he could dispose of glanced at one another wondering who it would be.

Ix Chebel, who every year carried in her arms the newborn boy destined to the new crops, whispered that it would surely be one of the boys who lived with her in the hut. They were both orphans and slaves, two of the main categories from which sacrifices were drawn.

Once, Gonzalo learned, she had offered up a child of her own; it was a sickly child who would not live long and who she was sure would be happier with the gods than on earth. Kanalsin, being pregnant, was not in danger.

Finally Chaac, Master of the Thunder, to whom the people of Ecab had given Captain Valdivia and the others, was moved to compassion and untied the knots of the sky before anybody was chosen. Once again the floor of the hut turned into a layer of mud; but Gonzalo no longer cursed it, for from that mud these people were molded into life at each season, and he with them.

Through the rainy months Kanalsin was confined indoors. There was talk among the women of the household that hers was going to be a difficult labor, for she was so small and the child seemed strangely heavy, taking after his father's big-boned race. Gonzalo felt for her, misshapen by that bulge that often wouldn't let her sleep at night and that kicked fiercely while she lay on the mat as if to push them apart. To ease her discomfort, after he returned from the cornfields he made her a small bed out of saplings woven together.

That work eased also his own deep and constant discomfort.

All kinds of thoughts tormented him as he braided together those saplings, like unwelcome guests that kept coming at the worst hours. Perhaps after the baby's birth she could be persuaded to escape with him, although the idea of attempting the crossing to Cuba with a woman and an infant was sheer lunacy; and God knew what he was going to do with them after he'd reach the islands, assuming they wouldn't all drown first. If Ponce could only see him now, Ponce who'd chided him so often for his indecision.

What sense he retained of himself as a Spaniard had slowly begun to erode. While Jerónimo still lived in the hut, he still had someone with whom he could speak his own tongue, even if in disagreement. Now he had no tongue but the natives', and to speak like them he had to think like them, often with the speed of desperation. The overseer might tap him on the shoulder with the single word *kan,* and he would have to decide in the space of an instant whether the man had told him to observe that the sky looked like rain, to drop four kernels of corn, or to watch out for a snake, since *kan* meant all at once sky, four and snake.

Time itself had changed. Jerónimo could keep track of its passing thanks to his breviary. Prayer by daily prayer, he went from Christmas to Easter and back to Christmas again. But with Jerónimo gone, time for Gonzalo was reduced to days of good weather followed by days of bad weather, hours of work followed by hours of rest. A feeling of unreality was beginning to take hold of him, the feeling that his life had turned into a blurry dream.

When there was time to talk, Kanalsin asked him to tell her about the land from which he came, the land where the Castilàn lived. Above all she never tired of hearing about those strange animals called horses, and how he'd learned to sit astride them.

It had been in Hispaniola, he began one more time, when he'd first landed in the island. Up to that time he'd traveled in ships or on foot. But captains would not hire men who couldn't ride, even though most of the newcomers were, like him, too poor to afford a mount. So a bit at a time, after many a fall and many a curse, he'd managed to become a fair horseman; but he still had no love for horses or mules or anything on four legs taller than he.

She listened very carefully, pitying him deeply for having to suffer such trials with those bad beasts. As she couldn't picture horses, she imagined them as big deer with no antlers and hair growing from their necks. And it was thanks to her that her idea of a horse became a companion to the gods painted on the walls of the shrine dedicated to Our Lady of the Rainbow, where she went to pray every month for the safe birth of her child.

After years of neglect, the shrine was being restored as a gesture of propitiation, since no news had been received of the expedition sent against Ecab and everybody in Tulum feared the worst. To Gonzalo the endeavor seemed strangely familiar. Just like the congregation in Palos when the parish church needed repairs, the whole town had willingly become the menials of heaven in hopes of obtaining its favor.

Men ground clay for the paint, women wove mats for the floor, children mixed water and sand for the plaster. While Kanalsin went in to confess to a priest her sins so as to cleanse from her all harm that might befall her, usually Gonzalo waited for her outside. Once, however, a priest beckoned him. Startled, since for him the sight of native priests was forever linked with the grisly rites they performed, he walked warily in.

It was the first time he set foot inside a temple. This one was cramped as a cave. Not until an attendant lit a taper was the full spread of the paintings revealed. Above his head was the figure of a winged being plummeting from the sky. Among unearthly blossoms and vines, gods and goddesses paid homage to one other with offerings of sacred bundles. A cold draft carried a smell of mold and damp plaster.

Gonzalo chose to wait for questions rather than ask them. To his relief he saw Kanalsin enter, followed by a man who must be one of the painters, for he held a brush made with the bristles of the wild boar and was all smeared with colored powder. The man pointed at a half-finished figure on the wall. The snaggle-toothed god Gonzalo knew well, because it was the same one to whom Leon's young life had been offered in the New Year ceremony, but the animal on whose back the god sat was none other than the horse he had described so often to Kanalsin.

"Is this a good likeness?" the man asked, proud of his skill.

Gonzalo shook his head. "The tail should be longer... and thicker, not like the tail of a monkey."

Huffing with annoyance, the painter started to retouch the figure.

"It's an unlovely beast," he commented as he worked. "I wouldn't want to face such a spirit myself. That's why I've made it a servant to Lord Itzamnà. He's the oldest and wisest of the Gods, he should know how to tame it."

Surprised, Gonzalo turned to Kanalsin. "Did you think I was talking about spirits?"

It was the priest who answered for her. "Indeed. She's very much afraid that you are being visited by an apparition of this shape. Didn't you tell her you were forced to wrestle with this creature, to sit on its back against your will?"

"Visions come from the gods," Kanalsin said earnestly, "and if they aren't returned to the gods they cause mischief and pain, so I— " She broke off in embarrassment.

More amused than irritated, Gonzalo addressed the priest. "But there really are such creatures. If you don't believe me, just go the islands, anywhere Spaniards are. I will willingly show you the way. I will show you all the unlovely beasts you want."

The priest looked him askance. "I know of no tribe called 'Spaniards.' You come from the islands, so of course you speak as a heathen and a liar. What else can be expected from savages who run around naked, keep no sacred days and even mistake their own dreams for reality?"

Gonzalo broke into a laugh. "My lord priest," he said in Spanish, "you sound just like Jerónimo when he talks about *you!*"

Appalled by the slave's lack of respect, the priest ordered him to leave. This Gonzalo did gladly, while Kanalsin kept begging him to be forgiven. But he held no grudge against her. After some protestations of good faith on her part and of truthfulness on his, they forgot the whole incident. Only, Gonzalo had to wonder what future visitors to the temple would make of Lord Itzamnà's mount—how they would explain a horse painted on a wall when no horse had ever come to this land that wasn't on any Spanish map.

THIRTEEN

By the time the corn was ready to be harvested, Gonzalo could no longer call the seasons by their names. He reckoned it must be around late October. To the natives it was the month of Xul, the End, when work in the cornfields came to an end.

The speckled corn was piled high, ready to be stored in underground pits. Stone altars and bowers of dry corn tassels were built, and thanks were given to the gods for granting abundance. Then, with the blessing of both their priests and their ruler, for four days and nights the people of Tulum happily took leaves of their senses.

The first night of the harvest festival Gonzalo was caught by surprise by the madness that seemed to have seized his captors.

Having finished his work, he lingered in the field only because no order had yet been given to return to town. At the other end of the clearing he saw Jerónimo glance at him with the same surprise. Then, when he saw the priests bring the idols from the temple, the fear took him that they were preparing a sacrifice, so he remained by the storage pits, away from the crowd. But it was a dog, fattened on corn, whose heart they offered to heaven.

The sun set, the priests left, and everybody still milled around in the fields. Food began to smoke on open fires. Games were played, amidst jokes and laughter. Painted mummers recounted the stories of ancient couplings between heaven and earth, blowing clay whistles shaped like women with large breasts and hips. Drunk in liberal drafts, the *balché* erased the boundaries of what was real. Men and women became like the gods and began to couple as freely as the gods, among the shorn cornstalks.

First a dance would begin, a circle of people twisting like a huge snake. Then the dance became a mimicry of sex, obsessively repeated to the sound of sticks rasped against human bones notched with grooves. Finally, when the dancers started to reel in a trance, they fell to the ground and onto each other in a tangle of limbs.

The same women who turned their backs when a man went by now lifted their dresses while calling the men to do the same with their loincloths. There were no longer husbands or wives, owner or owned. After days, weeks and months spent doing the endless things one must do, all these people cared for were the very few things one really wants to do.

Gonzalo was astounded. None of the overseers seemed interested in finding out where he or any of the slaves was. They too stumbled around laughing and drinking. At the other end of the clearing he saw Jerónimo crouching by a row of chili pepper plants. He didn't know Gonzalo was looking at him, or he might have been more careful in concealing the expression of fascinated horror on his face. He seemed transfixed by the drunken orgy before him. He looked like an old lecher peeping from behind a bush, aware that he can be found out yet unable to tear himself away.

Gonzalo couldn't quite take in the sheer excess that had burst out around him. He remembered people wearing masks and running through the streets of Palos the week before Lent, when the hogs were butchered and everybody ate his fill of meat, but nothing like this reveling. This was enough to make one lose his reason: the incessant trilling of the whistles, the moans of the women in the dark, the rustle of dry corn husks as if the earth had become a huge bed crumpling under the weight of a hundred lovers.

He hunkered down near the storage pit, shifting his weight and absurdly trying to hide the swelling under his loincloth while every other man seemed to be flaunting his own like a rare prize. The thought of Kanalsin now chafed him. If this was how her countrymen did their devotions, he'd be a fool to show himself less pious than they. The food at least, the food and drink he would have.

He glanced at the nearest altar, which sheltered the image of a handsome young god clasping an ear of corn in his hand. Beside it there was a small group of women tending a cooking fire. One of the women was holding over the fire a clay pot with a narrow mouth and a large belly; with her free hand she petted a tiny monkey. Once in a while the women jumped away from the fire, laughing and screaming. Out of the pot popped one after another in quick bursts like muffled firecrackers some white fluffy things that seemed alive and smelled wonderful.

Tentatively he walked over to the women to find out what sort of food could possibly leap and explode so. The women not only let him peek into the mouth of the pot, they had him bend over it. The next two or three white morsels popped up right in his face, giving him a start, while the laughter and the screams redoubled. It was just corn, they explained, but this kind was small and tapered, not square and almost flinty as the corn he knew.

Very much in high spirits, the women coaxed him into holding the pot over the fire. They listened to the sound of the kernels that danced and hissed. They poured balché for him; the more enterprising one pointed at his loincloth and whispered something that made the eyes of the others open wide.

Then the kernels began to burst open, and now the pot contained no longer corn but heaps of whatever those delicious bits were called. Gonzalo did away with a whole plateful. The women called him greedy and plied him with more. The little monkey ran up to get its share. It climbed all over Gonzalo's shoulders and head, tickling him with its soft tail. From another pot the women invited him to scoop out a dish of tender, savory venison.

At each sip of balché one more gloomy thought peeled away from him. He was determined to treat the powerful brew with more respect than he had the first time. Even so, the liquor washed all over him and slowly found its way to where the fear and the pain were.

The women were quite taken with the foreignness of him. Touching his face they wanted to know why it was so pale, and pointing at his eyes they asked him why they were of the same blue as the paint with which the priests daubed sacrificial victims. He didn't know what to answer. Until now the color of his skin and hair and eyes had never made much of a difference to anybody, in fact in the islands the pale skin of the Spaniards meant only terror and hatred to the natives.

But the feel of the women's hands on him was pleasant, the liquor worked, and he'd eaten well for the first time in a long time. Most surely this night would make the day after bleaker than ever. But he'd grown accustomed to forgetting there was such a thing as the day after.

Two men stopped by the fire. One still wore the mask in which he'd danced, a complicated affair decked with green plumes and deer antlers. The other was one of the overseers, so Gonzalo promptly stood aside, fearing punishment. But the two only wanted some of the venison stew, and instead of the cuff on the head with which they would have customarily ordered Gonzalo to get out of the way, greeted him with a vulgar insult that to them seemed funny enough. Then they grabbed two of the women and took them away.

Gonzalo remained alone with the woman who had the little monkey. She was looking at him in a way that could not be misunderstood, just waiting for him to do what the two men had done with her companions, and ready to respond with the same simple eagerness. The fire had become a reddish glow that gave everything the color of fever.

At the end of his restraint, Gonzalo pressed her down to the ground, fumbled briefly at her dress, and already he was inside her. Nothing had ever felt as good as that swift satisfaction freed from all proprieties and stripped of all ceremonies.

The woman spread herself underneath him, tearing at her own clothes for him. Even after reaching her peak of pleasure she kept pushing up against him, and when at last he fell on her catching his breath she still held on to him, digging her fists in his flesh as though the two of them should never come untangled.

The whistles started again, and the rattles sounded like the purring of beasts hidden in the jungle. The woman's hair was wrapped around his neck, and he could feel the wrinkles in the skin of her shoulders crisscrossed with tattoos. Suddenly he wanted to laugh like a child, delivered from all that was ugly. How wise of the ignorant savages, he thought. May God bless the godless heathen.

The woman opened her eyes and looked at him. A woman whose name he didn't know, whose kin he didn't know. A woman who could be the same age as his mother or his sister, as new to him as Eve must have been to Adam the first time they were together. She started to rock from side to side, and as she moved she rubbed her breasts against him with an air almost of challenge, because he was becoming hard again and she wanted him to.

In the last flickering light of the fire she was just a blur of features, no longer to be seen but only felt. Her breath grew thicker, and her thighs parted again. Again he was into her, slowly this time as though he had all the time, hoarding up his pleasure for the endless days that lay ahead, the days when again he would wish he'd never been born. The rattles spun and the whistles turned into a roar of crickets, drowning his cry. Then there was silence and sleep.

❖   ❖   ❖

Kanalsin knew the moment she saw him, but never spoke about it. In fact she seemed surprised when Gonzalo returned to the hut the next morning, since the harvest festival was far from over and no one wanted to cut short even of a minute that most welcome respite. Yet Gonzalo didn't go back to the fields, and instead waited out the celebrations as he would have the course of an illness. Ix Chebel praised him for this, but he felt neither proud of what he was doing now nor ashamed of what he'd done before. Naming what he felt had become a troublesome task, one he often left alone altogether.

Still, his early return to drudgery turned out to be an unwittingly sane thing, because four days later those who'd caroused to the fullest had a very unhappy time forcing themselves back to the tedium of daily life. The women got up first. They had to prod and nag their husbands, so the men complained and cursed them. Quarrels broke out; some became violent, refusing to leave. The overseers were fastest to resume their usual cruelty, venting out on the slaves their displeasure at the end of the revels.

The idols stood forgotten among food leavings and broken liquor jars, discarded clothes and torn sandals. What had begun as a joyful suspension of all rules ended, naturally enough, with their full and harsher reinstatement. It was pitiful to watch that disheveled mob of people being driven out of their own makeshift paradise amidst a noise of resentment and fistfights.

Only a few days later a much grimmer sobering came with the news brought by a ragged handful of survivors of the expedition sent against Ecab. The warriors dispatched six months before with such high boasts of victory had been utterly routed by the enemy in the jungle around Kantunil. Those who hadn't been killed in battle had been taken to Ecab to be sacrificed.

The news plunged Tulum from celebration into mourning. The same gods that had been thanked at the gathering of the harvest were now asked to guide the souls of the slain warriors in their dangerous journey through the caves of Xibalbà, the place of darkness and gloom. Kanalsin and Ix Chebel gave offerings on behalf of Ah Yax Ceh, who'd had his first and last taste of war in that ill-fated expedition. No one knew whether he'd been killed in the jungle or else in Ecab. Gonzalo, who'd liked Ah Yax Ceh for his good nature, wished for him that he'd been spared the ordeal of sacrifice and that he'd died the quick death of a warrior in battle.

For the time being then, while lord Ah Kin Cutz had to ponder the consequences of his rashness, life within the walls of Tulum returned to what it was. Though he was no longer needed in the cornfields, Gonzalo was always needed somewhere else. For a while he was given back to the slave master for whom he'd built canoes; then, because he'd told the man he'd once been a fisherman, he was finally assigned to the one task that seemed less like slavery since he'd been doing it all his life.

He was handed sturdy nets made with the fibers of the *henequen* plant, and sent out every morning aboard narrow, flat-bottomed dugouts made to pass easily over the treacherous reef that bound the coast almost without interruption. The reef teemed with all sorts of catch, and to these people all sorts of catch was food.

They caught not just haddock and crabs, cuttlefish and flounder and many other fish Gonzalo knew well, but also manatees, which the Spaniards had at first mistaken for mermaids because they suckle their young, and alligators taken with snares, and sharks that came voraciously by the dozen if only the water was pounded with an oar.

Upon their return they would clean and cut the catch, then smoke it on fires or pack it in salt. This was such easy work that it was almost rest. It was almost pleasant for Gonzalo to be on the beach, to steal a good morsel of cooked fish when no one was watching. The overseer praised him for knowing his job—indeed it was his to know—and didn't treat him too harshly.

There was comfort in repeating gestures that were familiar to him. With a net in his hands he could almost imagine that he was ten years old again and that his father was behind him to teach him how to cast the net into the sea. But the sea was of another color, jade-green and as fiercely clear as only the sea of these new latitudes could be; so he remembered that he was as lost to the world of his father as if he'd been buried with him. He then caught himself searching for his reflection in the water, as if to make sure he hadn't become someone else.

In those moments the old determination to escape rose again inside him. Fate had finally put him in the right place for that purpose. He was learning to navigate the coast and the openings in the reef, from where he could take to the open sea toward the islands. Often he was sent out with a single companion, and sometimes he was even left alone to watch the nets while the others moved on. The storm season had passed, and he felt strong now that his work was more reasonable and his food more abundant.

It was as if God were playing with him, he thought, waiting to see when he would finally seize the chance he was being offered. The baby first, he told himself; then he would give Kanalsin a choice, follow him to Cuba or stay behind. Even if she chose to stay, surely she wouldn't betray him. The more her time drew near the more he couldn't wait. Kanalsin smiled at his impatience, saying she'd never seen a man more anxious to become a father.

Her pains started when Gonzalo was out fishing. Later in the day Ix Chebel sent word to him by one of the young boys. As soon as he could leave the beach he hurried home, only to discover that the hut had become forbidden ground to him and to all males. In and out women went, bringing what they deemed necessary for the delivery. Even little girls helped out, but he was told repeatedly and unceremoniously to put himself someplace where he wouldn't be underfoot.

He argued with Ix Chebel, but Ix Chebel shrugged. Men usually didn't want to be present at births, she said, so men usually were kept away from births. It was neither a law nor a rule. It just was done that way, and everybody seemed to like it that way. He noticed the smugness in the old woman's voice and bristled with resentment. From the hut he heard Kanalsin's moans, punctuated by frightening screams. He paced up and down, angry at himself, at women and at the whole arrangement since Eve on down.

"It just takes time... and patience," Ix Chebel told him gently. "Will she be all right?" he worried.

Ix Chebel smiled. "If the Gods will it so."

As was the custom, she'd placed the image of Our Lady of the Rainbow under Kanalsin's bed and she'd laid her down facing the east, from which the sun was born and with it all new life. She would ease Kanalsin's pain with herbs; she'd been many times a midwife, and she knew what to do.

"You are kind," Gonzalo thanked her.

He waited in the courtyard a bit longer, thinking Kanalsin would ask for him, though he had no idea what sort of comfort he could give her. When no call came, he decided to return to the beach, where at least he could be useful. The men teased him the whole afternoon, and then began to speculate that the baby would be born with the most unheard-of features, perhaps even with his face covered with hair like his father.

Riled, Gonzalo rebutted that much more likely the child would look instead as ugly as they did, flat-headed like a fish. This wasn't just a cross remark but a misgiving that had worried him for a while. He'd never learned to like the strange shape of Kanalsin's forehead, and he knew he would not like it in his child, either.

The men laughed at his words as if he'd uttered the most witless thing, and if the overseer hadn't intervened the argument would have turned to fists. Then the overseer explained that he and his fellow natives were not born with flat heads but gave themselves that shape because it was most becoming. As soon as a baby was born, the mother wedged its head between two wooden boards, which after some time easily molded the soft bones. Kanalsin would show him how it was done, he concluded genially.

Gonzalo was appalled. "She will do no such thing," he replied hotly. "I will not let her torture my son in this unseemly way." Then, relieved that his fears had been unfounded and determined to prevent the child from being deformed, he went back to work without further discussion.

It went on all night. It felt like an endless time, he fretted in the dark, an excess of pain measured against the forgotten moment of pleasure that had started all this. As always, he thought, God seemed to have no sense of proportion. He finally dozed off toward dawn, when the rest of the men were getting up instead. Jerónimo, on his way out, looked at him with a long, hard look; that Gonzalo should be responsible for bringing into the world one more savage whose soul would be forever damned was something he could neither understand nor forgive.

Some time later Gonzalo woke up, not knowing whether Kanalsin's screams were real or a dream. But they were real, and hoarser now, a sound to make his hair stand on end. He could hear the voices of the women, no longer soothing as before but loud with frustration and worry. He must go see for himself.

He went to the hut's door, but had to stop there. Held under both arms by two of the women, Kanalsin was squatting over a pool of blood, naked and huge and twisting with the sort of agony that he thought must be deserved for the worst sinners in Hell.

The hut was full of the noise of the women trying to make themselves heard above her screams, debating opinions as to why the labor kept dragging on so. Ix Chebel insisted that the labor was just as long as it should be with a first birth, and that they were frightening Kanalsin for no reason. The only help needed, she went on, was the medicine she'd made for her as she had made it for so many others: four thorns snipped from the leaves of the *maguey* plant and boiled in water. Now she was lifting the medicine to Kanalsin's lips, saying she must drink it in four sips while facing the four cardinal points.

Kanalsin, helpless in the grip of her assistants, eased herself down on her knees and grasped the cup Ix Chebel offered. While Ix Chebel recited the same prayer four times, she swallowed the greenish potion. As she turned for the last time she saw Gonzalo in the door, and began to call him frantically.

He went in past the women, who raised a fuss at the intrusion, and took the place of the one who was holding Kanalsin under the right arm. He could not bear to look at her. She was no longer the girl who'd taught him words in the marketplace, brought him bread in the salt beds and slept with him on the mat only a few hours ago. This could not be her, not this woman convulsed with pain, blank-eyed with exhaustion and terror.

"It's an ill time," she stammered. "Zalo, I'm lost."

He turned to Ix Chebel. "What is she saying?" he asked the old woman angrily.

Ix Chebel kept pounding her herbs. "Today is the last day of the month of Chen," she whispered. "A most unlucky day, a day cursed by the Gods."

"Nonsense of pagans, lies!" he shouted in Spanish. "Don't the gods have any better pastimes than meddling in everything we do?" Then again his voice was overpowered by Kanalsin's.

He held her up, his fists contracting with almost the same violence as her womb. Her belly ridged in all its length, stretching and tightening as though she were possessed by some demon. The women kneaded her and told her to push. She wailed and wept and prayed with her throat scoured raw by the screaming. Ix Chebel cried out that she could see the baby's head. One more effort, she coaxed, one more brave push and it would be all over. But nothing helped. Kanalsin's face was crimson, grotesque. Again she fell back without breath, slippery with cold sweat.

Gonzalo stepped away and went to crouch in a corner. He wanted only to get out of there so he could no longer hear her. It seemed impossible to him that he should be the cause of so much suffering, that being born should be such hellish work. He trusted Ix Chebel to know what she was saying, but too many of the women kept calling her judgment in question.

"The child's too big," they repeated ominously at one voice. "You cannot pull a ripe pumpkin out of a green one."

If they were right—and looking at Kanalsin he feared they were—then she could very well be lost as she'd told him. Suddenly he felt hatred for the thing that was killing her, for the nameless featureless lump he couldn't think of as his child now and perhaps ever.

A little while later she started to call his name in a shrill voice, and he was forced to return to her side. She was straining for words. "Please," she begged him, "if I die you must bury me under our mat. Say you will do that for me."

He didn't understand what she meant, but at this point he was ready to make all sorts of promises. "All right, all right. But for the love of God, don't talk of dying."

She rested her head on the arm of the woman beside her. From the bottom of her throat another moan began, husky at first then rising to a shriek. With his hands in his hair Gonzalo went back to his corner, wishing he could smash the first thing he saw.

By midday she'd fallen into a limp, clammy stupor. Ix Chebel, finally admitting defeat, said they must send for the *ahmen,* the curer who would loosen the child from her womb with remedies he alone knew. So permission was asked from Citam, who would have to pay for the curer's services, and a wizened old man came to the hut carrying a bundle whose contents no one must look upon.

Neither the eagle feathers he touched her with nor the tobacco smoke he puffed at her were effective, and when the curer left the hut shaking his head at the evil he'd been unable to drive away, everybody understood that the gods had indeed abandoned Kanalsin and her baby on that ill-named last day of the month of Chen.

Too stunned to ask himself what he was doing, Gonzalo ran out and began to look for Jerónimo like a frantic man. You win, Brother Aguilar, he thought. You win this time. At last he found Jerónimo in a storage room with two other slaves.

"Brother Aguilar," he said hoarsely, "how would you like to make your first two converts today?"

Thinking he was making fun of him, Jerónimo threw him a hard glance and didn't answer. Gonzalo held out his hand.

"Brother Aguilar, I am in earnest. She's dying, and the baby too. Please baptize her, that she may be saved from the fires of hell."

Jerónimo held off nervously. "She may be saved from the fires of hell only if she has committed no mortal sin."

Gonzalo shook his head with a grim smile. He couldn't believe himself, arguing doctrine with Jerónimo in front of two bewildered heathens.

"I am quite sure she has committed no mortal sins, Brother Aguilar. Please help me."

Jerónimo still hesitated. "Anybody can baptize at the point of death, you as well as I. You need only to touch some water to her head and say the prescribed words."

Gonzalo clenched his fists. "I don't know what the prescribed words are. And I should have known better than to ask you." He turned to leave; but then Jerónimo followed him without a word.

When Ix Chebel saw them, she tried to stop them. Alarmed, she wanted to know why Gonzalo was with "the other one." As best he could Gonzalo explained to her the baptismal rite he wanted Jerónimo to perform for Kanalsin. Through his garbled words Ix Chebel took the rite to be some sort of powerful medicine the people of his race administered to those in danger of dying, and this she could not forbid. She ordered the women to put Kanalsin on the bed and cover her up, then she let the two men in.

It took Jerónimo a painful effort to walk in. No doubt to him the hut must seem like a suffocating cage full of the smell of female flesh condemned to give birth in pain and corruption. If not for the prospect of rescuing two souls in danger of their eternal lives, he would have never approached her.

When he kneeled by the bed, Kanalsin made a violent effort to get away and began to scream anew as if visited by an evil spirit. She babbled that he'd come to kill her and the baby, to finish his work of hatred against both. Angry, Jerónimo got up to leave. Ix Chebel fretted and the women muttered among themselves. Only Gonzalo could persuade Kanalsin to be still.

"Why is he here?" she panted. "Why must he touch me with water?"

Gonzalo didn't know what to tell her. Why indeed? Because there was nothing to lose, he thought, looking at her battered and warped on that bed he had made so she could rest a bit more easily. Because he was a coward and he too wanted to rest a bit more easily afterwards.

He brushed her hair away from her forehead. "Does it hurt much to have one's head shaped like this?"

But she didn't understand, and kept hanging onto his arm with a desperate grip. "Why must he touch me with water, Zalo?"

He searched for words of whose truth he was not convinced. "Because if you let him do that you can stay with me forever."

With that her face smoothed and she stopped struggling. "Stay with me now."

Gonzalo motioned Jerónimo to go ahead. Jerónimo asked for water. Ix Chebel took a cup and scooped some from a stone vessel she had prepared to wash the baby. Jerónimo blessed the water with the sign of the Cross and held it above Kanalsin's head.

"Brother Guerrero," he asked, "what do you want her name in Christ to be?"

Gonzalo looked at him wanly. Her own name was pretty enough for this life and the next, he thought, the first word he had learned in this hut. She'd told him once that it meant "yellow skirt," and that it was the name of a flower. Then he shrugged. "Maria," he said. Maria like his mother, like the girl he'd loved in Palos, the most common woman's name he knew.

On hearing the word, Jerónimo's entire demeanor softened. "Yes," he said with a smile. "There is no sweeter name than that of the Blessed Virgin." He poured gently the water on Kanalsin's head. "Through the grace of this holy sacrament I baptize thee Maria.

Renounce the devil and his works, in the name of the Father, of the Son, and of the Holy Spirit."

Only after the ritual was performed did he allow himself to show his gladness and gratitude for having been chosen as the instrument of the very first victory won by the true faith in this land. As he stood up he pressed Gonzalo's hands between his own, much as he would have done to congratulate the parents at a proper baptism in Spain. "Darkness cannot prevail upon her now," he reassured him quietly. Then he crossed himself and left.

Perhaps not the sort of darkness he meant, Gonzalo thought as he watched him leave with a clean conscience. But the truer darkness had prevailed already. Ix Chebel, who must have expected from Jerónimo some prodigious feat of curative magic, on seeing that his intervention amounted to nothing more than the same uttering of prayers the *ahmen* had tried before, gave in to despair. Some of the women left, while those who stayed sat exhausted and silent around the bed.

Gonzalo held Kanalsin's wrist, feeling the weakness of the pulse. It was so hard to understand how birth and death could have become one and the same thing, touching like the ends of a string looped upon itself. Why couldn't these people do something to save her? They knew how to cleave a man's chest and pull out the still- beating heart, but they had no surgeons to help a pregnant woman be delivered of her child.

Something that made no sense except that of desperation was telling him that perhaps he should borrow Citam's knife and cut her open himself. As it had been for her baptism, there was nothing to lose. But saving her soul had taken no more than the delicate gesture of a gardener sprinkling water on a flower, while trying to save her body would take the callousness of a butcher tearing into stubborn flesh. It was too savage a gamble, he told himself. Better to help her go gently at her appointed time than to watch her bleed to death for who knew how long. Better to let her end be God's doing and not his own.

He put his hand on her belly, as he'd done so many times to feel the baby kick. Now her belly was still, no longer rising and falling with contractions. Ix Chebel's mouth opened to say what there was no need to say. The baby was dead. Her old body bent like a cornstalk struck by an ax.

"Won't you give her something just for the pain?" Gonzalo asked.

Ix Chebel looked at her medicines and shook her head. "I have no herb strong enough. All that can help now is the drug we give to the ones chosen for sacrifice."

"Yes, I beg you," Gonzalo said gratefully. At Ix Chebel's gesture one of the women left, taking with her the cup that had held the water for the baptism.

It had grown dark, and very quiet. He knew that once he'd help her take the drug she would wander off beyond his reach, and for this reason he wanted to be close to her while he still could, talk to her while she could still hear him. He gathered her into his arms, and put his mouth to her ear. But no word could make it past the narrowness in his chest, only pieces of sounds, tatters of meaning.

She opened her eyes, but she seemed to be looking at a stranger. Why hadn't she looked at him like that before, he thought, when there was still time to stay strangers. She would have gained more from the terror of him she'd felt the first day that by the incomprehensible trust that had brought her to this.

"I so wanted to give you a son," she said. Her voice chilled him. It was like that of a judge pronouncing sentence without passion, only with the unflinching acknowledgment of waste beyond repair. He wanted to shout, I don't care about that, just don't turn your back on me after making me think that I could take anything from you and never have to repay you.

"It will be easy," she said then, as her face paled.

He didn't understand, and moved closer to hear.

"Easy to find your way back. The Gods... the Gods will help." Then she shivered against him and was still. Ix Chebel nudged him to hand him the cup full of the drug she'd brought, but then she saw that there was no need of it anymore.

Gonzalo hid his face in Kanalsin's throat and he thought that if only they let him stay like that forever he would be happy.

FOURTEEN

She was buried in the hut, according to her people's custom, and under the sleeping mat, according to her own wish. The women braided her hair and put ground corn in her mouth so she wouldn't go hungry on her journey. Citam dug up the floor and lowered her into the grave. Ix Chebel gathered the few things that could be buried with her: the small statue of Our Lady of the Rainbow, her yellow dress, the cup used to baptize her. First she smashed a hole in the cup to release its spirit from the clay, as Kanalsin's spirit had been released from her body.

They were already closing up the floor when Gonzalo took the sleeping mat and rolled it, so they could put that in too. As he did that he found the seashell that he'd taken from her and that he'd kept ever since. He let go first of the mat, then of the shell, which came to rest between her hands. Then he stepped aside, and while the earth was pressed over her the women started a loud wailing that made his skin crawl with the terror of the unknown into which she'd been taken.

The women stayed for the rest of the night. For this he was grateful, because he didn't want to be alone. He thought about all the things he'd lost in losing Kanalsin, the things that had kept him from giving up his dignity and his courage. If from now on he had to do without them, they might as well put a hole in his heart as they had done with that clay cup.

Desolate, Ix Chebel came to sit with him beside Kanalsin's naked loom.

"When she was willful," she said running her knotty fingers on the warp beam, "I would say to her that she was like one raised without a mother."

She tried to smile. "And she would say to me that she was not, that I had raised her."

Gonzalo didn't speak. The night seemed endless. From time to time he wondered why the women were wailing. Since the hut had been cleaned and the floor was smooth again, it was hard for him to remember what had happened. He kept waiting for the end of this strange time, when Kanalsin would walk in, bent under her water jar, and start patting the corn dough between the palms of her hands for the evening meal. He could hear that fast patting, slap slap slap while the water bubbled in the pot. It was always a good sound to hear at the end of the day.

"She is with the others now," Ix Chebel said then quietly.

Startled, Gonzalo turned his head. Her words sounded uncannily like the reminders of Christian immortality a priest would have used to comfort the bereaved. Jerónimo too could have said that Kanalsin now sat among the souls at the right hand of God and there was no need to shed tears for someone so blessed.

"With the others," he stammered. "Where?"

"In the Place of Peace," Ix Chebel said. "Where there is no hunger or thirst, where there is rest under the branches of the Great Tree." She whispered a psalm of resurrection. "So the Old Ones have said, when we die truly we die not, because we will live again, we will rise, we will awaken, and this will make us happy."

Gonzalo's shoulders shook as though he were starting to laugh. Heaven, he thought; same old thing with another name. He remembered begging Jerónimo to save Kanalsin's soul, and he felt like an utter fool. These people had their own schemes of salvation, They didn't need anybody else's. No matter where she had gone, she would be granted rest from pain, and what more could one wish for.

At long last the sun rose. He left with the first group of slaves, to load the nets in the dugout; then one by one the dugouts left the beach. Gonzalo went with the group of four boats that were usually sent farther, off Tulsayab where the shallows swarmed with the best catch. It was a beautiful winter dawn, billowy and mild.

He paddled with a good steady stroke. As he paddled he kept his eyes not on the sea or on the sky but on the gourd that lay between his bare feet. It contained his ration of *posol,* the only food he would have before returning to the master's house. He remembered Kanalsin's fresh bread, and the sight of the gourd filled him with loathing. Slave food, he thought, no better than dog's gruel.

He tried to imagine what it was going to be like eating that food every day for the rest of his days, doing every day what he was forced to do today. And the nights, when he would have to sleep on the naked floor of the hut while Kanalsin rotted away beneath him together with that baby whose face he'd never seen... He would die of his own nightmares, he would certainly go mad. No more, he told himself. Quite simply, no more.

He lifted the paddle again and again dipped it into the sea. He felt at peace, the same peace he'd felt when his father had died, pushing him out of Palos and into the New World. It was a feeling of utter freedom, like when he was a boy and stood at the edge of the cliff before diving. Nothing mattered anymore except the plunge he was about to take. Death seemed to have simplified a great many things for him. Kanalsin had said the gods would help him find his way back home; but with or without the gods' help, this was his last day as a slave.

Two of the dugouts turned into a small cove and were pulled ashore there. The third, with the overseer aboard, negotiated the reef and disappeared toward the island of Cuzumil. The fourth craft, carrying Gonzalo and his one companion, made for Tulsayab.

With each stroke of the paddle Gonzalo's mind became clearer. Finally now he would avenge every wrong he'd suffered in this land. Captain Valdivia and the other four, Leon, José, Felipe, Ponce, all of them would break free with him. Jerónimo too would be delivered, not by the mercy of his God but by the daring of a blasphemer and fornicator who'd lain with heathen women without a marriage contract and even without love. He was rowing so fast his companion told him to slow down.

Within sight of the tall carved stone that marked the cape of Tulsayab they steered the dugout toward the cliff and began to drop the nets. Gonzalo's companion gave occasional orders and made occasional remarks, to which Gonzalo answered only with a yes or a no. Once the nets were cast, he waited to see if the man left the boat to go ashore and carry out orders of his own, as he often did. But this morning the man gave no signs of parting company.

Some time passed. The sun climbed higher, and the nets began to shake with the first fish. Once in a while the man leaned to look into the water. Gonzalo's hands kept opening and closing around the shaft of the paddle. The man pointed at something under the water, something Gonzalo didn't catch because all that occupied his mind now was the thought of when he was going to strike. The man dipped his hand into the sea to make a ripple. Gonzalo lifted the paddle and swung it hard against the man's head. The man fell forward without a sound; blood started to ooze in his hair.

For a moment, stunned by what he'd done, Gonzalo stood still. Then, since the first move had been irrevocably made, everything came to him as easy as a dream, the one he'd dreamt for such a long time.

He considered a way to get rid of his companion. Tossing the man overboard to drown wouldn't cover his escape any more than leaving him unconscious, and he didn't want to burden himself with a needless killing. He began to row toward the cliff. He knew there were no beaches along that stretch of coast, but there were ledges and hollows where he could strand the man so they wouldn't find him for a good long while.

It seemed like an endless time before he spotted a sort of step in the cliff, high enough above water. It took him even longer to ease the dugout across the reef and then to maneuver it alongside the scalloped edge of limestone, dreading every inch of the way that he was going to wreck it. At long last he made it.

Struggling to hold the boat with one hand, he pushed and dragged the man onto the ledge, where he left him lying on the stone. Then he pulled away through the same narrow passage he'd used to get in. In the dugout there was still the gourd full of *posol,* together with a larger gourd full of water. He would rather starve than eat the posol. He threw the small gourd overboard. It floated along for a while, until he split it open with his paddle. Then he pointed the canoe toward the east.

In those first few moments he felt dizzy with his own strength, as though nothing in the world would dare stand in the way of a man reaching for his freedom. The sea itself should speed him toward Cuba and his birthright.

It was only later, when he stood alone in the middle of the empty water, that he began to feel the fatigue creeping into his limbs, the cold edge of the wind, and most of all the stubborn tug of the current that was pulling him northward toward Cuzumil, where he could no longer hide now that the men who went there to fish knew who he was. Already he could make out the strip of sand at the tip of the island, and he thought he could even see the fishing canoes beached there, among which there was surely the one that had left Tulum with him.

He veered around and tried to keep the dugout on its eastward course. He knew he must take to the open sea before anybody from the coast or the island would start wondering about that lone craft wavering in the channel. If only the current would let up a bit, so he wouldn't be forced to row so hard.

It was like trying to crawl out of a funnel, one painful yard forward and two backwards if he dipped the paddle only a little more slowly. Even the wind seemed to have a mind of its own, and now blew with greater force, congealing the sweat on his skin like an icy breath. Desperately he worked the paddle, sometimes beating it flat against the water in his frenzy, and cursing and praying all the while.

He had managed to regain some distance from Cuzumil when he saw astern a canoe, still nothing more than a black line on the water but headed unmistakably toward him. It came from the island, and at the speed at which it was approaching it wouldn't take long to catch up with him.

He stopped paddling to draw his breath in. His thoughts were beginning to mix up with fatigue and with fear. Perhaps he should let them catch up, and then lie. He could tell them that his companion was hurt and that he'd come looking for help. But perhaps it was no one who could recognize him, and the canoe was on its own business, and he would be a fool to give up so soon.

He took up his paddle again. He chided himself for yielding to panic, for thinking truly like a runaway slave. Then again he started to row, with new strength. For a while the current actually helped him eastward, and he could see the canoe becoming small behind him. He slowed down and pushed on at a less tiring pace. The sun was shining from between heaps of yellow clouds, and for a moment he allowed himself to daydream that Cuba was as close as one of those clouds.

Then the current caught him again. The dugout balked against it, twisting around in circles, and the paddle shuddered in his hands as if confronting an invisible wall. His breath came in long hard gasps that cut through his chest.

Turning his head he saw the canoe zigzagging on the water, dodging for the easiest course, and now almost flying toward him. The men in it must know what they were doing, having long mastered the same current that so stymied him. He was soon drifting on the sea like a plaything, while the canoe grew closer and closer and the faces of the men in it more and more distinct. When the two craft were a stone's throw apart, he heard someone calling out for him to stop and to toss his paddle overboard. It was the overseer, and beside him stood two warriors aiming their spears.

Sweat streaming down his face, Gonzalo watched his pursuers draw up alongside him and he knew he was defeated. He banged the shaft of his paddle against the edge of the dugout and cried out in despair, until the paddle broke in two and he threw the pieces away and he bent down, as if waiting for the executioner to strike.

Shortly before noon he was brought back to town together with the man he had abandoned at Tulsayab. The man, as they found out when they'd rescued him, had received a far worse head wound than Gonzalo could suspect, and had bled so badly during the time he'd remained unconscious on the cliff that he was now in danger of his life.

Vainly Gonzalo swore to the overseer that he'd never meant to kill the man, that he could have easily drowned him if he'd so intended. The overseer was unmoved. Gonzalo's rebellion angered him greatly. He had always treated Gonzalo with kindness, and Gonzalo had now repaid his kindness with treachery.

Gonzalo was dragged back to the master's house to receive his punishment, which the other slaves were made to behold as an example. With his arms bound and his mouth bleeding from a few cautionary blows, he stood kneeling before lord Ah Kin Cutz. Among

the men and women summoned to witness the judgment he saw both Ix Chebel, who looked at him in grief as if to ask why he'd done such a thing, and Citam, whose face was as always a blank wall. Jerónimo wasn't there.

Lord Ah Kin Cutz listened to the overseer's account with half-closed eyes. It occurred to Gonzalo that this was the first time he'd come face to face with his master since the day he'd been handed over to him in the marketplace. Having become a thing, he was to be brought to the master's presence only when he was no longer a usable thing.

The overseer answered the master's questions at length. What both men considered the worse crime was not Gonzalo's attempted escape but what they saw as his attempted murder of his companion. It seemed, Gonzalo was finding out, that these people detested the shedding of blood unless it was in sacrifice, and that they punished with equal severity assaults made on persons of all rank, including slaves.

Gonzalo was allowed to speak only once, with his face touching the ground before lord Ah Kin Cutz's feet. Almost unable to form the words in his terror and his rage, he could only claim one more time that he'd never meant to kill anybody. But he knew all the odds were against him. Never had he hated his captors more, and never had he felt more forsaken.

At last lord Ah Kin Cutz, satisfied that he'd heard all the evidence, lowered his staff of office and pronounced his sentence. "Send him to the priests."

Gonzalo had well anticipated those words, but he made the greatest effort to be silent. He would not grovel and beg for mercy before that despicable savage and his chattel. He was made to rise and to follow the overseer and his men out of the house. As he stumbled up he saw Ix Chebel standing by the hut, in tears, and unexpectedly he was comforted by the sight of the old woman and of Kanalsin's resting place. At least by someone in this land he had been loved, he thought, and by someone in this land he would be mourned. He wondered how Jerónimo would react when he'd come back and find himself the sole survivor. Then he was taken to the great temple.

He was fettered at ankles and wrists, so that he could take only small steps and perform only the simplest gestures needed for eating and drinking and relieving himself. Two men were put to guard him day and night. During the day the men worked at making headdresses for the priests, while at night they slept at both sides of him in a dank underground cell.

Despite his asking, he was not told when he would be sacrificed. All he could learn from the two guards was that he'd been chosen for the festival of Kukulcan, the Feathered Creator. Somehow, he thought, it was fitting that he should be given to the same bearded, white-skinned god he'd once briefly considered impersonating. There was a wicked logic in the way these people went about their worship, and it added insult to injury that he should have lived among them long enough to grasp that logic.

Nor was he told how he would be killed, so he feared the priests might have in store some fashion of sacrifice even harder to imagine than those with which he was already acquainted. Knowing he would surely die but not knowing when or how, his every hour passed in terror that it would be his last. In all this he was never harmed at all. The waiting alone was harm enough.

At first, seeing that his death was long in coming, he seized upon the smallest act or word to build a fitful hope. A milder look from the priests, a hint of sympathy from the guards, and he told himself a miracle could still happen. Then the next instant, on hearing the door of his cell being opened, he prepared himself to walk out, for this was surely the time. At night he lay between the two guards, listening to their breathing and rubbing his fetters with the unconscious motion of a calf in a butcher's backyard. When at dawn the guards got up once again, once again he readied himself to follow them to the altar of sacrifice.

Why had he waited so long to try to escape? he cursed himself.

Why hadn't he tried with Ponce, why hadn't he tried while he was making canoes, why had he been such a fool? Relentlessly he flogged himself with those questions, until they became a desperate jumble. Soon his mind emptied of all memory and all thoughts, except the memory that he'd been condemned and the thought that he was going to die.

By the fourth day, broken with dread and sleeplessness, he was fighting hallucinations. The faces of the idols melted into the faces of his mother and father, into the face of Kanalsin laughing and then shattering with a scream. The stone serpents that decorated the temple's door unhinged their huge jaws and crushed him between their fangs blackened with the blood of countless victims. So again he begged the guards to put an end to his misery. But the guards didn't know, so again he returned to his corner. And two, three more days spent like this, and three more nights.

On the eighth day, when Citam walked in, he found him lying on the floor with his face against the wall, crumpled and inert. At Citam's touch he made a small gesture of denial, like someone who doesn't want to be awakened from sleep just yet. Citam had to call out his name and turn him around. Still Gonzalo couldn't recognize him in the darkness of the cell. As he was being marched toward the door he nodded, understanding that finally now the time had come.

Citam prodded him out of the cell and on to the courtyard, where he had the guards remove Gonzalo's fetters. Blinded by the light, Gonzalo watched the ropes being untied with the same blank look as a newborn waiting for the cord to be cut. He looked at Citam and wanted to ask him what was going on. But he felt very tired and couldn't speak. Even as the fetters fell from his ankles and wrists he thought it was just another hallucination.

But then Citam began to prod him again, first toward the temple's gate then down the street and on toward the master's house. And then something even more strange happened, Jerónimo was walking with them. He put his arm under Gonzalo's and spoke some reassuring words Gonzalo couldn't catch.

They got home. When he saw the hut, Gonzalo shook his head. "No, not there," he begged. Citam and Jerónimo took him to the lodge behind the kitchen.

"Brother Guerrero?" Jerónimo asked softly, bringing him a cup of water. "Are you all right?"

Dazed, Gonzalo nodded. Citam motioned Jerónimo to explain.

Jerónimo smiled. "I asked Citam if we could find out what happened to the man you wounded," he said in Spanish. "He has recovered, and he will live. Then Citam persuaded the master to spare your life."

Citam looked down. "I will not lose a man for no reason," he said flatly; then, impassive as ever, started to walk away.

Gonzalo reached out to stop him, and before he could summon back his pride he was grasping Citam's ankles and sobbing at his feet. Unmoved, Citam made a sound of annoyance and shook him off.

Gonzalo put his arms around Jerónimo. His sobs and his broken words of thank you became one savage moan of relief.

"Stay with me, Brother Aguilar. Please stay here with me for a while."

BOOK TWO

THE HUSBAND AND THE FATHER

FIFTEEN

JANUARY 1514

If someone had told him he'd survived captivity for one more year, he would have called them a liar, for surely no one could do that. He had awakened, he had worked, he had eaten, he had slept. He had hoped and he had despaired and he had hoped again. From the day he'd been brought back from the temple he had pledged to leave his fate to God, no matter how incomprehensible His dawdling. Now he could only wonder how God could have allowed him to last this long.

He now lived with the rest of the slaves in the lodge behind the kitchen. He hadn't set foot back into the hut, and Ix Chebel had returned to the weaving room. The hut had eventually been turned into a storage room, its earthen floor hidden under stacks of feather brooms and grindstones.

When he left to go fishing or when he worked in the courtyard, he no longer looked in that direction. It was as if nothing that the hut meant had ever happened, neither the happiness he had known there nor the grief that had driven him from it. He no longer felt happiness or grief; there was only numbness. Finally he was living the way Jerónimo had lived since the first day of their captivity, with the same hardened patience that seemed to grow upon itself like layer upon layer of coral stone.

The rancor between the two of them had softened during the past year. As they both now seemed bent only on holding out, they found it easier to help one another in their common goal. Once Jerónimo had been sent to deliver a load that was too heavy for him. He had collapsed under the weight, and he'd been ill after that.

Gonzalo had taken over his chores for a week or so, to which Jerónimo had responded with some favor of his own.

Together they had outlasted one more harvest, one more dry season and one more rainy one. They had withstood hunger and fatigue and punishment. They had sat in the dark wondering what would become of them, content only to know that they were still alive.

By dint of his persistence with Citam, Jerónimo had finally been chosen to be among the men who guarded the weaving room. This was a position of some privilege. He was no longer sent out to carry loads or to chop wood or to fish; instead he spent most of his time comfortably indoors, making sure the women worked and kept their place. The first task entailed keeping a tight watch on all the weaving supplies that went into the room and on all the finished product that came out; the second meant keeping an equally tight watch on all those who might try to enjoy the master's females without the master's consent.

Before he could be granted this privileged position, Jerónimo had had to pass the test for which he had so often volunteered as proof of his trustworthiness in matters of the flesh. One night he'd been ordered to sleep on the beach with a fellow slave, so they could do their fishing in the morning without wasting time. They built a fire and put up hammocks. As Jerónimo was about to go to sleep, his fellow slave had vanished and in his place a young girl had appeared. Lying half naked in the hammock, she called him to join her where he would be sheltered and warm.

Jerónimo rolled himself in his ragged mantle and lay down by the fire. Again the girl called him and taunted him, saying he was no man and a fool. Meanwhile the slave, hidden in the dark, spied on the proceedings and tried not to laugh too loudly.

In matters such as these, however, Jerónimo could command ample guidance from his religious training, and the girl managed only to make a nuisance of herself. After a night spent fending off her attempts, he did his fishing and returned to the master's house, proud to have shown his captors that righteousness and chastity had their value even among savages. Of course by then the story was everywhere.

To Gonzalo Jerónimo's new status wasn't much better than that of a watchdog or of castrated prisoners employed as guardians of harems. But he could see how it made Jerónimo's life easier, and of this he could only approve. At first he'd even been able to make use of Jerónimo's position to obtain some small privileges for himself. If he tagged along with Jerónimo handing out weaving supplies or cutting reeds for new looms, Citam kept him in the house to complete these tasks instead of sending him out to do more strenuous ones. In the end, however, the real reason he was allowed in the weaving room at all was Ix Chebel's kindness, as the old woman hadn't forsaken him.

But when Ix Chebel had succumbed to old age, Gonzalo was banned from the weaving room once and for all.

Now left entirely on his own, he'd gone back to his undistinguished station among the other slaves. The only respites came with the unlucky days, when all work was forbidden, and with an occasional festival. On those days he took what comforts he could and tried not to judge himself too harshly for it, even when the greatest comfort of all turned out to be his own self-pity. If no one thought compassionately of him, he would do that to himself, for somebody must.

His body took care of itself—the sturdy, loyal body of a man of twenty-six that could go for days without the simplest mercy and still respond with the same good hunger and thirst, the same good allegiance to life. But his soul must be constantly tasked, or he knew it would be wrecked. He turned to memory as his only salvation, for memory was the one thing that had remained unchanged. To all his chores he added the most essential—holding onto the past. He told himself he must practice memory as diligently as he would have practiced horsemanship or gunnery, to be ready for when God would tap him again on the shoulder. He must not forget that freedom was like, so he would know how to reclaim it when the time came.

Sometimes the past visited him without pain, in dreams of home that were as sharp as a glimpse of sky from the bottom of a pit. Then through the day he went over the dream again and again until every detail was nailed down, until he could see every crack in the paint of his father's boat and every line in the face of his mother when she smiled.

During the most endless, brutally tedious chores, when at each repeated gesture it became easier and easier to welcome defeat, he began to dredge up the buried pieces of his other life. At times he hounded himself for hours to summon up what day of the week it was when the gypsies had come to town with their dancing bears or what he'd bought with his first copper coin.

More often he had to force himself to keep his past, no matter at what cost. After he was first warned not to talk back in his own tongue he did it again, and after he was punished he again persisted.

The punishment was well worth the reassurance that his captors could master everything about him except the way he thought and the way he chose to give sound to his thoughts.

Day after day and month after month, with enough of these small things his endurance was made, like a wall with enough small pebbles. The *Esperanza* had gone down and her log was rotting at the bottom of the sea, but he kept a log of his own that nothing could erase.

❖   ❖   ❖

It wasn't the first time that the house was being turned upside down by the arrival of guests. Lord Ah Kin Cutz loved to entertain with his lavish hospitality. Often he spent on a single banquet everything he'd acquired in a month, obliging his guests, as custom demanded, to give a similar feast in return. The household slaves had come to dread those occasions, with the taxing work they required.

The most exhausting celebration by far had been the full eight days of feasting when the master had taken two new wives with a single ceremony and even Citam, by the dawning of the seventh day, had allowed himself to lose his composure.

The guests whose arrival had been announced that winter morning must be important indeed, if Citam seemed on the verge of losing his composure again. His topknot almost undone, he was rounding up the slaves from every corner of the house and directing them to their tasks in great haste. Gonzalo was ordered to the front porch, where the floor must be swept and the stone benches moved and the vats refilled with water, all in the shortest time that Citam's patience allowed.

As he reached for a broom, he saw Jerónimo lead out of the weaving room a woman who carried two blankets just cut from the looms to be offered as gifts. Then two sitting stools and two painted bowls and two drinking cups followed. Since all the gifts came in pairs, the slaves began to mutter that perhaps the master was about to take two more wives. But one of the blankets was woven in the pattern commonly worn by women, while the other bore the design reserved to men. The joke spread that the master had developed a taste for wives of both sexes.

The preparations went on all day. The guests, however, didn't arrive until sundown. By then not only the slaves but the master and his principal wife and his two new wives had been waiting in the porch, all made miserable by the delay. As Gonzalo concluded while he hunkered down by the gate, these guests were exalted enough to keep even the ruler of Tulum waiting.

When the procession finally reached the house, announced from the beach by the conch shell trumpets, it was a respectable one; but the part that was let into the courtyard was only ten or so male and female attendants clustering around the two jade-encrusted litters. The rest camped outside, setting up hammocks in the palmetto grove.

Goaded by Citam, Gonzalo and three other slaves approached the two litters to help carry them. The guests couldn't be seen yet, as they were screened by white cotton curtains. Gonzalo put his shoulder under the heavy cedar pole of the litter closest to him. It must be the woman's, he thought, because it was scented with a perfume like ambergris and wildflowers. Outside the courtyard the sound of conch shells mixed with that of the drums and of the townspeople milling around.

For want of directions as to what he should do next, after the litter was lowered to the ground Gonzalo remained kneeling beside it, his right hand placed on his left shoulder in the customary gesture of subservience. He was uncomfortably aware of the stares he drew. If to the people of Tulum his appearance had become familiar, to these foreigners he was once again a source of wonder. Their servants were a well-fed and well-clothed lot, with good reason to also look down on his torn cloak and bare feet. In the first breath of wind of the evening the curtains on his side of the litter began to stir like the wings of a bird about to take flight.

Torches were lit all around. As though they knew this without having to be told, the two guests remained inside their litters for the time it took to complete the task. As he watched lord Ah Kin Cutz sweat stoically in his feathers and jaguar pelt, Gonzalo's curiosity was whetted even more. Who were these visitors who could humiliate the master with impunity?

The man emerged all at once, unfolding himself on long, powerful legs that must have been quite cramped inside the litter. He was at least as tall as Gonzalo; and, Gonzalo couldn't help adding in his mind, he was also handsome enough to make Gonzalo wonder when he'd ever stopped to think about another man's looks.

This man had none of the usual native embellishments, neither the crossed eyes nor the flattened skull. Still he was the sum of everything native, from the dark luster of his skin to the shape of his eyes to the high curve of his nose. There was something intensely, primally male about him, which seemed to come only in part from his privileged upbringing. Had he been the humblest corn farmer, he would have still carried himself with the same stunning grace.

His dress was that of the warrior more than of the ruler, spare and elegant. Next to him lord Ah Kin Cutz looked hopelessly provincial. In place of the cumbersome headdress that all native nobles fancied, he wore a single eagle feather in his long black hair.

The only other personal adornment were the tattoos that covered him from waist to chin—an impressive display of bravery, as Gonzalo could tell, having once witnessed the long, bloody torture of having one's skin painted like that.

Followed by an attendant waving a fan, the man brought himself before lord Ah Kin Cutz, offered his greetings, then listened to lord Ah Kin Cutz's welcome, which required that he, as the lesser of the two, recite the visitor's name, lineage and rank. Thus Gonzalo learned that he was in the presence of lord Hun Halal Nachancan, born of the House of Chan on his mother's side and of the House of Can on his father's side, ruler of the province of Chetemal with all that lay within it, and of Bakalal to the north and of Becan to the west.

Having said that, lord Ah Kin Cutz stopped rather abruptly, looking at the second litter to explain as courteously as he could that he didn't know the proper greeting for the lady. Lord Nachancan smiled, raising his arm toward the litter.

"Ix Ahau Na," he said, dispensing with all the expected flourishes. "My sister."

The look of pride and affection as he made this announcement seemed to disconcert lord Ah Kin Cutz, as if the visitor had committed an impropriety in paying such homage to a woman.

One more difference worth noticing, Gonzalo thought, between his dull master and the extraordinary guest. Then he turned slightly his head so he could look at her.

First he saw her hand parting aside the curtains. It was smooth as a sheet of copper yet strong, like the hands of some noblewomen back home who hunted with their husbands and could hold a stallion as surely as they. The wrist was surrounded by an exquisite gold bracelet of tiny frogs leaping one after the other. If her brother's looks were any indication, he thought, she must be as beautiful as that Queen of Cathay he'd dreamed of so many years ago. One thing he had never imagined back then, though, was that he would meet her as a slave, stooped low on the ground beside her perfumed litter.

The porter beside him reached out to keep the curtains open. The woman put out her head, her thick, lustrous, magnificently plaited hair brushing the cotton folds. She stood still for a moment, as though waiting for someone to come forward. Before Gonzalo could remember to bow down, she couldn't help noticing the only slave whose eyes were turned toward her.

If at the sight of the bearded stranger she felt any of the surprise which her retainers had manifested so plainly, it never showed, for as a woman of breeding she must be above such displays. But after the first unintentional glance she acknowledged his presence with another, deliberate look. Gonzalo didn't lower his face and held her gaze, almost challenging her to look all she wanted. She wasn't as beautiful as he'd expected, he thought, and not as young.

A second attendant, the one she'd been waiting for, rushed to the litter and dropped down on all fours, making of his naked back a step for her feet. She gathered the hem of her long white gown with the same hand that held a pleated paper fan and came out helped by one of her women. Lord Nachan-can motioned her to come stand beside him, not behind him as custom de-manded—a breach, this, that seemed most startling. As she complied, Gonza-lo saw that the two of them stood nearly shoulder to shoulder, a stately pair indeed. Her skin was lighter than her brother's and, by native standards, with no crossed eyes or flat forehead, she was as plain as he. She wore a necklace that matched her bracelet, only the little golden frogs had eyes of green jade.

Lord Ah Kin Cutz invited his guests to sit beside him and gestured to Citam to start showing the gifts. This was a tiresome ceremony calling for both host and visitors to look at each gift and praise it. Gonzalo wondered how much Lord Nachancan and Lady Ix Ahau Na could be impressed by these unimaginative offerings, since they seemed to own already all they needed and a good share of luxuries. Still, the blankets and stools and cups were accepted with graciousness, and all appearances saved.

Then the porters from the train outside began to file into the courtyard with the visitors' gifts. These were as elegant and unusual as their givers. First was presented a pair of jade pendants that, judging from size and weight, would drag down lord Ah Kin Cutz's earlobes with just the degree of showi-ness he favored in all things. Then came gold tweezers, which native men used to pluck out their scanty, unwanted beards. Then more large and small objects, all of the same reddish gold—beautiful jewels, fan handles, embossed disks and figures of animals and birds.

Looking at that astounding hoard, Gonzalo's heart began to race. What if *these* were the people of Eldorado? What if his dreams had come to call right there at his door? A strange panic swept over him. It had been a long time since he'd tried to grasp at freedom, since he'd last allowed himself the luxury of considering chances.

The riches that so amazed him, however, turned out to be only a minor introduction to the one gift that truly charmed the master: jar after jar full of honey, and log after log full of honeybees. Lord Nachancan had a servant open one of the jars and pour out in a dish the thick yellow honey, inviting his host to taste it. Lord Ah Kin Cutz looked like a child surrounded by all the sweets he can have. It was from honey, properly fermented, that the *balchè* liquor was made, and here there was enough for many a happy banquet.

Lord Nachancan pulled out the flint dagger he carried strapped to his arm and with it struck open one of the logs. Startled, Gonzalo anticipated the swarm bursting out in anger to sting all present. But the bees only flew out with a low hum, hovering for a moment like a cloud of gold dust suspended in mid-air, then rose above the wall and vanished. The sound of delighted laughter filled the courtyard, while the porters started to carry the heavy jars into the storage rooms.

Puzzled, Gonzalo looked up trying to see where the swarm had gone. But only a few bees remained, clustered greedily on the hand of the servant who'd opened the jar, no more of a threat to him than flies. These visitors seemed to have come not only from

Eldorado, he thought, but from some fabled land where honey flowed in plenty and even bees didn't sting. Then he saw that the woman, who was now sitting beside the master, was looking at him once again. It was a long, intent look, as though she'd chosen to make of him the only thing that deserved to be looked at.

The banquet went on into the night. To Gonzalo, busy at his tasks, it was nothing but a shuttling of tired slaves and a distant buzzing of voices from the porch. It was a warm, miserably humid night that sent trickles of sweat running down his back at every movement he made. Who knows when he would be allowed to rest, he wondered. Finally he curled up in a hidden corner and fell asleep, too tired to worry about being found out.

Some time later he was awakened by someone tapping lightly on his shoulder. He jumped up, muttering an excuse. But it was only the boy who fed the dogs.

"They need you," the boy said. "Outside, by the hut," and he left.

What did they want from him now, he thought, aching to lie down again. He squeezed his eyes in the dark. The room was empty, everything was silent. He walked out. The wind had died down, and the air was thick and heavy. The moon was still high, looking like a coin left at the bottom of a strongbox. By the kitchen door a woman was asleep, sitting up against the wall. The last splinters of *ocote* wood cast a feeble light on the empty dishes and the empty cups from the banquet.

By the hut, where he'd been told to go, he expected Citam or a fellow slave with news of some new chore. It was instead one of the visitors' retainers, a man of importance, judging from his dress and appearance. Thinking there must be a mistake, Gonzalo stopped. The man beckoned him to come closer.

"Who are you?" the man asked. His accent seemed oddly clipped to Gonzalo's ears, but he could understand it.

"Why should I tell you?" Gonzalo replied.

The man shrugged with a hint of contempt. "I'm only obeying orders. I'm not the one who wants to know."

"Then you won't know," Gonzalo countered, and turned around to leave.

"Wait," the man called sharply. "Are you happy here with your master?"

At that question Gonzalo had to glance around to see if someone was spying on them. "Can any man be happy as a slave?" he answered with a fierce edge in his voice.

There was a pause. Then the man walked into the hut, motioning him to follow. "We must talk."

Gonzalo hesitated. This whispered conversation in the night seemed unreal, like a meeting with a wayfaring spirit. What should he do? Go away and leave everything the same, or answer this strange call that might make everything different?

He went into the hut, after a full year since he'd last done that. He thought of Kanalsin who lay buried under the floor of that hut. He felt her loving presence, and he was no longer afraid. It seemed as if she were calling him there for a good purpose. His soul balked for a moment at the unexpected push, like a rusty door that nobody had opened in a long time, but it yielded of its own unbroken will.

In the hut the only light came from a moonbeam threading aslant through the open doorway. High under the roof, night birds made faint noises. He didn't know how long the two of them could go undetected, though he could invent some explanation or other. He must come to the point right away.

"Who sends you?" he asked.

"You speak our language well," the man remarked. "Who sends you? Tell me."

The man shuffled his sandaled feet on the bare earth of the floor.

"My master sends me, the Lord Nachancan."

Gonzalo shook his head. "You lie. Lord Nachancan hasn't set eyes on me yet."

The man might be surprised, but it was hard to tell. "The eyes of Lady Ix Na are the eyes of my master," he said.

Gonzalo caught his breath. So it was she, he thought. This was too strange to be true—a thing out of some Moorish tales he'd heard back home, of princesses and slaves and go-betweens skulking in the night.

"I'm sure Lord Nachancan's sister can find out about me from the man who owns me," he said.

"She has tried to," the man replied, "but all she has learned from your master is that he will not sell you to her. He must think highly of you," he mused, "because she named a handsome price." It was clear from the way he spoke that he himself saw no reason at all to be interested in the white-skinned one.

Gonzalo forced himself to go over those words again in his mind. Many a thing too strange to be true had taken place in the short time he'd been asleep!

"Yes," he whispered. "We must talk."

Clumsy with excitement, he groped his way to an uncluttered corner of the hut where they could sit down. He pushed aside a roll of matting, flinching at the noise that might give them away. Now he didn't know which question he should ask first.

"There are many slaves in this house," he began. "Why does she want me?"

The man tried to make himself comfortable in his bit of space, sniffing at the musty smell of the hut. "There are no other slaves who look like you," he replied.

That left Gonzalo wordless for a moment. Had the great lady chosen him for nothing more than an exotic difference in plumage and color? Was he to her some sort of freak to be gaped at?

"You're wrong," he said. "There is someone else who looks like me. Tell your lady she will be just as happy with him. We both have hairy faces, like monkeys."

The man clucked his tongue, very much annoyed. "She must be told you have a temper," he commented. "Hear me out. Lady Ix Na is not buying a monkey. You don't understand what you are being offered."

Gonzalo held out. "My freedom is the only offer you can make me."

Now it was the man's turn to be silent. In that silence a muffled sound of steps seemed to come from outside. Perhaps it was only the flapping of a bat.

"And even if I did want to change masters," Gonzalo asked, "how can I, since you say lord Ah Kin Cutz refuses to sell me?"

"He might agree if asked again," the man said. "Lady Ix Na and her brother are not easily turned down."

Indeed, Gonzalo thought, that lord Ah Kin Cutz should have turned them down was a mystery. He asked himself whether it would be wise to try to discover the reason why, perhaps from Citam, who surely by now must be familiar with the whole affair. But he would rather deal with the visitors on his own. The visitors too must prefer it that way, if they had sought him out without Citam's intervention.

"The matter of your freedom hasn't been considered," the man said at last. "But I will speak of it to the Lady Ix Na and her brother. Come back to this place tomorrow night."

Those words were enough to quicken Gonzalo's heart. But now that he'd become expensive merchandise, he didn't want the visitors to think they could have him for just a few glass beads of hope.

"I will come if I can," he said, "and if I can trust you. I will not risk my master's anger unless you make it well worth it."

In the dark the man's shoulders heaved, as if he were offended.

"I don't know where you come from, but it must be a distant place indeed if you claim not to trust the House of Can."

"Then listen closely," Gonzalo whispered. "I will tell you where I come from. I will tell you all you need to know. See that you understand it, for the sake of your lady."

SIXTEEN

It rained that day, an unusual occurrence for that time of the year. Everything had to be moved indoors, where the preparations for a second feast began as soon as the dishes from the first one were dry.

For once, Gonzalo was glad to have so much to do, because it would have been hard to sit idle with so many things on his mind.

When he'd slipped unobserved back to the storage room, he knew he no longer needed to worry about being caught sleeping now that everybody was resting. But he could not go back to sleep while inside the master's house the visitors' envoy was reporting his every word to Lady Ix Na and her brother.

This secret conspiracy brought him back all the sharp, fierce feelings he thought he'd lost. Much was still unsettled, and he was aware that from the nightly parley the visitors had learned about him more than he had learned about them. But that didn't trouble him. For the time being he'd contented himself with asking their messenger only two things—how distant their city was from Tulum, and whether it was in the inland or close to the sea.

The man had answered that Chetemal lay some thirty leagues to the south of Tulum, at the mouth of a most excellent bay on the same eastern coast. This, Gonzalo reasoned, meant he would be twice as far from Cuba as he was now; but if the visitors gave him his freedom, might they not also give him a boat and a crew? As he came and went under Citam's eyes he felt as though he'd become two people. One fetched and hauled and obeyed, and the other built a thousand plans and destroyed another thousand. This, he crowed to himself, had to be the most pleasurable building and destroying a man could indulge in.

Strongest of all was his wish to see again the woman who'd stirred in him this flurry of expectations. If he could see her again, with the attention he hadn't bothered to pay yesterday, he might discover something beyond any bits of truth she might grant him through her envoy. Who knows, he might even discover why she wanted him.

Even if she did want him only for his exotic appearance, so be it, he thought. Hurt pride was the smallest price he was willing to pay for his freedom. In fact, with a little goodwill he could very well decide that he was flattered by her choice, and even more by her insistence.

What exactly did she look like? he wondered. Was she really as haughty as she'd seemed yesterday, or was it only because in his mind a lady of her standing could be nothing but haughty? Her brother had called her by her full name Ix Ahau Na, which meant "She of the Lordly House," but her envoy had referred to her simply as Ix Na.

What would she make of what he'd told her messenger? She might not believe his claims that he came from beyond the sea, and decide that she didn't want a liar after all.

The hours seemed to have grown longer, all taken up by such a novelty. As time passed he had to fight the urge to go to Citam and try to find out from him whether lord Ah Kin Cutz had changed his mind. Then he chided himself for his unwise impatience. Soon it would be night, and he would know.

In the afternoon, while he was bringing to the kitchen a basket full of the squash seeds the cooks had requested for the stew, he came across Jerónimo, who relayed to him a few errands of no great urgency. He wondered whether Jerónimo had gotten wind of something. He knew the lady didn't want them both, and for this he thanked his good luck. If he was bought and made free, he would think of a way to help Jerónimo regain his freedom. For now, it was still each man for himself, and he put Jerónimo out of his thoughts. Better to think of what he would do if the master's refusal turned out to be final.

The only question he could ask around safely was how long the visitors would stay in Tulum. He approached a girl from the weaving room; from her he learned that the visitors had come to discuss an alliance between Tulum and Chetemal, and would remain at least two more days if the alliance was reached. So, Gonzalo thought while the girl chattered on about all the work this occasion was causing, he had at least two more days in which anything could happen. And something must happen, he vowed—if not something of their making then something of his own.

The rain didn't stop all day. It seemed almost like a bad omen, Gonzalo fretted. The cotton hangings at the windows of the house stayed drawn. Once in a while the shadows of those inside passed behind them. Then he heard

Citam's voice, which by now he could catch no matter where he might be: they had run out of firewood.

"You, you and you," Citam was shouting at random. "Go to the wood merchant. Tell him to send all he has." Before he could duck out of sight, the last summon fell on Gonzalo's back, followed by a jab of Citam's finger.

Damn him, Gonzalo panicked. It would take forever to bring the wood from the merchant's house, and by then it might be too late. But if Citam harbored any suspicions, to cross him at this point would be an even worse mistake. Without a word he followed the other two slaves.

All the wood the merchant had was quite a bit. Gonzalo couldn't tell how long he shuttled back and forth, welcomed at one end by the merchant's displeasure for having been roused from sleep, and at the other end by Citam's testy impatience. In his anxiety to get the chore done he almost didn't feel the weight of the wood that the merchant's helpers slammed on his back, the rope that cut into his flesh through his cloak soaked with rain.

When that was over Citam set him to undo the bundles and sort out the cords of wood that had stayed driest during the carrying. Tired and over-wrought, he wondered whether Citam was doing it on purpose, to keep him away from the hut. One by one he dumped the pieces of wood, swearing at the splinters. Finally Citam had enough wood, and Gonzalo was dismissed. He slipped into the hut and hid in the same corner as the night before. He sat against the rolled-up mats and listened in the dark for a rustle of sandals headed his way, struggling to keep his eyes open.

When would the man come? Why wouldn't he hurry now that the time was right? Were they reminding him with that anguished wait that he must keep his place? Perhaps he shouldn't have asked for his freedom right away. Perhaps he should have been happy with just the good fortune of much better owners. He started to doze off, jumping at each noise and then drifting again into sleep when the noises were followed only by the steady murmur of the rain. Soon he gave up, exhausted.

He woke up as if from those nightmares in which one reaches for the one thing that will save him and the thing draws back farther and farther. The moment he opened his eyes he knew something had eluded him, for reasons he couldn't fathom. From the courtyard came the sound of a bustle that must have started some time before. That he should have slept through it was a measure of how tired he was when he'd laid down on the bare floor of the hut.

He peeked out. It had stopped raining, and it looked like mid- morning. It looked as if the visitors were leaving. He could see the porters helping each other with the loads they'd put down only two days before, while in the palmetto grove hammocks were being rolled up and griddles stacked. Something must have gone wrong. If the visitors had come seeking an alliance, their early departure meant the alliance hadn't been reached. Now they would leave and he would never know what had happened. The hopes that had taunted him were about to vanish, like the flash of cape that set the bull running and then changed into the sword ready to strike.

No, he vowed. It wasn't going to be so simple. He didn't know whether it was rage, despair or foolishness, but whatever it was it was good, it drove away all fear. If the lady thought she could trifle with him because he was nothing but a slave, keep him hanging and then not bother to tell him that she didn't want him anymore, she would soon find out how wrong she was.

Quickly and determinedly he walked out of the courtyard and into the crowd of the visitors' servants. Here he brought down for a woman a basket she couldn't reach, there he lifted for an old man a bundle too awkward to shoulder. Nobody turned him down or sent him away. To the occasional question he replied with a show of stupidity. Let them look for him from the master's house if they wanted to, but he would not go back there.

The first few porters set out toward the beach. Gonzalo glanced at the gate of the house: the two litters for Lord Nachancan and Lady Ix Na sat there, still empty. So he kept on; he put a campfire out, untied a hammock from a tree, looked for a dog that had strayed away. By the time the two travelers stepped out of the master's house it was as if he'd always been one of that busy throng.

Lord Nachancan and Lady Ix Na approached the litters, followed by the man who'd come to the hut. The attendants helped the lady in, took hold of the wooden poles and lifted in unison. Armed men set themselves around both litters. The curtains were not drawn. As the procession started to move Lord Nachancan bowed his head at his host, while Lady Ix Na wrapped her white stole around her forearms and waved her fan in goodbye. The drums began, but to Gonzalo they were no louder than his heart.

What to do now? The question rapped at his mind like a fist at a stubborn lock, trying to force a snap of revelation. Everything was happening too fast, without the time to wrest a plan. Warily he started to walk with the crowd, keeping his head down. They got out in the main street. Townsfolk bent from windows to look, children rushed from the alleys. How far would he be able to go? he wondered. How long before the shout of alarm, the commotion bursting around him?

The two litters advanced slowly, hampered by the crowd.

Loads wrapped in matting and hardwood chests jostled one another on the porters' heads. A little further on they would come to the narrow gate that led out of the wall. There the procession would turn into a single file trickling out under the eyes of the guards.

Gonzalo stopped, letting the crowd push past him, waiting for the lady's litter to catch up. He couldn't call out to her. He must try to make her see him instead. He had to hold his ground against the flow of the procession. He had to push and shove, his face raised desperately toward the litter that swayed closer and closer.

At last she saw him. She seemed surprised for a moment. Then without the slightest hesitation she motioned discreetly to her man. On catching sight of Gonzalo, the man broke through the guards and reached out to grasp his arm.

"Take me with you," Gonzalo said under his breath. But the plea was unnecessary. The man was already drawing the guards around them with a whispered order not to interfere.

The gate loomed ahead. The first porters stopped, two within and two outside, so they could start handing one another the loads that would not get across any other way. With the smoothest of gestures Lady Ix Na slipped off her white stole and let it drop into Gonzalo's hands. Shielded by the guards, Gonzalo wrapped it around his neck to conceal the lower half of his face. She whispered something to the litter-bearer closest to her. The bearer stepped aside and Gonzalo took his place under the pole. Everything seemed to happen in the blink of an eye, so fast that he would never know how it had all come about.

The litter came to a halt. Gonzalo's heart wouldn't slow down. At every hard breath he took the scent of the stole wrapped around his face coursed dizzily to his lungs. He couldn't look at her, but he knew she could see him, his head a few inches away from where her legs bent under her on the cushioned floor of the litter.

Her voice floated to him, low and guarded. "Thank you."

Why would she thank him? he wondered. There was no time to think. Lord Nachancan's litter went through, then it was the lady's turn. No distance ever seemed longer to Gonzalo than the few steps it took him to get across, shoulders scraping against the stone, arms lifted high to hide his face. Then finally they were headed toward the beach. His hands relaxed. It should be easy now, he thought; now he was in her keeping.

The crowd thinned, but some people followed them all the way down to the canoes. Most of the craft had already been loaded. One was breasting the surf, the carved prow high above the water. Lord Nachancan was still unaware of all that had happened. He climbed aboard the largest of the canoes, the one with two seats shaded by a canopy woven of green and blue feathers, and waved some order to the steersman behind him. All around were the movement and the noise of the embarking, watched over by the sentinels stationed on the roof of the great temple.

His eyes riveted to the canoe, Gonzalo could barely keep the bearers' slow, rhythmic pace. It was true, he told himself again, he was truly running away. Of all the ways he'd ever envisioned this was the last one he could have imagined.

Again Lady Ix Na signaled to her man. "Paichè," she whispered, "my brother must be told before we join him, or he will surely object to having a slave sit beside him."

She chuckled behind her fan. "My proud brother."

Promptly Paichè hastened ahead, climbed aboard and spoke to Lord Na-chancan. Gonzalo couldn't see his reaction, but Lady Ix Na gave another small sound of satisfaction, like a girl who'd just brought about a clever prank.

With the others he put the litter down on the sand. Lady Ix Na held out her hand to him, to be helped out, and he took it. At that touch, so loaded with complicity, he felt a jolt in his whole being, as if they were secret lovers exchanging a pledge under the eyes of an unsuspecting husband. Her fingers were long and slim, with a good hard grip that made him trust her. Of course this was the best way for her to lead him to the canoe; but she could have just pointed him on, so he couldn't help thinking that she must like it that way.

Lord Nachancan beckoned nervously, looking at the guards atop the temple's roof. "Quickly, my sister, quickly," he said under his breath.

Almost tripping on the hem of her dress, she went in and sat down. Gonzalo crouched at her feet. For once it was good to have to shrink into the unobtrusive posture of the slave. The rowers started. At each stroke of the paddles Tulum slowly began to recede. Above the wall, the red and blue of its buildings seemed to grow dimmer, washed away by the sky. Gonzalo couldn't take his eyes off that sight. He had to remind himself that this time he wasn't leaving to go to the salt beds or to go fishing. This was new, this was forever.

"Stay low until we pass the watchtower," Lord Nachancan advised him. "Though I quite doubt the guards will notice you *now*... May the Gods be thanked for careless guards." He laughed, and suddenly Gonzalo laughed too, so hard he had to press his hand on his mouth for fear that he would choke on his own joy.

"You owe me ten *cacau* beans," Lady Ix Na said, pinching her brother's arm. "You know you shouldn't bet against me, Hun Halal."

"But if this morning you were sure you'd lost the bet!" her brother replied. "When he didn't go to the hut you said you gave up."

"But I did go to the hut, my Lord Nachancan, Gonzalo said. "I was there for the best part of the night."

Paichè intervened, surly-faced. "Then it must have been the wrong part of the night. I waited for quite some time, in the rain."

"I'm sorry," Gonzalo said. "I couldn't come any sooner. I was kept working."

Lord Nachancan smiled. "It's all clear now. Luck went against us last night, but now we're all here, a boatload of conspirators making off with lord Ah Kin Cutz's property right under his nose."

This time Lady Ix Na too laughed out loud. They hadn't been together more than a few moments, Gonzalo thought, and already she and her brother had welcomed him into their extraordinary intimacy.

Lord Nachancan turned to the steersman. "Faster, my good man. I cannot wait to put a hundred leagues of sea water between us and that old bore."

Lady Ix Na's foot brushed against Gonzalo's thigh.

"He is so insufferably stubborn," she said. "He refused to sell you just out of jealousy, to spite us."

Her eyes shone with delight. "This ought to serve him right."

She turned to her brother. "Do you think he will take this seriously, Hun Halal? Already he has granted that alliance with difficulty... Wouldn't it be like him to cause us trouble now?"

Lord Nachancan shrugged amiably. "I'll give him three of my *balchè* brewers as compensation," he said. "I'm certain he will have no objections. I will make sure the first thing they'll do will be to get him rolling drunk."

"Here's the watchtower," Gonzalo said, his voice still muffled by the white stole.

The sentinels near the squat grey beacon walked closer to the edge of the cliff to watch the convoy. One man waved his arm in salute. Lord Nachancan waved back.

"A little further," he said to Gonzalo, "and you can show your face."

"Then you did conclude your alliance, my Lord Nachancan," Gonzalo said. "Even though you stayed only two days in Tulum?"

"We had to give up some cornfields along the border," Lord Nachancan said, "but if we hadn't, we would have been forced to be lord Ah Kin Cutz's guests for who knows how many more days."

"Those endless banquets," Lady Ix Na echoed.

The canoe slipped swiftly along the coast, leaving the watchtower behind. Now they were at last far enough. Gonzalo unwrapped the white stole.

Lord Nachancan stared at him, his eyes sharp with interest. "My sister was right," he marveled. "I do believe you come from the other side of the world."

Lady Ix Na picked up her stole. She too looked at Gonzalo, a look that told him how grateful she was for his daring, and how proud of the instinct that had secured him to her. She motioned him to come sit in front of her.

"And to think that lord Ah Kin Cutz never bothered to find out anything about the other side of the world," she scoffed.

She leaned toward him eagerly. "There is so much that you must tell us."

"My Lady Ix Na, yes," Gonzalo said. "But will I be speaking as a slave or of my own will, as a free man?"

She laid her hand on her brother's arm, to signify that she answered for him also. "You should not ask us for your freedom. You made yourself a free man when you walked out of your master's house."

She nodded toward the canoe behind them, which carried the armed guards. "If you wish, you can leave now. Just tell the guards where they must take you. But we want you very much to stay with us, and only you would decide for how long."

Gonzalo looked at the guards in the canoe—his escort to freedom, the answer to three years of desperate prayers. His mind almost refused to believe it. Less than a week, and he would be back in the islands. But in the opposite direction there was an even more powerful lure, the same that had made him a sailor to begin with. For every thing he would tell them about his side of the world he would learn something about theirs. Now that he could choose again, there was nothing he would rather choose than to learn all these new things.

He smiled, bowing his head to her. "I can thank you only by staying, my Lady Ix Na. It doesn't matter to me for how long. Now it doesn't matter anymore."

SEVENTEEN

It took them five days to travel down to Chetemal, but for Gonzalo everything had changed from the first hour.

Again he was the first of his race among people who'd never known his race, and the only one as well. But now it was as it had been for the Admiral when he'd first touched the shores of San Salvador Island; he had become the guest of men and women to whom his coming was the cause of unending revelations. And the Admiral had never met so civilized a people; it seemed strange to him that he, a simple sailor, should be the forerunner of this encounter. It was a charmed crossing, one he wished would never end.

At the start it was almost hard to get accustomed to well-being. The first night he'd awakened from sleep, moaning in fear. The canoes had been beached in two great semicircles, with a fire burning at the center. On hearing Gonzalo call out, a servant came up to him and asked him if he needed anything. Gonzalo looked around in a daze. He touched the new clothes he had on, not knowing for a moment how he could be wearing such finery. The cloak was soft, the loincloth richly worked. The high-backed sandals felt oddly uncomfortable, since he was used to going barefoot. He fingered the thongs around his ankles, as if to make sure they weren't shackles.

Again the servant asked him what he could get for him—food, water, another blanket. Gonzalo drew his breath in. Yesterday night he was the one ready to answer all requests, carry out all orders. In such a short space had the wheel turned!

"No... nothing," he said at last. "I need nothing at all."

He lowered himself back into his hammock. Lord Nachancan was asleep under the next two trees, an armed warrior sitting on the sand as guard. He couldn't see Lady Ix Na. She was sleeping in the canoe, on a bed of mats laid astern. The only sounds in the night were the lapping of the waves and the crackling of the fires.

He stretched out in the hammock, making it rock. He thought of Citam, who must be turning Tulum upside down in search of the runaway; of lord Ah Kin Cutz, who'd been cheated by his own guests at his own crooked game; of Jerónimo, who no longer needed to pray for him now that he'd found a way out by the light of his own candle; and he thought of home, where he would be a few months from now, home with the gold that awaited him in Chetemal. He thought he would never sleep again, so he could think all these thoughts over and over.

At dawn he lay watching the sun, red as a Castilian petticoat.

The palm trees made lace out of the sky and frigate birds glided overhead, the sheen of their wings changing in the light. This morning seemed to him as blessed as the first morning he'd awakened in this land after the shipwreck. His life had been a chain of beginnings, he thought, a string of baptisms.

Three or four of the women were kneading tortilla dough. It occurred to him that all he had to do was call them, and they would bring him the first flat loaves hot off the griddle. But he would wait instead, this time because he chose to, not because he had to. Even in such small things his new freedom was exhilarating.

Some time later Lord Nachancan woke up, and the women brought breakfast: the tender flesh of the conch in its own peach- colored shell, big lobsters, corn bread, fruit of every pod and peel.

"When we reach home," Lord Nachancan said, "you will taste our *cacau* drink and you will tell me if it isn't the best you've ever had anywhere civilized people speak Mayathan."

"I am sure it will be the best," Gonzalo said with a pleasant grin, "since in my master's house I never tasted this drink."

Lady Ix Na grimaced. "Hun Halal, you did say *civilized* men."

Lord Nachancan laughed. Then his eyes took on a look of regret. "Indeed it seems that so far you have known only the worst of our land... Paichè told me about your five companions offered up by the people of Ecab. What a damnable waste! The people of Ecab are the reason why we sought this alliance with Ah Kin Cutz. We need to keep him between us and them. As long as the two of them wage war on each other, we might be left alone by both."

"Ah Kin Cutz might be unreasonable," Lady Ix Na added, "but the people of Ecab are in the habit of eating their prisoners first and asking questions later."

"How is it among the Castilàn?" Lord Nachancan asked. "Are you also at war with one another?"

"We were divided once," Gonzalo replied. "At war with one another, with our neighbors. Now we are one great nation, under one great king."

"And how many days is it from here to the land of the Castilàn?" Lady Ix Na asked.

He glanced up awkwardly. It still seemed strange to him that she should be so free with her speech, an equal to her brother. Lord Ah Kin Cutz's wives had always been without speech and without consequence.

"It's much more than days, my Lady Ix Na," he answered. "It takes about four of your months, if the winds help."

Her eyes opened wide. She threw her brother a keen look. "Four months! None of our people ever sailed four months into the ocean. Your canoes must be strong."

Gonzalo smiled. To see her so impressed made him secretly smug. It felt good to be a Spaniard, one of a people who had dared so much. He wished she could have seen him come ashore from a galleon under full sail.

"They *are* strong canoes, my Lady Ix Na," he said. "When the islanders saw them for the first time they thought they were mountains that moved on the water."

With an air of great irritation, Paichè stood up and walked away, saying he must see to their departure. Paichè had been silent all through breakfast. His manners toward Gonzalo had been contemptuous and cold since the moment the two had met.

Lord Nachancan's voice dropped to an amused whisper. "I think he doesn't like you too well."

"He's just jealous," Lady Ix Na said. "When our father and mother were killed he gave up a family of his own to be father to us."

From the look on her face at the mention of her parents Gonzalo saw that she and her brother were, like him, acquainted with the most savaging kind of grief, the one that comes too soon in one's years.

"My Lady Ix Na... how were they killed?"

She turned her head away for a moment. "Murdered in their sleep by the Xiu of Manì, along with our older brother. Hun Halal and I hid in a corn pit... Paichè found us in the morning... Hun Halal still had his hand on my mouth to keep me from screaming. I was ten years old."

There was silence. The thought of two children huddling together in a corn pit was as familiar to Gonzalo as his own memory of the night they'd come to take his father to jail. That these two should be so bonded seemed only the natural thing.

Lord Nachancan thrust back into its hide sheath the dagger he had used to eat. "To all that lives the Gods gave an enemy," he said. "To us they gave the Xiu, until the end of time."

He wiped his mouth and hands with a cloth. "They have no lineage among us," he added, sounding as if he were uttering the worst possible insult. "They are Mexìca, like too many of the foreign upstarts we must put up with."

He saw that Gonzalo didn't understand. "One of the people of Culhùa, to the north," he explained.

He touched the eagle feather in his hair. "Hun Halal means One Arrow. When I went into Manì to avenge our parents, I killed two of them with one shot."

A servant came to tell them the canoes were ready. Paichè had already gone aboard and was inspecting the craft for scorpions.

Lord Nachancan got up. "Now that we are speaking of names," he said, "yours also must have a meaning in your tongue."

Gonzalo smiled. His name was no hallmark born of a deed worth remembering. Who knows how long ago the last of his ancestors had died to whom that name had been more than a sound. He shrugged.

"Guerrero... I think you would say *holkan*... a warrior, or fighter."

Lord Nachancan and Lady Ix Na were mystified by the tone of self-mockery in his voice. Instead they both seemed genuinely pleased.

"Ah," Lord Nachancan said, nodding. "Then that is what you are. You are Ah Holkan, a great warrior."

This grand new name seemed so improbable to Gonzalo that he had to force himself not to laugh. Of course he had been trained to fight. He could fire gun and crossbow, he knew when it was best to stagger the fire, when to encircle and when to charge, where and how to build bastions and lookouts. But the fighting he'd witnessed in the New World was not the sort in which he wanted to seek distinction. The one among Spaniards was just endless squabbling, started by the party that shouted loudest and resolved more or less in the same way. No party was immune to the follies it imputed to the others, so he'd avoided them all. The war with the natives, on the other hand, wasn't war but a blood sport, one man on a horse chasing twenty on foot toward the mouth of the cannon.

Still, it was good that his hosts regarded him with approval.

Within moments the new name was on everybody's lips. He knew that for as long as he'd stay with the people of Chetemal he would not be called anything else. It would be fun, he imagined, back home in his old age, to tell his grandchildren how he'd once lived among the heathen and how they had bestowed upon him the title of great warrior.

Sometimes during the voyage a canoe would quietly catch up. The people in it would look at him, then quietly go back to its place in the convoy. At first, amused by this game, he had obliged by looking back and smiling. But when they were ashore, those people followed him around touching his skin and hair and beard, and the game became a violation.

Lord Nachancan, to whom this behavior was perfectly natural, didn't notice Gonzalo's uneasiness, and Gonzalo didn't know how to tell him without offending him. By the third day, however, the following and the touching stopped. Gonzalo remarked that he was glad to be no longer the center of attention. Lady Ix Na replied that he was still very much so, only she'd given strict orders that he should no longer be bothered. Relieved and surprised, Gonzalo thanked her.

Paichè had said her eyes were the eyes of Lord Nachancan. Indeed little seemed to slip by Lady Ix Na.

She must have noticed also how awkwardly Gonzalo responded to her presence. The most wonderful thing for him in all the voyage was the closeness of her. He loved to sit beside her in the luxurious hold of the great canoe, lulled by the ripple of the oars gliding in a sea made of green glass. Yet that closeness was both comfort and discomfort.He'd never been one to stumble all over himself because a woman was watching. With her instead he wanted to say the right word, make the right gesture. Perhaps because she was no young girl to be won over by a few common suavities; perhaps because she was a high-born lady of a foreign people, her habits doubly unfamiliar.

He began to observe Lord Nachancan, to copy his moves.

When sitting down, there was a proper way for a male to gather between his legs the folds of his *esh,* the long stiff loincloth that bore no resemblance to a commoner's plain wrap; when conversing among peers there was a soft throaty sound to be made as indication of respectful attention.

The rules of behavior were as complicated among these people as among the nobles of Spain. If he remembered those rules he was pleased with himself; if he thought he acted like an untutored barbarian he discovered a new strain of embarrassment. Though he knew she'd chosen him because he was different, he felt compelled to be like one of her people as much as he could.

Most of all he wanted to fulfill the expectations she'd Manifested when she'd offered lord Ah Kin Cutz three hundred *cacau* beans, three times the price of an ordinary slave.

On the fourth day they entered the territory of Chetemal.

Looking at the coast, Gonzalo was struck by two things: how beautiful it was, thick with jungle and cornfields, towns, roads and temples, and how it could have ever gone undiscovered for so long. Beginning with Don Cristóbal's own three caravels, Spanish ships must have sailed up and down this coast time and time again in their vain chase after Eldorado; still it had remained as if protected by an invisible shield for more than twenty years. This was something that he, a sailor, found very much a mystery. And what of that country of the Mexìca that Lord Nachancan had mentioned? The world kept increasing, room after room like an enchanted palace. So much to see, to map!

On the fifth day they turned from the sea and headed into a maze of sounds and coves the color of blue satin. At the clapping of the oars the coral sand came alive with thousands of birds, and the trees shook with wings. Herds of reddish-brown capybara grazed on the shores, then dived at an unseen danger. It looked like a haven for the gods.

Lord Nachancan swept his arm around. These were his favorite hunting grounds, he told Gonzalo, where his grandfather had taught him to stalk the one quarry truly worthy of a man, the jaguar whose choice food the capybara were. To both his father and his grandfather, he added, bow and arrow had been an undignified weapon, because it was preferred by those Mexìca who had invaded their homeland; but he had loved it since he was a boy, and in his hands it had become as proper as the flint-tipped spear of his ancestors.

Finally the city appeared, not cramped inside a wall like Tulum but spread out along a broad crescent of bay, its handsome white houses sheltered by hardwood trees. Hundreds of canoes lined the waterfront. Thatched stockrooms teemed with buyers and sellers.

Everywhere were the signs of a rich trading harbor. One saw temples, yes—Lord Nachancan pointed out the ones that honored Ek Chuah, patron of merchants, and Ah Cab, protector of beekeepers; yet the temples were less imposing than the warehouses. Gold and honey and jade had made the fortunate inhabitants of Chetemal less at the mercy of their divine rulers.

The drummers sounded to all the return of the convoy. The two litters were unloaded, then two more were brought for Paichè and Gonzalo. It was on the shoulders of four porters that Gonzalo came ashore at Chetemal, amid a happy din of people. The litter rocked and he wanted to hold onto one of the poles, utterly unused to being carried like that. But he was Ah Holkan, he joked with himself, and must be brave in the face of hardship.

The ancestral home of uncounted generations of Can lords, Masters of the Sea and Guardians of the Sand, rose inland, away from the crowded shore and fishing villages. It was a spot of paradise, at the far end of a lagoon whose water seem to have all the colors water can take.

Along the banks of the lagoon, lush with ferns and blossoms, were the prized beehives that made Chetemal's wealth—dozens of logs sealed with mud and piled into humming cities of gold. All around the house stretched *cacau* groves heavy with pods. Truly, Gonzalo marveled, money here grew on trees. There were no slaves and no slave quarters. The House of Can could afford to pay others for their labor.

"This is Xul Ha, Where The Water Ends," Lord Nachancan said with pride. "This is where I was born and, if the Gods grant it, where I will die, and my sons and my daughters, and their sons and daughters."

They were greeted by servants who had none of the skulking ways of lord Ah Kin Cutz's slaves. There was genuine pleasure in their welcome. Among the women were some young beauties who swarmed affectionately around Lord Nachancan, tugging at his mantle, touching his arms. One woman led a boy by the hand and carried a little girl astride her hip; another was pregnant.

Lord Nachancan tried to keep his composure amid the excitement, but when the little girl reached out to grasp the feather in his hair he gave in to laughter, picking her up from her mother's arms. Paichè was only annoyed at the noise, and Lady Ix Na asked about the well-being of the pregnant woman: had she remembered not to eat rabbit, so as not to mar the baby with a hare-lip? The only one ill at ease was Gonzalo, who'd recognized in this female throng a joyful counterpart of his old master's harem and who refused to believe, with a good deal of envy thrown in, that such harmony could be possible among a single rooster and so many hens.

One word from Lady Ix Na put an end to the whispers caused by the guest's appearance. They went into the house past a magnificent gate of carved rosewood capped by two jaguar skulls. All the rooms faced the lagoon; shrubs stippled with scarlet flowers graced the white stucco, their scent blending into an almost sinful breath of sweetness with that of the cedar beams set together without a single nail. The floors were worked with bits of jade and pearly shell. Swag curtains blazed with color against a sky that seemed to have been blue since the very first day. And since the very first day Gonzalo felt as though he'd lived there, since when he was old enough to dream of the one place after his heart. All this would be very hard to leave, he thought, if he already loved it so.

"Please see to our meal," Lady Ix Na told the women. "I will also need honey and *cacau* for the drinks." Giggling and whispering, the women left.

Before the food and the drink they must pay their respects to the rest of their kin, who'd been awaiting their arrival. Expecting an uncle or aunt, Gonzalo followed his hosts to a spacious main hall.

There, on an altar lavish with bowls of fruit and incense burners, stood an array of wooden statues, the likenesses of ancestors whose ashes they contained.

To these men and women who'd carried the name of the clan through the coiling of time, brother and sister affectionately made known their safe return, burning incense in their honor. Surprised but even more moved, Gonzalo became aware again of what precious small distinction these people made between life and death. With this custom of theirs, the living had the comforting daily closeness of their blood up to the farthest generation, and the dead merely became invisible.

Among the statues were those that guarded the ashes of the parents and older brother murdered by the Xiu. To one statue, that of a young man, only Lady Ix Na burned incense. The bond between them, Gonzalo inferred, must have been quite intimate. What puzzled him was how little of this intimacy her manners showed. She didn't talk to this image as she did to the others. She simply bowed, with all the respect of a wife or a betrothed but none of the fondness. He must know who this man had been, and why she bore him no tenderness.

He pointed at the carved figure, stumbling more than ever in addressing her. "My Lady Ix Na, was he... was he also killed by your enemies that night?"

Clumsy and perhaps inappropriate as that question was, she welcomed it eagerly, as though she'd been waiting for it. "Not him" she answered. "He was taken by an illness a few months after our wedding. He was a gentle husband... but he had been my father's choice, which I honored as it was proper for me to do."

It took Gonzalo some moments to grasp the meaning of her words. He could only guess her age, yet from only a guess he could tell that she'd been in the cheerless condition of a widow for over ten years, the prime years of her life. This struck him as unbearably unfair. Now loath to speak, he wished he could be far from this crowded room, from the empty eyes of the dead.

She lit more incense. "Ancestors," she addressed, "we bring you a guest of a people you have not known. Look kindly upon him. May the time of his staying be happy... and long."

They went to sit in a long patio that opened onto the lagoon, where hammocks and benches were set in the shade of the late afternoon. A woman brought what was needed for the *cacau* drink, but left everything in Lady Ix Na's hands.

"I won't let anybody else make it for me," Lord Nachancan said, sounding like a fastidious husband. "She keeps telling me that the reason I never married is because none of my women can match her *cacau*."

She knitted her eyebrows. "That is what you keep telling *me,* beloved brother!"

They teased one another while she worked, so much like husband and wife that Gonzalo was almost jealous. From a bowl she took a dark brown paste having the thoroughly unappetizing look of butter that had been rolled in mud.

"Taste this," she invited Gonzalo, with what an impish gleam in her eyes.

He put some of the paste on his fingertip, then on his tongue.

Against every rule of etiquette, he couldn't help grimacing. Never in his life had he tasted anything more hideously bitter than this stuff. It stuck to every corner of his mouth like the devil's own excrement.

Lord Nachancan laughed and handed him a cup of water. But even the water wouldn't cleanse that foulness. Was this the famed beverage his hosts had called "the food of the gods"?

Quickly Lady Ix Na mixed the brown lumps with honey. She whipped the mixture with a wooden beater, twirling the handle between the palms of her hands. She added water, then more honey and more water, until the bowl brimmed with a thick golden froth.

Again she offered him a taste. "Now try this."

Gonzalo forced himself to take the cup from her. But this time, if not by the food of the gods, he was rewarded by what must come closest among mortals, for this delicious wonder bore no resemblance to the substance from which it came.

Lord Nachancan sipped his drink with closed eyes, almost reverently. "It is like life itself... One moment so bitter you think you will not endure it, and one moment all goodness."

Indeed, Gonzalo thought. Five days ago he was a slave, and now he was knowing every human being's birthright. He looked at his hosts.

"May you only know the goodness," he toasted.

Lord Nachancan shook his head gently. "The good and the bad are one, and must be taken as one. That is the way it is, the only way it can be."

Gonzalo brought the cup to his lips. This too, he agreed, was the truth.

It was cool and lovely in the patio by the slow murmur of the lagoon. The two men stretched at ease in their hammocks, but Lady Ix Na sat upright on her bench with her hands in her lap. Now she seemed no different from all other native women when they sat demurely in the presence of men.

Her brother nudged her. "You have the look of someone with a question."

She threw him a sharp glance and stood up. "I will choose a room for Ah Holkan," she said. "And I will remind you that tomorrow the *batabs* are coming to discuss the tribute."

Lord Nachancan grazed her hand, asking with that gesture to be forgiven. "I should leave the ruling to my sister," he joked.

Then, as if being reminded of his duties had aroused in him a little boy's distaste, he got up, took off everything he wore and dived into the lagoon with the quick grace of his long limbs.

"You too, come," he called out to Gonzalo from the water, his black hair trailing behind him. "The *batabs* are the dreariest company of old men," he scoffed. "They talk of nothing but money."

Gonzalo hesitated, wondering what Lady Ix Na would think of his abetting Lord Nachancan's sudden playfulness. But what Lady Ix Na might reproach in her brother she might clearly condone in Gonzalo. She first smiled to him from the patio entrance and then she left, so he could follow his inclination without witnesses.

Once she was gone, Gonzalo didn't let Lord Nachancan call him a second time. Dropping all his clothes like him, he was in the water in an instant, with the uncomplicated joy of a holiday afternoon. The two men swam side by side for a while. The water was wonderfully warm, and the bottom was covered with a fine, white limestone powder that felt like silk against the skin. Lord Nachancan broke away, and Gonzalo went after him.

Lord Nachancan was a strong swimmer, but so was Gonzalo, who overtook him easily and didn't slow down for his sake but forced him instead to catch up in his turn. Well away from the shore, refreshed and alive with the exertion, they stopped, their silent challenge abated by the recognition of one another's equal power. The sun was setting, and the air was drowsy with the distant buzzing of the beehives. With a measured stroke they returned to the shore and sat down under a tree covered with large clusters of white roses.

"My sister does have a question she can't bring herself to ask you," Lord Nachancan said, "so I will ask for her. Do you have a wife?"

Gonzalo grinned to himself. For someone so sure of who she was, it seemed curious that Lady Ix Na couldn't bring herself to probe into her guest's personal matters. If she only knew how glad he was to answer her, he thought.

"My Lord Nachancan, I have no wife among my people or anywhere else," he said. He searched the face of his host to see how much he himself was interested in the same matter.

Lord Nachancan nodded. "She will be pleased to know this," he said, and his eyes seemed to say he too was pleased. "Shall I send you a woman tonight, then?"

Quickly Gonzalo shook his head. "No." Only as an afterthought he hastened to add, "Thank you, my Lord Nachancan."

There was an awkward silence. Of all the things Gonzalo had been offered, this was the first he had turned down. Aware of this novelty, he wondered what Lord Nachancan would make of his refusal. But for once he didn't worry about appearing discourteous. He found the thought of another woman in the same house with Lady Ix Na peculiarly distasteful. If he could not be with her, what pleasure would he get from some female sent to his bed the same as a pillow or a pair of slippers?

Lord Nachancan looked at him closely. His slightly puzzled expression changed into understanding. "I think she will be glad to hear about this also," he said.

The woman who'd brought the cups and bowls returned to say their evening meal was ready. She had cloths for the two men to dry themselves with, and a bone comb shaped like a bird. While Lord Nachancan put his mantle and sandals back on, she combed his hair and tied it. With a twinge of self-consciousness Gonzalo felt his own hair, wishing it wouldn't be still as short as a slave's.

"Will you sit in council with me tomorrow when the *batabs* come?" Lord Nachancan asked as they went in.

To that Gonzalo had no objections. These rich old men who ruled Lord Nachancan's towns would surely besiege him with questions, and some of the questions would be thorny enough. But this was the lot of every Spaniard in the New World, to face the chiefs of the land and test his skill in handling both their hostility and their acceptance. Both could be equally unreasonable, and so equally disastrous.

"I will be honored to sit in council with you, my Lord Nachancan," he answered. He noticed how his voice had changed now that it no longer conveyed just the fear and loathing of the slave.

The evening meal, served in dishes whose hollow legs were filled with dry seeds to make a pleasant sound, was lavish. So was his room, from which he could walk undisturbed out to the lagoon. Lady Ix Na saw him to the room, but at the door she let her women take over the care of their guest. Her look told him how deeply she regretted that the dictates of convention allowed her servants in but not her.

That night, while he lay down waiting for sleep and aching with the fullness of his heart, he discovered that he was no longer homesick. What had home ever given him that he could not possibly give up? he asked himself. Nothing, in truth—in all his life, not a small measure of what he had found here in a few days. The mere fact of this room was staggering. When had he ever had so much space of his own, and so much beauty of his own? Where had good people ever been ready to welcome him and not the nobility of his birth or the size of his money purse?

He closed his eyes. As he settled in bed, again a bed after more years than he remembered, he noticed something under one of the fat cotton pillows. It was Lady Ix Na's white stole, the one with which he had covered his face when he'd escaped from Tulum. She must have left it there when she'd chosen the room, or smuggled it in with one of the women.

He pulled it out. That scent of ambergris and wildflowers, the scent that forever and everywhere would mean her, lingered in the folds of the gauzy fabric. With all the names he had learned in this land, he had no name for what the thought of her did to his soul. But he knew he was going to stay in this land for a very long time, because nowhere else would he feel this way.

EIGHTEEN

The questions came, and thornier than he'd expected. Seated beside Lord Nachancan in Xul Ha's mail hall, he confronted not just the *batabs* but dozens of other officials who'd come simply to see him, the stranger. The *batabs'* assembly was made even more daunting by the copper hatchets the men carried as a badge of their rank. At one voice they asked that the matter of the tribute be set aside, so that all attention could be devoted to finding out just how much the Gods had kept from them for all those thousands of years.

Lord Nachancan presented his guest, adding only what he'd learned from Gonzalo himself—who he was, where he came from, where he had lived so far. Then he only listened; but Paichè seemed to find great pleasure in goading on the interrogators. It was he who asked the hardest question: what were the Castilàn doing in the islands?

This made Gonzalo wish he were a lawyer, a priest, or anyone versed in the complicated arguments on which his countrymen rested their claims to the lands they'd discovered. Most of all he wished he could, like his countrymen, believe that those claims were valid. He had learned to speak Mayathan well, but not well enough to convey ideas he knew would sound alien to his listeners.

As best as he could he summed up the document all conquistadors were required to read to all native people everywhere they went: the *requerimiento,* a formal request drafted by the most learned men in Spain for the benevolent purpose of spreading the only truth in the New World. Those learned men, however, were cast in Jerónimo's mold, not Gonzalo's. As a messenger from his Most Christian Majesty King Ferdinand of Castile, he knew he'd been quite poorly appointed for this task.

Long ago, the *requerimiento* explained, God had created the first man and the first woman. Their offspring had multiplied and scattered in many different lands. Though these scattered inhabitants might not know it, they were all God's creatures. God had then chosen Saint Peter as the supreme chief of all His people. Saint Peter's successor, the Pope of Rome, had given the islands and all new lands to the Castilàn. Therefore those of God's children who lived in these remote countries were subject to the Spanish king, whom they must acknowledge as their ruler. If they did so, the subjects would receive favors, honors and benign treatment, and they would know the blessings of the one true faith. If they refused, they would be considered rebels and as such they would suffer slavery, war, and execution. That, he concluded, was what the Castilàn were doing in the islands.

The last time Gonzalo had heard the *requerimiento* being read, in Spanish since there were no interpreters, was in the jungles of the Darién. Bewildered by a stranger uttering incomprehensible words and demanding by means of gestures that they all surrender at once, the natives had fled. The Spanish commander Gonzalo was serving at the time, Alonso de Ojeda, had seized three of them and had had their ears and noses cut off. This form of punishment had become a favorite with other commanders, although Alonso de Ojeda remained known as the one who had introduced it.

The same astounded panic Gonzalo remembered in the eyes of those naked tribesmen appeared on the faces of the *batabs*, of Paichè and of Lord Nachancan. He had expected it back then, and he was not surprised now. But then a thought came to him that was a flash of lightning. Back then he could do nothing except witness injustice, while now he could deal with the natives on his own terms. Until more Spaniards came, all that these people would learn was how *he* thought and acted. For all they knew, all of Spain, indeed all of Europe, was made up of men like him, men who did not believe in the one and only truth upheld by the lofty words of the *requerimiento*.

Paichè tried to silence the noise that filled the council hall. "Our own worst enemy would not speak as you have," he roared. "We already have a ruler, in whose house you are. You have lived in our land for only a short time and you know nothing about us, yet you want to give us other rulers and other Gods!"

Gonzalo didn't let that discomfit him. "My lord Paichè, you asked me what the Castilàn are doing in the islands. You did not ask me what *I* am doing."

Lord Nachancan gave a sound of approval. Despite his undeniable ability to startle, the guest was conducting himself well.

But Paichè was relentless. "And what are *you* doing here?"

Gonzalo spread open his hands. "Certainly not trying to give you another ruler or another God."

He was interrupted by one of the *batabs* from the far end of the room. "Then why have you told us about this... request that the men of your race make?"

"To warn you," Gonzalo replied without hesitation. "So you will know what to expect if the Castilàn come."

Another uproar rose in the hall. This time outrage was as strong as astonishment before.

One man began to shout. "What power of arms can you possibly have, to make such threats?"

Gonzalo didn't answer right away. He knew it was foolish to boast of muskets, horses, gunpowder and steel to people who had no notion these things. "I advise you to send scouts to the islands," he said then. "Let them see with their own eyes."

The *batab* struck with his fist the mat he was sitting on. "My Lord Nachancan, throw this foreigner out of your house and send warriors, not scouts, to the islands!" But another voice rose. "We cannot send him back to tell his people all that he now knows about us." And a third voice countered, "There are no such people as the Castilàn. This man is a liar, or else he's mad."

Lord Nachancan lifted his carved staff to restore silence. Then he turned to Gonzalo. "Ah Holkan. My *batabs* ask many questions, but I will ask just one question. Today you warn us against the Castilàn.

What will you do when you return among them?"

Gonzalo bowed his head. "My Lord Nachancan. Since you have granted me to stay here for as long as I wish, today I say also that I have no wish to return to the islands. I don't know whether the men of my race will ever find your country. I intend to just wait until that day comes."

Lord Nachancan put his hand on Gonzalo's arm. "I am content with your answer, Ah Holkan. I am content to just wait with you." He addressed the *batabs*. "My council must also be content."

Reluctant and far from silent, the council members got up and left. Paichè, defeated for now, withdrew with the others. Lord Nachancan and Gonzalo remained alone.

"My Lord Nachancan, thank you," Gonzalo said. "If there were anyone in my country to whom I could be as grateful as I am to you, I would return there."

Lord Nachancan smiled at the crowd that was leaving the hall. "I know why they are so afraid. Nothing will ever be the same for us from this day on." He looked at Gonzalo. "Perhaps I too should be afraid."

❖   ❖   ❖

In the days that followed, in private, the two men discussed what they couldn't properly pursue while being challenged by a roomful of agitated functionaries. As Gonzalo had suggested, scouts were sent to the island. Disguised as fishermen, they would observe the doings of the Spaniards and return with the information Gonzalo himself was eager to obtain after three years of absence.

Lord Nachancan provided him with maps. Together they scanned distances, features of the coast and boundaries of the mainland. Gonzalo discovered even the location of that reef of the

Víboras where the *Esperanza* had foundered. Something else he discovered was how truly lost he and his countrymen had been all that time. The Darién, for instance, where the horses broke their legs in the entangled vegetation and blood-hungry bats drove the men nearly insane with fear, was only a thin strip of land between the Ocean Sea and that western sea everyone had sought desperately for years. It would have taken only a few days for an expedition to cross it.

So that the scouts wouldn't return with more of the same delusions, Gonzalo instructed them on the unknowns they would encounter among the Castilàn, the unknowns he'd deemed unwise to disclose to the council. Horse, steel, armor and crossbow could be explained as different forms of dog, copper, quilted covering and spear-thrower; guns and gunpowder defied his power of description. From what he could explain, apparently the Castilàn were able to harness the might of the thunder and carry it in metal tubes against anything they wished to destroy. The scouts listened with a puzzled look, but Lord Nachancan understood he needed not wait for their return to know that Gonzalo was neither a liar nor a madman.

After the scouts left, Gonzalo remained looking at the maps spread around him. The country of the Mexìca, to the northwest, was thick with towns and cities. Their capital, named Tenochtitlàn, loomed as large as the navel of the world. It had far more people than any city in Christendom—prosperous people, well organized and fierce. If the Spaniards did find all these lands, he thought, they would also find themselves outnumbered in the midst of worthy adversaries. Despite the thunder they carried in their metal tubes, here they would do well to think twice before making war, because war would no longer be the slaughter of the islands.

And should the Spaniards feel no qualms in slaughtering the islanders because the islanders had no garments, masonry, writing or currency, here they would be stared in the face by all that the Spaniards considered civilization. Even the tenet of a single God would not be the sublime revelation they so yearned to bestow upon the rest of the world. As Lord Nachancan explained, his people were already familiar with Hunab Ku, the One Above All, whom they considered too high to be given a name, a gender or a shape.

Those thoughts tired him, as if he'd been forced to remember a load from which he'd tried to break loose. Everything seemed different now that he was a free man among free men. His opinion of these people broadened and changed almost by the hour. But for now, he decided, he would give these thoughts no more attention until the scouts returned.

The days at Xul Ha flowed like the honey from the beehives that surrounded it. As he had promised, Lord Nachancan sent three of his *balchè* brewers to lord Ah Kin Cutz and, at Gonzalo's urging, also a request for Jerónimo's freedom. If lord Ah Kin Cutz sold him his other white slave, he would pay him with three more choice servants.

The runners returned with the news that lord Ah Kin Cutz had accepted the brewers, but would not let Jerónimo go. For that, Lord Nachancan himself must come and steal this slave also from his house. Lord Ah Kin Cutz would not go back on the alliance he had granted, though he was tempted to forgo his scruples with a guest who'd so taken advantage of his hospitality.

Gonzalo was satisfied that he'd done all he could for Jerónimo; Jerónimo too would simply have to wait for the coming of the Spaniards. But while for Jerónimo their coming would be a deliverance, Gonzalo no longer knew by what name to call it.

Sometimes he wondered whether even Jerónimo, plied with all the blessings he'd found in Chetemal, would not stop pining for the dreariness of the islands, of seafaring, or of his father's butcher shop.

When she'd learned that Gonzalo had no wish yet to return to the Castilàn, Lady Ix Na had doubled her attention to him, certainly hoping his decision would become final before his countrymen arrived, if arrive they must. There was always a new present in his room when he retired—a new *esh* she'd woven herself, or one of those small mirrors that native men loved to wear in their hair.

Once she left jade earrings, but when she saw that his ears weren't pierced she asked him to accept the beautiful beads anyway, for it would give him pleasure just to hold them. Jade, he noticed, was singularly cool to the touch. No wonder such a stone was sacred to these people: it was like owning an imperishable drop of that water the gods granted only in exchange for human life.

Every evening there was a cup of *cacau* next to his bed. He had become so fond of it that he believed it had powers of addiction.

Sometimes he found a residue of powder at the bottom of the cup. As he became pleasantly drowsy in his bed he thought that perhaps she was putting some sort of potion in the drink. Not that he was apprehensive about it, only curious.

The drink came always in the same hands, those of a girl who went about the room in her white dress and black braids hardly breathing a word and hardly brushing the furniture. One evening, after she put the *cacau* by the bed as usual, Gonzalo told her to wait. He emptied the cup, then peered into it. Sure enough, the residue of powder was there at the bottom. The girl threw him a wary glance and headed for the door. Gonzalo called her again, this time with what he judged was the proper show of male displeasure that she must stop for. More than stopping she froze in fear. He showed her the cup. "Do you know what this is?"

She kept her eyes down. "*Cacau*," she whispered.

He put the cup under her eyes. "I meant this powder. Look."

She stood rooted to the spot. "I cannot say. My mistress told me not to say."

He tried the stern voice again. "But you must, or else I will be angry, and if I'm angry, your mistress will be angry."

The girl was trembling from head to toe. After a long silence, she finally gave in.

"It's the hearts of hummingbirds," she stammered. "A love charm."

Gonzalo's eyebrows went up. He didn't know whether he was more flattered or flabbergasted. At least it wasn't any of the loathsome ingredients women back home were said to use in their love potions. But all that slaughter of hummingbirds for his sake...

He gave the cup to the girl. "Give Lady Ix Na this message," he said gently. "Tell her there is no need for love charms."

The girl delivered the message. From that day on there were no more hummingbird hearts in his *cacau*. There was something else: whenever Gonzalo and Lady Ix Na met, their eyes carried the mutual recognition of the tie that bound them. She had become what no other woman had ever been for him, a longing that at times cast every other thought from his mind.

One of the first things that had been cast from his mind was that fevered mirage of gold that had dragged him from place to place like a beast on a halter. In conversation Lord Nachancan mentioned he must settle a dispute between two merchants about a canoe load of small gold objects. He added that he remembered Gonzalo inquiring about the metal.

Gonzalo made no reply. That talk of gold made him feel almost ashamed. Shame was what he'd felt when he'd learned that the Spaniards told the natives that they suffered from a disease of the heart that only the shiny substance could cure; and the gentle natives offered to help them look for it, only to end up dying of starvation in pits they were forced to dig or in the mud of rivers they were forced to pan, chained together and guarded by the mastiffs.

It was indeed a disease of the heart, he thought, as ugly as any real illness and for some men incurable. The only thing to have come out of that quest was the understanding at last of how foolish it was. Lord Nachancan explained that the only way to obtain that metal used for minor trinkets was to trade with distant tribes in the south—Tairona, Muisca, Sinù, tribes about which little was known.

Good, Gonzalo thought. Let them remain unknown forever.

Let the old ghost of Eldorado be laid to rest once and for all. He would never again ask anybody about gold. Since Eldorado was only a name, from now on he would give that name to what was truly precious, beginning with the woman who had reawakened in him the will to seize back his freedom.

Lady Ix Na might be rich, but she was hardly idle. If Lord Nachancan had a city of two thousand homes to look after, she had Xul Ha, a task no less demanding. Besides the workers of the *cacau* groves there were the household retainers and Lord Nachancan's women. After the daily chores had been put in order, she must see to her weaving, the one chore shared by native women of every status. Her status, however, appointed her to weave for the Gods—from the clothes that dressed the sacred images to the costumes worn by ceremonial dancers to the magnificent hangings destined to grace the walls of the temples.

Every evening Gonzalo found her at her loom, in a porch cooled by the breeze from the lagoon, with her brother's women and her brother's two children. The boy, a proud little warrior of nine, had just been given his full patronymic Ahau Can and broke into fits of temper if anybody dared to address him with his baby name. This his father would do sometimes just to delight in the boy's threats of mischief.

The girl was named Ix Sak Kukul, White Feather. At the age of six she was the loveliest child Gonzalo had ever seen. One more thing that bound him to Lady Ix Na was how fond of little Kuku they were. The girl spent more time with her than with her mother, learning to weave on a miniature loom, a battered cloth doll always strapped to her back. Of Gonzalo she'd been terrified at first, especially of the hair on his face and body. It took him much patience to win her over, patience he didn't know he had, since he'd never dealt with children before.

As he watched Lord Nachancan being catered to by his women, Gonzalo thought that that porch by the lagoon seemed to have been invented to make a man believe the sun rose and set for his pleasure alone. There was more than a hint of show when, after his daily swim, Lord Nachancan stood with arms and legs apart while two of the women rubbed him dry and covered him with a pleasant- smelling grease. The women enjoyed the slow, sensual stroking as much as he did. There was also some competition in the ritual, because the more skillful one received the summons to his bed. If he so wanted, both would join him.

The favorite was Ix Lolkin, the young mother of Ahau Can and White Feather. She was very beautiful, of a soft and lithe beauty, sweet-natured and sensible. She was also, according to Lord Nachancan, well versed in those arts that kept a man not just satisfied with the usual but surprised with the unusual.

Lord Nachancan had nothing but thanks to give to the Gods for having been born male in a world that prized males so. It showed even in the way he dressed, with the knot of the loincloth placed deliberately low on the groin, to show off the bulge and the swagger as he walked.

Although Gonzalo was happier in Lady Ix Na's private domain than in her brother's public one, he was called more and more to accompany Lord Nachancan on official matters. When the council didn't meet at Xul Ha, such matters were conducted at the men's house in Chetemal. This was a place of diverse uses, where after a hearty debate on politics or trade the various dignitaries could lounge around, eat, drink, or inhale the smoke of that brown leaf the men of the New World liked.

Lord Nachancan, who could leave his bed every time with a different woman by his side, claimed it was good for a man to be in the exclusive company of fellow men as often as possible. His opinion was shared by the elders, who in the men's house found escape from their many wives, but not by the bachelors. The latter were more than happy to find in the men's house the favors of the public ladies who could be enjoyed for a reasonable sum of *cacau* beans.

Be that as it may, Lord Nachancan concluded, the affairs of state were best handled by contented men, and contentment unfortunately sat with the opposite sex, whether because of its presence or because of its absence. Since in this land the affairs of state were intimately bound up with those of the heavens, the men's house was frequented by yet another group of people, the crotchety old day keepers who met there to render their verdicts on auspicious and inauspicious dates.

Lord Nachancan didn't particularly follow the day keepers' advice, but Paichè and most of his generation made no move without the approval of the *ah kinob.* The sending of the scouts, for instance, had been delayed twice because Paichè refused to begin the enterprise on an ill-named day. There had been some words between him and Lord Nachancan, until Gonzalo had mediated the argument and Lord Nachancan had given in for the sake of peace.

More serious disagreement between the two men Gonzalo could not mediate, since he himself was the reason for it. Growing more and more hostile each time Gonzalo sat with Lord Nachancan in public, Paichè had become the leader of all those who disliked the stranger, missing no occasion to stir up enmity against him.

This pained Lord Nachancan, who in private told Gonzalo it was sad to have an old ally become so unreasonable. In public he never hid his sympathy for his guest; and when Paichè asked what boon the stranger had brought that he should be treated so favorably,

Lord Nachancan replied that to have learned in time about a new race of men pressing at their door was boon enough, especially if those men were bent on enslavement and war.

Over a month had passed, and the scouts hadn't returned. They had been given no precise amount of time to complete their mission, so no one could say they were late. Still, with each passing day the delay seemed more and more ominous. Of course they might have run into trouble at sea. There had been storms, and the sea had "boiled yellow," as these people put it, for nearly three days. Even so, while he sat with Lord Nachancan and Lady Ix Na by the lagoon, or while he played with little White Feather, his mind wandered to the islands, gnawed by doubts.

He had advised the scouts to keep out of the Spaniards' sight, and these were men accustomed to passing through the jungle without alerting a bird to their presence. They also knew what to expect, so they would not be likely to panic like all those others who, unacquainted with the strangers, surrendered without resistance. But by advising the scouts to remain unnoticed he had advised them to treat the Spaniards as enemies; and how could he have told them to go as envoys, perhaps with gifts that would invite in a horde of greedy invaders?

Almost another month went by before finally one night a canoe docked at Xul Ha with a handful of passengers aboard: three of the eight scouts who'd gone out and the two fishermen who'd found them. The scouts had been adrift for some days in their leaky craft, half-starved, all branded on the forehead with a cross-like mark, and one of them with manacles around his wrists.

Lord Nachancan ordered the two rescuers to keep silent, but this inauspicious return would not remain a secret for long. After the fishermen left with their reward, the scouts were taken in and cared for. Lady Ix Na provided food and beds. Lord Nachancan had the manacles removed. Gonzalo pieced together the scouts' tale, which, just as he'd feared, bore out his every misgiving.

Even with their careful instructions, even these cool-headed men whose lives depended on reporting the truth as accurately as they could, had found themselves at a loss before the Castilàn. What they had seen were the most horrible creatures on earth, half man half giant deer, with a voice to stop one's blood and sparks flying from their paws. The man half and the beast half could divide at will, or else join into a single entity that ran like the wind and leaped like the lightning.

After a number of days spent trying to hide from these monsters, the scouts had split into two groups, with the intention of meeting at the place where they'd left their canoe. That was the last time the three survivors had seen their companions. The same day they'd been caught in snares set by the Castilàn and marched into a town surrounded by a palisade. There they'd been given as slaves to a man who owned many fields of a tall, sweet-tasting plant, which they must cut and harvest.

This they had done for the time they'd spent in the island, along with hundreds of other slaves, all branded with the man's sign of ownership, sleeping in the open fields and fed nothing but cassava bread. They had seen what the thunder sticks could do: tear the head off the body of a man and blow to pieces a house with everyone inside, from a distance far greater than that of arrow or spear and with a force that could not be imagined.

Once every seven days they were allowed to rest. They were then taken to a building in the Castilàn' town, where men dressed in long black robes showed them pictures of various people: an old man with a long white beard, a woman holding a baby, a young man fastened to two crossed pieces of wood. Once, five of the slaves were whipped because they had refused to kneel and join the palms of their hands in front of these pictures.

The same black-robed men who taught them, however, had then persuaded the owner of the fields to let those slaves who were ill go with them. Thanks to their kindness the scouts had been allowed to go to their house in the town, from where they had easily escaped. At the meeting point they'd waited in vain for their companions; finally they'd set out in their rickety craft.

Their tale ended, the three men were left to rest. Lord Nachancan asked Gonzalo and Lady Ix Na to follow him to his room. His face was taut as he listened to the ripple of the lagoon, holding the manacles taken from the scout's wrists. Gonzalo stood behind him in the dark. Strangely, all he could think of was that he wished Lady Ix Na hadn't heard anything. Nothing had changed in the islands.

Someone must have started to farm sugar cane, adding one more reason for horror.

Lord Nachancan's voice was soft and low. "The people of the islands have always had little to offer us. That is why we've always had little to do with them. But now I see there are other reasons why we meet them so rarely these days." He paused. "Are the Castilàn half men and half giant deer?" he asked.

Gonzalo shook his head. "No. They are men like you and me.

The horses are trained to carry them when they travel or when they make war."

"Who are the ones dressed in black robes?"

"Priests. They own likenesses of God, and of the Mother of God, and of the Son of God, who was killed on two crossed pieces of wood."

Lord Nachancan turned the round metal fetters in his hands. "Do the Castilàn die? Can they be killed by arrow, spear, or fire?"

Gonzalo felt an edge of fear. At a distance from him, Lady Ix Na stood still. He could hear her intent, rapid breathing.

"Some men of the Kuna once kidnapped one of the soldiers in my company," he said then. "They drowned him in the river, then stood guard by the corpse for three days to see if he came back to life. Three days because our captain had told them that the son of God came back to life after three days. On the fourth day the Kuna tossed the body back into our compound."

Another silence followed. Lord Nachancan stood up. "Ah Holkan," he said, "what would you do if while you slept something dangerous came close to you and to everything that you love?"

Gonzalo's eyes went to Lady Ix Na. "I would do what any man would do. I would defend myself and everything that I love with my life."

Lord Nachancan nodded. "I will send a warning to our friends.

Most live along the coast like us. They might be the first to be visited by the Castilàn. We will be ready to defend ourselves with our lives. We will not be taken by surprise."

"If your enemies will listen," Gonzalo cautioned, "they too must be warned. They would all too gladly ally themselves with the Castilàn, hoping to defeat you. I've seen it happen before."

"That is true. So be it." Lord Nachancan smiled tiredly. "I'm afraid there will be another noisy meeting of the council..." He held up the manacles. "What sort of metal is this? Is it the steel you told me about?"

"No. This is called iron. Not as strong as steel, but strong enough to make a man stay put."

With a look of distaste, Lord Nachancan pointed at the lagoon. "Throw it away."

"Wait," Gonzalo said. "With this we can make spear points and darts. You will see how much better than flint they are."

Lord Nachancan cocked his head backwards. "It seems that everything the Castilàn have is much better."

Gonzalo's lips stretched into a wry grin. "That is why the Castilàn think they *are* better than everyone else."

Lord Nachancan looked him in the eyes. "Yet you don't think you are better than everyone else," he said. "After what I have learned about your people, I wonder whether you are really one of them."

"Sometimes I wonder about the same thing," Gonzalo said. Lord Nachancan walked to the doorway. "We will sleep now,"he said. He turned to Lady Ix Na. "Sister, please see that nothing Ah

Holkan wants be kept from him. We have had many guests, but none to whom we are more indebted."

Lady Ix Na bowed her head in understanding. "Rest well, brother."

She followed Gonzalo across the porch. In front of his room, by habit, she stopped. Then she lifted the door hanging, standing aside to let him enter. Gonzalo went in. The empty room pained him, as if everything that quickened within him had ceased for a moment. She'd been told to see that nothing he wanted be kept from him. Did she know that he wanted her more than any other thing?

She made no move to leave, but her eyes showed how torn she was. He would do nothing, he swore to himself, nothing that would force her to choose between him and what she deemed proper. But when he saw her reaching out to drop the door hanging, he grasped it and held it as if he were about to drown.

She shut her eyes. Her hand, whose good strength he knew from the day she'd led him back to freedom, now felt strangely shrunken, submissive. The other hand went up to his face.

"Do you remember how people followed you around, the first days?" she asked. "How they kept touching your skin of another color, your hair of another color?"

He nodded, smiling. "You told them to stop. I remember." She touched his skin, his hair. "I envied them so."

With every strand of his being he wanted to tell her to stay. Yet he knew that that would bring her only confusion. If she could stay with him, he wouldn't have to ask. But something else he would tell her, with no expectation of anything in return: the long, hard, lovely words he'd carried with him through every hour of his waking and of his sleeping.

"*Tenn c'in yakuntik e'ch,*" he whispered. "There is an ache in my heart for you."

Her hand lingered around his mouth, as if stroking the sound. "And in my heart for you."

She stepped back. He knew she would, but less painfully now with those words given and taken, with the affirmation that the two of them stood together no matter where race, custom or propriety set them.

"If their coming will take you away from me," she said, "tonight and every night I will pray that the Castilàn never come. But one cannot be happy for long away from home, so I will pray only that you be happy."

As she left him, for a moment he felt that he was going to shout and let everybody hear him. He would be happy only here, only with her. He wouldn't be the first man to live well half a world away from home. But it was a promise he dared not make. How could he be sure that at first sight of a Spanish sail he wouldn't cast aside his native garments and dive into the sea, calling out his Christian name and the name of the place where he was born?

Her footsteps waned, and he was alone. He stayed awake for a long time that night, thinking of her, of the scouts, of the islands, of home, of heaven and of hell. The place within his soul from where those thoughts came seemed to have become the only place in the world where he belonged.

NINETEEN

There was indeed another noisy meeting of the council, when the scouts had recovered and could give their account in the crowded room. As always, Paichè led the dissenters' chorus. He was not at all surprised by what the scouts had found in the islands, he said. He had always been convinced of the evil nature of the strangers. How could Gonzalo not be of the same nature, since he was one of them?

At that Gonzalo let go of the anger he'd held in check until then. "My lord Paichè, when I first came among your people, I lost five of my companions and I was enslaved, like these men who have now returned. For a very long time I too was convinced that all those who live in this land could be nothing but evil."

Paichè was silenced, but Lord Nachancan was so displeased with him that he kept him out as he drafted the warning to be sent to the neighboring provinces. The warning went, as Gonzalo had suggested, to both friends and enemies of the House of Can. Among the first were Canpech and Chanputun, on the western coast, and Tulum. Among the latter were the hated Xiu of Manì, and Ecab, though Lord Nachancan remarked that the people of Ecab would most probably welcome a second visit by the Castilàn the way they'd welcomed the first by Gonzalo and his shipmates, the way they welcomed all strangers.

Responses from those warned would reach Chetemal one at a time according to the distance, and from Manì almost certainly there would be no response at all. But, Lord Nachancan said, he was content to have done for his neighbors far more than ordinary circumstances would have prompted him to do. All he asked from them in return was that they let him know the time and place of the Castilàn's coming.

Beyond this, he knew it would still be as it had been for many years in his land, each territorial ruler for himself. The last time they'd been a unified nation was during his grandfather's lifetime, long before he was born. He remembered his grandfather speaking of the walled capital of Mayapàn, the Banner of the Maya, from where the old warrior and his family had been forced to flee when the Xiu had seized power and the land had become a broken patchwork of warring provinces.

Lord Nachancan and Gonzalo traveled to Chetemal to see off the first team of runners. There they went to a coppersmith's shop, with the iron manacles Gonzalo wanted to be made into spearheads. It took them almost all day. The coppersmith knew his craft, but didn't know what was required of his craft with this tough new metal.

Gonzalo himself was no expert. The first blades turned out useless and had to be melted and beaten again. A crowd of men had gathered around to observe the proceedings.

"Look well," Lord Nachancan told the curious crowd. "Become acquainted with these new things, because they are going to stay with us, for good or ill."

When the first good blade finally hardened, he looked at it well himself, with mixed admiration and worry. If this was only iron, and could shear the toughest tapir hide with such ease, what must that steel be that Gonzalo had mentioned, or the bronze tubes in which the Castilàn carried their thunder?

For now, however, this terrible new magic was his alone, a gift from the stranger whose destiny had become intertwined with his own. Together the two of them returned to Xul Ha with several blades that Lord Nachancan showed to Lady Ix Na. She praised them, but by custom, being a woman, she was forbidden to touch all weapons.

The blades were fastened to shafts of *sapota* wood. Lord Nachancan, impatient to test them, began to teach their use to his guest, who was as unfamiliar with spears as his host was with crossbows and muskets. The rainy months had begun. They practiced under the roof of one of the many patios of the house. The targets, made of corn straw, were thick enough to simulate the average girth of a man's body; a patch of hide, no larger than the palm of one's hand, was attached at the height of the heart. With the spear-thrower—the simplest of tools, a flat stick three fingers wide and grooved to a third of its length—Lord Nachancan could hit that small patch of hide from forty full yards away.

Gonzalo thought that if he trained for forty full years he would never match that skill acquired since childhood. Even Lord Nachancan's nine-year-old son could find the mark more often than he did. But pride goaded him; it wasn't long before his aim made Lord Nachancan remark that he must have at least a few drops of native blood, for he'd never seen anybody learn so fast.

Gonzalo's favorite weapon was one for which he needed no training, a two-handed wooden sword set with splinters of obsidian glass. With that he could make Lord Nachancan stand back and watch. Like a two-edged Spanish broadsword, the *hadzab* was deadly for slashing; but without a blade at the tip it was useless for stabbing. He mentioned he flaw to Lord Nachancan, adding that it would take only a minor change to make the *hadzab* a more effective weapon.

Paichè was present that time. Lord Nachancan asked him what he thought of the idea, of which he himself approved.

"My Lord Nachancan," Paichè replied, "for more years that could be counted your ancestors were well served by the *hadzab* as it is. No man before you saw the need for improvements brought by foreigners."

He bowed stiffly his head. "But my advice seems to have become obsolete as well. Perhaps you might want to hear that of the *nacom*."

The *nacom*, a burly general whose prestigious office lasted for life, sided with Paichè. Who was this hairy-faced slave that he should presume to teach him his own profession? he seethed. Next the stranger with his fancy notions would persuade Lord Nachancan to make *him* war captain.

"If you persist in being so narrow, Ah Balam Tun, I might have to do just that," Lord Nachancan warned him.

With or without the assent of the *nacom*, a few of the *hadzabs* were fitted with a blade at the top, and a few others were made, shorter and lighter. Now they could be useful also when there was no room to swing them sideways.

Lord Nachancan was delighted. "You see, Ah Holkan. Your name means warrior, and a warrior you are. You can't escape your destiny."

Those words came back to haunt Gonzalo. What did Lord Nachancan know about destiny? he wondered. All he had done was point out some mundane changes, yet these people treated such simple novelties like forerunners of Armageddon.

Yet the praise he received was a powerful thing. The young warriors who'd first tested the new *hadzabs* in mock battles with one another now came every day to be instructed. Before he knew it, Gonzalo was teaching them swordplay, as he might have taught newcomers in the islands if by some twist of fate he had been the officer there instead of the sailor.

These young warriors were possessed of an almost religiously disciplined courage that any commander would have been proud to rely on, and they hung on his every word with wholehearted loyalty. Sometimes he watched them, hunkered down around him in their red and black paint, and he asked himself what had happened to bring him to this. He was giving orders instead of taking them, he was making others repeat the same gestures he'd been made to repeat until his arms dropped. To be so admired, even to be so resented by those who opposed him, gave him a faith in himself he'd never known before. He now knew what power was. The one thing he'd never imagined was how much he relished it.

He liked the way the smooth, polished shaft of the *hadzab* fit in his hands, and the way it cut the air, so much easier to handle than the heavy Spanish blades. There was a sensual pleasure in the shiver of terror he felt as he rushed toward the scalpel-sharp edges of black glass with nothing more than his own naked flesh.

This was a challenge among equals, not the awful imbalance he'd been forced to witness in the islands. It was a fair confrontation, a flowering of skills that took the most from both his body and his mind and in return gave him an almost intoxicating feeling of potency. As for what this training might become when the news of the first Spanish ship would sweep into this land, he forced himself not to consider just yet. The more he grew comfortable among these people, the less he asked himself what he would do when he would have to leave them.

After the first mock battles fought by his young warriors, he noticed that the skirmishes invariably ended in a way he found most peculiar. As soon as the man designated as leader was overpowered, the warriors conceded victory to their opponents. When Gonzalo asked why, Lord Nachancan answered that they were behaving as they would have in a real battle. The first aim of warfare was not slaughter but the capture of prisoners to be offered up in sacrifice. The most distinguished the captive, the more prized the sacrifice. This made of the leader the most fiercely protected man and the most fiercely sought after by the enemy.

"That seems unwise," Gonzalo said. "How can one man be more important than his entire army?"

Lord Nachancan frowned. "A body might live on without its limbs, but not without its head. Is it not so among the Castilàn?"

Gonzalo shook his head. "No. The Castilàn aim to kill, not to take captives. You must be aware of this, or else they will always have the advantage." Only a moment later did he realize how often nowadays he spoke of his own countrymen as "they."

One of the warriors drew closer. "Ah Holkan, what else must we know about the Castilàn? If we are to fight a new enemy, shouldn't we start to fight in a new way?"

Gonzalo's eyes clouded. "You ask too soon. And you ask a man who hopes not to fight, in an old way or a new one."

Lord Nachancan nodded. "*Kaynà*," he said, with the word that was a prayer of assent. "May it be so."

In the month of Muan the first two runners returned. The lords of Canpech and Chanputun had promised to be on the lookout for the Castilàn and to report immediately upon their arrival. Much later the people of Ecab sent their reply. They already knew about the bearded strangers, they said, and not just the ones who'd been offered up in the temple but also the ones who'd escaped. Merchants from Tulum had been carrying the news around for months. But if the

Castilàn were no better than the castaways who'd washed up ashore on their beach, they would send little boys against them instead of warriors. Lord Ah Kin Cutz responded in much the same way, saying he'd had Castilàn living in his own house and all they made were good menials.

In the month of Paax Lord Nachancan's third child was born, a boy. On the day chosen by the day keepers he was named Obsidian Blade, in honor of the new *hadzabs*. By now the warriors Gonzalo trained had increased in number, and the earliest group had become a devoted personal guard that accompanied him when he went to the men's house in Chetemal or when he sat in council at Xul Ha. The return of the scouts had persuaded many who at first had doubted him that the danger of which he had spoken was all too real and all too close. Now it wasn't only young men hungry for novelties who listened to him, but their elders as well.

Sixteenth in the round of the calendar, the month of Paax was devoted to the gods of war. People poured into the capital from all over the province to bring offerings to the temples, to watch the war dances and to eat and drink at the festivals. Lord Nachancan had summoned his two half-brothers, born of his father's lesser wives, from the hinterland region that they ruled in his name and that bordered with the lands of the Xiu. Much must be discussed with them, who lived so dangerously close to the enemy.

In the first four days of the festivities, after blessings and prayers, there were contests and games among the warriors. Paichè, though past the age of forty, threw one of the best wrestlers, and Lord Nachancan astonished with the marksmanship of his new iron spear. But everywhere one went the name most often heard was that of the man many had begun to call "the white *nacom*."

Those who saw him for the first time were disappointed in finding out that the name wasn't accurate. Gonzalo's skin, tanned by the sun of many years, had become almost as dark as a native's. He was dressed in their same garb, and his hair was now long enough to touch past his shoulders. One would have hardly known him for a white man if not for the beard, which he kept so as to be known for a white man.

The loudest and most contrary talk came from Ah Balam Tun, who'd been born and bred into the title of *nacom* from four generations of *nacoms*. Although he shared his office with a peer elected as the need arose, he'd already declared that he would sooner share it with a Xiu than with a stranger of a different race, different customs and beliefs.

Now he was sitting with Gonzalo and Lord Nachancan. As he watched Gonzalo's men line up against some warriors from Becan, he scoffed that those young fools Ah Holkan had stolen from him with his bragging and his lying would do better to surrender now, before their opponents showed them for the women they were.

"The number of blades on our *hadzabs* isn't enough for Ah Holkan's warriors," he sneered. "They need one more, so they can be sure they can strike an enemy somewhere."

Gonzalo's shoulders stiffened. He could feel everybody's eyes fixed on him. He knew what Ah Balam Tun wanted. The *nacom's* logic, as hard as the scars he displayed, was the same Gonzalo had seen in some Spanish captains who put their hands to their swords if only someone crossed their way in the street. The only settlement men like these understood was public and immediate confrontation.

Very well, he thought, feeling the blood rise pleasantly to his face. There was plenty of Spanish temper left in him to give Ah Balam Tun what he wanted. He stood up and planted himself in front of the *nacom* with the ritualistic posture everyone expected.

"You speak before you know," he said. "Fight me first."

Only too happy, Ah Balam Tun reached for his *hadzab*. The two lines of warriors stepped back to make room for the newest, unforeseen contenders. To sanction his support of Gonzalo, Lord Nachancan handed him his own *hadzab*. First he struck off the uppermost blade with the shaft of another weapon. "Now," he told the *nacom*, "you will not say that Ah Holkan needs a coward's advantage."

A conch-shell trumpet sounded to signal the challenge. It was a short, clean fight. Taller and faster than his adversary, Gonzalo let Ah Balam Tun see for himself that he was neither a fool nor a braggart. For the first time he was fighting in anger, against a man whose only aim was to humiliate him; and the anger worked, the fear of humiliation helped.

For a seasoned professional, Ah Balam Tun had little more than brute force on his side. Also, just as Gonzalo had anticipated, his handling of the *hadzab* was hampered by the native habit of swinging high and wide, so that by the time he regained his footing he left enough exposure to kill. When he finally realized this, the *nacom* began to lash out with frantic fury. He cut Gonzalo nastily enough across a shoulder, prompting a sound of disapproval from the crowd, but he paid for the blow with what must be the worst defeat of his life.

Livid with rage, he tossed his weapon and stalked away.

Gonzalo's men accompanied his exit with a whoop of derision. Then, spurred into unstoppable confidence, they fell on the warriors from Becan and quickly reduced them to what in a real battle would have been flesh for the sacrificial knife. When the skirmish was over they even mimicked that grisly culmination on their victims.

The conch shell sounded again, this time a signal to cheering and waving of banners. Gonzalo gave the *hadzab* back to Lord Nachancan.

"That was handsomely done," Lord Nachancan praised. "Men like Ah Balam Tun sometimes grow too full of their own worth. It's good that they be made humble."

He looked at Gonzalo's shoulder. "The cut is deep. Do you want to go home?"

Gonzalo tried to stanch the blood with a corner of his cloak. He grinned. "What will the men of Chetemal say if Ah Holkan goes home on account of a scratch?" But the cut still bled, making him tired and thirsty.

Lord Nachancan motioned his porters to get the litters. "The men of Chetemal will say nothing, because I'm going home too. I've already seen the best that today had to offer."

At home they were greeted by Lady Ix Na's pride in Gonzalo's defeat of Ah Balam Tun, and by her concern. At once she sent for Ix Lolkin, who knew how to treat wounds. While Ix Lolkin poured the juice of healing herbs on his shoulder, she besieged Lord Nachancan with questions about the challenge.

"My sister," Lord Nachancan teased her, "someone should begin to teach you what is seemly for a woman to talk about."

"My brother," she replied evenly, "I swear that on the day *you* will come home wounded I will not breathe a word. For now, please indulge my unseemly curiosity."

Gonzalo drank from the bowl of corn water she'd brought him.

"Really, my Lady Ix Na, there isn't much to tell, except that I was given a taste of the *hadzab*..." He winced at the sting of the herbal juice. "I can now say the Castilàn will find it a most respectable weapon."

She wrapped his shoulder with cloth. "You show the nature of the true *nacom*," she said in a low voice, her face coloring with passion and with the awareness that she was indeed speaking too boldly for a woman. "Were he in your place, Ah Balam Tun would make the Gods deaf with his boasting."

Lord Nachancan glanced at her intently. "As usual, my sister turns out to be my keenest observer," he said.

He turned to Gonzalo. "You have made an enemy you will have to reckon with," he warned him. "Unfortunately I cannot dismiss Ah Balam Tun without starting a rebellion, even from those who don't like him. His office is as untouchable as that of the high priest. But he will have to share that office with you... if you are willing to step forth as a candidate."

Gonzalo considered the proposal. Sharing the war captaincy with Ah Balam Tun would be like bedding down with a jaguar, after which Ah Balam Tun was named. He would have to watch the other's every move. Still, it was the second highest military rank in the land, sought after by the best nobility, a prize to put into any man the itch of ambition.

He felt the sharp pain of the wound. He remembered the viciousness that had caused it, the *nacom's* hatred and contempt for him for no better reason except that he was of a different race. Yes, matters between the two of them must be settled once and for all, he thought. Let Ah Balam Tun watch *his* every move.

He nodded. "My Lord Nachancan. I will step forth as a candidate. And I will serve you well if I'm chosen."

Some of Gonzalo's warriors had been waiting by the main gate. When he showed himself to say he was well, and to announce that he would become second *nacom* if enough men chose him, they raised a happy cry, swearing they would see to it that enough men chose him. They left still shouting and chanting war songs.

The women brought out the evening meal, a wonderful soup of shredded turkey meat, cherry tomatoes and sweet corn. There had been a rain shower, and now a rainbow arched from the water.

"I am certain that enough men will be found to elect you," Lord Nachancan said, and smiled with some slyness. "The most important vote is already in your favor."

He motioned a woman for another bowlful of soup. "You must know, however, that men will not follow a *nacom* unless he observes the rules of his office, which are many. For instance, this may be the last time you eat the meat of birds, and the last time you drink *balchè*."

Gonzalo was beginning to shrug, but Lord Nachancan's face showed no signs of levity. "For three years nothing must come between you and your readiness to fight. You must keep your weapons beside you when awake and when sleeping. You might not speak to all people, no woman may serve you, and... you may not always lie with a woman, even if she were your wife."

Lady Ix Na glanced at Gonzalo. That last word seemed to echo inside him with a sound louder than any talk of war. Everything slipped away from his mind and only that glance of hers was left, only that word—wife. He looked at her, trying to think of a reason why it shouldn't be so. No reasons came, instead the happy liberation ofknowing that he had only that choice.

They were interrupted by the rush of a man striding from the gate and calling loudly for Lord Nachancan. When he saw him he fell down on hands and knees before him. He had the desperate look of someone who'd covered many miles of jungle in a race against time.

"My lord, I am in the service of your brothers," he stammered. "The lord Natohcan and the lord Ekuneh..."

Lord Nachancan stood up. "I have summoned them to my house, yes. Are they here?"

The man's topknot skimmed the floor as he shook his head. "No, my lord. The Xiu have crossed the border near the swamps... before dawn, without warning, in their usual way of men without honor —"

"Crossed the border!" Lord Nachancan shouted. "This goes past all bounds, even for the Xiu. Are my brothers safe?"

"Your brothers are well, may Itzamnà be praised. But their town is cut off. They beg you to come quickly, with all the warriors you can muster."

Lord Nachancan motioned the man to rise. "We will be there.

Do you know precisely in what place near the swamps they have crossed?"

"Yes, my lord."

"Then you will lead us there. Go now, rest. Be ready to march with us tomorrow."

The servants showed the messenger out. Lord Nachancan sat back before his unfinished bowl of food, waving away the woman who served him.

For a moment nobody spoke. The two children, Ahau Can and White Feather, peeked from behind a carved pillar, wondering why their father didn't call them to join him as he always did after his meal.

Finally Lord Nachancan turned to Gonzalo. "Ah Holkan. The matter of your election to second *nacom* is now a formality we can dispense with. You already have a good number of men under your command. I have the archers and spearmen. Ah Balam Tun has his own warriors, and Paichè also leads a company. Should discord arise among us, we will be evenly split, and they will be against the territorial ruler of Chetemal. Tell me your intentions."

Knowing that what he was about to say would sound utterly incongruous, Gonzalo made his words as plain as he could.

"My Lord Nachancan. How does a man go about asking for a woman in marriage among your people?"

Lady Ix Na's eyes darted up, startled. Lord Nachancan was also taken aback.

"There is a way for lords and a way for commoners," he said, "but..."

"The commoner's way, for that is what I am."

Lord Nachancan was still baffled. "A man will go to the woman's father, or to her oldest male relative, and spend some time in service to him as payment for the bride. If a farmer he will tend his cornfield, if a fisherman he will tend his canoe, and so on."

"If a warrior, can a man offer his skill in battle toward making the woman his bride?" Gonzalo asked.

Lord Nachancan's confusion vanished. "He can, of course."

Gonzalo drew his breath in. "Then, my Lord Nachancan, I ask you that you consider my service against the Xiu as service toward your sister, Lady Ix Ahau Na."

Again she lifted her eyes to him. This time they were filled with the brightest, the most perfect joy.

Lord Nachancan smiled broadly, with a hint of archness. "Have you forgotten already all I told you before, about the abstinence required of a *nacom* in times of war?" He put his hand on Gonzalo's arm. "You will make a most discontented bridegroom, Ah Holkan."

Gonzalo clenched his fists to keep his own heartbeat from smothering him. "My Lord Nachancan," he promised, "by the time of our wedding your enemies will have suffered such a defeat that for the next three years we will know nothing but peace."

TWENTY

They left before noon, on a sweltering hot day. Paichè and Ah Balam Tun understood that Gonzalo's presence as second *nacom* was a test of their obedience, and didn't complain for the time being. But they marched side by side to show that they were of one mind.

Looking at them over his shoulder, Gonzalo knew this army was as much at war with itself as it was against the Xiu.

The man sent by Lord Nachancan's brothers led them. With him went the scouts, who from time to time disappeared, returning later to say what was ahead. The first and last thing one saw of them were the weasel tails hanging from their belts. Weasels they were called, for their keen eyesight and their cunning.

Gonzalo walked between Lord Nachancan and the standard- bearer carrying the Can insignia. He had forgotten how hard it was to make one's way through the jungle, and the jungle that surrounded Chetemal was particularly harsh. No road or trail marked it, only the trails of the fire ants and the hidden lairs of the scorpions.

This was where survival took on its oldest face. He could feel himself scenting out the dangers that awaited him. The whirrings and screechings and rattlings around him were a constant onslaught of noise. His ears strained to make sure he could still sort human voice from beast's. Though he tried not to think about it, there was fear in the way he kept grazing the *hadzab* strapped over his thigh. Something else he was trying not to think about was Lady Ix Na's eyes, with her love in them and her prayer for him to return safely to the wedding.

That morning she had made offerings of corn and flowers to the Gods of war, the fearsome Gods painted red and black for blood and death. Then she had walked into Gonzalo's room, with one of her women. She had roused him from sleep and she had presented him the badge of his war captain's rank, a belt set with small human heads carved out of bone.

Her usual reticence gone now that she was pledged to him in the eyes of the world, she'd tied the belt around his waist as her whole body seemed to shake with emotion. It hurt him to remember how beautiful she looked, and how much he'd wanted to clasp her in his arms before his men had called him away.

The shuddery sound of a dead branch falling to the ground brought him back to the present. He wiped the sweat from his face and looked at the belt he was wearing. A fitting emblem for a war captain, he thought. Who knows how recently those startlingly life-like human heads had been real ones, shrunken and cured like the heads that some tribes south of the Darién prized highly.

"My brothers' messenger tells me the Xiu have come in near the ruined temple," Lord Nachancan said. He glanced behind him. "Paichè finds it an ill omen, because the temple is haunted by the *aluuxob,* the spirits bent on mischief. What do you make of it, Ah Holkan?"

Gonzalo shrugged. "I think it's foolishness, my Lord Nachancan. Paichè worries too much about things he doesn't see."

"Still, such things must be given their due," Lord Nachancan countered. "Don't you mind any of them?"

"Not if they distract me from things I do see."

Lord Nachancan made no reply. But by now Gonzalo knew that when he let a point of discussion drop, it meant he agreed but was too proud to say it.

They marched on in silence. Each man had to fight his own battle against fatigue and thirst. After some time they stopped at a natural well that the new rains had nearly filled. Some of the men clambered down the limestone walls to get fresh water. They ate parched corn and dried fish. Sitting at a distance, Paichè and Ah Balam Tun talked between themselves with the hushed, reticent tones of men with a secret. Gonzalo and Lord Nachancan watched them, in a way to make them see they were being watched.

The march resumed. Gonzalo hadn't been told how far the must go, and he would not ask for fear of sounding too easily discouraged. Secretly he was daunted by the thought of having to engage in battle after so many hours of walking through that sweltering jungle.

At sunset Lord Nachancan called a halt, and the warriors prepared for the night. They cleared patches of brush so they could sleep on damp earth instead of thorny undergrowth, and they lit fires to keep at bay jaguars and other prowlers. With the coming of dark the heat let up only a bit, and the noise of the jungle seemed to increase, a constant whistling of crickets punctuated by the roars of beasts that sounded close enough to make the hairs on one's neck bristle.

As he lay down by the fire, wrapped up in his cloak against the mosquitoes, Gonzalo wondered how these men could muster enough strength for war against each other when most of their strength had to be spent warring their own unforgiving land.

At dawn they were ready to march again. This time Gonzalo didn't even try to keep track of how long they walked. He staved off fatigue and fear with the methodical gestures that preceded battle—gathering his hair into a topknot and greasing it to make it drop forward; dipping into the common pot and covering his face with paint. He could tell these were almost magical transformations: what he was to his friends disappeared behind what he was to his enemies.

After one more short rest, after some more marching, at last the scouts returned from their silent foray with the news everyone was waiting for. They had spotted the enemy, near the ruined temple.

Lord Nachancan called a halt. "There is enough of a clearing around the temple for us to fight them in the open," he said. "That is good. That is where I want to fight them, not under the trees."

He raised the Can insignia high. "Remember," he shouted, "their name means Grass, and grass is to be trampled underfoot!"

He was about to start out when Gonzalo stopped him. "My Lord Nachancan, which one of us will stay to the sides? If you will allow it, my men are best suited."

Lord Nachancan eyed him quizzically. "Why must you stay to the sides?"

"To close in around the enemy, of course..." Gonzalo began.

He paused abruptly. One of the most disastrous shortcomings of the islanders was the haphazard simplicity of their fighting. They too massed all in a body, spending themselves in wave upon wave of straightforward attack. He had assumed the people of the mainland must be more sophisticated in their military skills, since they were so superior to the islanders in everything else.

"Just let me put my men in two wings at the sides of your warriors," he said. "I will tell them what to do." Out of the corner of his eye he saw Ah Balam Tun jerk up his head.

Lord Nachancan was silent for a while. Then he nodded. "Ah Holkan, I don't understand, but you may lead your warriors any way you see fit. Take also my spearmen, they are most able."

With that Ah Balam Tun stormed forward. "The spearmen have always gone into battle with the Halach Uinic... the True Man, the territorial ruler from the House of Can!" he seethed. "My Lord Nachancan, must we like children follow without questions that which we cannot even comprehend?"

Lord Nachancan looked him in the eyes. "Ah Balam Tun. I am the one from whom you take your orders. You will do as you are told, or you will let everyone here know that you are a man I cannot trust."

Ah Balam Tun shook his *hadzab* violently up and down.

Paichè took him back to his place, both men's eyes flashing.

Silently the four columns drew closer together. Gonzalo motioned his warriors to stand aside, and the spearmen to join them. He prayed to himself that these men would carry out his instructions swiftly and precisely. Though yesterday in the flush of his gladness he'd promised victory to Lord Nachancan, he knew he would not have it without their obedience.

But as they gathered around him he could see on their faces the same fierce loyalty he'd always commanded. He saw that they understood, and he was reassured. Now was the time to prove himself, for a most worthy prize. Into his heart came an impatience, almost a lust to fight that swept through his fear like a clean fire.

The bulk of the army began to march toward the temple.

Gonzalo's warriors fanned out into two wings—spearmen in front, their shields made of tapir hide pressed against one another to form a wall, swordsmen in the back. Lord Nachancan's face showed bafflement mixed with admiration. Although Gonzalo had had no time to tell him, what he was facing his enemies with was nothing more than the standard formation of Spanish infantry troops.

The ruined temple, its top lopped off and choked with vegetation, could have been mistaken for a small hill if not for some enormous sculptured faces, gods or men staring from the sloping walls, snakes' fangs curling from their lips. Watched by those stone faces, the Xiu were camped in the confident manner of invaders certain of being already masters of the land on which they'd trespassed. Surely,

Gonzalo thought, Lord Nachancan would make the most of their confidence and pounce on them with the advantage of surprise.

The Can warriors emerged from the canopy of trees at the same even pace and in the same perfect silence, like actors taking their place on a stage. Within the bristly cocoon of his archers, Lord Nachancan stood still before his enemies, like a priest summoning his chosen victims to the sacrifice. There was a moment of eerie quiet as the Xiu looked up to find themselves surrounded. Then the conch shell sounded the alarm. In a surge of noise they merged at the end of the clearing.

The two armies sized each other up face to face. The Xiu *nacom* was a distant mask of black paint framed by huge disks of jade. Still Lord Nachancan gave no signal. Gonzalo understood that he wanted the Xiu to come forward, and in his mind he praised his good judgment. He could feel the hesitation among the Xiu, their uncertainty at that bizarre formation of warriors that resembled the open pincers of a crab. Come on, he thought, come on and be crushed.

At last the Xiu started to rush onward. The archers on both sides began their volleys. The narrowing distance whistled with the pelting of the feathered spits. Within moments the center of the Can army was a furious hand-to-hand melee. Lord Nachancan, Paichè and Ah Balam Tun were engulfed. But Gonzalo's wings withstood the assault with just a few gaps that the spearmen closed by regrouping.

Thwarted by the unexpected barrier, the Xiu could only fall back into the center. Those who tried to make their way around the wings were quickly felled down.

Grasping his *hadzab* in both hands, Gonzalo slashed at them as they came. A number of his best men fought by him in the customary way they always guarded their *nacom* in battle. Soon he and they were slippery with blood, the enemy's and their own. The vicious glass splinters of the *hadzab* did damage everywhere they fell. One Xiu who'd leapt at Gonzalo was only a blur before his eyes; yet even before Gonzalo became aware that he'd struck him, he saw the man's severed arm fly off like a dry cornstalk in the wind.

Even sooner than he'd hoped for, the Xiu became a seething mass battering itself against the center, too doggedly bent upon breaching that one familiar spot to pay attention to the wings. If they had felt hesitation before, now he could see that they'd been overcome by panic. This wasn't war as they knew it, this was a mockery of every rule they'd ever abided by.

Gonzalo gave the signal. The spearmen began to close in, a living rampart spiked with flint blades. Those enemies the spearmen couldn't stop, the swordsmen mowed down with little trouble. The ground between the folding wings became a place of crowded slaughter where the spears could not be pried loose from the dead bodies. In that confined space the new *hadzabs* with the stabbing points wreaked the most havoc. Gonzalo had surged ahead and was fighting alone, while his guard tried to catch up with him and called to each other, nearly as confused as the enemy by yet another change in their rules of warfare.

At the core of the crowd the Xiu commander and his guard still held out, lunging again and again at Lord Nachancan with the courage of desperation. Knowing they were lost, their only aim now was to take the *Halach Uinic* with them and leave to the Can a victory of mourning. But the wings kept drawing inexorably closer, and Lord Nachancan was well protected between Paichè and Ah Balam Tun. Surrounded by all sides, that last and most valuable enemy remnant was captured and stripped of weapons. The Xiu insignia went down and was trampled.

Some who'd retreated up the steps of the temple were chased and seized as they climbed. Gonzalo forced down three men whose jade ornaments made them captives worth taking. To bring them to Lord Nachancan he had to step over many corpses and pieces of corpses he didn't want to look at.

The bandage around his shoulder had come undone and the old cut was bleeding along with many new ones. The heat and the stench seemed to rise up at him like a wave. Yet he had never felt more alive. He pushed his three prisoners down and shouted a cry of savage gratitude to whatever lords of heaven or hell had seen him through the carnage. His warriors thrust their hadzabs at the sky and threaded his name into a heady ramble of praise, re-joicing and taunts of the defeated Xiu.

It was some time before order returned among the men, for there was a sort of madness in them that none of their commanders could stop. The ones who'd stayed coolest began to help the wounded to their feet and to gather the weapons littering the ground. Others were busy stripping the dead of their jade. A group of Paichè's warriors cut some of the heads and carried those off along with their lootings.

Finally the madness burned itself out and Lord Nachancan could speak, his foot on the neck of the naked Xiu hunched before him. "On a day like this day the Gods will be called most gracious. With a new *nacom* we have defeat-ed an old enemy, and in a way that will be remembered for many years to come."

The men cheered again. Lord Nachancan silenced them with a sweep of his arm that pointed at Paichè and Ah Balam Tun. "Let those who have shown ill will toward Ah Holkan learn from this victory that he has given the House of Can. Let them know that the only thing they can do to prove their loyalty is to give me a victory greater than this one."

The men broke into a louder ovation. Whether sincere or simply fearful because of Lord Nachancan's warning, Paichè's and Ah Balam Tun's warriors joined in. All that could be wrung from their two commanders was a stiff bow that spoke of the old hatred. But the impotent rage on their faces made them look as if they too were chastened captives, which gave Gonzalo a dou-ble feeling of triumph. Lord Nachancan was right, he thought. This was a day he would remember long into the future. Proudly now he would return to Xul Ha, to the woman he had won as his bride. Nothing and no one could harm him.

Lord Natohcan and lord Ekuneh welcomed them with the most thankful acclaim. For days they been waiting to see the Xiu march up the road from the ruined temple, and all they had to hold the town with was a bare handful of men. Orders went out to retrieve for burial the bodies of the dead and to make ready all that was needed by the living. The captive Xiu were given a locked room in the house the two brothers shared, and the food and water that would keep them able to walk to the sacrificial stone in Chetemal.

There was much the two Can lords must be told. Gonzalo let Lord Nachancan fill them in on the many news, including the news of Gonzalo himself. For his part, he gave himself over to the cares of four very capable women—one to wash him and salve his cuts, one to bring him fresh clothes, the third to see to his drink, and the fourth to make sure a free pair of hands remained available for anything else. As heluxuriated in their deftness, he told himself that perhaps the mayhem of the life of a Can warrior was worth it, if after it came such comforts.

Restored to himself, he was taken to join his hosts. Lord Natohcan and lord Ekuneh, having been told not only who he was but also who he would soon become with his impending marriage to Lady Ix Na, treated him with twofold respect. If they harbored any uncertainty about the stranger dropped among them on the heels of such a rescue, they never let it show. The talk around the rich evening meal was of nothing but happy things.

Before it was over they honored Gonzalo with many gifts, including the four women, since he had so praised the women's good services. Over cups of *cacau*—too thick and too sweet for Gonzalo's tastes, a far cry from Lady Ix Na's perfection—the last subject pursued was the best spot around the lagoon at Xul Ha on which to build the home of the new couple. When he pulled down the hanging at the door of his room, he was as tired and as pleased with the world as he thought he'd ever be. In the afterglow of this fortunate day the future seemed full of hope.

Certainly Lord Nachancan had informed his half-brothers about the Castilàn in the islands, and about the warning that had gone out against the coming of these men. But the Castilàn were very far from him right then. All that mattered in that sultry night in the middle of the jungle was the thought of his wedding day. What he had looked for all his life he had finally found where he least expected, like treasure gained after jumping a fence that others said was too high.

Even the Castilàn wouldn't blame him, he thought. After all they were men, and all men seek happiness. Once they would just see her, and see how blessed he'd been to meet her, they would surely leave him to the life he'd chosen, a life after his own manner. Sleep came with the swiftness of an easy promise.

When the noise woke him up he wondered first how far into the night it was, then why the guard who sat outside his room was making such a raspy snoring when he should be wide awake. He listened for a moment. There was silence again—the guard must have dozed off—and he lay back down. An instant later something caught him around the throat, a grip of bare arms that knocked the wind from him and made him open his mouth into what he wanted to be a shout but was the same raspy sound he'd heard from the guard outside.

He rolled off the bed, taking the man down with him, his hands working frantically to free himself. He could feel the man's legs kicking around his feet, trying to pin him down. A stool was thrown aside; on it he'd left his *hadzab* and his flint knife. Either would have been useful, but he must have the man alive or he might never find out who was trying to kill him.

At last he managed a good hold of the man's arm, and enough breath back into his lungs to keep the hold, pull the arm down. They were right in the doorway, with the curtain slapping between them, still no one seemed to have seen or heard anything. He hung his whole weight onto the man's arm, and twisted until he felt the arm go limp at an angle. The man slumped against him with a cry of pain, then was up again and trying to tear himself away. Gonzalo began to shout. Finally a flurry of steps told him the guards had been alerted.

The man made a last effort, breathing hard in pain. Gonzalo threw him into the arms of the men who were coming with drawn knives. Lord Nachan-can followed, calling out to bring torches and to wake up his brothers.

"Ah Holkan... are you hurt?" He ripped off the torn curtain, got the overturned stool out of his way, and reached out to help Gonzalo to his feet. Gonzalo motioned he was all right. He'd been forced out of bed naked; one of the guards hastened to find his clothes for him. Within minutes the room was full of men and of questions.

The only one silent was the Xiu *nacom,* pinioned between two guards and stiffly holding his arm against his side.

Lord Nachancan's eyes swept accusingly over his brothers. "I was told you had our prisoners well under guard. Will you tell me how this could have happened?"

Lord Natohcan and lord Ekuneh gave signs of the utmost bewilderment, demanding in their turn that the guards give an explanation. The guards only added to the confusion with their own claims of innocence.

Lord Nachancan silenced them all. "None of this is reasonable," he thundered. "Someone has let this man out, someone has told him where he must go and whom he must kill." Again he addressed his brothers. "Someone in your household knows as much as this man does, and must be made to answer. Find him, my brothers, or I will hold you both as traitors."

"And how are we ever to find this traitor?" lord Ekuneh pleaded. "I beg you, Hun Halal, think of what you say before you accuse your own kinsmen."

Gonzalo wrapped his cloak around his hips in place of the *esh* he didn't want to waste time with. "My Lord Nachancan, lord Ekuneh speaks well. We must search among our own men, the ones we have led into your brothers' town."

The warriors of Gonzalo's personal escort began the same protestations of innocence. One hit the Xiu with his fist, enraged that on account of that hated enemy Gonzalo should have come to suspect his most loyal men.

Gonzalo stopped them. "Some are not here who should be," he said. "They are the ones I accuse."

There was a moment of silent perplexity. Then Lord Nachancan walked out of the room.

"Send for Ah Balam Tun," he ordered. A moment later, painfully, he added, "And for Paichè."

When they got to the main hall it was almost dawn. Paichè and Ah Balam Tun came not with the subdued manners of men accused of the worst crime against the House of Can, but embattled, shrill in their defense of themselves and of each other. Gonzalo could see how much Lord Nachancan was torn between granting them some good faith and cutting to the heart of the matter.

"Paichè," he questioned, "wasn't it you whom I entrusted with taking the captives to the place of their keeping? Wasn't it you who locked them in last night?"

Paichè glanced at the Xiu *nacom*. It was a glance of venomous contempt, as if reproaching the man for failing to do his job.

"Yes, I locked them in," he answered. "But what will that prove, my Lord Nachancan? I have served you all my life. I have risked my life in battle for you, and always gladly. Have you ever had reason to be displeased with me?"

Lord Nachancan looked away. His voice dropped. "No, Paichè. Not until today."

Paichè's eyes flashed. "Not until you let the stranger blind you, as one would with a handful of dust!"

Ah Balam Tun joined in. "When has there ever been such division within the House of Can?" he asked indignantly. "How easily you trust this foreigner, and doubt of us."

"You are both wrong about Ah Holkan," Lord Nachancan said. "And you both must think me a man of small heart, who could not love old friends along with a new one." He sat down, as though he were tired. He looked at Gonzalo.

"Ah Holkan. I want to find the truth, but I don't know how. Tell me what you would do, what would satisfy you that enough has been done."

Gonzalo paced back to where the Xiu was crouching between the guards. Of course he would get nothing from Paichè and Ah Balam Tun, and neither could be coerced. But the Xiu was entirely in his hands, still very much attached to life and with no love to spare for those who'd send him in the night to do what they themselves didn't have the stomach for.

He looked into the eyes of the man who'd tried to kill him. "What were you promised?" he wondered. "Escape?" The Xiu stared back without moving a muscle. "Well, the ones who made you that promise will not step forth to save you now. You will pay alone, and you will pay for them, too."

Fear came into the man's eyes. Gonzalo smiled; fear was what he wanted. "The way of your dying will be unlike what you'd expected," he said. "It won't be in sacrifice, where you might have gone with some honor. It won't be quick, and it won't be clean." He paused, to let the fear sink in. "You will have much time to think before dying."

The Xiu looked up at him, and for a moment he seemed about to speak. But even before Gonzalo had motioned the guards to take the prisoner away, his warriors appointed themselves to the task of torturers with grim relish. They started to pull and to gouge at the Xiu, thrusting their knives at his groin and swearing he would die as nothing resembling a man. There was such hatred in them that Gonzalo feared they would kill the man before anything useful could be gotten from him. Paichè and Ah Balam Tun looked on impassively. Gonzalo knew that if only they could, they would tear the Xiu apart themselves, to silence him forever.

The Xiu moaned something. The men thought he was begging for mercy, and punched him and kicked him harder. The Xiu cried out again. "There are the ones who came to me," he gasped, "the ones who promised..."

Gonzalo had to put himself between the Xiu and his warriors to make them stop. The Xiu crumpled to the ground, his face and hair bloody. Now he was bawling, his one sound arm raised. "There are the ones you want!" Paichè and Ah Balam Tun, at last discovered before all, remained stonily side by side, shoring each other up with their silence.

The Xiu spat at them through cracked lips. "I could not have hoped for such good fortune," he rasped. "Two that I could not kill in battle will now go down with me of their own doing."

Lord Nachancan's eyes became narrow with hatred and pain. He turned his back to Paichè and Ah Balam Tun and faced Gonzalo. His voice was weary.

"Ah Holkan. You may do with them as you wish. I ask you only that you remove them forever from my presence." Without waiting for an answer, he left the room.

Quiet, stunned to be doing such a thing to two of their own highest chieftains, the warriors began to strip the traitors, as it had been done to the

Xiu captives, as it must be done with all those who stood beyond the pale. Everything was taken from them: mantles, daggers, even the thongs that fastened their hair, until they stood naked and unkempt, no longer human beings but objects of shame.

As he looked at them Gonzalo felt none of Lord Nachancan's hatred, only something like a weariness of soul. He too wanted to be away from the two men. What should he do with them? he wondered, though in truth there was little to debate. He could have them jailed for life, or send them into exile. But alive they would remain forever a danger to the House of Can. Besides, why should he show compassion to cowards who'd tried to kill him as he lay in bed naked and alone?

Paichè held his gaze with an air of challenge. "Why do you wait?" he scoffed. "Is the slave so used to receiving punishment that he doesn't know how to give it?"

"May the Gods save us from the hairy-face's mercy," Ah Balam Tun spat out.

Paichè twisted his mouth. "Your judgment means nothing, Castilàn. If we must throttle one another with our bare hands we will not live to see you married into the House of Can."

Gonzalo picked up the two daggers that lay with the rest of the things stripped from the traitors. "Here. These are much faster than bare hands." He placed each dagger in front of its owner. "It's not a choice I give you, and it's not mercy. I too don't want you to live to see the day of my wedding."

It was a little while before Ah Balam Tun could bring himself to gather up his dagger. Paichè did it right away, as if ready to carry out Gonzalo's order on the spot.

"Lock them all up," Gonzalo told the guards.

The Xiu limped away. Paichè and Ah Balam Tun followed their guardians without a word, for all the world unaffected by what they'd done and by what they would have to do. Only lord Natohcan and lord Ekuneh remained, mumbling apologies and offers to provide the guest with anything he might want. But all that Gonzalo wanted was to be left alone in his room for the rest of the day, unless Lord Nachancan called for him. This, his hosts assured him, they would do with the utmost care.

As he went back to bed it occurred to him that finally he'd rid himself of his two most dangerous adversaries. But the thought gave him no pleasure. When he'd hoped for their defeat he'd never imagined that that would mean watching their bodies being carried away in secret to be buried in the swamps, with their own daggers in their hearts.

❖   ❖   ❖

It wasn't the happy return everybody had so anticipated. Paichè and Ah Balam Tun had cheated them of their triumph. The Can army marched back to Chetemal with only the necessary words spoken, disturbing little the noisy quiet of the jungle. At the end of one column were twenty Xiu captives. Behind the warriors went lord Natohcan and lord Ekuneh with their porters shouldering bridal gifts.

Gonzalo had never seen Lord Nachancan in such a joyless mood. Even his battle guard kept at a distance from him. Only when they rested shortly after midday, and together they sat apart from the others, Lord Nachancan broke his grim silence.

"In our house he was like the father we lost," he said, speaking of Paichè whose name, like Ah Balam Tun's, must no longer be spoken. "What will my sister say? She will see the shadow that this thing casts upon us. Better for us and for them if they had died in battle four days ago."

In the silence that followed Gonzalo mulled that last sentence over. "Yes," he agreed. "But must the truth be told this time? If every man here can be trusted to obey an order, no one in Chetemal will have to learn of the treason."

Lord Nachancan raised his face. He didn't need to ask Gonzalo what he meant. With him he could agree without the help of words. Gonzalo motioned two of his men to come forward. The instructions he gave them were spoken so softly that even Lord Nachancan couldn't hear them. As the two spread the order, a silent ripple of surprise went through the entire army.

Gonzalo called a halt. He pointed at random for one of the warriors to come forward. The young man crouched down before him.

"What is your name?" Gonzalo asked. "Nine Deer, son of Ah Tzap."

"Say where your company leader is, Nine Deer."

"He and Ah... he and the old *nacom* were killed four days ago, in the battle against the Xiu."

"And if anyone says otherwise?"

The young man looked flustered. "If anyone says otherwise... he will join them in the World Underneath," he blurted out.

Gonzalo nodded. "Go back to your place, Nine Deer."

Lord Nachancan glanced at Gonzalo and kept silent. He spoke again only when they were almost home.

"Ah Holkan. As the Gods know my heart, this time I'm not sure how to thank you. You see, even before we learn to speak we learn that we must not lie... Yet even for your lie I am grateful."

Gonzalo acknowledged his words with a nod. "I just want you to be at peace, my Lord Nachancan."

Lord Nachancan finally smiled. "I am at peace," he said. "We will no longer speak of sad things, Ah Holkan. And you will begin to call me by a relative's name. We have a wedding to do."

TWENTY-ONE

After the twenty Xiu captives were displayed in Chetemal amidst the general celebration, Nachancan sent them to the temple of Ah Cab, as a gift to the brotherhood of beekeepers. As for Paichè and Ah Balam Tun, they were now among the honored warriors dead in battle, and their bodies rested in the town they'd helped save from the enemy.

Ix Na grieved for Paichè, blackening her cheeks with ashes mixed with her own tears. In private, when only Gonzalo and her brother were present, she could not hide her delight in the safe return of both men, the dearest to her heart, and her pride in the one who would soon be her husband. With Ah Balam Tun gone, Gonzalo was now *nacom* for life. If and when necessary, the

Can warriors would elect the lesser captain who shared the office; but for now, as Nachancan said, these matters of war could well wait.

At a spot where the lagoon curled into a hidden cove, stonecutters and carpenters had set to work on the new house, raising timbers of lush red hardwood and stucco walls graced with fine carvings. Often Gonzalo and Ix Na would walk down to the cove to watch the workers. Those days it took to finish the house were the longest and the happiest of their lives, wonderfully impatient with all the expectations that would surely be fulfilled in that house. Every one of his dreams had come true after all—like in fairy tales, Gonzalo thought, where the youngest son, the one to whom nobody pays heed, ends up marrying the daughter of a faraway king and getting half the kingdom for a dowry.

Wherever he went people gathered to pay him homage.

Mothers pointed him out to their children, old warriors praised him. The tale of how he'd led his men against the Xiu had spread throughout the province. What seemed to impress the most was that he'd fought without the protection of his battle guard, which was only what he'd always done among the Spaniards.

At times it was too easy for him to grow smug. Whatever proof of manhood these people demanded, he had delivered. He would enjoy their admiration, although he only looked on uneasily when the warriors set the severed enemy heads on a platform built for no other purpose. True, this time the praise had been earned at the expenses of men he didn't even know; but he was among the Can now, and those who threatened the Can threatened him also.

For the first time his new name took on for him the truer meaning these people intended. His very scars now told that he was Ah Holkan, a warrior proven in battle. He sent for the tattoo man and had the handsome characters of the name drawn on his chest, above the heart where many warriors wore their own name with pride.

It was an endlessly excruciating time before the design was rubbed into his skin with ink and with his own blood. Even Ix Na's hand wiping the sweat from his face seemed to bring him torment instead of relief. But when it was finally done he understood why these people marked their flesh with a living record of themselves. If he could strip himself of a Spanish uniform, he couldn't cast off an identity so permanently engraved. Even in death he would not be one of the unknown bodies the Spaniards tumbled into their common graves.

Ix Na mopped one last time the beads of blood on his chest. "May this name protect you," she whispered, happy that the ordeal was over and that he'd borne it well. "May it be one with the heart underneath... forever."

The day keepers were called to set the wedding date. In the month of Pop, after the New Year's ceremonies, there was a day 'special for anything one might desire'. That was to be the one. All of Chetemal buzzed with the preparations. Vats of *balchè* were brewed; the potters kept their fires stoked for new dishes and cups, and the mat-makers' fingers blurred around silky new mats. Everything must be new for the new couple, the first of the New Year when the whole world started fresh.

Nachancan's women furnished rich clothes for both, but left to the bride the most important garment. Ix Na's loom blossomed with the most beautiful lengths of cotton she'd ever woven. The wedding dress was made of four strips of cloth sewn together. Four were the corners of the world, four the colors of corn, the life-giver.

When she would don the dress, her head emerging from the center scoop, Ix Na would stand at the sacred crossroads of heaven and earth, ready to receive their blessings.

At the close of the day, when the air smelled of jungle loam and hung with mist from the last thundershower, the faint clicking of the loom led Gonzalo to where she was. He would sit down behind her, not on hammock or bench but cross-legged on the floor. He didn't know why he liked to sit like that. She was some years older than he, and she looked stately as she worked, a lady of high breeding. When he was among men he had no trouble assuming the overweening posture of men; but in those evenings alone with her it gave him a strange pleasure to serve her, as though he were still the slave who'd kneeled by her litter in Tulum.

Without a word, anticipating her commands as a good slave must, he would fetch her a skein of cotton or the knife she used to cut the thread. Then he would just watch her for long rapt moments, waiting for the next small task. She'd glance at him, caught in his mood, understanding how excited it made him to behave like that; until he tossed aside skein or knife and pressed her to him, made her cleave to him as if to heal something that had been missing since he was born.

Like the women of the islands and like Kanalsin, she didn't know about kissing. But neither the women of the islands nor Kanalsin had ever really liked it. To her instead, of all the new things he brought this that they alone shared was the most wonderful. Just to see her lift her mouth toward his, with such desire every time, was enough to set his heart pounding; until they were interrupted by someone walking into the porch, Nachancan fawned upon by his women or little White Feather with a flower she'd plucked to show them.

Thirteen days before the New Year Nachancan began the ritual fast that all men undertook before this celebration. The one meal he took at night had no salt, pepper or spices. He also slept apart from his women. Gonzalo had never sacrificed his body for the sake of his soul, but he joined in the fast. The men spoke of it not as the self- denial of penitents but as the test of endurance of warriors, and this he would not shirk.

When the New Year came, they washed themselves and painted their bodies with red paint. In their new garments they brought offerings of food, drink and incense to the temple of Ah Cab in Chetemal. Four priests stretched a cord at four corners around the men, fencing away evil. Then they lit the new fire high on the roof.

From the top of another temple, across the dark pelt of the jungle and the white stretch of the seashore, another fire blazed in response, and yet another and another, until the news was everywhere. Helped by the remembrance of its children, time had set out in one more coil like a benign heavenly serpent. The fast was broken with a banquet and with the rekindling of the ties that bound each to each other.

Finally the wedding day arrived. The morning was full of measured, meticulous gestures. For many years afterwards what Gonzalo would remember most clearly was the time he spent getting dressed for the ceremony. Such a stir in his heart, and such quiet arranging of garments, such slow tying up of knots. He didn't know how many times he'd straightened the crescent of gold and copper on his chest, or tugged at the strips of jaguar skin wrapped around his elbows and knees.

How well he liked himself in that warrior bridegroom's finery, more than he would have in any velvet back home. And how far from home this was, he thought; perhaps his own kinfolk would no longer recognize him as the reflection in the obsidian mirror that the servants were holding for him. The sound of flutes and drums reached him from outside. I'm ready, he rejoiced in his mind as he strode out, ready for whatever is in store.

First came the priest with his attendant, carrying the pouch of sacred tobacco whose fragrance would nourish the gods; then Nachancan, sumptuous as a peacock in his crown of nodding green feathers; then Ix Na looking like a queen. Her hair was piled up to resemble the roof of a temple and her throat weighed down by a double strand of huge jade beads, Gonzalo's wedding present to her, the stones he'd taken from his three Xiu captives.

He took his place beside her and walked into the hall, where the images of the ancestors were waiting to witness the newest branching of their clan, this time into the blood of a race they could have never foreseen. He sat down on the wedding mat and let himself be enveloped by the solemn rhythms of the ceremony.

The ghostly clouds of sacred tobacco seemed to rise and fall at one with the drone of the priest calling out benedictions as old as the centuries. Though he couldn't understand their meaning, or perhaps just because of that, the words compelled him to the awe he'd long ceased to feel in the rituals of his own religion. It was almost as if talking to God became easier in a tongue not his own, through worship not his own, as if God were now someone other than the one forever linked with the terror and the tedium that he remembered from his childhood.

There came a trembling inside him, of joy mixed with foreboding, and he turned to look at Ix Na sitting beside him. Who was he? he wondered. What was all this, what had happened?

Someone must have cast on him a spell that made even the most foreign things seem familiar, like this woman he could not have invented in his wildest imaginings yet he was now taking for his wife.

Ix Na glanced at him with a serene look. He smiled, to her and to his own doubts. If he was under a spell, he thought, so was she. She had made her own irrevocable choice. She had given her life to a man who tomorrow could desert her and return to his people; she had entrusted her children to the bloodline of another race about which she knew nothing. Nachancan too had entrusted his future to a man who tomorrow could betray him into the hands of foreign invaders.

Perhaps they were all under a spell, he thought, all caught in a dream conjured up by the smoke that curled up towards the faces of the dead. Something told him to let go of all thoughts, to surrender.

The priest's hands drew a circle of divine protection around the wedding mat. He took a corner of Gonzalo's mantle in his right hand, a corner of Ix Na's mantle in his left hand, and tied the two corners together. It was done.

From that moment on, it was a whirlwind of people clustering around them, noisy with good wishes. The drums beat and the flutes blew loudly, to warn the evil spirits that there was no place for them in such a happy crowd. At the main gate Gonzalo's warriors were clamoring to see him and Ix Na together. Together Gonzalo and Ix Na stepped out to meet them. What the men saw must truly please them, because their cheering went up to the sky.

A throng of people had gathered. No one could tell if among them there were some who doubted this stranger who dressed like them and spoke like them. If there were, they would not be heard from today. Today, all Gonzalo could hear was the sound of goodwill. Even the priest seemed only a dignified old man, if one could forget that his long hair was matted with blood. Gonzalo's mind went back to the islands, where he'd first seen natives and Spaniards mingle within the same walls: there it had never been like this, never as one people.

A little girl rushed from the crowd to offer Ix Na a spray of scarlet *plumerias* symbolizing the pleasures of the flesh. The women drew closer around her, brushing her face with quick touches of blessing. Nachancan invited all to sit down. Food and drink would be sent out soon. Then husband and wife led the way down the new path covered with white flagstones that linked Xul Ha with their house by the cove.

After the priest purified its threshold with incense, they stepped in for the first time, passing under the masks of Itzamnà, Father of Heaven, and of his consort Ix Chel. The wedding banquet had been spread in the inner patio of the house, lavish and bursting with color.

From the perfume sprinkled on the mats to the tiny gold bees placed around the rims of the serving bowls, it was a feast for each of the senses. Nachancan's two half-brothers particularly enjoyed themselves. While they emptied many dishes of food and many cups of *balchè,* Gonzalo could barely taste the delicacies they kept pressing on him: wild turkey, corn-fattened dog, tender slivers of boiled cactus leaves. Ix Na too bore up bravely, nodding her thanks to the gifts the servants brought for her to look at.

At long last the sun set, and the threat of a thunderstorm hastened the end of the revels. Thoroughly intoxicated, Natohcan and Ekuneh toasted their hosts one more time, then tottered back to Xul Ha while bantering with Ahau Can and White Feather, who seemed more than ready to go to sleep. After them the patio quickly emptied of all save the few who belonged there.

Ix Na's waiting women escorted the bride into the house.

Almost leaping up to follow, Gonzalo caught himself only at the last moment, as he wondered how long it would be before custom allowed him to join her. From his mat, where he was lying in the arms of his youngest concubine, Nachancan saw him and tried to suppress a good-natured laugh.

"My brother... for I can call you that now... I was never so impatient to go to a woman, and I know I never will be. You put envy in my heart."

Envy, Gonzalo thought with a smile, from a man who could have any woman he set his eyes on. He'd never seen him so candid, so almost painfully open.

Nachancan got up, holding onto the girl. He looked at her. She seemed too young to have attained any other accomplishment except her youth. His voice turned into a hoarse whisper.

"Be on your way, my brother, and we will be on ours. May Itzamnà bless your bed."

Now alone, Gonzalo started in the direction he'd seen the women lead Ix Na. This was his house, but it was new to him, and it was a big house. In his eagerness he went back on his steps twice, and all the time he thought it was like searching for treasure in a dimly-lit maze. The thunder began. With it he caught the faint music of flutes from the other side of the lagoon.

Then he saw one of the torches the women had taken with them, set in the wall to show a door. There, he thought, there, and he was almost running. Everything he wanted in the world was waiting for him behind that door garlanded with flowers. There he would find perfect shelter from all unhappiness and evil.

Ix Na stood by the bed. For a moment he wondered whether it was her: her back was turned and all of her nearly hidden under a cascade of hair. Loosed from the braids and ribbons, it rippled down to the back of her thighs, thick and heavy, with a sheen like black oil's. One of the serving women, the only one left, was combing it with a single sweeping motion.

Seeing Gonzalo enter, the woman stopped. Ix Na turned around. How different she seemed, like a young girl with her hair like that. She'd taken off her wedding dress and wore only a white shift. But she hadn't removed her jade beads, and he thought they must burden her, each stone almost as big as a robin's egg.

He dismissed the woman with a wave of his hand. It wasn't necessary, since the woman was already leaving; but he was remembering all the times he'd had to stop at the entrance of Ix Na's room while her women followed her in. This time, he seemed to be saying with that gesture, this time and for all time *he* was the one who could go in whenever he pleased.

Ix Na welcomed him into her arms. There was nothing of the coy young bride about her. She had waited too long for this happiness. Pressing him to her, she sought his mouth with hers, as she unfastened the knot of his mantle. She nodded her pleasure at his body. She caressed him not with the tips of her fingers but with her palms open, wanting the most from that fearless touch that delighted her so.

He, who had come with the secret worries of all new husbands, was first reassured by her eagerness, then fired in his very soul. To a woman who received him with such unaffected passion he could do nothing wrong. His mind seemed to stagger with the thought of how completely he now had her.

Quickly he pulled down his loincloth, then lifted her shift over her head. Her hair flicked against him like long, tangled strands of raw silk. She took a step backward so he could see her, for she would take pride in her body as openly as she did in his. She saw great gladness in the way he looked at her.

How perfect she seemed, a woman in the ripeness of her years.

He couldn't help draw his breath in at the exquisite tattoos drawn all over her chest. He thought he'd never seen anything more arousing than that intricacy of swirling blue lines, from which her breasts stood out round and full. Even to think of the pain she must have endured stirred him with the knowledge that she was brave.

There was a clap of thunder, like the summons of a heavenly drummer. Soon they could hear the squall beat past the palm trees into the ruffled surface of the lagoon. But in the house, their house, it was warm and it was safe.

Gonzalo lay down with Ix Na on their bed, on the great jaguar pelt spread over the mats textured like finest fabric. He'd never felt his heart so strong inside him, full of a love that didn't seem to stop at her but only to be summed up in her, the sheer love of being alive and lacking nothing under the sun.

With his hands he reaped the harvest of her firm, sweet flesh.

With his mouth he tasted of her, from her taut black nipples to the warm folds opening wetly between her legs, where his tongue lingered until he heard her breath come in gasps full of wonder, for he knew she'd never heard of such a thing being done.

When he went into her she was still shuddering with pleasure. Her arms coiled around him, tighter at each new thrust of his. Her hair had fallen wildly this way and that. It snaked between their bodies, saturated with that perfume he'd breathed from her even before he'd seen her the very first day.

He seemed to be hearing her voice as if from a great distance, her voice that called him in a strange language. From this woman he would have children, he thought while his life spilled into hers and he fell into the most intense pleasure ever afforded him by something as simple as lovemaking. From this woman he would have children, and this woman and her children would make of him something he'd never dreamed of.

❖   ❖   ❖

Those were the only days in his life in which nothing marred his happiness. He knew that well, just as he knew that these days would end and never come back.

Above all there was Ix Na, with him in the day and at night, when the gods gave rain and when they gave dry weather. He couldn't remember what it had been like to be alone. When he did, he didn't understand how he could have lived like that for so many years.

Left to themselves by the world as it was proper in this time, they missed nothing of the world. Often Gonzalo lost all sense of time as he lay with her in his arms in the hammock slung by the lagoon.

Nothing to do but be together, take pleasure in each other as each pleased; sleep all morning if they wished, and in the dead of the afternoon, when the air lay still over the still blue water, wake up to a new surge of desire and find one more way of quenching it, as though their bodies held inexhaustible wonders.

The first time Nachancan came to call on them it was like greeting a beloved guest they hadn't seen in a long while. The news he brought sounded like those from a faraway place, good news of a full harvest soon to come, of new trading posts established in the southern lands of the Kuna, of peace all along the border. Not a stirring from the Xiu, no word of the Castilàn anywhere yet. Only half in jest Nachancan complained to Gonzalo that they were both going soft for lack of something to worry about, and only half in jest Gonzalo replied that Nachancan had better not tempt the gods with such complaints.

Still, wanting to nudge Gonzalo from his ease, Nachancan took him along on the first jaguar hunt of the season. Gonzalo followed him reluctantly, but once they were out in the jungle his reluctance vanished. Their eyes nailed to the tracks, their breath pent up inside them and their muscles coiled around the flint spears, the two of them were once again drawn into that bonding they knew from having gone to battle together. If Nachancan cherished this intimacy more than that of a woman, it was because he'd never known what Gonzalo had with his woman.

The stalking took all of a long, hot morning. The jaguar led them around like a cat playing, unseen as if made of the same substance as the jungle. Finally the quarry was found, surrounded. Gonzalo got first try at the spear, and in that try he put all he had, beginning with the fear that sat like a stone in the pit of his stomach. In a whirlwind of torn leaves the jaguar sprang up from its hiding place and lunged straight at him. The spear twanged in the motionless noon air. It went clean into the animal's flank, and the full-grown body dropped down cut in mid-leap, the last of a growl caught in its throat.

It was a glory to return to Xul Ha carrying the great bloodied beast across his shoulders, to toss it down at Ix Na's feet while her women sang out and she made the gesture of welcome as though offering him her soul in her hands. The rest of the afternoon was still a man's thing, spent cutting up the animal with Nachancan and the servants. The head was fastened to the main door of Gonzalo's house, the skin stretched on pegs to be made into a cloak, the claws gathered into a necklace. The heart was cooked and eaten for courage, after the spirit of the creature was appeased with the proper prayers.

The sun set, Nachancan left, and all of that manly bustle ceased. Gonzalo took his customary evening bath, then walked to where Ix Na had their evening meal brought out if it wasn't raining. She was waiting for him in their hammock, her eyes half-closed as she listened to the waves lap softly the shore. The food was on a low table, in the lovely bowls of black onyx shaped like water birds, and Gonzalo should have been hungry after such a day. Instead the sight of her lying in the hold of the hammock, swaying to herself with her arms raised to frame her face, set all other thoughts out of his mind.

"*Etan,*" he called. "My wife."

She heard him, and was about to rise, but he shook his head. Something wild was coursing through his veins, something the hunt had awakened with its sweat, its smell and its blood. He pressed his hands on her shoulders and made her lie down again, with her arms raised as he'd found her, in that attitude of complete surrender. There was a guarded look in her eyes, because she could feel what was inside him and she knew he would not stop. Nothing of her moved as she stared up at him, only her breasts rising and falling as if she were fighting for air.

He straddled the hammock, planting his feet apart and holding it still between his thighs. He pulled her gown up to her belly and let the wide folds of his loincloth cover her instead. Underneath them, his flesh pressed hard against hers—shifting at first to find her, then plunging in all at once, then withdrawing so he could plunge in again, his eyes open and fast into hers as though wanting to fix well in his mind from whom it was that he could draw a pleasure as searing as this.

She'd caught her lip between her teeth to keep from crying out, but her throat shook with a low, drawn-out sound almost like that of the jaguar when he'd driven the spear into its flank. It was only at the end that he closed his eyes, when he let himself down and the hammock sagged under their bodies.

Slowly, everything that had been blotted out returned—the ripple of the lagoon, the calls of the last birds before nightfall. A few lights burned already inside the house, where the servants must be discreetly waiting for them to come in. But the air was sweet on the shore, the first stars were appearing, and they didn't want to leave the coolness of the hammock.

Gonzalo made himself snug against Ix Na, his arm across her chest. How good life was, he sighed to himself, how good. Everything around them was luxury, contentment. One room at a time the house was filling up with as many beautiful things as anyone would wish to possess; the servants went about their chores, well treated and uncomplaining; the *cacau* groves flowered and ripened in due time; the beehives hummed with their orderly work, yielding their sweetness without fail.

How long before the gods noticed this happiness they had let slip and ask them to pay for it in full? Ix Na never spoke to him of the Castilàn. It was as though the least she knew of his other life the better.

His other life had become a burden for him too, a life where everything seemed to have been a mistake.

Now in the midst of his peace the thought of his countrymen came back to him for the first time in a long time. The same day he'd find himself among them, his marriage to Ix Na would become invalid, and Ix Na would become nothing better than his whore. The Church dictated that a native woman could live with a soldier as his slave or his mistress, but never as his wife. There was only one door to salvation, he thought, and Spain kept the only set of keys.

Ix Na noticed how silent he was. "My husband," she whispered. "Come back."

He breathed out hard, as if casting from his body the poison of those worried ruminations. If there was no place for them among the Spaniards, there was a place for them here, a place from which he would keep the Spaniards if he had die for it.

He took Ix Na's face between his hands and kissed her. "*Etan,*" he told her, "I didn't go away. I never will."

TWENTY-TWO

Shortly after the onset of the dry season Ix Na became pregnant, and Gonzalo became the most exacting of husbands. The moment Ix Na told him, the memory of Kanalsin jumped to his mind at once with his joy, as though after Kanalsin childbirth had turned into a promise of death for every woman.

Because she knew about illnesses and cures, he assigned Ix Lolkin to attend her. When Ix Na showed any discomfort, he slept elsewhere while Ix Lolkin took his place. Neither Ix Na nor Ix Lolkin liked the arrangement, and Nachancan grumbled whenever he sent for his favorite concubine and was told she'd spend the night in his sister's room. But Gonzalo ignored them all. What good was it to have gained power if he couldn't use it to fight some of the terrible fears he'd known when he didn't have any power at all?

He sent for the priests of Ix Chel and had them tell him what must be done for a safe delivery. As for the many taboos they listed for him, he would observe them all and make everyone else observe them as well. Soon the word spread that Castilàn women must be quite frail, if their men worried so.

After the first four or five months, Gonzalo's fears were made worse when he noticed how quickly Ix Na was putting on weight.

Though she was no slight young girl like Kanalsin, like Kanalsin she seemed unusually burdened. He had the *ahmen* come to see her right away. The old curer confirmed Gonzalo's observations, in fact praised him for his sharp eye. Ix Na was putting on more weight than expected, but because she was carrying two new lives instead of one. She was perfectly well, the *ahmen* concluded, and with the help of the Gods she would stay well into old age; only, she would be a busier mother than she'd thought.

The news of twins soon to be born to the House of Can stirred a rush of excitement, for reasons that Gonzalo had to be explained as soon as he himself had taken in his own surprise.

Nachancan, Ix Lolkin and about a dozen women rushed to Ix Na's bedside, crying out their happiness and blessing both parents-to-be.

Twins, Ix Na told him, were the luckiest of births. He had seen the images of handsome twin boys honored in the books of divine revelation. The most sacred of these, the Book of Counsel, spoke of how the First Gods had sent the brothers Hunhapu and Xbalanke to make the world safe for the human beings they were about to create. Brave, cunning and selfless, the Twins had even harrowed hell to defeat its fearsome rulers. From that day the lords of the World Underneath had agreed that they would loose their evils only upon the wicked.

For the rest of the day no one in Xul Ha spoke of anything else—of how like the Hero Twins these two lucky babies would be, handsome and brave and destined to fame as warriors and as hunters with the blowgun. The thought that it might be twin girls escaped everyone's mind, beginning with Gonzalo's.

Not that Gonzalo's worries ceased after that day. He thought the *ahmen* had spoken too assuredly, as a man accustomed to saying what would please listeners of high rank. There were things over which he would never gain power, things over which he would fret all his life like the last corn farmer in his hut.

Ix Na yoked a second loom next to the one on which she'd been weaving her baby clothes, and started going from one to the other in what must be the perfect rehearsal of the busy times she had ahead. If she'd always hated being idle, she now seemed possessed of boundless energy.

"You have made me happy, husband, happy," she whispered to him as they lay together in their bed. "In all that you have given me, you have given me joy. I tell you now, my father and my brother have taught me the meekness that becomes a woman, but when the Castilàn will come for you, I will be like a man."

On that day, Gonzalo added in his mind, he too would fight to keep what she had come to mean for him in a world he'd always damned as having no meaning at all. With each passing day he could feel himself sinking deeper into this land. It was no longer like being swallowed up, but like the settling of a seed of corn in good earth ready to welcome its new roots. Strange, he thought, how even the scars from his years as a slave couldn't hamper that settling.

All those times he'd sworn that if he ever regained his freedom he wouldn't as much as look back once at the place of his trials… Could one really change so, start down a road and then turn when another one beckoned? Yes, he answered himself, one could; sometimes perhaps one must. If he hadn't taken the other road, he would have known nothing in this land but the desperation of the slave.

He tried to imagine where he would be now, what he would be doing, if he'd accepted the canoe ride to the islands that Ix Na had offered him when he'd escaped from Tulum. There were only two choices: carry the secret of this land to his grave, or lead a ship to this land with the usual cargo of cheap trinkets and death. He was happy he'd never had to make a choice.

During the winter months the peace with the Xiu held, although after the battle at the ruined temple no formal truce had passed between Nachancan and the new Xiu ruler. No one had survived the battle to tell the Xiu that the rules of warfare had changed in Chetemal. Nachancan rested confidently in the knowledge that he still had over his enemies the full advantage given him by Gonzalo's innovations.

Perhaps too confidently, Gonzalo warned him. Natohcan and Ekuneh had been instructed in the new way of fighting, but they remained too close to the border. Their unprotected town was a weak spot that the Xiu would certainly try to breach again. Already before the wedding Gonzalo had mentioned to the three Can lords the need to fortify that crucial spot, and Nachancan had advised his brothers to use the ruined temple as a lookout.

To Gonzalo that was far from enough. He thought of the bastions so common in Spain, of the wooden palisades the Spaniards put up in the islands, and he had to wonder why there were no such barriers here. Small as it was, Tulum was much better guarded by its wall than sprawling, prosperous Chetemal. He made known to Nachancan what occupied his mind: stockades to be built around Natohcan's and Ekuneh's border town and around every other place worth defending. The corn harvest was over, and the people could be summoned to common service.

By now Nachancan accepted everything that came from Gonzalo's mouth in matters of warfare even before he'd fully grasped what Gonzalo meant. He sent instructions to his half-brothers and to the *batabs* in Chetemal. Construction of the stockades must begin at once in every town and village lying within ten leagues from the border, and the border must be secured once and for all by means of posts manned by warriors and scouts.

In less than two weeks a stout wooden wall was raised around Natohcan's and Ekuneh's town, and the first post of warriors was established. Soon more border villages followed. All over the hinterland was a noise of flint axes felling down trees, shaping stakes, hammering the stakes into the earth. Farmers volunteered to keep the wall clear from the constant growth of the jungle.

Gonzalo and Nachancan spent most of the spring traveling from place to place to oversee the construction of the stockades. For Gonzalo it was a wearisome time. He couldn't bear to be away from Ix Na. Should something happen to her, he worried that he wouldn't know for many days. Each town and village looked alike to his eyes, and each offered the same amenities. There was no local chief who didn't greet them with a choice company of young women. The perkiest ones were invariably sent to Gonzalo, surely with instructions to discover and divulge the intimate habits of the bearded stranger. He had to learn quickly how to divert his share to Nachancan without raising a fuss.

These incidents reminded him of something he had forgotten since he'd become Ix Na's husband. As a Can noble, he could have any of those young women not just for a night's pleasure but as concubines or secondary wives. At a time when all of him longed to be reunited with Ix Na, the idea struck him as a perfect enormity.

Nachancan, on his part, had no trouble at all honoring each one of the young women at least once in the course of their stay. He made no remarks about Gonzalo's restraint; but some mornings, when the two of them walked out to their litters to resume their travel, Gonzalo thought the sated look on Nachancan's handsome face was expressly calculated to weary him more.

The worst was the stop in Becan, where the priests consecrated the new fortifications by offering up a man in sacrifice. After enduring the sacrifice, Gonzalo could only endure a bit longer while the priests poured a bowlful of the man's blood into the furrow that would receive the wooden stakes.

Before being led to the stockade the man asked to be blessed by Nachancan and by the new *nacom*. His manners were calm, willing, but Gonzalo's hand shook as he placed it on the man's forehead. He looked into his eyes, trying to fathom the man's soul, and he thought that no matter how long he would live in this land, in many ways it would remain forever alien to him. Away from Ix Na, who made everything easy to understand, at times he felt as lost as he'd felt at the beginning. When they started back to Chetemal, in his body and his mind he was more than ready to take refuge in her arms.

For many nights after his return no one but the two of them slept in their bed. Big as she'd grown, she received him with the same passion as always. The prescription of abstinence given by the priests was joyfully broken more than once. By now the twins had become a restless pair, kicking lustily as if impatient to come to the light.

When he put his hands on her belly he could feel the small lumps of their skulls, and sometimes he even imagined he could hear the double beating of their hearts. How he loved to lie next to her great soft body. In having sired two at once there was an ingenuous satisfaction that made him feel more than equal to Nachancan's displays of tireless manhood.

Not long after his return, Natohcan and Ekuneh sent word that two Xiu scouts had been captured while trying to plumb the new defenses around their town. A month or so later, runners from another town reported that the Xiu had sent out a large war party, which the much scantier garrison of that town had been able to throw back like a pack of craven dogs. Only the man who'd tried to set fire to the palisade was left alive. His hair shorn and his fingernails torn out, he'd been sent back to tell the Xiu that the border was no longer the same they'd dared to breach the last time.

The news caused much joy in Chetemal. In the city's crowded main plaza, Gonzalo and Nachancan received the gifts the town's *batab* had sent to show his gratitude and loyalty. Among them were the jaws of two Xiu dead, stripped of flesh and ready to be worn. Nachancan helped Gonzalo slip one of them on. After the first queasy moments Gonzalo thought it didn't feel much different from the necklace of jaguar claws he already wore.

His memory went back to the day he and his shipwrecked companions from the *Esperanza* had been captured on the beach by the people of Ecab. The warrior who'd seized him wore a jaw just like this one. He could still see it, its teeth like long yellow pearls. Who could ever imagine that some day he would be carrying that same trophy.

They returned to Xul Ha at sunset, surrounded by warriors in ceremonial feathers. At the gate they were met by Ix Lolkin with the news that Ix Na's pains had begun around midday. She'd already been taken to the room set aside for the birth, and Gonzalo wondered how long it would be before he could see her again. But the curer was on his way just in case, Ix Lolkin told him, and there were experienced women with her. The day keeper had been called as well, and he'd given good omens for both this day and the next.

There was nothing else for him to do but go sit in the shade playing at beans with Nachancan. He was familiar with the waiting, but it weighed on him no more now since the first time had become such a harrowing memory. Nachancan fidgeted, too. While his third child was being born they'd played at beans too, but back then he'd wanted to finish his hand before seeing the baby; now instead he kept absentmindedly losing game after game. As he cocked his ears to catch the sounds from the house he blurted out softly, "Such busy lives men lead… We hunt, we fight, we speak in council… yet we must be utterly idle in these long hours."

Whether Nachancan had spoken in jealousy, concern, or irritation, Gonzalo couldn't tell. How very true, he sighed. Had he been even the most skillful of curers, this time she would do all the work and face all the risks.

They remained hunched over the game long after the daylight faded, until both thought they would never want to look at another playing bean again. The servants lit torches and brought their meal. Ix Lolkin came out once to say nothing had happened yet but everything was going well.

After some time Nachancan went to take his bath, and Gonzalo drifted off to sleep in his hammock. All sorts of unquiet dreams crept up to him in the fitful stretches of time he was able to rest. Once he dreamt that he was back home, showing his sons to the neighbors who'd come to congratulate him. Their delight turned to horror when he opened the blanket and the babies were revealed to be shriveled little corpses only half-human, with the tails and paws of some unknown jungle beast. He bolted up in the hammock at the sound of his own strangled cry. It was almost dawn.

The twins were born without a blemish, healthy, perfect, and perfectly identical. When the woman called him from the house, his first question was about Ix Na. He rushed in more eager to have her back than to look at his sons. But when he did look at them, he understood that their lives had changed forever, and even something beyond their lives. These were the first of a whole new race, he thought. They looked like her, smooth dark skin and thick, shiny black hair. The native strain had won; but what distant blood ran through their veins, the blood of a man God had let fall beyond the rim of the world and fished back up on the other side.

He stood by the bed, grasping Ix Na's arm and staring with new awe at her, at what he had made with her. Around them the whispers of the women sounded like those of people to whom something from another country is shown for the first time, a bird of a color never seen before or a plant with flowers no one's ever imagined.

Ix Na, with her arms full, was the portrait of pride. He knew she expected no words from him now, amidst the common noise. The true words would come later, when the two of them would be alone. But he must say his relief, because it had been a wait full of worry, and in the joyful tumult of his heart all he could think of was the expression of thanksgiving he'd heard most commonly in this land.

"May Itzamnà be praised," he let out with a deep breath. "It's over. You are all right."

Nachancan came in like a burst of wind from the lagoon, so boisterous with excitement one would have thought him to be the new father.

"My brother, my sister, double blessings upon you!" He pushed the women aside and bent down to press his lips to Ix Na's bare throat. He sounded out of breath, tipsy. What a display for the True Man of Chetemal, Gonzalo marveled.

"Look at them," Nachancan said, flipping away the cloth that covered the twins. He felt the boys' arms and legs and buttocks, sizing them up for the warriors they would grow into.

"Strong, handsome, big…. Big! My brother, I will send you my women, and you will give them more Castilàn babies."

Nachancan seemed to have spoken in earnest. There was an explosion of laughter and squeals from the women in the room. Ix Na handed the twins over to them so she could pull herself up and point a warning at him.

"Hun Halal," she said with a smile that too was in perfect earnest, "the only Castilàn babies in Chetemal will be these two and the brothers and sisters of these two. If you want more, you will have to let more Castilàn into your land." She put her hand on Gonzalo's as if to add that this Castilàn belonged to nobody but her.

A hush fell in the room. She had spoken before her husband, with her usual boldness, and she had spoken for him. Gonzalo could feel what everyone was thinking; Nachancan too, whom he knew would never tolerate such frankness from any of his women.

Yet he didn't try to lift his hand from under Ix Na's. In fact, there was something in her touch that shot to the very core of his being, like that day in Tulum when she'd taken his hand to lead him to freedom. That he was hers he had known from a long time, and that he was hers alone he had learned the first time Nachancan had offered him another woman and he had refused. Bold Ix Na was, yes, and he wouldn't want her any other way.

Awake and hungry, the boys began a loud crying. Nachancan looked at the parents with a good-natured shake of his head.

"You too are of one nature," he grumbled. "Selfish."

When the twins were eight days old, Gonzalo and Ix Na took them to Chetemal so the priests would read their future and prescribe names for them. Each holding a boy, they sat on the floor of the temple of Ah Cab while the old men took out their books of divination and carefully, slowly, turned the great folding pages of painted bark. At last the prophecy came.

These two, the books said, would be swift and powerful runners. Their names must be chosen from those of birds: Pa'ap for the brown jay, and Akil for the white crane. They would be loving, dutiful, agreeable sons. They would bring much joy to the House of Can. But then the words of the priests became obscure, their voices tinged with a gravity that put fear in the parents' hearts.

Though these boys so resembled each other, the books said, their lives would resemble none of those that had come before. In their childhood they would belong to the familiar world of their mother; before reaching manhood they would pass into the world of their father, a world of great upheavals. Nothing more and nothing clearer would the priests say. Eventually, sad and angry, Gonzalo put some jade beads in their hands and left the temple with Ix Na in a hurry.

Outside a crowd had gathered, eager to see the twins. The people of Chetemal seemed to have lost their hearts to the boys. A woman had brought a present of reed flutes, and some youths had made toy bows and arrows for them. Everyone wanted to be the first to look at them, the first to repeat the expressions of wonder his neighbor had uttered before. Even the staidest elders couldn't keep smiling, if nothing else at how one small face mirrored the other in its tiniest twitch and crease.

Not at all disturbed by the crowd, the boys snuggled peacefully in their blanket. They had nursed robustly that morning. How grand and lovely Ix Na looked, Gonzalo remembered, with one of them at each breast like one of those images of the goddess of Plenty from back home.

Surrounded by so much love, the new parents should have felt like a royal couple presenting their offspring to adoring subjects.

Instead they stood back, close together as if buttressing each other against a common danger. Damn those heathen customs of horoscopes and such nonsense, Gonzalo thought angrily.

When the crowd had had its fill of looking and praising, they returned to Xul Ha in an uneasy silence. They took their meals, then again Ix Na's bared her full breasts to the twins' hunger. Nachancan came in to ask about the names and the forecast. The names she disclosed, the forecast she shortened into the good news only.

Gonzalo was so vexed he barely spoke.

Nachancan too wanted his fill of looking at the boys. He dangled before them one of the toy bows, making all kinds of sounds.

"This one is Pa'ap, and this one is Akil... Am I right?"

Ix Na shook her head with a weak smile. "Pa'ap is the one with the brown strip of cloth around his wrist, Akil the one with the white strip. It was Ix Lolkin's idea."

"The priests chose good names," Nachancan said happily. "When they'll be old enough they will take also the Can surname."

He pulled on the string of the toy bow. "Ah Holkan, I can't wait to take these two hunting with us," he winked.

As soon as Nachancan left and the twins were again tucked into their crib, Ix Na dismissed everybody from the room, pulled down the door hanging and asked Gonzalo to sit with her. She made herself small in his arms. Together they watched the boys sleep.

Then she sighed. "My husband," she said, "the priests spoke plainly enough. You know it, and so do I."

She looked resigned. Her eyes seemed to see the years that would come, that must come as it had been predicted.

"Before our sons will reach manhood, the Castilàn will arrive and turn everything upside down. We cannot keep it from happening, and we cannot pretend it will not happen."

Gonzalo knew she was right. His mind ranged with a clarity that was unbidden and unbearable. He let himself imagine that this wasn't the mainland, still safe from the Spaniards, but one of the places that had already been turned upside down by the Spaniards and would never return to what it was neither in good nor in evil, since good and evil had been switched around forever.

He let himself imagine that his sons were only two more of the numberless half-breed children who swarmed around every trash heap in the islands—ragged, despised, fighting each other for a piece of bread while their mothers must work the cane fields or tend the pigs or lie with the soldier who'd raped them.

This was his world, he thought savagely, the world into which his sons would pass, as the priests had forecast, when the Spaniards would come. And yet Ix Na's world could be no less full of horror.

Once the boys would grow into the great warriors everyone wanted them to become, they would also become the captives most sought after by their enemies. They might end up on the sacrificial stone, their hearts torn out and their jaws worn on the arm of some Xiu chieftain just like the jaw he himself wore.

"*Etan,*" he breathed, saying her name as if it were an incantation against evil. "We cannot live in fear. We cannot raise our sons with omens hanging over our heads. Now we are here, we are happy. Never again will we listen to the words of those who say they own the future."

But the fear that his words wanted to deny was right there in his voice. And Ix Na, clinging to him, could only nod her own uncertain assent.

TWENTY-THREE

Only a year passed before the first of the upheavals forecast by the priests swept into the land like an ill wind.

Long ahead of the expected time, the twins had started to walk without help—surely, everyone agreed, a sign of that excellence that had been willed upon them even before their birth. According to native custom, they would be allowed to nurse until old enough to ask for the breast in perfect Maya-than. This was a prospect which concerned Ix Na but which Gonzalo praised. He was sure it was the richness of her milk which made the boys so healthy and strong.

With five children now growing in the Can household, Xul Ha had become a place of lively noise. The stretch of shore between the two houses was a playground full of the children's games and arguments, of their laughing and crying, of all the sounds that were the promise of abiding life.

Gonzalo was the most tender of fathers. It was he, not Ix Na, who fretted at the scraped elbow, at the sneeze in the middle of the night; he who badgered the servants if a strange dog scared the boys or if they let them wander off too close to the lagoon. Patient even when Ix Na's patience flagged, he looked after them while she rested or saw to her chores. She was both moved and mystified by this man who could return home after a day spent drilling troops for warfare and, once he'd hung his weapons on the wall, turn to whispering singsong into the cradle.

He loved the sight of them, handsome and quiet; the mystery of them, that bond that made them two and one at the same time; and the feel of them when something saddened them and they snuggled close to him for comfort, one under each arm, the flesh of their small bodies soft next to his own scarred one. In them he found completeness, the closing of a circle. Nothing made him prouder than his having become the protector of these two and of the mother of these two. Nothing heartened him more than the thought that upon him, upon his strength these dear ones would rely in times of danger.

The danger came not from the Xiu or other familiar enemies, not from the anger of the Gods, but from a remote and elusive source, like a murderer who travels a great distance to commit his crimes where no one will know him.

In the month of Cumhu a merchant's slave was found lying on the sand behind a warehouse on Chetemal's waterfront—drunk, it was thought at first, until his master came to rouse him and saw the blisters that covered him, as if sea worms had bored into his flesh and left slime oozing from the sores. The body, too repulsive to be buried, was thrown into the sea and the man forgotten, as he was just a slave.

About fifteen days later the man's master was found dead in his home, covered with the same blisters. Then the merchant's father had followed, then his wife and his concubines and his sons and his daughters. Within a few days a household of ten people was wiped out, and the house left open to looters who carried off the merchant's possessions. By the time the looters and their families were dying of the stinking sores in their turn, all of Chetemal was in a terror about this *maya cimil,* this easy death no one had ever witnessed before and even less knew how to stop.

First curers were consulted, and when they failed, practitioners of magic. Sacrifices were rounded up to appease whatever evil force had let this illness loose. In one village terrified neighbors shut all those with the signs of the disease into a house, with only food and water left every morning by the doorway, until one morning no one was left to take the food and water in. Finally, two *batabs* were sent to ask for help from Nachancan in Xul Ha. They brought along the one man who'd so far survived the mysterious illness, a thief sentenced to death but then pardoned in hopes that his recovery might explain what had spared him.

Gonzalo and Nachancan were in the kennel inspecting a new litter of hunting dogs when the two *batabs* were announced by a servant, who detailed the nature of their business. Irritated by the unexpected visit, Nachancan told the servant to turn the men away.

"Tomorrow," he ordered. "I know nothing about this illness they speak of. Forty-three people dead in a single street in a single day? Surely they lie."

Gonzalo was of another mind. The servant's account of what the visitors claimed was happening in the city awakened in him an all-too-familiar dread. "Do let them in now," he advised. When the two *batabs* prodded in the survivor, a young man who looked as if he would have most gladly avoided the attention, one look at his face pocked with small round scars told him right away what was that the twice-lucky thief had escaped.

His apprehension turned to panic. "Stay where you are," he shouted to the two *batabs.* The older one was coming to take Nachancan's hand "Don't touch him!" Frightened, Nachancan backed away.

The two *batabs* fell on their knees, crossing their arms in the gesture of supplication. The older one, who'd been denied the customary greeting of his lord, was fighting tears of shame like a newly-discovered leper. Even the dogs seemed to scent the presence of death, whining in discomfort.

"*Yumeh,*" began the older *batab*, addressing Nachancan with the ancient title of Father of his people. "A blight is on the face of the land. None of our forebears ever saw anything like it. Give us help.

Give us counsel."

"We have prayed," the second visitor said. "We have asked the Gods to tell us in what we have been remiss that we should be punished so. But there is just no answer."

At a loss himself, Nachancan turned to Gonzalo. "Ah Holkan, your actions tell me the Castilàn have a name for this blight."

"Yes," Gonzalo said grimly. "Smallpox."

Both *batabs* began to talk at once, pouring out questions and pleas. They seemed very much relieved to hear that Gonzalo knew about the *maya cimil*, as if this alone would put an end to it.

Gonzalo cried out his own helplessness above their voices. "Only a name, I have nothing more. The Castilàn too die of this disease, for no reason they can find." He nodded toward the young thief. "As for why he survived, the gods alone know."

There was silence, while the two *batabs* remained bowed in their grief and Nachancan stroked the puppy he was holding with an absent gesture, as if seeking comfort in the softness of the small warm body.

Piercingly aware that the two visitors may have brought the disease to Xul Ha, Gonzalo struggled to regain his calm and to pursue whatever facts could be garnered. What he wanted to find out first of all was where the smallpox came from, though he knew there was little good in that except the bitter satisfaction of learning where the fire had started while the house was already burning. What had happened to usher in such a disaster?

It had been a peaceful, prosperous year. There had been no contact with the islands, so that source could be dismissed. Trade had moved instead southward. Scores of canoes built of Chetemal's fine hardwood had left the piers to be sold in the Valley of Ulùa, whose broad river flowed among cacau plantations like a great vein pulsing with wealth. Back from Ulùa had come feathers, jade, and those beautiful vessels of cut marble made nowhere else.

With the overland routes Chetemal's merchants reached even farther than that. They went to the highland country of Cuautemàllan, to the lake of Nicarao; and, he remembered it, to those newest trading posts Nachancan had told him he'd established, soon after his wedding, in the southernmost lands. Those southernmost lands were the country of the Darién, where the Spaniards were.

He turned to the two *batabs*. "You said the man who found the dead slave on the waterfront was a trader?"

The two nodded. "He was the slave's owner. They had just returned with a load of gold and copper jewelry—"

"Kuna jewelry," Gonzalo finished. He smiled painfully. "I wanted to trade for some of it myself when I was among them..." He looked at Nachancan. "That is where this blight comes from. The Kuna have long been acquainted with the Castilàn, because of their gold jewelry."

"And is there nothing we can do?" Nachancan asked.

Gonzalo shook his head. "Very little. All trade with the Kuna must stop, in fact all trade with the south. All trade goods must be considered tainted, and no one must be allowed into the province."

"But that is impossible," Nachancan countered. "Trade is our mainstay. The people will starve even before they die of the *maya cimil*."

Gonzalo couldn't bear to look into Nachancan's frightened eyes. "Still we must try," he said.

After a moment Nachancan turned to the two *batabs*. "You have heard," he told them. "All I can do is shut us all in, just like those villagers you told me about. Let the traders know. Burn all they've brought in within the past month."

"Mind that no one touches any of it," Gonzalo said, "or anything that belongs to the dead and the diseased."

The two *batabs* stood up to leave. Nachancan motioned them to wait. "I will come to Chetemal with you," he said. "I too must pray to the Gods... and to the God of the Castilàn, if he will hear me."

In the temple of Ek Chuah protector of merchants, in the presence of a terror-stricken crowd, Nachancan stripped himself naked and, assisted by the priests who cooled his agony with fans, drew a rope knotted with *maguey* thorns through the flesh of his body, beseeching heaven to be content with his suffering and not demand more from his people.

His blood, gathered drop by drop, was smeared on the stone lips of the Gods. It was the *pa'chi* ceremony, the Opening of the Mouth. After him every man followed with the same warm, red gift. No god was left hungry, no power of earth, sky or underworld overlooked. The priests exhausted themselves listening to the sins that the people dredged up from their souls. For each sin atonement was made with enough blood and enough tears to move to compassion even the hardest among the Makers.

Then what trade goods could be found were seized, and all the possessions of the dead were taken from those who'd appropriated them. They were piled up in the main plaza and burned. Most gave them up willingly, many had to be coerced. It wasn't only stunned merchants who fought to keep the means of their livelihood. It was also the widow who refused to give up her wedding gown, and the old man who wouldn't let go of his dead grandson's playthings.

The rumor spread that Ah Holkan, the white *nacom,* was the one responsible for the *maya cimil,* and that *his* possessions should be confiscated and burned. Only Nachancan's presence prevented a riot. In many towns the order to destroy all foreign goods recently imported was received with an uproar of conflicting responses; in many places it was ignored altogether.

Gonzalo didn't go to the city for the *pa'chi* ceremony. His nature afforded him no comfort in prayer or penance. His task was to do for Xul Ha what Nachancan was trying to do for the whole province. Xul Ha must become a closed citadel where the House of Can, from which the whole province depended, might be sheltered from the plague and perhaps survive.

With Ix Na he inspected the corn pits and the storage rooms, assessing their supplies and the number of mouths to feed. Ix Na knew all about the inner workings of Xul Ha. Her help turned out to be his most valuable resource in a time of confusion that threatened to become chaos. She devised the rationing among the servants, according to how hard each one worked;

she charged trusted retainers with making sure no one cheated or stole; and she closed the main gate.

After that they could do nothing but wait to see if anyone showed the signs of the smallpox, the aches and chills that began mildly enough, until the boils appeared all over the body and one seemed to die merely of the stench and horror of the disease. Their only link with the outside world were the runners who came every day but stopped at the safe distance of the shore to shout their news, news that each time grew more and more dismal.

Despite all precautions, the smallpox was spreading. The lords, who could still command either loyalty or fear among their subordinates, had someone to bury them if they died and someone to nurse them back to health if they survived. The common folk could only rely on the kindness of their neighbors and this, because of the appalling ease with which the plague went from one to another, had all but disappeared.

The runners told of huts where only the dogs remained to guard the dead, of entire families cut down within hours of each other in their own hammocks. Whole villages remained empty, as if the Gods had taken a broom to the world. Those who recovered were scarred for life, and many were blinded. Even survival meant the birth of a maimed generation.

The new corn rotted in the fields, the canoes sat abandoned on the beaches. Priests couldn't be found to send the dead on their journeys with the proper rites. After a while the bodies were simply pushed with long poles into common ditches covered with lime. In one town a woman was accused of spreading the disease through black magic and hacked to death; in another, many were crushed when a starving mob sacked a corn pit. The simplest compacts of everyday life were coming apart. Nothing could hold, when a mother refused to go near her sick child.

Xul Ha was like a castle under siege. Shut in, living in fear, Gonzalo could feel the madness that was taking hold of him and of everyone else.

Nachancan, who since childhood had been trained to face death in war, in sacrifice, in the fangs of a jaguar, of this rotting death was utterly terrified. Some days he shut himself up in his rooms, refusing to let anybody in. He slept apart from his women in self- imposed abstinence, as though he'd bargained with the Gods to yield to them his pleasure in exchange for his life.

It was anguish for him to be unable to hearten his people with his presence. What pained him most was that his people were dying without knowing why. He understood death that one called upon himself because of his sins. Death that came for no reason was like a flogging given to a child by parents who won't tell him why he's being flogged.

Ix Na found little solace in whatever personal safety her rank granted her. Her composure began to give way to anxiety. She wouldn't let the twins out of her sight. She spent most of her time with them and with Gonzalo in their room at the core of the house. The merest whimper from the boys made her rush to their crib, then spend hours watching for spots or other symptoms. She wept bitterly for thosemothers who were mourning their dead children even as she thanked the Gods that one more night had passed and her own were still alive.

All of Gonzalo's feelings seemed to have pooled into overpowering rage. Even the numbing fear that took him when he allowed himself to think of Ix Na or his children dying was easier to bear if he turned it into anger toward the cause of his anguish—the men of his race, among whom he'd once counted himself.

They hadn't even set foot onto the mainland, he thought, and already the devastation that accompanied their coming had preceded them. They tainted everything they touched, as they had tainted those Kuna trinkets of copper and gold among which a new way of dying had come ashore. It wasn't enough for them to have exported to the New World wholesale slaughter and the bonfires of the Inquisition; they brought the very ills that rotted their blood. Despite all he was doing to keep them away, they'd managed to worm their way to his own door, cutting a swath hundreds of miles long through people whose existence they didn't even suspect. Not that these people were unacquainted with catastrophic scourges; but at least until now they had died of their own.

Twenty days into the siege the man who'd brought in the two *batabs* from the city came down with the signs of the smallpox and was dead by the following sunrise. The servants gave in to panic. If Nachancan hadn't threatened them with an even swifter death than the *maya cimil,* not one of them would have been persuaded to carry the body out and bury it in the *cacau* grove.

One month into the siege the runners brought the news that Natohcan was ill and Ekuneh was doing what he could to assist him. After lingering for a week, Natohcan died calling on the Gods to curse the race of the Castilàn, even though a Castilàn had once saved his life. Ekuneh recovered, but his face would bear forever the disfiguring marks of the smallpox.

In the room at the core of the house time passed between boredom and fear. Ix Na whiled away the hours weaving. The two boys strained at being confined, and she was snappish with them and with Gonzalo. A month and a half into the siege Nachancan's youngest concubine died. It was hard to tell whether Nachancan had loved the girl. As he and Gonzalo watched the terrified servants make again the trip to the *cacau* grove, Gonzalo heard him whisper that to see a lovely young body turn into a mass of festering sores was enough to strip all sweetness from lovemaking for the rest of one's life.

Two months into the siege the food supply began to run low. Nothing had come into Xul Ha for all that time, not the corn or the fish and the game that the people always brought in tribute. The servants were allowed to pick whatever could be found on the trees and vines, and even to help themselves to the honey and the *cacau* that no trader was coming to buy.

In the room at the core of the house Gonzalo, Ix Na and the boys had become prisoners. Nachancan came by less and less often; so did Ix Lolkin, who used to bring White Feather and Ahau Can to play with the twins. The disease threatened not only their lives but also the bonds that tied their lives together. Sleepless nights passed without a word spoken or a touch exchanged.

Two months and a week into the siege Akil woke up one morning hot with fever. When Ix Na shook Gonzalo awake, Gonzalo became acquainted with a sickening dread he hadn't known even an hour before battle. Nothing became possible except panic. Screaming at being separated from his brother,

Pa'ap was taken immediately to another room. They could hear him call and call. His small voice shrill with fear tore at their hearts.

Ix Na paced around the crib like a mother jaguar around the pit that traps her cubs. Gonzalo held Akil's hand. There was no sign of blisters, but both knew it was a matter of hours. Ix Na began to say they must look for a curer. There was one in a village not too far away who was very highly thought of, he'd once saved a woman everyone had given up for dead. Gonzalo made no answer, not wanting to encourage her unreasonable hopes. Perhaps the best thing to do, he told himself, was to bring back Pa'ap, lie down all together and quietly wait for the end like all those other families he'd been told of.

Ix Na, now on the verge of hysteria, kept talking about looking for a curer, prodding him to go to that village she'd mentioned, to that man who could work miracles. The boys must not die, they just mustn't, and wouldn't he hurry up and go, the village wasn't far, please, not far at all—

"Wife," he blurted out, "I would let myself be flayed alive if that could save my children. Don't tell me where I must go and who I must look for."

Ix Na stared at him as if disbelieving that he could give up so easily. Then she accepted what she'd known all along. Her shoulders sagged, and her mouth stayed open for a last word that never came. Gonzalo didn't move. Ix Na walked toward the doorway, then back, then turned again as if trying to find her way. Finally she sat down, her arms slack against her body. Akil opened his eyes and moaned. She dipped a cup in the vat and handed it to Gonzalo. Gonzalo lifted the boy's head and held the cup to his lips.

The light burned on in the room. They didn't know whether it was still daylight or not, whether it was still raining or not, whether it was time for the morning meal or the evening meal or what else. Akil's small hand in Gonzalo's was limp and sweaty. In the next room Pa'ap had cried himself to sleep. Ix Na sat glassy-eyed under a niche in the wall where an image of Ix Chel stood covered with flowers that had long wilted. When she heard Nachancan coming, she told one of the servants to stop him. But Nachancan went in. He looked haggard.

"My sister," he said. "I am tired of waiting alone. Please let me stay here."

Ix Na began to protest, then she burst into tears and Nachancan took her in his arms.

Grieved for the way he'd snapped at her before, Gonzalo looked up at her, asking with his eyes to be forgiven. Her tears were good, washed away the silence between them. She and Nachancan came to sit by the crib with him. She peeled a fruit for Akil, coaxed him to eat it and was comforted when the boy didn't refuse it.

As the Gods willed, another night passed and another dawn came. Akil's fever rose. He was racked with chills, but there were still no blisters. Toward midday he fell asleep. Ix Na went to stay with Pa'ap in the next room for a while. Gonzalo nodded off and Nachancan had the women bring in some food.

Then, as suddenly as it had come on, the boy's fever broke. Ix Na and Gonzalo could not take that as a good sign, not yet. Numb as they were, it seemed only that the Gods were playing in their cruel and inexplicable fashion. In the afternoon Akil was well enough to ask for Pa'ap. Torn between granting his wish and trying to keep at least one boy safe, Gonzalo and Ix Na argued again. Finally they gave in to the twins' unhappiness, and Pa'ap was reunited with his brother. The boys fell asleep in each other's arms. Now the parents were sure they would both die in each other's arms.

Instead, not only did Pa'ap not catch his brother's illness, but Akil kept on getting better. There was no more fever, and there had never been blisters. Whatever illness that was, it had never been the *maya cimil*. As soon as Gonzalo and Ix Na at last accepted their good fortune, a pall seemed to lift from Xul Ha. The women of the household couldn't stop mouthing their wonder. Like the Hero Twins of the sacred Book of Counsel, Akil and Pa'ap had defeated the Lords of Death and had left the Dark House unscathed, to show the others the way out. Exhausted, relieved and thankful, both parents let themselves believe in the impossible.

Some days later the runners came with the only good news they had brought in months. The *maya cimil* seemed to have moved on from the province, certainly from the city of Chetemal, where the people were beginning to put their lives together again. Revived by the news, Nachancan and Gonzalo went to the city.

Along the way, as the two litters passed through the country scarred by the pits of the common graves into which so many had gone, Gonzalo felt as if he'd just stepped out of the Ark after the Flood. But surely Noah had known only gratefulness at being alive in a world cleansed of mankind's sin, not sorrow for all the lives lost or blighted. No one came out to greet them; no children played; no women walked to the well with their water jugs. The rain had battered the empty houses, ruined the seed for the next planting. For many there would be hunger and no shelter.

It wasn't much better in the city. Many traders had gone bankrupt, others had profited beyond decency. Refugees squatted in the houses left vacant, causing no end of quarrels with their neighbors. Boys left orphans had turned into thieves, and girls swelled the crowd of cheap whores who made their living on the waterfront. Only the Gods knew how long it would be before peaceful, prosperous Chetemal would remember what it had been like once.

Nachancan went into the men's house to see who among his chieftains had survived, and to begin to bring a measure of normality back to the province. Gonzalo made a first count of those who'd been left alive among the warriors. He wasn't relieved to surmise that for each man killed or blinded by the smallpox someone had been removed in the same way from the enemy's ranks. But it was most comforting to see the men welcome him with the old love and trust, which not even a Castilàn disease had been able to destroy.

It was a long day, bittersweet with reckonings and reunions. The tasks that loomed ahead were huge. Nachancan put together a first edict: those traders who'd profited from the *maya cimil* must, on pain of execution, contribute a good portion of their new wealth to the common reconstruction. The people had risen from disasters before, he said to Gonzalo. Indeed they were so intimate with Death that they'd made it one of their most familiar deities, its fleshless jaw gaping on every temple wall, roadside shrine and child's toy.

Ix Na had been standing by the doorway, listening to their footsteps. Gonzalo took her under his arm, kissed her eyes wet with tears, and went in to his children.

BOOK THREE

THE WARRIOR AND THE REBEL

TWENTY-FOUR

MARCH 1517

The news came from Ecab. Only a few years before it would have caused the world to stand on end and the people to gape at the arrival of beings too powerful to resist. Now that one of those beings had been living among them, perhaps the people could face the intruders unafraid.

It was a sweltering day toward the end of the dry season.

Under the thatched roof of the pavilion built between the two houses, not even the nearness of water brought relief, or the great round fans that the servants waved with a drowsy slowness. Flat jungle lay under flat sky, not a thing stirring. The canoe that approached was at first only a black wisp against the molten silver of the lagoon, and the voices of the oarsmen calling out for permission to dock sounded as if muffled by layers of soggy cotton.

The man was escorted to the pavilion with the respect due to his rank but also to some sorrow that made his steps falter. Ix Na and Ix Lolkin began to collect the children, ready to melt away with them as they always did when official business came to call. But Nachancan and Gonzalo motioned them to stay, as if knowing already that this particular business touched everyone's future.

The man's name was Nakehya. He asked to be received both as a chieftain of proven lineage sent by the True Man of Ecab and as a father who'd just lost his only son. He was made welcome and comfortable. His attention was all on Gonzalo. He peered at the mixture of familiar and foreign in Gonzalo's appearance, the jade earrings with the blue eyes, the tattoos with the hair on face and body. As he looked at him he shook his head in grieving wonder.

"So, so… You were among the ones who were found on the beach, who were offered up in the temple… Is it to take vengeance for those captives that your companions have come? Is that why the *Kashlàn* have taken my son?"

Nachancan traded a quick glance with Gonzalo. Immediately both understood. "*Kashlàn*, Castilàn… They came to Ecab? When?"

"Ten days ago... We fought them, we wounded many. But they took my son and another captive." His words were strained with desperation. "My son is only a boy. I will give you all I have if you return him to me."

Gonzalo's frame had stiffened. Nothing in it showed his turmoil. The Spaniards were at the gates of the mainland. They had at last discovered this place where until now only two white men had survived—he and Jerónimo de Aguilar. As a castaway and a slave, he'd hoped for no other news; as Nachancan's war captain, he'd pushed it out of his mind. What would he do now, he asked himself, as a husband and a father? First he must hear the tale Nakehya had brought all the way from Ecab. Quietly he motioned the man to speak.

Ten days ago, Nakehya began, the first light of dawn off the coast of Ecab had revealed two immense ships heaped with white sails and bristling with the faces of strangers in strange clothes. Immediately the townspeople had put out canoes to meet the strangers. The first one aboard was Ah Yuntun, the True Man of Ecab, with more than thirty of his men. Among them were Nakehya and his young son.

They had been allowed to wander about the ships, to touch and smell and look. The Kashlàn seemed well disposed. They had given each man a string of jade beads, a lavish gift which to the givers was a mere trifle, for they owned whole coffers of the stone of life.

For the people of Ecab that had been a day of wonders. The Kashlàn too could hardly hide their surprise, but more like hunters' dogs that have stumbled upon a fat prey.

Throughout that first encounter Ah Yuntun had been all smiles. But he knew where he wanted the newcomers. He'd signaled that they should come to his town, where he would provide them with everything they needed. Persuaded by that show of goodwill, the Kashlàn had gone ashore. On this day Nakehya and his son were among the warriors Ah Yuntun had placed behind some hills with orders to destroy the newcomers. A large force had been lying in wait all morning. True to his reputation, the ruler of Ecab would not stop to ask strangers what they were doing in his land.

"We were of many minds," Nakehya said. "I and others thought the Kashlàn should be received with the same generosity they had showed us. But Ah Yuntun does not take chances. And he remembered the warning sent a long time by someone named Ah Holkan..."

He grasped Gonzalo's hand. "If not for that warning you sent us, I wouldn't have come to ask for the life of my son. Now I have seen you, and you truly seem one of us. You truly seem our friend."

Gonzalo remained silent. Then he told Nakehya to go on. Nakehya paused to drink a sip of corn water and resumed his tale.

The Kashlàn approached the hills where Ecab's warriors were waiting. When they were close enough, Ah Yuntun ordered to attack. The archers wounded thirteen with their arrows; then the whole body of warriors rushed out, and a fierce combat began.

With the advantage of surprise, the men of Ecab might have left no Kashlàn alive. But if the men of Ecab knew whom they were fighting, they didn't yet know that they were fighting with sticks and stones against gunpowder and steel. After the first shock the Kashlàn quickly recovered, and let loose the terrifying power of their weapons. Smoking, deafening thunder erupted. From nowhere the eyes could discern, it cut a swath through the massed warriors, mowed them down like weeds in a cornfield, scattering blood and torn flesh.

"At that moment," Nakehya said, "we just didn't understand anything anymore. We just ran. I, my son, our best warriors, our own ruler and king... all turned into children by the Kashlàn." Another pause followed. After ten days Nakehya's voice still shook at the memory of what the Spaniards had done to the bodies and the minds of the people of Ecab.

Again Gonzalo prodded him to say what happened next.

When Ecab's warriors regrouped, Nakehya discovered that his son had disappeared and another boy was also missing. He couldn't find them among the dead. He went to look in a temple that rose near the hills where the battle had been fought; perhaps the two boys had taken shelter there.

What he found out instead was that the Kashlàn had sacked the temple for everything made of gold that was there—images of the Gods, ceremonial headdresses, sacred offerings, everything. What wasn't made of gold they had smashed to pieces. As he was told by a terrified priest who'd been hiding in the temple, along with these lootings the Kashlàn had also taken Nakehya's son and the other boy.

Exhausted, Nakehya signaled he was done and reached thirstily for his cup of corn water. From a pouch he carried he took out the gift he'd received aboard the Kashlàn ship, and put in on the mat for his hosts to look at.

Nachancan picked it up. He liked the round, polished beads, but he couldn't decide what they were made of. "Surely jade never felt so light," he wondered, "as if only the outer skin of the stone were left."

Gonzalo knew what it was. A look of contempt came on his face.

"Glass," he said to himself, in Spanish because there was no glass in this land. "Green glass marbles strung together." He shook his head. "My brother, you're right. This is not the stone of life. It's just a child's cheap toy." No wonder the Spaniards were so generous, he thought, handing out treasure by the pound. Already they had bought thousands of human lives with the same hollow currency.

He gave the string back to Nakehya. "Keep it if you wish. Were it mine, I'd give it to my sons to play with."

"My lord, I no longer have a son," Nakehya reminded him with urgency. "What will the Kashlàn do to him?" He was asking not only whether the Kashlàn would sacrifice the boy as it was customary with captives, but whether the Kashlàn's treatment of war captives went beyond anything he'd ever considered customary.

Gonzalo felt a kind of dark amusement. Once, as a prisoner of Ecab's people, he too had wondered whether they would simply put him to death or else put him to death in some way he'd never imagined.

"I think the *Kashlàn* will have a far greater need of your son alive than dead," he answered. "When I arrived in the islands I learned that our first need was for someone who could be taught our language. Without an interpreter, we might as well have arrived on the moon...

Young people were usually chosen, for their quicker mind."

Nakehya's face brightened with hope. "Then my son could have been taken for this reason?"

"And the other boy, yes," Gonzalo said. "Two minds are more reliable than one."

Nakehya breathed in. "You must certainly know," he said, a bit relieved. "You must know."

Nachancan shifted on the mat. "The people must be told of this coming..." He addressed Nakehya. "When the Kashlàn left Ecab, could you see in which direction they were headed?"

"Westward," Nakehya answered, "towards the towns of Canpech and Chanputun. They kept close to the coast always, at times too close to the reef."

He lowered his face. "In my heart I hoped the ships would get too close to the reef, sink with everyone aboard."

Nachancan could no longer sit. He got up and paced under the dappled shade of the pavilion's roof. Little White Feather followed him giggling like in a game of catch as he went about restlessly.

"I don't know how fast these ships are," he mused, "how long it will take them to reach Canpech or Chanputun."

He turned to Gonzalo. "But there is no doubt they will reach Canpech or Chanputun, is there, Ah Holkan?"

Gonzalo shook his head. "That gold the Castilàn found is the perfect bait. They will not rest until they have more."

Nakehya made the supplicant's gesture. "My lords, I beg you to let me stay here until news is received. I will sleep among your menials. I will eat their leavings."

Gonzalo didn't wait for Nachancan's response.

"You will stay in my house," he said. "You will eat at my table."

How strange it felt, he thought while Nakehya blessed him, to play host and protector to a man from the same people who'd once put him in a cage to fatten for their next feast.

In all of this Ix Na had been silent. Gonzalo glanced at her. He saw how she was holding the twins, as though they were about to be taken from her as

Nakehya's boy had been taken. For the first time ever he read in her eyes something he neither understood nor liked—mistrust of him, fear that he might harm her and her children. For the first time ever she seemed a stranger, one who would think of herself and her children before thinking of him. She excused herself with the men, and went to see to Nakehya's lodgings.

❖   ❖   ❖

Something had come into Ix Na's soul. That night while she prepared Gonzalo's bath and then brought him his meal she seemed watchful, coiled. All the questions she had never asked him about his former life began to slip into her talk, one here one there as if prompted only by a woman's desultory curiosity. She would not be content until Gonzalo gave her the full answer, if she had to pry it from him with a woman's subtle perseverance.

"What were you among the Castilàn?" "Less than nothing."

"Could you become something among them now?" "Only if I did one thing. I need another cloth." "Only if you did what?"

"Only if I erased from my mind that you are my wife, that you are the mother of my children, and that I love you and my children."

"Please hand me that dish. Did you like the chili sauce?" "Same as I always did, why?"

"I used a different kind of chilies. Would you be higher among the Castilàn than here?"

"No, and I wouldn't be happier, either. I'm bringing the boys back. You know they don't like to sleep in the next room."

After the questions, a strange silence settled in her. Gonzalo lay down, listening to the noise she made as she went about the room. It seemed that she would never come to bed. He caught her staring at herself in her mirror, like a woman who worries for the first time about what her age is doing to her looks.

When she finally lay down beside him her eyes seemed fathomless. He made love to her slowly, attentively, as if coaxing her to remember that she

279

trusted him and that she could open herself to him. But she remained muted and distant. He heard her toss about until late.

In the morning he made up his mind. Today he would go to Chetemal with Nachancan and Nakehya to discuss the coming of the Castilàn to Ecab. He would not reveal his decision to her. But sharp as she was, she may have understood already when he told her that today he would wear the full *nacom* regalia.

If she did understand, she gave no sign. She helped him put on the heavily knotted *esh,* the belt with the *hadzab,* the jaguar-skin collar, the armbands and legbands, and the feather headdress. He must look good to her; her face shone. The twins gaped in awe and a little in fear at this tall proud man who was their father.

In the men's house, after Nakehya gave once again his report, it was a seething of opinions. It wasn't hard to believe Ecab's envoy; but it was hard to believe that the Castilàn posed a clear and immediate danger not only to Ecab but to Chetemal and to all of the mainland.

So what if these strangers went snooping around the coast? If Ah Yuntun had been able to throw them out of his town, any other ruler could do the same, and none better than the ruler of Chetemal. In vain—and Gonzalo knew just how in vain—Nakehya reminded the council that he'd witnessed the power of the Castilàn with his own eyes. Until the people of Chetemal witnessed it with their own eyes, he knew such appeals would remain fruitless.

When Gonzalo stood up to announce his decision, the mood among the men packed together in the brutal heat of the day changed. The danger must be real indeed if Ah Holkan now proposed to travel to Canpech and Chanputun, where the Castilàn ships were headed, and fight the Castilàn there himself. Even if force would not be needed, Gonzalo added, he would still go, to advise the rulers of Canpech and Chanputun on how best to deal with these strangers who were no strangers to him.

Nachancan put himself unreservedly on Gonzalo's side. So did Gonzalo's warriors; far from being cowed by Nakehya's description of the Castilàn' weapons, they seemed inflamed by the challenge, boasting that they would pile Castilàn heads on the skull rack. Nakehya too was happy at that announcement. He would travel with the Can army, and be there when those who'd kidnapped his son would come ashore again on the western coast.

With this support behind him, Gonzalo hurried home to Ix Na in the mood of a lover bringing to his beloved the gift that would make everything good again between them. Once she would learn that he was ready to battle the Castilàn, her doubts would be nothing, her fears would be dust. He could feel her in his arms already, made soft again by her faith in him. How he would tease her, he thought, for thinking he could ever abandon her and her sons to the Castilàn's mercy.

He walked in engrossed in plans with Nachancan and Nakehya. He couldn't talk to her right away. While she welcomed them he knew she was listening to them. As soon as she would grasp what they were talking about, she would look at him with the same approval as her brother. He could do nothing more to prove his loyalty to them both than pit himself against the men of his race, who came as murderers and robbers to a land that had never invited them in.

Nothing came from her. After she grasped Gonzalo's intentions, her manners became even more strained, her silence more inexplicable. Puzzled, he sounded her for a response with a few good- natured prods.

"Woman, leave us and send for my wife. I haven't heard from her all night."

Ix Na smiled with a coyness unnatural for her. "It's good that you haven't heard from her," she replied evenly. "What would you do with a woman's opinion?"

Gonzalo's puzzlement became annoyance. He took his leave of Nachancan and headed for his home down the path along the lagoon, knowing that she must follow.

Calling him, waving their arms, the twins ran out to greet him—a flurry of love to melt his heart, their hands tangled around his neck, their faces sunk in laughter against his chest, and Akil's toy blowgun poking sharply his side. For them he would fight not just the Castilàn who'd come with two ships but the whole Castilàn fleet. Why was their mother so hard to persuade?

He went into the bedroom and put the boys down. They wanted to play, so he let them chase him around with the blowguns as if he were a quarry in the jungle. The boys blew small clay pellets at him and climbed on him when he lay spread out on the floor, a dead jaguar felled by their true hunters' aim. Only then, tired and happy, did the boys go to bed, without complaining.

Where was Ix Na? he wondered. What could she still be doing in her brother's house? This time he was sure he would have harsh words for her. Her husband was about to go to war, and this woman behaved like an ill-disposed slave. At last he heard footsteps, and her voice while she told her waiting women they could retire. As he waited to see her come in, Nachancan appeared instead.

"What is it?" Gonzalo asked. "What's wrong?"

Nachancan hesitated. "My brother, nothing's wrong." He smiled to lend truth to his answer. He went to look at the boys in their bed, picked up the toy blowgun they'd left on the floor. "I've been thinking about this expedition," he said with another flicker of hesitation, "and it seems to me that it's not necessary for you to risk your life there when the Castilàn are still so far away. The rulers of Canpech and Chanputun command many warriors. Mok Kouoh, the True Man of Chanputun, is well known for his warlike disposition."

He paused. "Ah Holkan. Your decision to go shows a truly brave heart. The people could not think more highly of you for it, or I. But I have made up my mind that my *nacom* is too valuable to have him fight in such a distant place."

It took Gonzalo a while to gather the meaning of Nachancan's words. It was like trying to find out what lies under the surface of clouded water; the more he dipped his hand in, the cloudier the water became. Nachancan's behavior mirrored Ix Na's. Some unspoken hostility had grown in the two people he most loved and trusted. Then there was a beginning of clarity. Ix Na had lingered in her brother's house instead of following him home. Something had passed between them in that time, something that had made Nachancan change his mind.

Without a word he strode out to find her. A servant told him she was in Nakehya's room. Into that room he went; who knows, he told himself hotly, perhaps even Nakehya had changed his mind for the same incomprehensible reason.

"Wife," he called her.

Ix Na was startled, and ashamed that he should be confronting her in the presence of the guest. Her hands were shaking.

"What is this all about?" Gonzalo asked. "First nothing but silence from you when I give you news that should please you, now this change of heart from your brother."

He took her arm. "What did you say to him while you were with him just now? I know he listens closely to your words. What words were there this time that you saw fit to hide from me?"

She wanted to shrink away from him, pulling to free her arm.

Then she looked him straight in the eyes to show she was sincere. "My husband. The journey to the west is an unnecessary risk... but not in the way Hun Halal has explained. He and I know you can fight the Castilàn and survive. The risk is another..."

She interrupted herself for a moment. Nachancan came in and was about to say something, but she stopped him. Nakehya, the unexpected witness, could only sit and watch, confused.

Gonzalo let go of her arm, but that was all the reprieve he was willing to give her.

"Go on," he pressed her. He had understood what she meant, but she must say it to his face.

"The risk is ... that once you will be close to the men of your race, once you will see them..." She sounded panicked, as if chased by an enemy. "It's in the nature of men to want to go back to their homes. It's just there in their hearts." Her eyes welled up.

The anger Gonzalo had held in check crowded his heart. For a while he couldn't speak. His eyes darted at Nachancan. Now he too seemed a stranger. Something was very wrong, he thought. Some crossing of intentions had made the three of them as cagey toward each other as thieves trying to split booty. For the first time since he'd come to Chetemal he felt caught in a trap.

"My brother," he said, "my wife," and he made both words full of meaning. "If I told you that I intend to travel to the west regardless of your fears, would you stop me by force?" His face became hard and closed. "Would I find out that for the past three years I have been a prisoner in your house?"

Overwhelmed, Ix Na could only shake her head again and again. What Gonzalo had said seemed enormous to her. She had never thought he would react this way. But the rift had been open. In desperation she turned to her brother.

"Hun Halal... please tell my husband he's wrong. Please explain to him the only reason why I came to speak to you... the only reason why I don't want him to travel to the west." Then she turned slightly her back, in the gesture women made when they had no business being in the presence of men, and fell silent.

Nachancan too looked sad and puzzled. "The only reason is the love she... the love we both bear you," he said, and even in his anger Gonzalo could appreciate the effort it was taking Nachancan to expose his feelings, something he found hard to do with his own children. "When you find something precious, a piece of jade that falls into your hands unexpectedly, or some of that gold your people values so much... would you not hold it tightly, would you not refuse to let go of it?"

Gonzalo's turn had come to claim his good faith, which had gotten so tangled up in misunderstanding. "But that is just the reason why I want to go." His voice rose with the urgency of his heart. "I know that precious thing you speak of. I have it here in this house, and I don't want the Castilàn to steal it as they stole the gold from Ecab's temple."

He turned to Ix Na. "You question me, you doubt me. I could think of no better way to crush your doubts than to fight the men of my race. But if staying will do that instead, then I will stay. I will do what will convince you. Name it, but not behind my back."

The pain in his last words was too much for Ix Na. She tried to say something, then she almost ran out of the room.

Nachancan was silent. Gonzalo looked at him. "I will do what will convince you," he said again. He then addressed Nakehya. "I will give you an escort of warriors to Canpech and Chanputun. You will go without me. I ask you only that you send back a runner as soon as you have any news."

Nakehya could only nod. Gonzalo muttered a good night and turned around to leave. Nachancan reached out to stop him, but Gonzalo had nothing more to say.

The bedroom was dark. She lay in bed with her back to him, stiffly. He undressed and lay down. For the first time since he'd known her he wished he were away from that familiar presence that all of a sudden made him feel bridled, tied down. It was such an ugly thing to feel.

The hurt rankled for days. Gonzalo spoke to Ix Na only about everyday private matters, and to Nachancan only about everyday public ones. He spent a great deal of time out of the house, drilling his warriors. It was a bad time for war games. The heat alone could utterly exhaust a man; the warriors grumbled openly at the relentlessness of his orders. He drove them as though they were in a real war, the war against the Castilàn that he'd had to give up.

Being in the dark as to what the Spaniards were doing made him ever more unhappy. He tried to speculate how long a captain would let his men go thirsty before venturing ashore for fresh water, or before giving in to greed for more gold. At times he daydreamed about the two ships, following them in his mind as they negotiated the uncharted waters of the New World, two leaky nutshells full of raw newcomers like he himself had been. After a while he came to understand what wounded him the most about having to stay away from his countrymen—he would not be able to prove that Ix Na's doubts were unfounded.

She had talked of him simply seeing those men and their ships, but that seemed like such a paltry temptation. Could it be that just a familiar sight had the power to wipe out three years of happiness, to destroy an allegiance he thought he'd pledged once and forever? All this he would not know. Not for now, he told himself, because the day and the hour of his knowing would most surely come.

A month went by in such a strained mood before the runner returned from the west. The first thing he told was that the Castilàn had been beaten from the land so badly that they might never come back, may the Gods be thanked.

"I wouldn't start burning incense yet," Gonzalo muttered.

Nachancan pointedly ignored him. Not a word passed between them while they listened to the man's report.

The Castilàn had reached Canpech fifteen days after leaving Ecab. They had come ashore with all their weapons and with some wooden casks, and they'd stopped at a well to fill them with water. While they were so engaged, a group of Canpech's *batabs* had come out to meet them peacefully and to find out where they came from. But although they were asked repeatedly whether they were Castilàn, they didn't seem to understand that word.

So the *batabs* of Canpech had decided the best thing to do was warn the visitors that they must leave. They had some slaves make a pile of firewood, and two bands of warriors draw close. The *batabs* ordered the slaves to set fire to the wood, then motioned to the strangers that they must leave before the fire burned out. To explain what would happen if they didn't, the warriors began to sound their trumpets and drums.

Frightened already by the rough welcome they'd received at Ecab, the Castilàn had needed no persuading. Immediately and in good order they'd withdrawn to their ships, with nothing to show for this second encounter but some casks full of well water.

Nothing so peaceful had taken place at Chanputun, where the ships had anchored a few days later. Again the Spaniards had gone ashore for fresh water; again they didn't understand when they were asked whether they were Castilàn. But Mok Kouoh, the True Man of Chanputun, whom Nachancan had said was known for his warlike nature, had wasted no time. When the Castilàn had decided to stay the night, his answer had been an army of warriors that outnumbered the strangers two hundred to one. At the break of dawn the warriors had fallen on them with the sole intention to kill.

The battle had lasted an hour. Unlike the people of Ecab who'd fled at the first salvo from the guns, the warriors of Chanputun remained undaunted by the Castilàn's thunder. Mok Kouoh had given orders to keep charging. As one line of men was felled, another rushed on with spears, darts, stones, bare hands. It was as if they had made up their minds to fight first and be terrified later.

The Castilàn were surrounded. More than fifty had been killed, two had been taken prisoners, and most of those who'd survived had received two or three arrows. They could do nothing but retreat.

Ranged closely together, they broke through the encircling warriors who still came at them in full force. Wading, swimming, they reached the boats and jumped in. The boats started to sink. As they rowed away, the survivors clung to their sides, half drowned.

At this point one of the Castilàn's ships had come to their help. Only after the cannon was fired from her bow into the thick of the warriors, after the surf was awash with red, did Mok Kouoh's men give up the fight. They dragged the two Castilàn prisoners where their companions could see them and summarily cut their hearts out, tossing their bodies among the hundreds of Chanputun dead that lay on the shore. From what anyone could tell, more Castilàn would die on their way back, of thirst if not of their wounds, because in their run for the boats they'd left behind the water casks. As for the Castilàn captain, whom the warriors had in vain tried to capture, he was bleeding from several wounds and most certainly would not reach the islands alive.

Here the runner ended his tale. He seemed very satisfied with it.

"Lord Mok Kouoh," he said, "has charged me to bring both of you his gratitude for having warned him about the coming of these strangers. He hopes that soon he might meet the True Man of Chetemal and his *nacom,* the one they call Ah Holkan."

Nachancan nodded. "Yes, yes, of course. We too hope to meet him soon."

"What of Nakehya's son?" Gonzalo asked.

"He couldn't be found, or the other boy," the runner said. "Either they were kept aboard the Castilàn ships all the time, or else they were dead before reaching the west. Nakehya left Chanputun the same day I did. He seemed a broken man."

After some silence, Nachancan motioned to a retainer. "See that this good man be paid for his services. Give him three pieces of jade." The messenger bowed while the retainer escorted him out.

Gonzalo was the first to speak, and none too gently.

"So, my brother. For the second time we just sit and listen to news of war. We must be thankful for the good fighters of Chanputun. It's our luck that they could push back the Castilàn for us, even if at the cost of so many lives."

Nachancan's eyes flashed. "I will not talk about any of this while your heart is still bitter."

"How can you expect my heart not to be bitter?" Gonzalo countered. "I should have been at Chanputun. Perhaps there wouldn't have been so many dead."

He threw up his arm, as if to stop the desperate charge of warriors rushing toward the smoking muskets. "Outnumbered two hundred to one and still they were able to break through!" His voice carried disbelief and anger. "Do you see now? Do you understand what sort of an enemy the Castilàn are?"

Nachancan said nothing.

Gonzalo was pacing back and forth. "If only one soldier returns to report what he saw... the gold, the cities and everything else, in a year or so they'll send another expedition. More fake jade, more muskets, more cannons. If that expedition fails, they'll send another and another."

"And mind you," he added, "if that one soldier is smart enough to remember that he and his friends were called 'Castilàn' over and over, then they will know there are Castilàn in this land. They will remember the ship that was wrecked years ago, and this time they will come looking for her survivors... They will come looking for your war captain, my brother, the one who stayed behind while others fought."

Nachancan's face was grim. "And what do you think we will do when they come looking for my war captain, Ah Holkan?" he asked. "Do you think we will tie you up and hide you where they can't find you? No. Three years ago you came to us of your own will, and you have remained with us of your own will. You chose to become one of us even before we tried to make you into one of us."

He took Gonzalo's arm in the gesture that had always meant solidarity and love. "It's true that we fear to lose you. We fear to lose you to the Xiu, to illness, to the bite of a scorpion... or to the Castilàn. Truly, it never made any difference."

Something inside Gonzalo's soul gave way, a dam of feelings that had been there too long. He thought of Ix Na, of the days of enmity the two of them had endured. It was time for all of that to heal; or else, he told himself, the Castilàn had already wrested him back into their grasp.

He put his hand on Nachancan's. "My brother, let there be no more anger between us. Let everything be as it was. The Castilàn took twenty years to come to this land. May it be another twenty before they return."

Smiling at last, Nachancan nodded. He noticed that Gonzalo seemed to be in a hurry to leave. "Go to her," he said. "She has news for you. She couldn't tell you in the midst of all these other things. So she told me... the night she tarried in my house to beg me not to let you go to Chanputun."

Gonzalo looked puzzled. "You are to become a father again," Nachancan said, and he was barely finished when he was alone, listening to Gonzalo call her loudly as he dashed out of the room.

TWENTY-FIVE

In the month of Muan of the following year Ekuneh took a wife. She was plain, dutiful and tightfisted. Ekuneh was very pleased with her and with having fulfilled his duty to marry.

The wedding and the four days of feasting took place at Xul Ha, where Nachancan had offered to host his half-brother and his bride. Among the guests was Mok Kouoh, who a year before, after confronting the Spaniards in the first pitched battle fought in the New World, had expressed his wish to meet Nachancan and his *nacom*.

Mok Kouoh was a short, heavily scarred man who took great pleasure in recounting how he'd driven the intruders away from Chanputun after riddling them with arrows like practice targets.

Among the men there was hardly another topic of conversation but the coming of the Castilàn and their defeat. Mok Kouoh started to laugh again each time he told of how the two Castilàn they'd captured called their companions in the boats before they were cut open, and how his warriors had smashed the Castilàn's water casks and danced around them as if around great smashed skulls.

He also made no mystery of being disappointed by Gonzalo. He seemed to have expected a white demon seven feet tall and entirely covered with hair, which was what every Castilàn had become in Chanputun's year-old folktales. In turn, Gonzalo found Mok Kouoh a loud-mouthed, rough-mannered man who didn't seem to like or to understand much besides warfare.

According to Mok Kouoh, it hadn't been easy for him and his company to travel to Chetemal for the wedding. He claimed that they'd been followed and harassed by Xiu scouts, and that at one time he'd thought they would be attacked before reaching Chetemal's border. Often during his stay he hinted broadly that he should be given protection when he and his company would return to Chanputun. Nachancan didn't want to displease his ally, but he found the request improper. He made no promises, hoping his guest would change his mind.

On the eve of his departure Mok Kouoh presented his request again, this time addressing Gonzalo directly and in such terms as to make clear that the future of his friendship with the House of Can depended on having an escort of Can warriors traveling with him at least part of the way back home.

Even more irritated than Nachancan, Gonzalo was forced to decide that they couldn't afford to lose Mok Kouoh's favor over the minor inconvenience of an unforeseen march through the jungle. The number of warriors of the escort was agreed upon, and the time of departure. That evening Gonzalo went home with Ix Na and the children before everyone else, so they could be together for a few hours before his leaving.

Their third son, Temah, had been born six months before. Remembering how upset they'd been to hear the twins' horoscope, Gonzalo and Ix Na had not taken him to the priests. Instead they'd named him themselves, with a happy name that only spoke of how pleased they were by his arrival, and they'd refused to seek any omens, good or bad, for his future.

Temah was not as big or strong as the twins, nor as lusty in his suckling. At first Gonzalo feared there might be something wrong with a baby who was willing to wait for his milk without awakening Ix Na in the middle of the night with his crying. He'd been ill as an infant, too, making them worry for a long and harrowing month that he would never reach babyhood.

It was clear from the start that Temah would never be like Akil and Pa'ap. It was clear also that Akil and Pa'ap would never accept him into their society of two. Even when left alone, Akil and Pa'ap still had each other; Temah seemed to have learned quite early that he must rely first and foremost upon himself.

For this reason Gonzalo loved him of a deeper love. Of the twins he could be easily proud, because they were perfect. This little one instead moved him with his determination to come through despite his weakness. No one had invoked the sacred books at his birth, no one had pressed toy weapons in his hand. Gonzalo and Ix Na had no idea what his calling would be, though they could tell he would be no warrior like his brothers. The twins' lives had been all but foreordained. Temah's destiny would be entirely his own, like his father's had been.

Ix Na put the baby to bed, in the twins' roomy old crib, then started to gather the things Gonzalo would need for his trip, with the usual exception of his weapons. She was very much annoyed by the prospect of this unexpected separation from him. As she went about the room she spoke a steady stream of uncharitable remarks about Mok Kouoh and his bad manners.

She'd kept some of the stoutness of her last pregnancy, and her breasts were full again with the nursing of the baby. Her hair now reached almost to her feet, and when she piled it up she seemed to be wearing a crown made of black shiny metal. Now more than ever she looked like the mistress of Xul

Ha, the one female to whom all other females of the household must answer and, on occasion, the males as well.

A few days before, one of the young waiting women who'd come with Ekuneh's bride had caught Nachancan's eye, and he'd manifested an intention to add her to his concubines. Ix Na had observed the young woman closely, and found in her the signs of a nature much too vain to bring happiness to Nachancan or anyone else.

Right away she'd warned him against taking such a person into the household, where he would see her only when the fancy struck him while she would have to put up with the newcomer during the rest of the time, the time of her pregnancies and the time when Nachancan would tire of the novelty. So Nachancan invited the vain young beauty to his bed once during the revels for the wedding, made her a present of jade rings and reluctantly gave her up.

"You will be careful," Ix Na was now telling Gonzalo as she hunted for another pair of sandals to add to his baggage; and it wasn't a plea, it was a demand.

Gonzalo bowed his head, smiling. "Yes, my Lady Ix Na. I will be careful." He handed Pa'ap a small cake from the wedding feast and watched the boy split off one exact half for Akil.

"They call Mok Kouoh a great warrior," he said with sarcasm, "But his fears of Xiu lying in wait for him are almost those of a coward. He has an escort of his own, yet wants more men around him..."

"And he's inconsiderate enough to ask his hosts for them," Ix Na put in resentfully. She went to the doorway to call a kitchen servant.

"I'll have them pack plenty of that dried venison you like. Please don't go to bed yet." The two of them lay together awake for some time. She clung to him as though he were leaving for war, not for a journey, and fought sleep until late.

Mok Kouoh had decided to set out before dawn, to spare himself some of the morning heat. His armed escort went ahead, mixed with the Can warriors. While everyone else walked, Mok Kouoh sprawled at ease in his litter. He dictated the schedule. Sometimes he decided to go hunting, and left Gonzalo and his men waiting for hours in the blistering heat of an improvised campsite.

If at first Gonzalo had been annoyed at having to serve the ruler of Chanputun, for the rest of the journey he was galled by a constant grudge that sharpened every smaller discomfort. He hadn't been ordered around in a long time. Since then he'd grown a pride of his own, and pride seemed to make everything harder.

The farther away from the coast they moved, the more inhospitable the country became. Towns and villages grew more and more apart, more and more lost. Next to these impoverished villages

Gonzalo could see the relics of a past that must have rivaled the past of Athens and Rome.

Huge broken buildings, as beautiful as they were strange, lay smothered in the rampant roots of the jungle. The flagstones of roads that hadn't been traveled in centuries emerged here and there. Mazes of courtyards and vaulted rooms echoed with the scurrying footsteps of monkeys. Who had ordered those palaces to be built? Gonzalo wondered. How long had all that eerie and magnificent rubble stood abandoned? It made for a melancholy passage, like tramping through a forlorn graveyard where the graves bore no names.

He was cheered by one of his men reminding him that tomorrow they would reach the point where they'd agree to leave Mok Kouoh and start back to Chetemal. He had appointed this man, one of his battle guard by the name of Ah Dzan Chi, as second-in-command for the journey. The man had first come to his attention during the battle at the ruined temple. Since then he'd become one of Gonzalo's most trusted warriors and a good friend as well.

Ah Dzan Chi was young, smart and eager, sometimes perhaps too eager. He had been ridiculed since childhood because he had lost some of his teeth in a bad fall. Gonzalo suspected he had molded himself into so determined a warrior to silence his tormentors. He was still known as Ruined Mouth, but now the name was spoken without any of the old scorn. He never curried Gonzalo's favor, like some other men, and he never asked for more recognition than he deserved. With only a little more experience, Gonzalo was sure Ah Dzan Chi would make him a good second *nacom*.

"Those Xiu warriors the True Man of Chanputun spoke of must have been ghosts," Ah Dzan Chi mocked, nodding at Mok Kouoh ahead.

Gonzalo let out a sound of derision. "One more day," he grinned, "may the gods be loudly thanked. One more day and you will be returning to your lovely Bird Woman."

Ah Dzan Chi turned his head to hide his look of longing. "She does sing like a lovely bird," Gonzalo praised, remembering the girl who'd delighted the guests at Ekuneh's wedding with her beautiful voice.

Ah Dzan Chi's face fell. "If only her father didn't think so little of me," he said. "I just wonder whether I'll ever have the courage to ask for her again... whether I'll ever do anything to make the old man approve of me."

He was silent after that. Gonzalo wanted to say something encouraging, but he knew that Bird Woman's father, Nachancan's chief tribute collector, had refused the young man's proposal to marry his daughter.

The last day of the journey seemed to Gonzalo almost pleasant. Nothing could ruin his good mood. He would have carried Mok Kouoh on his shoulders to hasten his deliverance. By now they'd advanced so far into the hinterland that all signs of human presence had faded. If the rest of the province had been lived in and then abandoned, this savage heart of the jungle seemed to have always been a desert.

Mok Kouoh spent the evening of that last day arguing with Gonzalo that he should accompany him a little further on, at least for another day. Gonzalo, who'd rather expected this final vexation, had a hard time holding Mok Kouoh to his word without compromising his friendship. At last Mok Kouoh relented. The following morning the goodbyes still managed to be polite and formal.

Gonzalo anticipated an easy trek back to Chetemal. Even without his order the men put themselves at a jog; they all must be as impatient to get home as he was. If common caution didn't forbid it, they would have started to sing as they marched.

They'd been gone for only a short time when out of the jungle the Xiu rushed at them before a bird could shriek an alarm. Two men next to Gonzalo were cut down while their hands were still on the handles of their *hadzabs*.

They just seemed to peel away from him, leaving him to face the enemy on his own. All he could see as he dodged down to reach for his weapon was that Ah Dzan Chi was not one of the dead. In an instant it became all too clear that the Xiu had waited for them to be separated from Mok Kouoh to attack them, and that Mok Kouoh was being attacked at the same moment.

There was no time to think about Mok Kouoh's predicament, only time for each man to try to save his own life first. Having been so taken by surprise, Gonzalo could barely keep the Xiu in check. He couldn't even tell if he was outnumbered. Panic made it seem so, panic that had him swing around blindly like a novice. Most of all he had to struggle for control of himself. His mind had been too much at ease, too full of homecoming thoughts. Mok Kouoh's fears had been sound, and he had disregarded them too quickly. Even if he came out of this ambush unscathed, he would certainly have to consider the value of humility.

The Xiu who had him engaged was fast as a cat. The only blows he could land on him smacked on his armor of brine-toughened cotton. He kept after him, chased him around a gnarl of naked roots until the Xiu stumbled. When the Xiu stumbled he sank the *hadzab* into him once and was done.

Before he could regain his breath another Xiu leapt at him, with no more warning than the tip of a spear slicing the air a finger's width away from his forehead. Trying to parry, he managed only to shatter two of the blades of his *hadzab* against the shaft of the spear. Black glass flew into his enemy's face. It was enough to blind him for a few instants, and for Gonzalo to find unprotected flesh.

Looking back he saw that Ah Dzan Chi had remained at the far end of the column with perhaps twenty warriors. Unlike Gonzalo, Ah Dzan Chi was having no trouble holding the Xiu at bay. He'd already gotten rid of a good number of them. But instead of forcing his way through to where the thick of the fighting was, he kept retreating more and more, waving his men along.

It took Gonzalo only a moment to understand. At the first break Ah Dzan Chi would run back to where they'd left Mok Kouoh. This meant Mok Kouoh would get the help Gonzalo needed just as badly; but that was their duty, and in his heart Gonzalo praised the wisdom of his second-in-command.

In his anxiety to check on Ah Dzan Chi's actions, he wasn't paying enough attention to his own. He'd been pushed into a bad spot, cut off from his battle guard. The Xiu had him with his back against a tree. As he struggled with all he could muster, the thought of being captured alive sank in as a terrifying possibility. He began to shout for the closest of his warriors. Even though he could see that the man was himself holding out with the strength of desperation, he called him at the top of his voice, fear pounding inside him. Wasn't he their *nacom*, wasn't he the man they'd been trained to protect with their lives?

Two of the battle guard managed to shake off their attackers and come to his rescue. It was too late. Before he could push away his enemies with the ruined edge of his *hadzab,* the Xiu landed a blow to his head that sent him staggering backward, blinded by a pain that ran through his whole body like the clang of a great bell. His two men jumped in front of him, kept him from a second blow that would have finished him off, and cried out to him that he was safe.

Before he lost consciousness he could glimpse Ah Dzan Chi and his warriors slipping away unseen, as if sopped up by the green folds of the jungle. He hoped they would not be followed, he hoped they would reach Mok Kou-oh in time. As he felt somebody's arms come between him and the ground where he was falling, he told himself that if Ah Dzan Chi succeeded, Bird Woman's father would have to take good notice of the young man who'd asked for his daughter in marriage.

For a long time the world was a shadowy place of half- remembered nightmares, a thick sleep he kept giving in to even when it was time to wake up. Sometimes a word would pierce through to him, sometimes a touch that he wanted to answer but couldn't.

His head throbbed unbearably, as though he were lying next to the great *tunkul* drum that called with the booming voice of the Gods. There was always a great fatigue, an overwhelming heaviness in his limbs. All that his mind could scan was pain followed by pain; and a feeling of dread, of being trapped in a place he must leave at all costs.

He came to at the prompting of another kind of pain, a sharp biting stab in the flesh of his arm. The first thing he saw upon opening his eyes was the face of an old man, crisscrossed with wrinkles and cowled in a white head-dress—an old worried face he vaguely knew, he must know. He became aware that he was in a bed, perhaps his bed.

He could see his arm, where the biting pain came from. Something else he could see was the rattlesnake the old man was holding to his arm, both fangs fastened in like needles and blood running from the two punctures.

Terror brought life back to his body. He jerked his arm away, shaking it furiously. The snake's fangs remained planted in his flesh and the blood ran and he tried to scream as the old man held him down. The old man pulled the fangs out and showed him that the snake was dead, saying something he couldn't grasp. When he saw Ix Na's face bending over him he began to moan for her help.

She hushed him, stroked his chest, gently pushed him back down on the bed. "It's just to treat you, it's just to bleed you and make you well again."

Her voice was muffled by the cotton bandage around his head, but he heard every word. His body relaxed and his mind found reassurance. Her he could trust. If she was there, everything was all right.

The old man was waiting, concerned. Now Gonzalo recognized him; it was the *ahmen* who'd helped Ix Na in childbirth. He wanted to nod; but his head—now he remembered also why it was bandaged—felt like a stone pressing him down. He held his arm out, let it hang limp for the old curer. When he felt the rattlesnake's fangs bite again into it, he grasped Ix Na's hand and closed his eyes.

He could tell she'd been crying. He wondered for how long, he wondered how long he'd been unconscious.

"The men..." he whispered with a great effort. "Ah Dzan Chi..."

"Ah Dzan Chi is well," she answered. "He keeps a vigil by your bed every night. You lost nine men. Mok Kouoh lost more, but he has reached Chanputun safely."

He wanted to say something else, but she stopped him. "None of this matters now. You must be well again. Nothing else matters."

He squeezed her hand and didn't try to speak anymore. She was right, he must be well again. Dying was unthinkable, for how could he go where she wasn't?

There was another long interval of pain and of heavy, helpless sleep. He could not move, he could not speak, he could barely see or hear. Even his thoughts were crippled by hallucinations that sometimes mixed present with past, this life with what had once been his life. He saw himself back on Hispaniola, standing in front of a gallows where he and his shipmates had been made to watch a woman being hanged; only the woman was Ix Na, in the dress he'd last seen her wearing, her arms bound with rawhide and her broken neck dangling in the noose. He couldn't even scream out his horror or his relief when it vanished, leaving him soaked in cold sweat.

Ix Na was his only link to reality. To keep his mind alive she spoke to him all the time, told him everything that went on. She brought the children to him and made him squeeze her hand if he understood what he heard, until the world had again a meaning and a shape. When he held her hand he had no doubt that through it came the strength to survive. If he'd ever thought the children could claim a greater share of his love, he'd been wrong. She was his life.

He didn't notice Nachancan's absence for many days, and when he asked her about him, he realized she'd been bearing not one but two burdens of worry. Enraged to learn of the ambush in the jungle, Nachancan had left with a full army the day after Gonzalo had been brought home wounded. Ekuneh had joined him. All-out war with the Xiu had resumed, after the four years of peace that Gonzalo's victory at the ruined temple had secured. The latest runner said her brothers were well and holding their ground behind the stockade that protected the border.

Gonzalo felt helpless. His recovery was taking a long time. He understood how close to dying he had been. He feared that he would never fully recover, that he would spend the rest of his life half blind and half deaf as he was now. But Ix Na was there to take the fear away. Day by day, untiring, she made him better. She coaxed, showed, commanded if she had to. And then one day, when the curer announced that Gonzalo's wound had closed cleanly and he was out of danger, she gave him the news she'd kept for him.

Ah Dzan Chi had just finished recounting what had happened after he and his men had rushed to help Mok Kouoh during the ambush in the jungle. He told how he had managed to wedge his men between the Xiu and Mok Kouoh, how they had encircled the enemy the way Gonzalo had taught them, and how they had finally routed them. But when they'd gone back the joy of their success had been dashed by the sight of Gonzalo lying on an improvised stretcher with his head split open.

It did Gonzalo good to listen to the young man. Ah Dzan Chi spoke with a pleasant modesty of his intervention, which had in fact saved Mok Kouoh's life. He even made Gonzalo laugh when he told how Mok Kouoh, instead of expressing gratitude for the help received, had berated at length both him and Gonzalo for paying no attention to his warnings and for abandoning him in the middle of a wilderness crawling with bloodthirsty Xiu.

Public praise must be paid to this young warrior who'd behaved so bravely in an unforeseen predicament. Gonzalo promised Ah Dzan Chi that as soon as he'd be well he would honor him in the men's house in Chetemal. Before leaving the men's house, he advised him with a smile, it would be a wise idea to walk over to Bird Woman's father and present again his suit for the girl.

When Ah Dzan Chi left, Ix Na sat down by Gonzalo's bed with a cup of *cacau* she'd whipped for him. She looked at him without any of the agonizing worry that had pinched her face in the past long days. She knew he would soon be whole again.

"I have news for you," she said then quietly. His senses rallied to attention.

Five days ago, she began, when Gonzalo was still too weak to sit up in bed, two messengers had come to Xul Ha, one on the heels of the other. The first came from Tulum, the second from Chanputun. In the absence of Nachancan, she had decided to receive them herself instead of sending them to the *batabs*.

"You had to know first," she said. "The *batabs* might be in charge of the affairs of state when Hun Halal is away, but you are the most important man here after the True Man."

Gonzalo's forehead crinkled in surprise under the lighter bandage he now wore. Left without the aid of both her brother and her husband, the only surviving female of the House of Can had taken it upon herself to rewrite Chetemal's customs according to her own wisdom. Not that he was displeased; but he had to wonder what the *batabs* would say when they'd learn of this novelty.

"All right," he said. "Tell me this news."

She put down the cup. "The Castilàn have returned." Her face showed none of the distress that had been so plain a year ago, when she'd begged Nachancan to keep Gonzalo away from the men of his race. This time she knew she would not be abandoned.

Gonzalo had expected this news. It made him think of the way hounds keep returning to a den they have scented. He told himself he mustn't start to think like a trapped fox.

She gave him first the news from Tulum—rather, from the island of Cuzumil, which lay within Tulum's rule and where the Castilàn had landed this time. The runner had come not from Ah Kin Cutz but from the priests of the temple of Ix Chel. Upon sighting the four ships that made up this second expedition, the priests of Ix Chel had all fled into the jungle. Two of them, too old to run, had hid in a cornfield. These two the Castilàn had found and brought to meet their captain. With the captain were Nakehya's son and the other kidnapped boy, who were now the Castilàn's interpreters.

Ix Na was silent for a few moments, taken by some thoughts of her own. "You did say the two boys would become the Castilàn's tongue. I am glad that they are both alive... The runner said they wore Castilàn clothes and were called by Castilàn names. The name of Nakehya's son sounded like Mel Ko, and the name of the other boy like Hu Lian."

Gonzalo tried to nod. It was still hard for him to make full movements without pain. "Julián is a Castilàn name. The other name could be Melchor. I had a shipmate named Melchor. He was one of those sacrificed by the people of Ecab."

Ix Na's face became grim. "It's a bad omen for the boy to have been given the same name as your companion. It means he too will be sacrificed."

Gonzalo made no reply. Like her people, she was given to seeing connections where he saw nothing but coincidence, especially in that business of names. She was always careful not to cross him with too much devotion to her ways, but he knew she'd never given them up for his sake. There were news she must finish telling, he reminded her.

Speaking through Nakehya's son, the Castilàn captain had given the two old priests of Cuzumil some green glass beads, and he'd sent them to summon those he called "the *caciques* of the town." The old men had left, but had never gone back. When the Castilàn had finally understood that nobody would come to parley with them, they'd returned to their ships and sailed away. Ah Kin Cutz had been told about all this, but his reaction was not known.

Gonzalo's mind went to Jerónimo. He remembered the old quarrels with him, Jerónimo's staunch conviction that the Spaniards would soon come to rescue them, and his own rebuttals that the Spaniards had better things to do than look for common castaways. If Jerónimo was still alive, it must have been maddening for him to learn that he'd been only a few miles away from Spanish ships, from that rescue whose thought had kept him alive through seven years of captivity. Jerónimo had been right all along, Gonzalo thought. Worse, Gonzalo was no longer a common castaway but a man many a Spanish captain would go out of his way to find. Suddenly he felt keenly that sense of danger he'd tried to ward off before.

Ix Na noticed his face. "What's wrong?" she asked.

He made an effort to smile. "Nothing, *etan*. It's nothing. I was thinking of how long it would take for ships of that size to travel down here from

Cuzumil... With a good wind, in this season... three days at most." He seemed to shiver. "So close."

Ix Na was silent. For a while both of them were silent, as if intent upon listening to a faraway sound.

"Well, but they didn't travel here," Ix Na said then. "The runner said they sailed west, like a year ago. I wonder why."

Gonzalo sighed. "Because to sailors a half-known route is better than an unknown one. What happened after they sailed westward?" he asked. "You said you spoke also to a runner from Chanputun. They must have landed there again."

"Not there but close by," she answered. "At a small town where no one had ever seen Castilàn before. That must be why everybody ran away and left the town to the Castilàn for three days."

Gonzalo pulled himself up on his elbow. The abrupt movement made him dizzy, but he was too angry to care.

"What are you saying? A few old priests on Cuzumil might go hide in the bushes, but not the neighbors of people who fought back the Castilàn with their bare hands!" His head swam with passion and with the effort to speak. He would not lie back down under Ix Na's hands.

"It was four ships this time," she said. "And also, when the people of the town sent out warriors, the Castilàn used those great weapons you call..." she faltered after the name, "cannons, yes?... cannons, and those other weapons you call muskets and crossbows. They killed more than two hundred warriors with those weapons, Ah Holkan."

"And how many Castilàn died this time?" he asked. "Seven."

"Seven! Against more than two hundred on the other side!" With his fists clenched, he refused to understand.

"Deserters, cowards," he damned Chanputun's neighbors. "Cannons and muskets didn't stop them before. Where was Mok Kouoh in all this?"

"Still traveling home with you. He was told about it when he got there, but by then the Castilàn had left."

Gonzalo seemed to calm down. Perhaps, just perhaps, Mok Kouoh's absence could acquit his subjects in that small town that had never seen Castilàn before. But their flight was a bad omen. He imagined the Castilàn camped at ease in the deserted town and his blood rose again. It was the islands all over again. A burst of gunpowder, and hundreds of grown people scattered like terrified rabbits, leaving everything behind. There was something obscene in that, he thought. No human being should be made to cower that way. It was something that scorched him with the will to fight to his last breath.

"Damn my head," he muttered, giving in to the pain that was starting again. "When did the curer say I can leave this bed?"

"In about a month."

"That is impossible. A week's too long already." He shifted for a more comfortable position. "Let the *batabs* know about this news you told me," he said. "Tell me right away if there are any more news. I was quite careless this time," he reproached himself. "I must stay whole for my beloved countrymen. I must stay healthy to throw them out of my land. This is one place the greedy bastards will not touch."

Ix Na, her back turned to him, stopped what she was doing.

She could hear in his voice a determination that was beginning to sound like an obsession, and that frightened her. Then she spoke no more, and drew the door hanging behind her.

TWENTY-SIX

For a year after that there was no more news of the Castilàn. Again it was as though they'd sprung out from a nightmare and then had vanished, leaving no other trace of their coming but the graves of those they'd killed.

Around the borders of the province the war with the Xiu dragged on. As soon as Gonzalo recovered, he and Ah Dzan Chi went to join Nachancan, who was still entrenched behind the stockade. The enemy were stubborn, the heat fierce, and tempers among the men short. Supplies had to be brought from Ekuneh's town, and if the porters were delayed the men went without food. From Ekuneh's town came also their only curer, a man sorely tested by the many wounded or sick with the innumerable diseases of the jungle.

Gonzalo saw Ix Na and the boys only a handful of times, whenever he could persuade himself to leave Nachancan, trek back to Xul Ha and spend a day or two with his family. During those visits there was barely time for him and Ix Na to fill each other in with news. But there was never the time to lie together, since she was adamant about the abstinence required of a *nacom* in times of war, convinced that it was most unwise to break that rule.

One time, however, he came home too tired of fighting, too tired of sweating and bleeding and sleeping on the ground and eating old corn and watching the daily batch of prisoners being cut open. He told her angrily that jaguars mate only once every two years, not men, then he took her despite her protests; and all the while it took him to be finally, savagely satisfied, in his mind he kept defying anyone to prove that a warrior would get bad luck if he touched a woman, if he reacquainted himself for a few hours with all that was the very opposite of war.

Afterwards, Ix Na said nothing. But she looked sad, which made him briefly sorry he'd forced her. It was only when he returned to the jungle that he saw the wisdom of that rule. The hardness of heart needed for war seemed to have left him. He ached too much with the memory of those few hours of sweetness. A man could be driven insane trying to be a husband, a father and a warrior all at once. There must be a separate time for each thing, and he understood why Nachancan had never gone home since the start of the war. After that he didn't go home again. Painfully, doggedly, one dead enemy at a time, he remade himself into the single-minded machine that he must be in order to stay alive.

Seeing that the fighting at the stockade had turned into a deadlock, he persuaded the others to help him in a plan which once again demanded that they abandon old ways for new ones. Whether because of the difficult terrain or because of some ancient taboo, these people never waged war at night. But Gonzalo had decided he would lead a night sortie to the back of the Xiu camp, pin the Xiu against the stockade, and cut off their escape. Ekuneh, if not Nachancan or Ah Dzan Chi, took some coaxing. This breach of customs seemed too much. War was bad, he argued, but war outside the accepted rules was a sin.

Too impatient to bother with diplomacy, Gonzalo reminded Ekuneh that a breach of rules had allowed him to defeat the Xiu at the ruined temple and save Ekuneh's life. So, cowed more than convinced, Ekuneh agreed to do his part in the night attack.

With only Ah Dzan Chi and the best of his men, Gonzalo started out before dawn. At an unguarded spot he climbed over the stockade and began the slow, stealthy march through the jungle. There was barely enough light, and they must be utterly silent. But that wasn't too hard for a man who'd once escaped at night from a cage where he'd been waiting to become somebody's Sunday meal, and his warriors were the flower of the Can army, soundless and sure as the great spotted cats with which they shared their land.

Easily and quickly they reached the back of the Xiu camp, got rid of those who were asleep without waking up one of them. Then Ah Dzan Chi gave the signal to light the torches. Gonzalo and his men fell onto the unsuspecting enemies and subdued them even before Nachancan and Ekuneh arrived to finish the job. There were so many captives that they had to use the Xiu's own hair thongs to tie them all up. Among them were also the two Xiu *nacoms,* whose rank would make them first at the sacrificial stone. It was a complete triumph.

Now at last they could leave the border to the guards and go home. As always, only one Xiu was allowed to go free as a messenger of defeat. This time Gonzalo made sure the messenger would say clearly the name of the one who'd defeated him: Ah Holkan, the white *nacom,* the brother of Hun Halal of the House of Can.

When they entered the gates of Xul Ha, followed by the long train of bound captives, a great crowd came to cheer wildly. So many offerings, so much to please the Gods with, and peace once again.

Never had Gonzalo ridden more securely the tide of success. Finally he belonged, as he'd always wanted to, and as a cherished member. He lingered at the gate for a long time, with Ix Na and his children beside him, basking in the glory of the day.

When a week later Ah Dzan Chi invited him to his wedding to Bird Woman, he went as the guest of honor, the highest man in the land after the

True Man. He sat down to the wedding banquet among people who loved him and whom he loved, and told himself that something good, something right had come into his life the day he'd traveled to this place he could no longer leave.

❖   ❖   ❖

Ix Na, not the retainer who usually announced visitors, came to tell him there was a man who wanted to see him, a man whose name she couldn't pronounce properly but which sounded like Jerónimo de Aguilar. She looked so upset that Gonzalo made her repeat what she'd said to make sure he'd understood, and even then he shook his head, because she couldn't possibly have pronounced the name right, it couldn't possibly be Jerónimo de Aguilar.

Nachancan that evening wasn't there. He had gone to a nearby town on official business, and wouldn't be back for some days. Gonzalo had taken his bath and had remained in his hammock eating his supper, watching the twins play and listening to Temah try out new sounds in the crib set by Ix Na's loom. Nothing in that peaceful evening, the first cool evening they'd had in months, could have prepared him for this garbled news that jolted him in his whole body as if someone had rammed a fist into his stomach.

"Who is this man?" Ix Na asked as she followed him. "His dress his so ragged you couldn't tell him other than a slave. He says he comes from Tulum, with a very important message."

Gonzalo strode on so fast she could barely keep up with him. "Do you remember the other Castilàn who was with me in Ah Kin Cutz's house? The one I asked Nachancan to ransom from Ah Kin Cutz? I never told you his name... if that's the name I think I just heard."

The visitor was sitting cross-legged on the ground by the main gate, with the two oarsmen who'd rowed him there, also slaves from Tulum, from what one could tell. His canoe, pulled ashore on the bank of the lagoon, was a poor-looking craft that must usually transport firewood or other kitchen supplies. His hair was close-cropped. He wore a ragged cloak and a worse loincloth. He was barefoot, and carried his rope sandals tied to his belt. Bundled up in a corner of his cloak was a dog-eared book. It could be none other than Jerónimo. It was Jerónimo.

Gonzalo stopped in his tracks, as if he'd just seen Lazarus called back from the grave. Without warning, in this blessedly cool evening, he was being confronted by a ghost dredged up from the most unpleasant corner of his past.

For the moment Jerónimo seemed to be plainly astounded by the place he'd come to visit. Wide-eyed, he observed the two stately houses rising along the shore, the humming beehives and well-tended *cacau* trees, the sturdy whitewashed huts where the servants lived. Gonzalo could almost read his mind. As someone who in this land had known mostly Ah Kin Cutz's grubby courtyard, Jerónimo had never suspected that anything made by heathens could be so lovely.

When they caught sight of Gonzalo, Jerónimo's eyes included him in their sweep of the surroundings as one more object of wonder; it was only a moment later that they clouded over with condemnation, the old unmitigated condemnation that had begun the first time Gonzalo had ever approved of things native. Only this time the frown was deeper than ever, since this time Jerónimo could see that Gonzalo had himself become a thing native.

But then he must have remembered some good news that offset his displeasure, because he jumped to his feet and spread open his arms as if expecting Gonzalo to embrace him like a long-lost friend.

"Brother Guerrero!" he cried out, "may the Lord and His Blessed Mother be thanked for letting me find you alive and well!" He was out of breath with genuine goodwill and overwhelming excitement.

Gonzalo drew back, nearly bumping into Ix Na who followed at his heels. Jerónimo's Spanish, though broken by the many years of Mayathan, sounded alarmingly strange to his ears—stilted, unnatural, a foreign tongue. He didn't know what he would do if Jerónimo came any closer. Fortunately Jerónimo didn't; he dropped his arms and then just smiled and smiled, as his hands went to the prayer book tucked in his cloak, to the faithful talisman. He looked over Ix Na without much interest, as if she were only a minor hindrance, then returned his whole attention to Gonzalo.

"They told me you'd become a principal man in this tribe, but I could never imagine... this," and he waved his hands around. He looked at Gonzalo's clothes, but the contrast with his own rags didn't mortify him in the least, as though he deemed it nothing more than a temporary difference soon to be corrected.

At length Gonzalo realized he must let him in. He mumbled, "Well, Brother Aguilar, welcome," and showed him to the porch. Ix Na, who couldn't understand a word they were saying, seemed pained with confusion, and when Gonzalo asked her to bring something to eat she stood there for a good minute before she could bring herself to leave the two men.

The twins stopped playing, curious about the visitor. Temah, who'd sat up in his crib, ceased his dreamy warbling. If Jerónimo had looked at Ix Na perfunctorily, he now glanced at the three children with visible embarrassment, only because their presence could not be ignored.

Gonzalo chose a bench in the shade of a flowering tree and sat down leaving plenty of space between him and Jerónimo.

"So," he began awkwardly, "I'm told you bring important news. Indeed it must be, if you were allowed to travel all the way to my house."

Jerónimo's hands were gripping the tattered covers of the prayer book with impatient joy. "From this day on, Brother Guerrero, I am free to travel wherever I please, and so are you. The Lord has heard my prayers. He has delivered us from the hands of the heathen."

Then, before Gonzalo asked anything, he let everything out in one headlong speech. "Two days ago our Christian brethren came to the island of Cuzumil. A glorious expedition, the pride of our beloved country, with Captain Cortez as its leader. Do you remember him from Hispaniola? I do, and quite well. He is now a man of importance, and yet he went out of his way to look for us, because he heard our plight and he was moved to compassion for us. May God grant Captain Cortez all that his heart desires!"

He opened his prayer book and took out a small piece of parchment. "But here, Brother Guerrero. Here is the letter Captain Cortez sent to Tulum, to the man who was once our master."

Ix Na was back with a servant who carried a dish of fruit, meat and *cacau*. She motioned the servant to leave the dish on the bench, then dismissed him. She looked anxiously at Gonzalo.

"My wife," Gonzalo said, "please sit here with me." He showed her the piece of parchment. "I have news from the men of my race."

Ix Na said nothing. She glanced at Jerónimo with a look almost of threat, as if warning him to mind what he was doing. Then she spotted a stool near Temah's crib, and there she sat, stiffly.

Gonzalo opened the letter and read it out loud.

"Gentlemen and brothers, here in Cozumel I have heard that you are captives in the hands of a *cacique*. I beg you to come to this place at once, and for this purpose I have sent a ship with soldiers, in case you need them, and also a ransom to be given to those Indians with whom you are living. The ship will wait for you for eight days.

Come as quickly as you can, and you will be welcomed and looked after by me. I am staying at this island with five hundred soldiers and eleven ships in which I am going, God willing, to a town called Chanpoton."

Gonzalo made an effort to hide how he felt, then he asked himself what was the use of such an effort. This was precisely the day he had awaited so long, the day he would finally be able to tell the Castilàn how he felt about them and their glorious expeditions. His hands began to tremble around the crumpled piece of Castilàn parchment they were holding.

He looked again at the letter and shook his head to himself. Cuzumil had become Cozumel, Chanputun had become Chanpoton. Over twenty years ago don Cristobal Colón had come to the conclusion that the land he'd stumbled upon was not India, yet everybody kept calling its people Indians, lumping them all together as if they had no names of their own that were worth calling them by.

Bent forward, Jerónimo was waiting for a response. Gonzalo returned him the letter. "Thank you for the news,

Brother Aguilar. What will you do now?"

"I will leave with the ships, of course," Jerónimo said. "And if God grants me that I should be of any help to Captain Cortez, I will serve him loyally to the end of my days. But you, Brother Guerrero?" he asked urgently. "I've come to take you with me. There will be just enough time for us to travel to Tulum and then to Cuzumil. Captain Cortez sent some green beads with the letter, and in exchange for those not only did lord Ah Kin Cutz set me free, but he also gave me the canoe and the two rowers you saw."

"Lord Ah Kin Cutz..." Gonzalo said. "What did he do when the ships came?"

Jerónimo gave a smug little laugh. "He was in terror, Brother Guerrero! I saw that barbarian cower before our countrymen's might like the Philistines before the Lord of Hosts, and my heart rejoiced." He fumbled in his belt and took out a string of green glass beads. "These are for you, for your ransom."

Gonzalo took the beads, arched his eyebrows and smiled. He showed the beads to Ix Na. "The men of my race want me to go back to them," he told her in Mayathan, and he was giving her the password to something the two of them had settled long ago. She looked at him and nodded once.

Gonzalo drew himself up. "Brother Aguilar, I am married and have three children. They look on me as a chief here, and as a captain in time of war. My body is tattooed and my ears are pierced. What would the Spaniards say if they saw me like this? You go, and God be with you. But I will not come."

From the look on Jerónimo's stunned face Ix Na understood what her husband had said. And from the look on her husband's face she understood how much peace and how much strength the uttering of this refusal gave him. She'd seen him lead the best warriors in battle and the best speakers in council; she'd seen him rise above his enemies and go first among his friends. But she'd never seen him more sure of who he was, or more proud.

Jerónimo's entire demeanor was thrown into disarray. His smile vanished, his hands left the prayer book. "What you are here does not matter," he said with great force. "What the Spaniards will say about your appearance does not matter. I knew all this already, and I came anyway. I even knew you sent a warning against our countrymen to the chiefs of this land... The only thing that matters now is that you will be finally restored to the world."

Then he added earnestly, "You and I have argued in the past, but there can be no arguing now. If you won't come because of your family, you can take them with you. Many soldiers take native wives and have children by them. It is no sin. It's a necessity of the times. There are no Christian women in these lands, so of course —"

"Of course one must do with whatever's at hand," Gonzalo put in, his voice thick with sarcasm. "Brother Aguilar, my family to me is not a necessity of the times. It's where I've belonged for the past five years, and where I intend to belong for the rest of my life. You seem to think that all I did since I left Tulum is just the straying of a child when the parents are away. Now the parents have returned, and are ready to welcome the child back and to forgive him for his escapades... for the tattoos and the pierced ears... and the wife and the children."

He pointed at his own chest. "Brother Aguilar, when I had these signs painted on my body, I knew I could never erase them, and when I took a wife among these people, I knew I could never cast her off." He smiled lovingly to the twins and to the baby in the crib. "And look how handsome my children are!"

He reached out to hand the twins the string of green glass marbles. "I will give them these beads you brought, and I will tell my children that they were sent from my country. I will tell them this trinket is what the Spaniards consider a fair price for their father."

He stood up. "I have no other answer for you or for Captain Cortez. If there's anything you need for your journey back to Tulum, I will see to it gladly. But my mind is made up."

Jerónimo, who wanted to avoid the arguments of the past, now could see that his rescue mission had turned into the most savage of all arguments; so he stood up in his turn and gathered into his voice the old, inflexible vehemence of convictions.

"What of your immortal soul, ?" he demanded. "Will you destroy that for the sake of an Indian woman? Will you let yourself be cut off from God's grace for the sake of your Indian children?"

The way Jerónimo said "Indian" made Gonzalo's blood boil. For a moment he thought he would lift him up and toss him out the gate, give that scrawny would-be priest the taste of a man's strength.

Then instead he told himself that he'd waited too many years to speak his mind to a Spaniard.

"Brother Aguilar," he said, "my immortal soul is none of your concern. You are neither my priest nor my confessor, and you know nothing about these people, because you never bothered to find out anything about them. The name by which an "Indian" calls heaven to me is worth precisely the same as the name a Christian gives to it.

In Hispaniola, in fact, I saw a chief named Hatuey who was about to be burned at the stake for refusing to be converted, and a friar who was telling him that if he became a Christian he would go to the Christians' heaven. And chief Hatuey asked if he would find Spaniards there, and the friar said he most certainly would, and chief Hatuey replied that in that case he preferred to go to hell rather than ever seeing another Spaniard again. If to stay with these people I have to go to hell, then I will go to hell like chief Hatuey of Hispaniola."

Under the impact of Gonzalo's passion, Jerónimo had to keep his peace for a few instants. He too seemed to be debating with himself whether he wanted to stalk out of the gate or else say all he had to say while he still could. Then he quieted down. "I have come a long way," he said, "and I don't want to leave without you. But if I must leave without you, I want at least to understand why."

Gonzalo nodded. "Very well. I doubt you can understand even if we talk all night. Just the same, I'm more than willing to explain."

There was a long silence, like the lull two wrestlers grant each other before the next lunge. Then Gonzalo turned to Ix Na. "*Etan,* our visitor will spend the night here. Will you please prepare a room?" He walked with her to the doorway.

At the doorway she blurted out her thoughts without bothering first to find out whether Jerónimo could hear her. "I don't like this man, Ah Holkan. He talks too noisily and he's too stubborn. Why do you let him stay? Why don't you just send him out now, before he can provoke you with more of his noisy talk?"

He put his mouth on her forehead, felt her smooth skin. "He'll be out tomorrow, *etan*. His talk means nothing to me. Go now. Take the children, and go to bed."

Ix Na glanced at Jerónimo one more time, as if to make sure she trusted him to be with her husband, then she picked up Temah and called to Akil and Pa'ap to follow her. The twins would not leave for bed without the usual hug from their father, so she let them run to Gonzalo and climb on his knees and whisper their goodnight in his ears as they always did. Akil noticed that his father was hugging them too tight, as if with a special meaning, and complained with a laugh that it hurt. A moment later they were gone.

Gonzalo returned to the bench and motioned toward the dish of food. "You haven't eaten or drunk, Brother Aguilar," he said without looking at him.

Jerónimo studied the dish, sorting out its contents with his eyes. He peered into the *cacau* cup, wondering what that muddy-looking beverage could be. Then he chose a slice of pineapple, mostly to demonstrate good intentions.

"The meat is good," Gonzalo cajoled him.

"But today is Friday," Jerónimo said.

"So?"

"I eat no meat on Friday, the day of Our Lord's Passion," Jerónimo reminded him primly.

"Ah, yes," Gonzalo said without irony, in fact rather surprised at himself for having forgotten something that had once been so familiar.

"You still know what day of the week it is," he added with the same quiet surprise. "Tell me... what month is this, and what year? In the Christian reckoning, I mean."

Jerónimo looked very proud of himself for having kept faith all those years with time as he knew it. "It's the end of February of the year of Our Lord 1519," he answered carefully.

Gonzalo mulled those words over, as if tasting a food he was no longer accustomed to. Then he shrugged. He didn't know how far back the Christian calendar went, but he knew that the calendar used by the people of this land went back many thousands of years.

"I can see you have lived very well in this place," Jerónimo said then, without any discernible tone of censure.

"Indeed I have," Gonzalo replied. "And I doubt any reward from Captain Cortez could match it. Besides, his reward would be something he stole from these people. I didn't have to steal anything instead."

Jerónimo chewed his pineapple and swallowed. "You do know, of course, that if you don't come with me you will be considered a traitor and treated accordingly," he said, and now his voice was no longer as toneless as before.

Gonzalo scanned the darkness that was coming to envelop the house, the trees and the lagoon. "I know," he nodded. "I know that is what they will call me, not what I call myself."

Jerónimo's thin body bent forward, as if impelled by an inner demand. "What has happened to you, Gonzalo?" he asked, sounding like an honestly concerned physician inquiring about a patient's illness. "Were you coerced in any way, were you given no choice?"

Gonzalo shook slowly his head, with something of a smile playing around the corners of his mouth. "No, Jerónimo. I've just come to see what we are doing in these lands through the eyes of the people who live here. In whose house we do the fighting has come to mean a great deal to me. I guess you're right... to see things from the other side is the worst treason. As for being given no choice, I'd say I have given myself no choice. In the end a man can take only one fork in the road, you know. That's the trouble with human beings... there aren't enough choices to go around."

A servant leaned in from the doorway to ask Gonzalo if anything was needed. "Some light," Gonzalo answered, and a little later the servant returned with lighted splinters of *ocote* wood.

"But you are a reasonable man," Jerónimo pressed. "What can you gain by siding with these people? They're bound to be defeated. If you stay with them, you'll only be destroyed with them."

"I imagine so, yes," Gonzalo said calmly. "Anybody facing cannons and horses and smallpox without any defense is bound to lose in the end. Here to the Spaniards, somewhere else to the French or the Portuguese or the Dutch or the English, it really doesn't matter." He sighed deeply, tiredly. "I know I won't save these people. I must have known it all along, since the very beginning. Perhaps..." and he groped after the right words, "all I do want to save is my self- respect."

Another long, hard silence followed. The house around them had grown very quiet, as if deserted. Gonzalo's mind went to those townspeople who'd fled from the Spaniards, and for a moment his thoughts flashed with the vision of his own house abandoned and left wide open like those houses. He mustn't do that, he reproached himself. He mustn't think of defeat. Hatred rose up again in him against Jerónimo and the others behind Jerónimo, who were making him think of defeat. He wished he'd sent Jerónimo out right away, as Ix Na had told him to do.

Jerónimo's forehead was creased with the effort to comprehend, to break through the wall. He started to say something, couldn't give form to it and gave up, but only for a moment. "You've been treated too well," he said then scathingly. "I can see you've had time to do a lot of thinking, and thinking is done on soft beds, on a full belly. You've been seduced by these people, bought with their heathen luxuries. You have no Spanish pride left."

"No, Brother Aguilar," Gonzalo rebutted. "I have no pride in being Spanish, rather. Not if the Spaniards go about doing what they do."

His finger was pointed accusingly at Jerónimo. "Ever since they have thrown open the doors of the earth, the good Christian men of our race have become the great busybodies of the world," he said harshly. "We take people from America and move them to Europe, we take people from Africa and move them to America. We find hunters and change them into farmers, we find worshippers of trees and change them into worshippers of crosses. Well,

Brother Aguilar, here is one man of our race who used to be a good Christian and now wants no part in all this changing."

Jerónimo let go of all diplomacy. "Learn!" he shouted. "You're talking about people who offer human sacrifices to please their gods! What can one possibly learn from such barbarians?"

"We offer our own human sacrifices, Brother Aguilar," Gonzalo countered. "They are called *autos de fé,* and they too are made to please our God."

He cut off Jerónimo's next objection. "You ask me what we can learn from these people. I can answer you only with what *I* have learned. I have learned that they are our equals. That they match us virtue for virtue and vice for vice. I have learned that they are entirely unlike us and at the same time entirely like us."

He grinned. "I'm afraid I can't explain this last thing. But you are used to mysteries. You understand how the Father, the Son and the Holy Spirit can be three and one at the same time, and how Jesus can be human and divine at the same time. So, it's something like that."

He knew Jerónimo would break off the argument at any hint of blasphemy, and when Jerónimo rose from the bench, he felt again that old pleasure he always felt whenever he could so shock his pious adversary that the latter left the arena.

"Brother Guerrero," Jerónimo spat out, "I have no choice but to spend the night in your house, and this I will consider the very last night of my captivity among the savages. With the grace of that God whom you revile, tomorrow I will be on my way back to rejoining men who still know the meaning of decency and righteousness and loyalty to one's country. I have nothing more to say."

Gonzalo too stood up, but at his leisure. "Neither do I, Brother Aguilar." He waved in the servant who stood by the doorway. "If you will follow that savage, he will show you to your room. And please be assured that no creature of the female sex will come within a league of it. I will give the strictest orders in this matter." He watched Jerónimo turn around stiffly, red-faced, and walk away behind the servant; then he too went into the house.

Ix Na had been awake all that time, awake and angry. "You two had much to talk about," she said when he came to bed.

Gonzalo yawned. "Yes," he said pleasantly, "and I can't tell you happy all that talking has made me." It was good after all, he thought, that he'd confronted Jerónimo instead of some other would- be rescuer he'd never met. It was good that all the words which had piled up in his soul during the past years had finally been spent on someone who embodied so many of the things he hated about the invaders.

But Ix Na didn't hear him. "I want that man out of this house by dawn," she said. "Not by midmorning and not by noon. Or else you shall see what even a woman can do when her patience's at an end."

TWENTY-SEVEN

When Gonzalo woke up he saw that Ix Na had left the bed before him and had taken Temah with her. The servant who'd shown Jerónimo to his room now walked in to announce that the visitor was in the porch, ready to leave. And in the porch Gonzalo found him, but not quite ready to leave.

It appeared that Jerónimo had decided he must fight for Gonzalo's soul one last time. He was meek and mild once again, as if last night he'd heard nothing he couldn't change. But last night Gonzalo had finally learned to ignore that old nemesis who used to irk him so. This morning all he felt was amusement at his tenacity. If Jerónimo did go on to take his final religious vows, he thought, woe to the poor sinners who came under the care of such a perseverant fisher of souls.

"I hope you slept well, Brother Aguilar," he said with a hint of irony. "I trust the fans kept some of the heat from you?"

"Some of it, Brother Guerrero. But I'm used to the heat," Jerónimo replied politely, buying time.

Gonzalo sat down to the breakfast the servants had left in the usual place, wondering where Ix Na and the children were. "Eat with me, Brother Aguilar," he told Jerónimo. "You have a long way to go. There's no sense in leaving on an empty belly."

Clearly Jerónimo had been waiting for just such an invitation, just such a chance. He sat down on the mat and welcomed the food with that this time looked like genuine appetite.

"I myself slept badly last night," Gonzalo said then.

Jerónimo looked up as if hoping to hear that Gonzalo had lain all night listening to the pricking of his conscience.

"I had a rather unnerving dream..." Gonzalo said. "Frightening is a better word for it. Would you like to hear my dream, Brother Aguilar?"

Jerónimo's anticipation turned into a testy knitting of eyebrows. But a moment later he summoned back his patience. "Yes, I think I would like to hear it."

"Well," Gonzalo began, "I dreamed that I was home in Spain, in fact that I had never left. I dreamed that I had lived all my life within the boundaries of my homeland and that like all good Spaniards I loved my country as I love my own mother."

Jerónimo ate and listened.

"Then one morning," Gonzalo went on, "some sort of... flying ships appeared in the sky, huge, all covered with iron, and —"

"There are no such things as flying ships," Jerónimo interrupted nervously, his mouth crinkling with suspicion.

"You're right, Brother Aguilar," Gonzalo said. "There are no ships that can fly. But who knows, some days maybe there will be. The people of this land had never seen galleons before we came. They too thought there could never be such things. Besides, you know that in dreams all sorts of strange things happen."

Jerónimo was having a very hard time trying to hold on to his courtesy. But Gonzalo was too caught up in his own storytelling, as the sailor he'd once been.

"From these flying ships," he went on, "these ships more terrifying and more powerful than anything you or I had ever seen, came men unlike any you or I had ever seen... Not quite of the handsome sort, I must add, with an unpleasant smell about them, and... imagine, Brother Aguilar, their skin was green, like the skin of toads!"

Jerónimo could no longer sit still. "Brother Guerrero, please let's talk about serious matters, not of fairy stories and dreams," he blurted out. "Our countrymen are waiting. How can I return to them alone? I beg you for the last time to listen to me."

Gonzalo nodded. "But do listen to me first," he said. "Sometimes dreams reveal things of importance, and this one is about the matters you speak of."

Jerónimo relented a little, holding onto the tattered shreds of his patience. But he stopped eating, as if suddenly full.

Gonzalo too stopped eating. "The very first thing these strange men did," he continued, "was to tell us that all of Spain and all that was in Spain was now the property of their king. We were asked to give up our homeland, because it was best for us to be subjects of their king, who they said was a very wise man.

"The second thing they did was destroy every crucifix, every statue of saint and every holy image they could find. They smashed crosses to pieces, saying they were evil objects. They burned our Bibles, claiming they were abominations. They lopped the head off the Christ of Compostela and off the Virgin of Seville. They called Mary a heathen whore and Jesus a fiendish deceiver, who'd let thousands of people die horrible deaths, devoured by lions, pierced by arrows, roasted on fires... because he'd promised eternal reward to those who sacrificed themselves in his name."

At that, predictably, Jerónimo stood up in a rage; but Gonzalo signaled the servant who'd followed him to the porch to come stand by Jerónimo's side. Frightened by that sudden move, Jerónimo stopped where he was and blanched.

"Brother Aguilar," Gonzalo said quietly, "you are a guest in my house. Be kind enough to indulge my talking. For it's just talk after all."

Glancing at the servant, Jerónimo put his hand to his prayer book and then lowered himself again onto the mat. He looked all around him, as if in fear of invisible henchmen.

"I came here as a peaceful messenger from our brethren," he said in a strained voice. "You wouldn't dare kill me like this, like..."

"Like a savage?" Gonzalo offered pleasantly. "By means of treachery, trampling on the sacred laws of hospitality, and all of that. For that is how the savages kill, of course. The only way they know."

He waved the servant away. "You have nothing to fear, Brother Aguilar. I have no wish to kill you. I'm only asking you to hear me through, so that perhaps when you return among the Spaniards you'll give them the full and true account of my... treason."

Ashen-faced, Jerónimo sat waiting.

"Well then, where was I?" Gonzalo went on, slapping his hand on his thigh. "Ah, yes. Now. The strange and powerful men who'd come to us in flying ships tore down all our Christian images and in their place put images of their gods... all green, of course, and all looking like toads. Those were the proper gods to worship, they said, not our misshapen idols. Naturally we good Spaniards would never pray to a green toad, and this made the visitors very angry.

"Actually, Brother Aguilar, it seemed that just about everything we did madethe visitors angry. It was... it was a little like trying to please very stern teachers.But no matter what we did or didn't do, no matter what we said or didn't say, these men simply could not be pleased. Why would we wear hair on our heads, for instance, when the only civilized way was to be bald, men women and children? And why in the name of God would we kill and eat lambs, those poor sweet creatures that didn't hurt anybody and were so soft and trusting... when everybody knew that fat, juicy flies were the only proper food?"

Jerónimo swayed on his mat, as if caught in tight fetters. The way he was now looking at Gonzalo made clear that he thought Gonzalo had plainly and completely gone mad.

"So," Gonzalo went on, "because we simply could not please these men, the third thing they did was send some sort of fire from their flying ships, some all-consuming destruction the likes of which we'd never seen before. A single blast of this fire, and whole cities were flattened, thousands of people killed. We didn't know how to resist such a thing. We tried, with our puny cannons and guns, but their fire melted our cannons and guns as it touched them. We could do nothing, Brother Aguilar, nothing to keep our beloved homeland from becoming the property of these strange men.

"After only a few years of this, after our people had been starved and tortured and decimated, Spain as we knew it no longer existed. And because our wives and sisters and daughters had been mated to the strange men from the sky, even the newborns they gave birth to were no longer our own. You see, Brother Aguilar, they all had green skin. We wondered at those babies, but the men from the sky liked the green skin very much. It was the only good color, they said, the only one that made a true human being."

Emptied out, all passion finally poured from him, Gonzalo fell silent. Now he wanted to lie down in a clean pool of water and forget all he had said, all he had seen and heard in his life.

In the eerie silence that now reigned in the porch, the faint sound of Ix Na's bare footsteps was just a ripple of wind. She appeared out of the shadows of the house, her head held high.

Perhaps she'd been there all along, out of sight.

Jerónimo saw her. He got up, broken at last in his stubborn hope. He looked at Gonzalo with a mixture of compassion and horror. "May God forgive you," he said in Mayathan so that Ix Na would understand, "because no one else will."

Ix Na took a step forward. On her face was an outrage she could no longer bear in silence. "Who is this slave who comes to call my husband away?" she cried out, her voice choking. Her arm was raised toward the gate. "Out of here, and let us have no more of your talk!" And she was shaking with rage, as if ready to throw the intruder out of her house with her own hands.

Jerónimo drew back. Never in his life had he heard an Indian woman dare to give orders to any man who wasn't a slave—and a slave she'd just called him contemptuously, though she must know he was now a free man. For the first time he seemed ashamed of his appearance, humiliated and furious that he couldn't show himself to this heathen shrew dressed in the clothes of a Spaniard.

He walked to the main gate and pushed it open. The two oarsmen saw him and got into the canoe. He climbed aboard, sat down, put his prayer book between his hands. The oarsmen started to row. Soon the canoe was only a small black thing becoming smaller in the distance.

Gonzalo and Ix Na watched it disappear. Ix Na's shoulders still heaved with anger under Gonzalo's arm. "I wonder what he'll tell the others," Gonzalo said then slowly. "I wonder what he'll remember of all that I told him... Quite probably nothing more than the simplest things, the things most easily twisted around. He'll say I stayed because I was ashamed of my appearance... he'll say I was tied to the apron strings of my Indian wife..." He shrugged. "What does any of this matter?"

He called the man who'd been with him in the porch, and the man came forward with three more. The three wore the insignia of scouts; the man who'd pretended to be a servant was also a scout.

"You have your instructions," Gonzalo told them. "I want him followed where you can, how you can, and for as long as you can. I want to know his every move, and the Castilàn's every move. Go," and the four scouts filed out to the canoe that had been ready for them since the night before.

Ix Na was first to turn from the gate. "Ah Holkan," she said tautly, "I know I should ask you to forgive me for speaking to the Castilàn, but I can't. I'm not sorry I did it."

For the first time in two long days Gonzalo's sinews relaxed. "Neither am I, *etan.*"

It was some time before the memory of Jerónimo's visit began to cool and to settle. At first there was a feeling of panic, a dread of the future. He knew he was alone now, and very much a prisoner again since now he could never leave this land. He thought of Captain Cortez and of the others, to whom he was now a traitor and a renegade, the lowest of men. From this day on there would be a price on his head. If news of his refusal reached Spain, his name would be spoken with contempt within the very walls of his father's house, the house he would never see again.

But when Gonzalo thought about his father's house, he thought also about what had driven him from it, and that gave him peace once and for all. His father was a good man, but a defeated one. His goodness, that Gonzalo remembered so well, had met betrayal so many times that by the time his life came to an end he was convinced the two would always go together. By the time he faced the ultimate betrayal, he had accepted the knowledge that he would never be given a fair chance.

When someone falsely accused him of being a thief, after the first surprise he offered no struggle, as though he'd always known that it would come to that. But Gonzalo, not yet a man and no longer a boy, raged for the whole week it took the accusers and judges to destroy his father on the torture rack.

The last time he'd seen his father, buried alive in a cell half- swamped with the stinky backwash of the harbor, he had refused to believe that that was indeed his father, a man who just sat waiting to die, almost content to die in fact now that the worth of goodness had finally been revealed. He wanted to scream at that defeated man, not at those who'd destroyed him. He wanted his father to stand up before his death and die whole. But his father had died as silent as a snuffed- out candle.

So Gonzalo had left home; left his father, left Palos, left everything. Surely in the New World there must be some new ways, some possibility of redress. He understood now that when he'd sailed away what he was truly looking for was not gold or glory or love, but for the chance to begin the universe again, with a new set of rules that would not reward goodness with betrayal.

Perhaps that chance had now come. It still wasn't a fair chance. Like his father, the people he'd chosen as his new kin faced too vast a conspiracy of injustice. But if he knew it wasn't a fair chance, he also knew that he would not stand by in silence and watch his father be crucified again on the same cross. Now everything was clear, he told himself. If his was a lost cause, then never in his life had he been married to one he loved most.

❖   ❖   ❖

Nachancan returned the same day the first news sent by the scouts reached Xul Ha. Gonzalo had just finished telling Nachancan about his meeting with Jerónimo when the messenger from Cuzumil asked to be received.

While the messenger spoke, Gonzalo's mind wandered back to the years of his captivity in Tulum. How often had he heard Jerónimo say that God, his God, was going to reach down from heaven to pluck him out of his misery? And now, as he listened to the tale of Jerónimo's rescue, he could almost believe that God, Jerónimo's God, had personally removed each and every obstacle from the path of his faithful servant.

Jerónimo had reached Cuzumil too late. The eight days Captain Cortes had given him had elapsed. He'd easily found the place of the Castilàn' landing, for it was marked by a number of wooden crosses. Captain Cortez had also broken up the statues of Ix Chel that were kept in the ancient shrine and had rolled them down the steps. In place of Our Lady of the Rainbow there was now a lady with white skin.

So Jerónimo, after tarrying to pray to the image, had returned to Ah Kin Cutz's house. But the fleet had gone only a short distance when one of the ships sprang a leak and the Castilàn were forced to go back to Cuzumil. Having heard about this, Jerónimo had immediately set out with his canoe. A large piece in the side of the craft was rotten, but on the beach he'd found an oar that fit in the ruined space; and in that rickety canoe that no one would have trusted to stay afloat for an hour, he'd crossed the treacherous waters of the channel between

Tulum and Cuzumil, the channel Gonzalo had once tried to cross and failed.

At Cuzumil the Castilàn were waiting for their ship to be repaired. The inhabitants of the island, who'd once fled at the sight of the strangers, had now been bringing food to them and to their horses and to their dogs. Sometimes they brought also offerings of flowers to appease the animals' neighing and barking.

Captain Cortez was sitting at a table eating when he was told a canoe was approaching from Tulum. Once ashore, Jerónimo had spoken to the Castilàn in their own tongue. At their reply he'd burst into tears and he'd fallen on his knees. Captain Cortez hadgiven him Castilàn clothes and food and drink. Gonzalo's name had been spoken between them. Jerónimo had shaken his head, and Captain Cortez's face had taken on a look of darkest anger. He'd shouted something, hitting the table with his fist.

Then Jerónimo had been taken to meet Nakehya's son. The two had spoken to one another in Mayathan, and this had enormously pleased Captain Cortez. The following day, when Captain Cortez had given a speech to the people of Cuzumil, Jerónimo and no longer Nakehya's son had stood by him to translate his words.

The speech had to do with the image of the white-skinned lady the Castilàn had put on the altar in place of Ix Chel. Jerónimo had told the people of the island that they must honor the lady and pray to her, for she had it in her power to grant every wish to those who asked with all their hearts. He'd spoken well, the messenger added, with now forceful now flattering words that persuaded and touched.

A few days later the Castilàn ships had left Cuzumil, sailing in the same direction as all previous expeditions: north-west, toward the land of Culhua where the Mexìca lived.

Gonzalo dismissed the messenger with the usual reward. "And so good riddance to Brother Aguilar," he mused. "Seems he has instantly become a man of importance... He might end up a bishop yet!"

Then he addressed Nachancan. "My brother, it's clear the Castilàn won't come looking for me, at least not right now. We might be left alone for a while. Is there much gold in this land of Culhua?"

"I know there's much more there than here," Nachancan replied. "They are a gaudy people, the Mexìca."

Gonzalo scratched his beard, lost in thought. "If the Castilàn reach Culhua, this gaudiness you speak of will be the end of the Mexìca," he said.

"What sort of rulers do the Mexìca have?" he asked then. "How is their land held?"

Nachancan motioned a servant who stood by the doorway. "Bring us a map." When he had it, he spread the painted cotton cloth before him on the floor. "It's not like here, where each lord holds sovereign power over his own province. There one man is sovereign of all, and his name is Motecùzoma Xocoyotzìn. Many of his subjects are unhappy with the heavy tribute they must pay him, but too afraid to rebel."

Gonzalo considered these facts in silence. "What do you know about this Motecùzoma Xocoyotzìn?" he asked.

Nachancan's face showed distaste. "He is a brave leader in war, but he is also too fond of brooding and meditation, and much preoccupied with visions and omens. Once in the middle of a military campaign he ordered his counselors to return to the capital and put to death all the teachers and nurses of his many children. He claimed he was directed by a dream."

Gonzalo frowned. "There's danger there. A man like that could all too easily be turned into a puppet, and God knows the Castilàn are good at fabricating omens."

"One of his greatest fears is said to be the prediction that in the year One Reed lord Kukulkan will return and wreak destruction upon the Mexìca,"

Nachancan continued. "I don't even know how many of our people still pay heed to that prophecy. It's a Mexìca belief, not one of our own."

Gonzalo looked up. "Kukulkan... the Feathered Serpent?" he wondered. He'd heard that name before, long ago... Kanalsin, yes. She was the one who'd told him about the god who had white skin and a full beard and who would some day return from the east—the god to whom he was to have been offered in sacrifice, after he tried to escape, because he resembled him so.

"You know," Nachancan said, "this is the year One Reed... Strangers with white skin and full beards, arriving from the east in the year One Reed, armed with tools of destruction..."

"The people of Cuzumil, afraid as they were, knew right away the Castilàn are men and not gods," Gonzalo put in. "Even Ah Kin Cutz, who doesn't have the wits of an eagle, never invoked the supernatural."

"True," Nachancan said. "But if I did believe in the supernatural as strongly as Motecùzoma does, I would have to say the coincidence is astounding." He laughed uneasily. But in his eyes, and in Gonzalo's eyes, there was a startled apprehension.

❖   ❖   ❖

And astounding was everything that happened after the Castilàn set out for the country of the Mexìca.

Over the following two years and a half, from the mouths of messengers who came almost without breath to the gates of Xul Ha, Gonzalo heard a tale so frightful he would have thought it a lie, if messengers were not punished with death for reporting false news.

Most incredible of all was to learn just how quickly a nation of millions could be wiped out by a handful of strangers.

In March, at Cintla, the Castilàn defeated a body of forty thousand warriors in two days. Nakehya's son had escaped at night from the Castilàn camp, leaving his Castilàn clothes on a bush, and had urged the people of the town to attack the invaders. After they were defeated, in retaliation for his bad advice the people of Cintla cut the boy's heart out, which was the fate Ix Na had predicted for him. Then, speaking through Jerónimo de Aguilar,

Captain Cortez told the people of Cintla that they must renounce the worship of their false idols and embrace the Christian creed. He broke up the statues of the gods, rolled them down the steps of the temples and erected a cross in their place.

In September, at Tlaxcala, the Castilàn conquered a city of one hundred and fifty thousand families in three weeks. The people of Tlaxcala, who hated their Mexìca king, joined the Castilàn in their march toward the capital of the kingdom. Speaking through Jerónimo de Aguilar, Captain Cortez welcomed the allies and put them under the protection of the Castilàn king, of whom the people of Tlaxcala knew only the name, Carlos, Then Captain Cortez broke up the statues of the gods and erected a cross in their place.

In October, at Cholula, during a peaceful festival the Castilàn massacred six thousand unarmed people in a few hours. The people of Cholula threw themselves off the tops of the temples trying to escape the cannon fire. The survivors were forced to clean up the streets of the city choked with bodies. Then Captain Cortez broke up the statues of the gods and erected a cross in their place.

In November the Castilàn entered the capital city of the Mexìca, Tenochtitlàn. As Nachancan had predicted, Motecùzoma Xocoyotzìn took Captain Cortez to be the returning god Kukulkan, offered no resistance and received the strangers with every honor. Nine days after being received into Tenochtitlàn as a god, Captain Cortez walked into the king's quarters and, speaking through Jerónimo de Aguilar, told Motecùzoma that he was under arrest and confined to his own royal palace. The Castilàn filled room after room with gold given to them by the Mexìca king and destined to be sent over the ocean to their country.

In June of 1520 Captain Cortez attacked Tenochtitlàn. By now, after seven months of captivity, Motecùzoma Xocoyotzìn whose subjects were not allowed to look him in the face, had become the victim of his own beliefs in omens and of the cunning strangers he'd let into his house. His own people reviled him for his cowardice, and his captors humiliated him daily. He understood nothing of this, except that everything had been foretold long ago and must therefore be suffered. During the attack a stone flew to his head, whether thrown by Castilàn or by Mexìca, no one could tell. Speaking through Jerónimo de Aguilar, Motecùzoma refused to be seen by doctors, refused to be baptized, and let himself die.

The battle for the capital raged on after his death. The Castilàn were forced out and had to retreat to Tlaxcala, their faithful ally. From there they raided the city of Tepeaca, killed sixty thousand of its inhabitants and sold into slavery the surviving women and children after branding them on cheeks and lips. Captain Cortez renamed the city Segura de la Frontera; and in recognition for the service Jerónimo de Aguilar had rendered him throughout the conquest, he made Jerónimo councilman of the city. By then Jerónimo had completely forgotten his religious vocation, and was looking for a Castilàn wife of suitable status. His first act as councilman of Segura de la Frontera was to break up the statues of the gods and erect a cross in their place.

In December smallpox broke out, killing thousands upon thousands of people all over the Mexìca kingdom. In June of 1521 the Castilàn launched their final assault on Tenochtitlàn. The capital was now defended by Cuauhtèmoc, a warrior even the Castilàn respected for his valor, and a man far different from Motecùzoma. But not even Cuauhtèmoc's valor could save the Mexìca now. Out of three hundred thousand people sixty thousand survived the battle, the siege, the starvation. Women and children were reduced to eating the bark of trees. None of the dead were touched. The Castilàn, on the other hand, during the siege fed the bodies of slain Mexìca to their dogs.

On August 13, 1521, the richest and most beautiful city in the New World surrendered, a heap of smoldering ruins. Its surviving inhabitants were parceled out as slaves among the conquerors.

Cuauhtèmoc was captured and tortured to reveal whether he'd hidden any gold. Tenochtitlàn was renamed the City of México. Captain Cortez broke up the statues of the gods, rolled them down the steps of the temples and erected a cross in their place.

The day Gonzalo heard about the fall of Tenochtitlàn was a beautiful autumn day rustling with the new corn almost ripe on the stalks. When the messenger left him, the last one he would receive from the country of the

Mexìca, all he could do was walk to a spot on the bank of the lagoon where he could be alone.

A thought went around his head like an evil spell. Two and a half years, he thought. In two and a half years a people had gone who had endured for centuries; and not a people of weaklings, not a people of ignorant peasants. During those two and a half years, on the island of Cuzumil the wooden crosses left behind by the Castilàn had rotted away, and the image of the Virgin they had set up on the altar of Ix Chel had peeled into oblivion. It would be easy, he told himself, to think of those forgotten traces of the Castilàn's coming and to say that what had befallen the Mexìca could not happen in this land. It would be easy and it would be the worst folly.

He didn't hear Nachancan approach him softly. Nachancan sat down beside him and for some time both of them were loath to break the silence. Silence at least was a peaceful thing. But then Nachancan said what had to be said, what had to be faced.

"They will come for us too. Perhaps ten years from now, perhaps tomorrow. But they will come for us too." Gonzalo winced. He turned his face away.

Then Nachancan asked, "Tell me something, Ah Holkan. Do the Castilàn know why the world was made? Why some things and some people are evil, why there is unhappiness and disease? Why there is death in the end?"

There was no hint of challenge in his words, no contempt for the people he spoke of. "Because if the Castilàn did know all this, I would open my arms in surrender and I would say with all my heart that we are indeed an inferior people, that we must accept the wisdom of the Castilàn as a child accepts the wisdom of a grandfather who can lead him out of a very bad predicament."

Gonzalo shook his head. "No Castilàn has the answer to any of these things."

"Not even Captain Cortez?"

"Least of all Captain Cortez. When it comes to such answers, every man on earth is a child without a wise grandfather."

"But then why do they win?" Nachancan wondered quietly. "Is it because they're good at making so many things? The powder for the guns, for instance... It's just some crushed rocks, isn't it? Yet they discovered it, and we never did."

"My brother, that it not the same thing at all," Gonzalo said. "Knowing how something works is not the same as knowing why it works. And all the Castilàn do know is how. It isn't much they know. Sorcery, that's all... of a luckier sort than most."

He smiled. "Often enough what they know they stole.

Gunpowder? They didn't invent that. Somebody brought it from a country called Cathay."

Nachancan kept his peace for a few more moments. Then he looked toward the two houses on the banks of the lagoon. "My oldest son and your oldest sons have grown old enough to hate the Castilàn," he mused. "I hear them when they play... they no longer hunt the Xiu."

"Neither must we," Gonzalo said. "We all have a common enemy now... we, the Xiu and everyone else in between." He stood up. "My brother, it's no use to sit here and mourn. We have work to do. We must seek a permanent peace with our enemies and strengthen our ties with our friends. All these small wars among us make us weak for the one war that matters. Perhaps what happened to the Mexìca will finally convince the people of this land that we must be one against the Castilàn."

Nachancan nodded. The two of them walked back to the house.

As he went, Gonzalo's mind couldn't help returning to the horrors that had poured in from the country of the Mexìca during the past two and a half years. He thought of Nakehya's son, who had paid for his courage with his life; of the unarmed young men in their festival finery mowed down by the cannons at Cholula; of the starving women in Tenochtitlàn who stripped the bark off trees for food; of the children branded on the face with hot irons and sold as slaves at Tepeaca.

A shudder came from the depths of his being. "My God," he murmured, "there is nothing a human being won't do to another."

Nachancan shook his head. "If only it were that simple, Ah Holkan... There's also nothing a human being won't do *for* another," he said, and his smile spoke of gratitude and love.

TWENTY-EIGHT

When the twins turned twelve and Temah ten, Gonzalo and Ix Na took them to the temple of Ah Cab, protector of beehives, for the *emku* ceremony; Nachancan took his youngest, Obsidian Blade, who'd just turned thirteen.

The four boys stood straight and proud all through the ritual, the blessings and chants, the cleansing with virgin water taken from tree hollows in the jungle. Each threw his handful of ground corn into the fire with a well-rehearsed gesture, and each received with reverence the flowers and the pipe that made him a man and wished him a sweet life.

But when the ceremony was over and the parents came forward with their presents, while the twins and Obsidian Blade cried out delightedly over the full-sized bows, the jaguar-skin quivers and the new hunting dog, Temah stood engrossed in the sacred books and the prayer stick jingling with rattle-snake bells that had been used during the ritual.

The youngest of the four priests nodded toward Gonzalo and Ix Na.

"This one looks down a different path," he said with a pleased smile. He handed the boy the prayer stick. "Take it, it's yours. The Gods will favor you, Temah Can."

Temah reached out his hand, but then looked at his parents as if asking their permission. His blue eyes, the only one of Gonzalo's features to have been passed down to Gonzalo's children, and a bit startling in Temah's hand-some brown face, were full of desire mixed with fear. This wasn't the first time he shunned the usual playthings that spoke of the hunt and of the battle-field. He'd always been fond of reading, of asking questions and of wonder-ing, as he was wondering now about the shape of the prayer stick, about the sound trapped inside the rattlesnake's tail.

Ix Na motioned him to take the gift, and thanked the young priest. Gon-zalo, however, gave no sign of approval. Not that he frowned on Temah's choice: there was a seriousness in the boy, a depth of soul that pleased him as much as the twins' physical strength and comfortable grace. But he'd seen Temah pay too often for his difference with loneliness, and this was what pained him.

All the way home from the temple the twins and Obsidian Blade so teased the boy for his prayer stick that finally, right in the middle of the ban-quet that followed the *emku* ceremony, Temah quietly got up, went into the house and shut himself in. Another boy might have thrown away the prayer stick and spent the rest of the year trying to make the others forget he'd ever owned one; but Temah loyally took it with him into exile.

Gonzalo forbade Ix Na to go to him. Perhaps that way, he thought, Te-mah would learn that the unspoken laws of the clan left him with little to gain from being different, like the branch that sticks out of the tree and gets hacked out of the way.

Yet in his heart he knew that Temah was perfectly happy to be alone, even on this day in which he'd just been formally welcomed into the clan.

Temah was a survivor, and would survive within or without the clan's protective circle. That night when Gonzalo and Ix Na would go home, they would find him rattling his prayer stick with the solemn bearing of a priest and repeating word for word the ancient chants that were meant to be understood only by a chosen few.

During the banquet the twins and Obsidian Blade were toasted and indulged. The three of them were great friends. They were already good swimmers and runners, and they'd started to train with the spear under Ahau Can, who was now a slim, sinewy man of twenty-two. Today Ahau Can wanted to show the fruits of his training, so he lined up the boys and had them throw his own spear with his own spear-thrower.

The boys needed no coaxing. When it came to a challenge, they jumped to it with an enthusiasm that warmed the heart. If the man-sized spear demanded too much from them, it never showed. Obsidian Blade made a good clean throw; Pa'ap with his sure arm came closest to the center of the target, which caused Akil to hit it only a few well-calculated inches from his brother's mark.

The parents cheered the boys, the guests sang out their names. Ahau Can voiced his satisfaction, at his pupils as well as at himself, for he was not one to hide his own merits. The mother of Obsidian Blade, who was sitting beside Nachancan as a sign of honor and was pregnant with Nachancan's fourth child, patted affectionately her son's arm.

The twins basked in their parents' praise. They spoke seldom and to the point, while between themselves, like most twins, they barely needed to talk to understand one another; and if they like most twins didn't finish each other's speech, it was because they'd come to the unspoken agreement that it was not fitting for one man to take away the words of another.

Then White Feather honored the three boys by serving them food and drink. It was the first time they were served by a woman other than their mother, and White Feather's perfect manners made her every gesture even lovelier to look at. At nineteen, she was by far the most beautiful woman in Xul Ha. Nachancan was fiercely proud of her, and possessive enough to have so far scared away every young man who even mentioned her name to him.

He bought her the finest jade and the finest dresses—nothing homespun for her, nothing common. Had White Feather been less wise than she was, he would have easily made of her a spoiled little queen.

Ix Lolkin grumbled at Nachancan for this excess of love that kept their daughter still a virgin at an age when most young women were mothers. Ix Lolkin had raised her with the proper strictness, rubbing stinging chili pepper on her if she smiled to a man; but now that the time had come for White Feather to smile to a man, not one man was allowed to court her. But Nachancan wouldn't change his mind.

The past six years had all been filled with the growing up of the children. The rites of passage that must be observed for them, the ceremonies unaltered since centuries, blessed life with continuity in the midst of unwanted and unholy change. The Castilàn had come, sown terror and death; but within the walls of Xul Ha everything was as it had been in the time of the ancestors.

Scouts from all over kept Gonzalo and Nachancan well appraised of the Castilàn's doings. By some miracle, for the past six years Chetemal had remained outside the reach of the invaders; but the invaders were all around Chetemal, like beasts of prey still distant in the night. In the north, the country of the Mexìca was now forever in their possession, a land where men and women who'd once been princes and the consorts of princes labored as slaves in the estates and mines owned by the conquerors. In the south, after a swift and merciless campaign the highland country of Cuautemàllan had also been vanquished, its leaders killed, its priests burned at the stake and its people enslaved.

From Cuautemàllan the Castilàn had gone on to establish a settlement in the valley of Ulùa, near the mouth of the great river. For generations the valley of Ulùa had been the main destination of Chetemal's merchants; but now that route had been cut, and Chetemal had become poorer over the years, the waterfront crowded with canoes that no longer went out to sea.

But as long as the Castilàn stayed away, everything could be put up with, even the arrogance of the Xiu, who had finally agreed to parley for peace after Nachancan had traveled in person to Manì, putting himself in great danger.

After five days of talks he had persuaded the Xiu to cease hostilities and to send a warning if the Castilàn came. As a gesture of friendship he'd given them a stretch of good land where they could plant corn or hunt peccary and deer. The five days had ended with a banquet of celebration, and when Nachancan had returned to Chetemal he had assured Gonzalo that the Xiu would keep their word.

Alliances had also been strengthened with Ecab, where Ah Yuntun remained firm in his determination to fight the Castilàn even before they would land; and with Tulum, where the craven and unpredictable Ah Kin Cutz needed to be shored up in his resolve.

Tying all these bonds had been slow and laborious work. While Nachancan received embassies or traveled back and forth, Gonzalo had carried on a different task within the province itself. He had taught some of his men as much of the Castilàn's language as would be necessary to grasp the Castilàn's intentions, anticipate their moves, lie to them and mislead them.

Ah Dzan Chi, who was now Gonzalo's second *nacom,* Bird Woman's husband and the father of two children, had learned especially fast; and he'd learned not only the words but also the attitudes and gestures that would make the Castilàn think he was just a simple-hearted, well-intentioned Indian who could take them to a cache of gold by the shortest route. If the Castilàn ever landed at Chetemal and asked for directions, Gonzalo's men were now able to lure them into that part of the province where they would most easily be destroyed.

Chetemal seemed ready, as well protected as it could be—and even better than by men, by the hostility of the country itself, the snarl of swampy jungle on one side and the almost uninterrupted reef that barred the coast on the other. There was nothing else to do now but wait. Forget, if possible, the news of disaster brought in from countries all around, remember that they lived in the only unconquered country on the mainland, and get on with life, while the children came of age and everything was still the same.

❖   ❖   ❖

In the hazy November dawn sunlight knifed through the trees in long slanting rays, smoky with the moisture that rose from the floor of the jungle. Crouched under a strangler fig tree, Gonzalo and the two boys had been silently waiting, while the only thing that moved was the sweat trickling down their backs. It had been a long wait, yet the three of them could wish for nothing better than more of those hours spent away from the world.

Akil and Pa'ap, their hands steady on the five-foot-long blowguns, kept slowly chewing gum made from the milky clotted juice of the *sapodilla* tree. The slightly tart substance that one must keep working between one's teeth was a passion with the boys, and today

Gonzalo too was acquiring a taste for it; it helped him remain alert, as all hunters must during the wait.

"There, father, there's one," Pa'ap whispered then excitedly.

A swift clapping of wings had stirred the green canopy above them; a fleeting whirr of scarlet feathers had disturbed the arrangement of light and shadow.

"It's the female," Gonzalo whispered back. "Steady now, my son."

Carefully Pa'ap put his hand into the small bag of deer hide he carried at his belt and felt for the clay pellet of the right size, the one that would stun but not kill the macaw. He nodded to Akil, who was doing the same, in anticipation of success.

"Her mate's on that other tree, I can hear him," Akil said. A half-eaten fruit fell indeed to the ground, dropped by the male feeding high in the branches.

Pa'ap loaded the clay pellet into the blowgun. Presently the female's head became visible, the great round eye staring and the curved beak busy around a large seed. Pa'ap lifted his blowgun and took aim, a portrait of determined concentration. Gonzalo's hand went up to the boy's arm to correct the angle, but then withdrew. The try must belong entirely to Pa'ap. A few paces away Akil kept his sight on the male, knowing the second shot must come as close as possible to that of his brother.

When he was ready Pa'ap drew all his breath in, held it for an instant, then blew it out with all his strength. A small scarlet meteor plummeted from the tree, and even before it came to rest on the ground Akil was bringing the male down, with a soft thump of ruffled feathers.

Shouting in triumph the boys rushed out to gather up the pair, tie the legs together before the birds revived. The female, less incapacitated by the shot than her mate, attempted a blustery escape, squawking so loudly that Akil was startled and almost let go of her, as he arched away from the vicious beak. But in the end the bird had to give up, having lost one of her brilliant feathers, which Akil quickly scooped up. The feathers were the reason why the two macaws would spend the rest of their lives inside a cage; the twins anticipated with joy the beautiful headdresses they would wear, after the birds' first molting.

Gonzalo called the two servants who'd accompanied them and took from them the water gourd, but had the twins drink first as a sign of honor. His smile told the boys how proud he was.

"Your mother won't like the noise, but we'll find a place away from her loom," he winked. Then they headed home, with the boys carrying the birds themselves and recounting their feat to each other.

Ix Na was careful to praise the twins without making Temah feel humiliated for not having joined his brothers. Temah, who wasn't handy with any weapon, had refused to go hunting with them and had spent the morning following her around, as he often liked to do. She tried to discourage this attachment, yet another one of Temah's peculiarities, although she was also pleased to have his company whenever the other three men if the house were away. It was almost like having a daughter, she often said, and this worried her as much as it comforted her.

The large wicker cage was hung near the boys' favorite playing spot. Akil and Pa'ap danced in celebration around it, filling the air with their joyous cries. Temah instead observed the macaws with a somber look, in silence. The twins didn't pay him much attention, surely thinking he was jealous; but Gonzalo felt compelled to draw closer to Temah and probe the boy's inward-looking soul.

He hunkered down next to him. "They are a beautiful pair, aren't they?" he said awkwardly, mostly as an invitation to talk.

Temah nodded. His face showed pity for the two birds that kept beating their wings against the bars, frantic. "Yes, father, but their beauty has made them captives," he said. "Surely now they must wish they were plain as quail... and free."

Gonzalo didn't reply. Temah, unfortunately, had spoken the truth. He stroked affectionately the boy's head and sighed to himself. How much simpler it was to seize the day as Akil and Pa'ap did, he thought, whose happiness was like that of healthy young animals, uncomplicated by remorse.

He let Temah go, rose and walked over to Ix Na. She slipped under his arm, her thick black braids pressing against his skin. She smelled of *cacau* and *ixtahtè,* the lovely perfume made from the resin of the sweet gum tree. She was wearing the necklace with the golden frogs that she wore when they'd first met in Tulum, and she seemed to him not a day older than that day.

"It is so good to come back to you," he whispered, kissing her. "From war or from a day of leisure, it's the same thing..."

But Ix Na only smiled wanly, and turned away with a face even more somber than Temah's before.

Gonzalo frowned. "What's wrong?"

She started to walk away, not toward their house, but toward Nachancan's house. There was something ominous in that, and in her reticent words. "Hun Halal wants to see you right away. He's in the council room, with Ah Dzan Chi and some of the *batabs.*"

Gonzalo doubled his pace. All the pleasure of the morning left him. He could tell it was bad news; and bad news these days meant one thing only—Castilàn.

In the council room Nachancan, Ahau Can and Ah Dzan Chi were gathered with three *batabs* and with a man Gonzalo had never met but whom he recognized, from the insignia of the wild turkey, as a messenger from Ah Kin Cutz. He had the eerie, unpleasant feeling he was seeing again something he'd seen before.

Nachancan greeted him with a worried smile. He too seemed to be repeating a scene from the past.

"Ah Holkan. This man just came from Tulum. I'll let you hear the message from his own mouth."

Gonzalo sat down and looked into the messenger's face—young, earnest and concerned. Before the man finished his greeting to him, he interrupted him.

"How many ships did the Castilàn bring this time?" he asked. Tulum's messenger cleared his throat. "Two ships, my lord, and one hundred and eighty soldiers, from what we could tell. They also have horses, and some dogs."

"Scanty forces," Gonzalo said. "They must think poorly of us."

Nachancan's face was grim. "It was enough for Ah Kin Cutz," he said, and caught himself before he blurted out anything more disparaging about his neighbor in front of his neighbor's envoy.

But the messenger had a mind of his own. "It was indeed ill- advised of him to let them land. Lord Ah Kin Cutz feared for his life. He thought it would be prudent to welcome them peacefully, but I see no prudence in such a decision."

Now it was Gonzalo who had to make an effort not to lash out at that cowardly old man who worried more about himself than about his people. Why of all men did Ah Kin Cutz have to be ruler over the stretch of coast the Castilàn had chosen as their landing place? he wondered angrily.

"I see no prudence in such a decision, either," he muttered. He waved his hand at the messenger. "So, tell me what happened this time," and he thought of the past six years in which nothing had happened except what everybody wanted—they had been left alone.

"We have learned a few things about the man who leads this expedition," Tulum's messenger began, "although surely I won't be able to say his name properly. It's a very long and very difficult name... Francisco de Montejo Adelantado Por Vida De Yucatán—"

Gonzalo stopped him. "Wait. *Adelantado* is not a name. It's a title... like True Man, or *nacom*."

"And what does the title mean?" Nachancan asked.

"It means a governor, or ruler, and *'por vida'* is 'for life.' But I have no idea what *'yucatán'* means."

"It's what the Castilàn call our country," the messenger explained. "When they came ashore they asked if this was 'the land of Yucatán.' We'd never heard the name before, but what they described was our land."

Gonzalo shook his head. "God knows where they got a name like that... They have such a gift for twisting words, never bothering to find out what the right one is! Please go on," he told the messenger. "What we have so far is a perfect stranger who's been given someone else's land in perpetuity even before setting both feet on it," he summed up sarcastically.

Tulum's envoy resumed his tale. "When the Castilàn landed, not at Tulum but at Xelha, a short distance away, they made us watch a ceremony of theirs. They had an interpreter, but still we couldn't understand much of what they were doing. One man planted a banner in the sand. Another read to us from a piece of paper..."

"The *requerimiento,* of course," Gonzalo said. "They wouldn't want to snuff out a few hundred thousands of us without making a request in writing first."

"Then Francisco de Montejo Adelantado took out his..." The messenger groped for the word, helping himself with gestures.

"Sword," Gonzalo said.

"Yes. He took out his sword and made three slashes in the trunk of a tree. Then he cried out three times, *España, viva!* and all the Castilàn cheered. When this was over, Francisco de Montejo Adelantado told the people of Xelha that the whole of the mainland now belonged to the Castilàn."

Gonzalo slapped his thigh. "Hah! Well, señor don Adelantado, that was the easy part. Now come and get it, the whole of the mainland!"

Nachancan wasn't laughing. "Say what happened next," he prodded the messenger.

"Lord Ah Kin Cutz has allowed the Castilàn to settle at Xelha and has promised them friendship. But there were some quarrels among the Castilàn, so Francisco de Montejo Adelantado had the two ships burned to keep the men from deserting. The Castilàn are now landlocked. They have begun to build a settlement, and lord Ah Kin Cutz sends them food and slaves to help with the work."

"And the people?" Gonzalo asked. "Do they agree with him?" "Far from it. No one in Tulum wants to keep feeding and housing an army of invaders," the young man added, again in his own words and with a clear tone of outrage. "They do it only for fear of lord Ah Kin Cutz, and lord Ah Kin Cutz does it only for fear of the Castilàn."

"Then our task is easier," Gonzalo said.

"There is only one mind to change. My brother," he said to Nachancan, "if you are with me, we will leave for Tulum as soon as the warriors are assembled. Ahau Can and Ah Dzan Chi will keep them ready just across the border until we'll have obtained Ah Kin Cutz's permission to enter his province. We will destroy the Adelantado," he vowed. "With Ah Kin Cutz's help if he can be persuaded, without it if he can't."

There was a sound of eager assent from all the men. Ahau Can and Ah Dzan Chi left immediately to summon the warriors.

"He lets them build a settlement," Gonzalo said between his teeth when he was alone with Nachancan. "He might as well throw open the door of his house and let in a pack of hungry jaguars... His own messenger shows better judgment!"

Nachancan's hand on his shoulder cooled some of his rage. "We'll soon be on our way, Ah Holkan. Let's get ready now."

It was hard saying goodbye to Ix Na and the boys. Only the thought that he was leaving to make them safe could allay some of Gonzalo's sadness. The twins helped him gather his weapons—gravely, like grown men, made older still by their hatred for the enemy that was causing their father to go to war.

"Soon we will march at your side, father," Akil said eagerly. "And fight the Castilàn with you," Pa'ap echoed.

Ix Na, whose face wore the dark look of her own sadness, tightened up even more at the twins' enthusiasm, at the knowledge that in a few short years her sons would be of warrior age.

"Four men the Gods gave me," she said, her face turned away. "Four men and the prospect of much war."

Temah, who wasn't helping his father like the twins, tugged at her dress. "I will stay with you, mother. I don't like war."

Those words made Gonzalo stop what he was doing. He put himself in front of the boy and took him by the arm.

"My son, hear me out. I also don't like war; no man with any sense does. But this is a war we must make, so we can be free from the men who come into our land as masters. If need be, you too must leave those you love and go to war. Do you understand me, Temah Can?"

Temah was silent for a moment. Then he nodded.

"Yes, father. I understand." But there was something hostile in his answer, a distant refusal underneath the dutiful "yes."

Ix Na said nothing. She busied herself with Gonzalo's things, as she'd done so many times, but there was a particular heaviness in her gestures. Gonzalo could all but hear her thoughts. This was the time that had so often almost come and had now had come for real. This wasn't against the Xiu. Against the men of his own race Gonzalo had now no better advantage than that of any native warrior facing cannon and steel with flint stone. This was the hard truth that must be acknowledged, the inevitable outcome of his having placed himself with her people.

That night, while he lay next to her in the dark, unable to sleep, a terrible disquiet crept into him, as if he would never again see her or the boys. He wanted to cling to her and tell her, like Temah, that he would stay with her, that he would never leave her. He caught himself wishing it was already dawn and he already gone, wrenched loose from that bittersweet pull.

But then Ix Na without a word took him in her arms and did what she'd never done before. She started making love to him, started what he had always started, with the same confidence that would not be denied.

He let her do all she wanted. She straddled him like a man and lowered herself onto him and rocked him between her thighs, her breasts grazing against his chest, her hair hanging around him like a net. In her hands was a wisdom that knew precisely what and where, all that she had learned through the years about his body and what pleased it. She held him under her, sheathed and shielded, as her warm weight heaved gently but with a steady, unstoppable power; until he cried out freely like a woman and the cry, like the sound of the sacred rattles, chased away the demon of fear.

In the morning when he left, he carried the memory of a night unlike any they'd ever shared, one they would remember the way they remembered their first one together. At the main gate he turned his head toward her one last time and smiled. It was as if last night she had performed a charm, marked him in his flesh for her own so that death would stand warned not to encroach.

TWENTY-NINE

The oarsmen pulled the great canoe ashore on the beach of Tulum under a low dark sky crackling with thunder. With only two guards and Ah Kin

Cutz's messenger, Gonzalo and Nachancan walked up the road to the wall. By the time they were in sight of Ah Kin Cutz's house the rain started again, driven by a cold wind from the sea.

The voyage had been uneventful, but they'd been delayed by bad weather. They'd been forced to seek shelter at a village on the coast and wait out the storm there. That delay had been hard on Gonzalo. He knew that when it came to the Castilàn there was never a moment to waste. They were like a disease that must be eradicated immediately, before it spread; even a few days could mean too late.

He also had to deal with a host of emotions roused by his being back in Tulum and about to face the man to whom he'd once been handed at spear's point as a slave. The walk from the beach was like the fragment of a dream. These were the steps he'd traced so often, the steps loaded with hunger, fatigue, despair. Time was warped, squeezed into layers of two, three different lifetimes. Which lifetime was this? he panicked. Who was he this time?

Then he breathed in deeply, looking at the house he was about to enter now for the first time after he'd spent years in the shadow of its walls. Confidence returned to him with the sting of the rain on his face. This time he would face Ah Kin Cutz as an equal.

There was a sense of sweet vengeance about it; the past had turned out well after all. He knew who he was.

Not Citam but a woman let them in and brought them dry cloaks, as the messenger went to tell Ah Kin Cutz that he had guests. While they waited, Gonzalo kept staring at the hut in the courtyard. The thatched roof was falling to pieces, the plaster peeled away in large patches.

"This place is so rife with memories," he said under his breath.

The messenger returned, escorted them in. "Is Citam still here?" Gonzalo asked.

The messenger shook his head.

"Citam died last summer. No one has taken his place yet." Gonzalo smiled to himself. No one could take Citam's place, he thought, Citam who had driven him, punished him without mercy and finally saved his life.

The inside of Ah Kin Cutz's house seemed to Gonzalo quite modest compared to his own. Like every other building in Tulum, it was cramped and low-ceilinged, as if built for dwarfs. Through this house he could now walk at ease, even swagger.

The woman ushered them into the room where Ah Kin Cutz was. Ah Kin Cutz had been expecting only his messenger back from Chetemal, and he still hadn't recovered from his surprise upon hearing about the visitors. When Gonzalo and Nachancan walked in, the stunned look on his face was quite telling.

He lay on a low bed, propped up by pillows. Aside from the usual love of showy ornaments, little remained of the man Gonzalo remembered. All the extra flesh he used to carry was gone. The eyes were filmed, the hair had grown white. At an age when most men were old, the True Man of Tulum had become decrepit.

While Gonzalo and Nachancan sat down, he jerked himself up as if approached by enemies. "I wasn't told about this. My Lord Nachancan... You..." The last word was directed at Gonzalo. "You," he repeated, flustered. "You were once a slave in my house, and now you come to me wearing the dress of a *nacom!* They say you are a Can now, they say you are called by a new name. Is this true?"

Gonzalo could have smiled at this feeble old man's confusion, if he weren't thinking about the Castilàn only a few leagues way, in the settlement this feeble old man was letting them build. He made the gesture of salute among peers. "My lord Ah Kin Cutz, what you have heard is all true. I am Ah Holkan, my brother's war captain in Chetemal."

Ah Kin Cutz squinted. "But why are you here?" he asked apprehensively, as if fearing retaliation from the former slave who'd risen to prominence under a powerful neighbor. "Why do you come to me unannounced?"

"Because we must discuss the matter of the Castilàn you have welcomed into your province," Gonzalo replied. "Long ago my brother and I warned you against them. You seem to have forgotten that warning, my lord Ah Kin Cutz."

Ah Kin Cutz's frown deepened along with his bewilderment. "Castilàn?" he wondered. "Who are these Castilàn?"

The messenger bent toward him. "The Españolesob, my lord."

"Ah," Ah Kin Cutz said wretchedly. "The suckers of *anonas!*"

The first word was easy to understand; the second puzzled both Gonzalo and Nachancan, who asked for explanations.

Ah Kin Cutz's mouth puckered with resentment. "They eat *anonas* by the basketful," he whined. "They say they've never tasted a sweeter fruit in the whole world. Every day I send them *anonas,* and every day they ask for more!"

"If you're so unhappy about these strangers," Nachancan asked, "why do you let them build a town? Why do you feed them and treat them as your friends?"

Ah Kin Cutz slumped down on his bed again. "What choice do I have? They are too powerful. I've seen with my own eyes what they can do... One of them is worth a hundred of us! Men like that can only be appeased, not crossed."

With a great effort Gonzalo stifled the sneer that was coming to his lips at the old man's fear.

"My lord Ah Kin Cutz," he said then with quiet force. "Do you remember those slaves a hunter brought you years ago? If you had met us while we were on our ships, you would have thought we too were invincible. You would have made obeisance to us and let us walk across your land like kings. Instead we were starved, wounded, barely alive... we were defeated. The Españolesob *can* be defeated, my lord, and that too you have seen with your own eyes."

Ah Kin Cutz said nothing, but his face showed that Gonzalo's words had breached through to him.

"Remember the rout at Chanputun," Nachancan added. "It can be done again. Our warriors are waiting beyond the border. You won't have to risk the life of a single man of your own if you so wish. You won't even have to break your promise of friendship to the Españolesob. It will be as though you knew nothing of this. Let all retaliation fall on us. We ask you only that you let us march on to Xelha, where the Adelantado is."

"I know the Españolesob, my lord," Gonzalo pressed. " I know how they think, how they act. Now that they are without their ships, lodged all in one place and assured of protection, killing them will be a game for boys."

Ah Kin Cutz's face was screwed into a grimace of uncertainty. "But the Adelantado is not in Xelha anymore," he said then, "and the Españolesob are not all in one place. The Adelantado left two days ago for Ecab... There are now only forty men in Xelha, and twenty in Polè. The rest went with him."

At that Gonzalo's temper flared. He slapped his thigh once, twice as he thought of the storm that had delayed their arrival. A few days had made again a crucial difference. In his mind he damned both Ah Kin Cutz and the Adelantado to the everlasting torments of the World Underneath.

Nachancan's frustration was no less obvious.

But after some thought he said, "Ah Holkan. Perhaps this is for the best after all. Divided, the Castilàn are an easier target. We'll have to strike in two places at once, that's all."

Gonzalo was beginning to put in something, but Nachancan anticipated him. "As for the Adelantado, we will send word to Ah Yuntun in Ecab that the Castilàn have crossed into his province, and that he must attack them immediately. Ah Yuntun can be trusted to act swiftly," he added, not unaware that his words were a tacit reproach to Ah Kin Cutz's quailing indecision.

Gonzalo had to agree. But Ah Kin Cutz still hadn't agreed to anything, so again he turned to him. "My brother speaks well. But we can do nothing without your help, my lord Ah Kin Cutz. Will you let us send a message to Ah Yuntun? Will you let us march on to Xelha and Polè?" he pressed.

Ah Kin Cutz looked as though he were lying on smoldering coals. "What if you fail?" he demurred fretfully. "What if Ah Yuntun fails? Whichever group of Españolesob is left alive will surely seek vengeance... And what shall I do then?"

"Hand over to the Españolesob those of us who survive, as you would do with any of your war captives," Nachancan replied.

"Or rise up after us and throw these invaders out yourself," Gonzalo blurted out hotly. "Your people will be behind you already, all too eager to fight!"

Ah Kin Cutz was silent for long, hesitant moments. Only the sound of the rain and of the thunder could be heard in that interval. Gonzalo's eyes were fixed on Ah Kin Cutz's face, while in the back of his mind he was already shaping a plan to circumvent his refusal.

Then Ah Kin Cutz gave a quavering sigh. "I understand nothing about these strangers. They are like dangerous beasts I've come across in a bad dream." He looked at Gonzalo. "And you... You I understand even less. Years ago the other slave, the one I let go for a ransom, told me you'd refused to return to your people, but I thought he was lying... You are even more strange than they are!"

His eyes went from one to the other unbidden visitor who'd come to spur him into action. "You do promise I will be safe," he reminded them. "You do promise I will not be blamed..."

"We do, may Itzamnà be our witness," Gonzalo said at the end of his patience.

"Then," Ah Kin Cutz stammered. "Then..."

"Then by tomorrow morning our runner will be on his way to Ah Yuntun in Ecab," Nachancan said, "and our warriors will be on their way to Xelha and Polè."

"Mind you, my lord, the Españolesob must not be given the slightest hint," Gonzalo warned. "Whatever they expect from you, you will keep providing. No more, no less."

"Lumber and thatch they want," Ah Kin Cutz complained, "and fish they want, and corn and fowls and firewood and—"

"And *anonas*, yes," Gonzalo finished. "Send them all the *anonas* they can eat, for soon they will choke on them!"

A burst of thunder seemed to underscore his words. It had grown dark. Beyond the wall the sea pounded against the jagged cliff like a battering ram.

"All right," Ah Kin Cutz surrendered. "Your warriors can cross the border when they wish. Your runner can go to Ah Yuntun by the quickest route across my province."

He raised his hand, half in warning and half in plea. "But see that you do not fail."

The two visitors got up. "My lord Ah Kin Cutz, we will not fail. Thank you," Nachancan said with relief. "The Españolesob may have landed in your province, but they are a threat to all of us. We are surrounded by people who were once masters in their own country and who are now the lowest of beings because of these strangers. We cannot let ourselves be crushed also. We cannot be made to follow their fate."

A flicker of spirit finally came into Ah Kin Cutz's eyes at those words. "No, no, we can't," he said.

"I will send scouts to Xelha and Polè," he added then. "They will let you know what to expect there. Tell me in what other ways I can help."

"Yes," Gonzalo said, bowing his head in thanks. "We will talk of that when our warriors will have joined us."

"But will you leave at this late hour?" Ah Kin Cutz asked. "Our guards will find shelter for us," Nachancan answered.

Ah Kin Cutz stopped them. "Please remain in my house." He motioned the messenger to help him up from bed, then tottered toward the door. "My women will find rooms for you. Women are all I have... Four wives and not one son!"

Before stepping out he turned and peered into Gonzalo's face. "You are the only one of my slaves who ever escaped from this house," he said. "The only one of my slaves whom I remember among the many who have crossed my threshold. The Gods do play the strangest tricks upon a man!" he mused with an air of wonder, and it wasn't clear whether he meant the man who'd once been the slave or the one who'd once been the master.

Three days later the Can warriors crossed the border. Gonzalo and Ah Dzan Chi led the group destined for Xelha, Nachancan and Ahau Can the one destined for Polè. The two towns lay only a few leagues away from Tulum and very close to each other. For this reason they must be attacked at the same time, before any alarm was raised. It must be, Gonzalo thought, like the double blowgun shot with which Akil and Pa'ap had captured the two macaws.

At midday the two groups were ready—their weapons concealed, mixed in with the townsfolk Ah Kin Cutz sent daily to deliver food and supplies to the Castilàn. Beside this cover, Ah Kin Cutz had furnished twenty of his warriors.

Outside the wall Nachancan and Gonzalo parted. Nachancan prayed for the favor of the Gods, then embraced Gonzalo and wished him luck.

"Leave no Castilàn alive," Gonzalo said with his farewell.

The settlement at Xelha was reached without incidents. It was nothing grander than a cluster of thatched huts ranged around a larger building still unfinished, certainly the Castilàn's future council house and headquarters. It rose at some distance from the town, and it was surrounded by cornfields, some of which hadn't been harvested yet.

In those cornfields Gonzalo found the perfect place to hide, while the supply-bearers went past the Castilàn sentinels with their baskets and their firewood. Soon the women would light fires and start to cook; soon the soldiers would sit down to supper. Gonzalo crouched among the shaggy stalks, with Ah Dzan Chi beside him, and settled down to the wait.

There was a moment, when he first glimpsed the Spanish flag waving above the roofs, when his mind faltered. How many times had he dreamed of this day? he wondered. He couldn't keep his heart from pounding as it did, and not just because of the usual reasons before battle. Between this day and the day he'd last seen Spaniards a break had occurred, a change to make anyone tremble. Could these men suspect that not far from them was hiding one of their own who was no longer one of their own, one they called a traitor and a renegade?

His eyes took in every detail of the settlement with an intensity that went beyond the warrior's need to have every detail under control. So familiar everything looked, and at the same time so alien. He could see the men, many bearded like him; some mended their clothes, some lounged in hammocks, some bantered with the women in the way of soldiers around women.

They seemed confident, at ease in this new place, even without their leader; it was the confidence he knew so well, the self- assurance that made of each Spaniard his own leader, responsible only for his own chosen fate. For a moment it was all too easy to imagine himself back among them, to hear their voices speak the first language he had ever learned, to laugh at the old jokes. He also had to marvel in admiration at this handful of adventurers who in the middle of nowhere, outnumbered and at the mercy of shifty hosts, still managed to look like the masters of the place.

But the moment only lasted until he remembered what these men had come to do, and in the name of what intolerance; until behind each face he could see the stakes smoking with burning flesh and the gallows heavy with bodies and the garrote and the chains and the branding irons. From these same men all these things came, these same laughing ordinary men who ate *anonas* with a relish like children's, dripping sweet sticky juice all over their shirts. From these men who were and would remain his enemies.

The sun began to dip toward the horizon. His hand on his weapon, Ah Dzan Chi shifted about, impatient for action.

"It won't be long now, Ah Holkan," he whispered.

He watched the Castilàn wide-eyed, confronted with a pageant of strangeness. Only one thing about them was familiar: the covering of quilted cotton stiffened in brine, adopted from the natives in place of their heavy steel armor.

The women began to bring steaming pots from the fires and stacks of hot tortillas from the griddles. One stocky, pock-marked Castilàn sounded the supper call, and the men began to form a single file, gourd bowls in hand. As they filed past, Gonzalo counted them. Ten, twenty, twenty-five, twenty-eight. After the twenty-eighth man the line stopped.

He waited for the rest of the soldiers to join their comrades, but they never did; for some inexplicable reason, twelve of the Castilàn would not have their evening meal, or would not have it now. Ah Dzan Chi shot him a worried glance that wondered about the same fact.

"Why didn't the scouts tell us about this?" Gonzalo muttered angrily. Then he signaled one of his warriors to approach him.

"Find out where the other Castilàn are. Be careful and be quick." An instant later the warrior disappeared into the cornfield without so much as a rustling of dry leaves.

The last man in the line took his ration and sat down to eat with the others. Tense moments passed as Gonzalo waited for his warrior to return. His mind kept envisioning alternatives, chasing after the missing detail. Ah Dzan Chi looked nervously over his shoulder and whispered an oath at the unexpected delay.

Suddenly there was a commotion among the Castilàn soldiers. The pock-marked one who'd sounded the supper call began to shout at one of the women; from his hiding place Gonzalo couldn't tell what he was saying. Before the woman could reply anything, the soldier struck her so hard that she fell. Even as she cowered on the ground he hit her and kicked her, and now the woman's cries could be heard even in the cornfield, and the cries of the other women trying to stop the soldier.

Presently a boy rushed out of a hut and put himself in front of the woman, shielding her with his body. The soldier called out to his companions, who seized the boy and dragged him away. On the ground the woman screamed, her mouth bloody. The soldiers tied the boy to a post; one brought out a whip and began whipping him until the boy's back was a grating of red welts.

Gonzalo's eyes shrank to slits. Whatever the woman might have done could not possibly have caused such punishment for her and the boy. It was sufficient for the Castilàn that the two were Indians, as he knew well. The way the Castilàn dealt with these people could be so simplified as not to leave the slightest chink, like a brick wall.

Anger swept through him, anger that dimmed all sense and caution. Without waiting for his man to return, ignoring Ah Dzan Chi's alarmed whisper, he jumped to his feet and gave the order to attack. Out of the cornfield he raced, impelled by the strongest hatred he'd ever felt for another human being.

He went straight for the soldier who was hitting the woman, leaving to Ah Dzan Chi the one who was whipping the boy and to the others the rest of the Castilàn, many of whom had put away their swords before eating and had no time to reach for anything but their daggers. He struck the Castilàn across the neck as the Castilàn was about to kick the woman again. One blow of his *hadzab* was all it took him, and his own pent-up wrath exploding.

Upon seeing the pock-marked soldier fall dead at Gonzalo's feet, the people of Xelha arose as one, armed with whatever they could get —wooden mallets from the unfinished huts, smoldering brands from the fires, the stone *metates* on which the women had been grinding corn. In an instant Gonzalo found himself surrounded by a mob whose hatred of the invaders matched his own. Those soldiers who escaped him did not escape the mob, and died a worse death. A hut was set on fire, and from its roof the flames began to spread to the other dwellings.

Amid the smoke he saw the man he'd sent out from the cornfield. The man was trying to make his way through to him, but with a strangely halting step. Gonzalo got one more Castilàn out of the way, knocked down a third who was coming at him, then rushed to the man. When he got to him he saw the man's hands pressed on his belly, the blood seeping between the clenched fingers.

As the man collapsed in his arms, he saw also that the wound was the single ragged hole only a musket could make. The man had found the missing soldiers, and they had found him. There remained in him only strength to point at the direction from which he'd come: the outskirts of town, the first tall buildings of painted stone.

In that direction Gonzalo began to run, followed by Ah Dzan Chi, his battle guard, and Ah Kin Cutz's warriors. Some men of Xelha joined him. They were armed with axes, and they were shouting to him to stop. In his impatience, he paid them no attention. Only when he was almost in the town, facing the sloping stairway of a temple, did he become aware of what he'd been warned.

There was a crackle of gunfire from the cell atop the temple; he felt something hot hissing past his neck, singeing his hair, and he saw five of his warriors thrown back as if struck by an invisible fist. He grabbed Ah Dzan Chi by the arm, pulled him behind the cover of a tall stone marker. The rest of the men had to scramble for whatever protection they could find. Two of Ah Kin Cutz's warriors weren't fast enough. One was shot in the head, the other took a ball in the chest.

Behind the marker Gonzalo had grown still as the stone that hid him. He could hear Ah Dzan Chi's rapid breathing, and the frightened whispers of one of his battle guard huddled behind the trunk of a tree. What should he do now? he wondered. Inside the cell at the top of the temple he could see only darkness. He seemed to have forgotten that the first thing the Castilàn did upon entering a town was to set up their guns on a high position, and here they had found the ideal one.

Perhaps all twelve Castilàn had muskets, perhaps only a few. But even a few would be enough. Certainly they also had food and water stored up there. They could hold out for days if necessary, or until the Adelantado returned, which as far as he knew could be that same night.

Would he send his men up the steps of the temple, where the guns would pick them off one by one as they climbed? The Castilàn were staggering their fire, as he himself would have done: one man fired while the other reloaded. By the time one of his warriors would reach the top, ten, twenty would lie dead on the stairway.

Yet he'd assured Ah Kin Cutz that the Castilàn could be defeated, and he'd ordered Nachancan to leave no Castilàn alive. Would he now retreat with only half of his mission accomplished? With this last thought like the tip of a spear pressing against his side, he was in a torment of indecision.

Ah Dzan Chi stood up behind him.

"Ah Holkan, why do we wait? Let me be the first to climb up!" Before Gonzalo could stop him, Ah Dzan Chi motioned the rest of the men to follow him and broke out of cover. The instant movement was detected, again the guns smoked from the temple top. Ah Dzan Chi let go of his *hadzab* and fell. Two warriors managed to gain the first two steps but went no further. One, wounded, rushed back to the tree trunk trailing blood.

Cursing to himself, Gonzalo bent low and dashed toward Ah Dzan Chi. He grabbed hold of him, pulled him back to safety, but not before a musket ball found flesh. There was a sound like a whistle's, and a fierce burning in his right arm. He crouched behind the stone marker without breath, Ah Dzan Chi crumpled to the ground beside him. He couldn't tell whether Ah Dzan Chi's wound was serious; all he could tell was that he wished he'd stopped him in time.

"We must retreat," he said then grimly, and wanted to erase the words even as he uttered them. He felt helpless, naked. His first imperative was the safety of his men, too many of whom had already died for nothing. Later, later he would try to understand why he'd been defeated, and pray that he could accept that.

"Can you walk?" he asked Ah Dzan Chi. Ah Dzan Chi's face was ashen, beaded with sweat. He nodded yes.

Gonzalo put Ah Dzan Chi's arm over his shoulder and strapped his *hadzab* to his belt, as it would be of no use now. The closest shelter he could see was a thicket of trees interspersed with boulders, perhaps fifteen paces behind him. It would be fifteen long paces, he thought.

He signaled the men that they must make a run for the trees. "Not in a straight line, but like the rabbit," he added. He asked Ah Dzan Chi if he was ready, then the two of them started to run.

As if caught unprepared this time, the guns didn't start until most of the warriors were halfway to the thicket. Slowed down by Ah Dzan Chi, Gonzalo was among the last to dive behind a boulder.

There he found the one man who hadn't made it alive. Then the guns were silent. The Castilàn would not waste powder and shot on a retreating target.

From the thicket back to what up to a few minutes ago had been the Castilàn' settlement, the path was easy. The people of Xelha were going through the bodies of the dead, stripping them of their foreign clothes and gathering up their foreign weapons. Women emptied the soldiers' pockets and argued over their contents. The boy who had been whipped went about the smoldering huts waving a bloody Spanish shirt on a stick.

Stretchers were put together for Ah Dzan Chi and the other wounded. There was nothing else to do but return to Tulum, where they were to meet Nachancan, and hope that Nachancan had had better luck in Polè. A great weariness overtook Gonzalo, the spent aftermath of what had raged through him. Here at the settlement everything looked like victory—not a Castilàn standing. But those twelve who'd driven him away from the temple were the true winners, he thought, no matter what he would say to justify himself.

Something Ah Kin Cutz had said three days ago about the Castilàn came back to him. It was something that he had scoffed at, and that now seemed to be scoffing at him. "One of them is worth a hundred of us," the decrepit old man of Tulum had claimed. And it almost rang true now, as Gonzalo set out for the old man's house in a mood as foul as the thunderheads that were gathering again from the sea.

Nachancan made it back to Tulum at the expected time, and with good news. All of the twenty Castilàn lodged at Polè had been killed, and their horses as well. These Castilàn had no muskets, so there had been only a few dead among the Can warriors. Nachancan was proud of himself, and justly so.

Gonzalo congratulated him, made his own brief account, then left Nachancan to answer Ah Kin Cutz's fretful questions and went to see Ah Dzan Chi, who was being tended by a curer. But he might as well have attempted a forecast himself, since the curer knew nothing about the damage inflicted by musket balls. The wound was close to vital organs; only time and the Gods would tell whether Ah Dzan Chi would survive.

All night long, exhausted as he was, Gonzalo waked by the bed of his second *nacom,* denying himself relief from his worry, his despondency and the pain from his own wound. He went over each moment of the attack again and again, scourging himself with the same obsessed thoughts that yielded no way out, no easy salving. Nothing reasonable he tried to tell himself could convince him that he hadn't failed, and even more shamefully so in view of Nachancan's complete victory.

What haunted him the most was the memory of his warriors marching behind him from Xelha in silence. It wasn't merely the dejected silence of trained fighters who'd been kept from their goal. It was a shocked stupor like that of children when the priests went about the streets dressed as the Lords of Hell.

Never had he seen his warriors like that; and as he remembered both his warriors and all those others who'd fled in terror from the Castilàn, he understood what his real enemy was—not powder and shot, but that onslaught of terrible newness that made of powder and shot something beyond comprehension, something to be feared not as mere artifacts of men but as the anger of gods who permitted no appeals.

THIRTY

He brooded over Xelha for days, beginning with the days they waited in Tulum for the Castilàn' next move, which never came.

The twelve soldiers remained barricaded in their temple lookout, firing at anything that moved. They would never be caught off guard. Theirs was the desperate resolve Gonzalo knew well himself, the ability for survival that had so often gotten the Castilàn out of the worst predicaments. Eventually the people of Xelha had to give up trying to smoke them out. Of course, however, they cut off all supplies.

During those days nothing came from Ecab. Ah Yuntun either could not or would not give a reply to the message he'd been sent. After waiting in vain for an answer, vexed beyond endurance by Ah Kin Cutz's fears of retaliation, Gonzalo and Nachancan sailed back to Chetemal, with Ah Dzan Chi still fighting for his life.

Ix Na welcomed home a man sorely cast down. She told him that she didn't think the attack was the failure he deemed it to be, and that she was happy enough with what he had accomplished while also staying alive. But in his gloom Gonzalo slighted her words as a woman's narrow-minded inability to understand warfare, and afterwards sought even more to be alone with his own dejection.

It got even worse after the messenger to Ecab finally returned, more than two months later. The Castilàn, the messenger related, had been intercepted by Ah Yuntun and engaged in battle; but they had crushed Ah Yuntun's forces and inflicted a great loss of men. Ah Yuntun had surrendered to the Adelantado, and his neighbors had followed his example. Four northeastern provinces were now under the control of barely a hundred invaders. The news made Gonzalo so furious he nearly struck its bearer.

From that day on the pursuit of his goal took on the tenacity of an obsession. He ate, he slept, he drilled his warriors and he thought of nothing else—when, where, how he could defeat the Castilàn. His mind remained locked around it until it left no room for other concerns. The only consolation in all of this was that Ah Dzan Chi recovered and after a long convalescence was once again fit for combat.

What Gonzalo wanted was another chance to measure himself against his enemies. If only this time his enemies would come straight to him, to his land. There he would be able to lure them to the place most favorable for victory instead of having to go looking for them in unfamiliar territory. There he would be able to muster all the resources at his disposal instead of having to beg permission from cowardly allies like Ah Kin Cutz.

For such a chance he would mumble prayers and seek out diviners like the last slave woman. Nothing else would heal his unhappiness, cleanse the humiliation that poisoned him: to be able to wage war on his own premises, war as his heart desired.

He got his wish.

One spring morning, while he was swimming in the lagoon with the twins and Temah, he was called to meet the one messenger bearing the one message he'd hoped to receive. Ix Na had to run after him with something to wrap around his hips, or he would have greeted the visitor naked. Naked the twins and Temah followed their father out of the lagoon.

Dripping, his hair plastered on his shoulders, he grabbed the messenger's arm and steered him to the nearest bench. "A ship?" he blurted out. "In Chetemal's harbor? Are you sure?" He turned to Ix Na. "Is Nachancan coming to hear this?" And when she nodded yes, again he took hold of the man's arm. "Great lord Itzamnà. Start talking, man."

The messenger couldn't speak fast enough. First he explained that while he was out at sea fishing the Castilàn had captured him and pressed him into service as an informant. They'd asked him whether this was the Bay of Chetumal—so they called it—and whether a white man lived here as war captain to the local *cacique*. When he'd answered yes to both questions, the Castilàn had made him go ashore as message-bearer. Gonzalo's heart was racing. Francisco de Montejo, Adelantado for life of Yucatán, had come in person to Chetemal for no other purpose but to meet him.

While the messenger spoke, Nachancan came in. Again there was a letter. Like Captain Cortez before him, the Adelantado had thought he would best impress Gonzalo with a written plea. Gonzalo nearly wrested the piece of paper from the messenger's hands. First he read the letter to himself, then he translated it for Nachancan, for Ix Na and for his sons.

It was a long one, and full of flowery Spanish expressions that didn't carry over well in Mayathan. Some sentences he had to leave out altogether, for they were Spanish conceits which would be wholly incomprehensible to his loved ones.

"Gonzalo, my brother and special friend. I count it my good fortune that I have learned of you through the bearer of this letter.

With it I want to remind you that you are a Christian, bought by the blood of Jesus Christ our Redeemer, to whom I give, as you must give, infinite thanks."

"You have a great opportunity to serve God and the Emperor our Sovereign in the pacification and baptism of these people; and even more than this, you have the opportunity to leave your sins behind you, with the grace of God, and to honor and benefit yourself. I shall be your very good friend in this, and you will be treated very well. Thus I beseech you not to let the devil influence you and to do what I say, so that he will not gain possession of your soul forever. On behalf of His Majesty I promise you to do very well for you and to comply fully with what I have said.

"On my part, as a noble gentleman, I give you my word and I pledge you my faith to keep my promises to you without any reservations; to favor and to honor you, and to make you one of my principal men and one of my most select and beloved in these lands. Therefore I beseech you to come without delay to my ship, or to the coast where I can meet you, to help me carry out, through your counsel and guidance, that which seems most expedient.'"

Gonzalo lifted his face and gave a little sardonic laugh. What seemed most incredible in that incredible letter was that the Adelantado addressed him with the formal *vos* reserved to noblemen instead of the *tú* to which Gonzalo had been accustomed all his life as a commoner. Another intriguing bit was the word "pacification," a favorite of the Spaniards, although it had certainly been used long before by others who also thought of themselves as a race of masters; once they reduced a country to a desert they called it peace.

He shook his head. "This is most amazing," he said. "What a valuable man I have become to the Castilàn, that they keep trying so hard to win me back!"

Ix Na sat with the boys serenely in her place. Akil asked her to explain something he hadn't understood, and she answered him at length under her breath.

But Nachancan seethed at what he'd heard. "This scum from the sea, who think a load of words can turn a man away from his family and his people!"

Gonzalo turned over the sheet of paper, laid it on the bench and smoothed it with the palm of his hand. "Oh, but my brother," he said, "such a fine load of words deserves a fine reply. We must not leave the Adelantado waiting."

On the bank of the lagoon were the remnants of a fire the twins had built to sharpen the tips of the wooden spears they played with. He searched for a piece of charcoal among the cold ashes, found one that suited him, then with it started to write on the blank back of the Adelantado's letter.

He made it simple, so that even an illiterate man would be able to grasp his response. Only sarcasm could match the Adelantado's request, and only an outrageous lie would show what he thought of the Castilàn's offer of redemption. When he was done, he translated into Mayathan for his brother, his wife and his sons.

"*Señor,* I kiss Your Grace's hands. As I am a slave, I have no freedom to join you, even though I am married and the father of children. But I do remember your God, and both you and the Spaniards will find in me a very good friend."

Ix Na crossed her hands in her lap. "*Your* God," she chuckled. "I like that."

Then Gonzalo spoke to the messenger. "You must be anxious to return to your fishing. Go then, my friend. Someone else will deliver my answer to the Adelantado." Flushed with relief and gratitude, the man hurried to leave.

Gonzalo stood up and gathered his clothes. A rush of anticipation now carried him like a great wave. After Xelha he'd laid awake for many a night mulling over plans. Finally the time had come to put all those sleepless nights to good use.

The first thing to do was plant eyes and ears among the Castilàn. He sent for Ah Dzan Chi. Disguised as a common townsman, Ah Dzan Chi would deliver Gonzalo's answer to the Adelantado, then offer his services to him. The second thing to do was make sure the people stood united behind him and ready to carry out his orders.

An hour later he was ready to leave for Chetemal with Nachancan and Ahau Can. At the main gate he said goodbye to Ix Na and the boys. He didn't know when he would see them again. He hugged them as if before a long journey, lingering to remember their closeness, drawing strength from their love.

The boys crowded in his arms, quiet but clinging. Ix Na put her hand on his chest. She could feel how taut he was, and she didn't delay him with her worries.

"It will be well," she said. "It will be as you wish."

Three hours later he was at the edge of the water looking at the big brown ship that rocked lazily under furled sails, surrounded by a swarm of canoes full of curious people. She was a handsome, sturdy- looking brigantine fitted for long stretches away from land and armed with light cannon. She was anchored close enough for one to see the sailors going about their chores.

The crowd around him was ranged like a thick palisade—merchants, craftsmen, corn farmers, beekeepers, all marveling in a constant murmur of apprehension. There would be no need to go to the men's house, since the entire council of *batabs* was already there. Good, Gonzalo thought, for he wanted every man in Chetemal to hear his call to war. He turned his back to the ship and faced the crowd.

"Hear me out," he hushed it. "The more you marvel at this thing, the weaker this thing makes you. If your spirit is strong, then you will see this thing for what it is, just wood and fabric, just metal and rope."

He raised his arm as if to bar the ship's way. "We must keep these men from landing. Even if they remain here for months, we must make them understand that they will never be welcome among us. And we must protect the city if they try to land by force. We must build a wall, and pits for the horses."

He paused to gage the mood of the crowd, and what he saw pleased him. The *batabs* were brandishing their ceremonial copper axes like true weapons. Some were calling for an immediate attack.

Nachancan raised his carved staff of office. "Are we one against our enemies?" he demanded. "Are we one body and one mind?"

From every corner of the shore a cry rose that answered him yes. Even the Castilàn must have heard it, because the deck was now dark with men thronging to see what was happening.

Summoned from their cool inner chambers in the temples, the priests hurried down to the shore, carrying the images of the Gods of war freshly daubed with the blood of animal sacrifices. The crowd sat Gonzalo on his litter and carried him in procession as every *nacom* before him had been carried, among cheers and shouts and the smell of the *copal* incense that the priests wafted toward him to call down upon him the favor of heaven.

Four hours later the waterfront was evacuated, and work began on the fortifications. Slaves and freemen toiled side by side digging trenches, dragging sharpened stakes from the jungle, heaping barriers of stone and thorny cactus. It was the Spaniards' own way of fortifying their towns in the New World. They called such fortifications *albarradas*. Should they try to land, they would find their own sort of defenses blocking their way.

Moving back and forth to direct the work, Gonzalo seemed possessed of the energy of a jaguar before the pounce. This time it would be quite different from Xelha, he thought. No one would build huts for these Castilàn, no one would bring them food and supplies. If the Adelantado had any sense in him, he would sail away and never come back within a hundred leagues of Chetemal.

Five hours later Ah Dzan Chi was able to relay through runners in canoes the first intelligence he'd gathered aboard the ship—and it was a rather extraordinary piece of news. If Francisco de

Montejo had come such a long way to get his hands on Gonzalo, it had been at the prompting of none other than Jerónimo de Aguilar.

The two of them had met in the City of Mexico, where Jerónimo was dying of tumors, assisted by his daughter. During their meeting Montejo the newcomer had asked Jerónimo the veteran where in Yucatán he should go look for gold; and Jerónimo had replied that he should go to Chetemal, where he would find not only gold but also the white traitor who lived among the Indians.

In the midst of the bustle of war, Gonzalo had to pause for a moment to consider what he'd just learned. Jerónimo's malice toward him was so relentless that it had found a way to strike even from a deathbed. It had been a very long time since he'd last thought about Jerónimo. Now he conjured up the thin, fever-eyed young man who'd once shared his captivity, and he plumbed his own soul to see what remained after so many years.

All he could find was a vague feeling of compassion for the way Jerónimo had ended up, eaten alive piecemeal by disease at the age of forty. After that, he hoped with all his heart that Jerónimo would not die before learning how the man he called a traitor had tossed the Adelantado out of the land he called Yucatán.

The rest of Ah Dzan Chi's report had to do with the Adelantado's reaction upon reading Gonzalo's answer scrawled in charcoal in the back of his own letter; it was a very predictable reaction. Another bit of information was that before coming to Chetemal the Adelantado had stopped at Xelha to rescue the twelve surviving soldiers from the destroyed settlement. One thing Gonzalo never found out was where this third ship came from, since the Adelantado had burned two others.

By sundown the *albarrada* was beginning to take on a definite shape, and certainly a definite meaning to the men aboard the ship.

Sentries were posted, and signal fires lit. With these, should Gonzalo decide to attack, he could alert within minutes the five companies of warriors that he kept ready behind the deserted warehouses of the waterfront.

As the sun sank down there was a pause for rest and a meal brought by the women from the city. Gonzalo ate with the people, of the same simple but tasty fare. Then he went back among the workers. If he couldn't make himself understood, he put his hands to rope or log and showed them what he wanted them to do by doing it himself.

The men were tireless. They had vowed to stop only when it would get too dark to see. When it did get too dark to see, he gave the order to stop. After the great noise of the day silence fell, and the breeze from the sea made them forget the fierce heat in which they'd sweated all day.

Gonzalo lay down in his hammock and stared at the ship across the water. Against the dappled, streaked, immense reach of the sky the hull curved as gracefully as a slack bow. The sailors had lit lanterns on deck. Aft was the brightest one, under which Gonzalo imagined the Adelantado looking out at the shore.

From the next hammock Nachancan tapped his fingers on his arm. "Ah Holkan," he said under his breath, "if the Castilàn don't land by force, how long do you think they will be willing to wait?"

Gonzalo smiled. "My brother, it doesn't really matter. Time is on our side... time and Ah Kin, the Lord Sun. Let's see how much of it the Castilàn can take when they run out of water, with no other shelter but their own sails. For all I know," he said, "this ship can become their coffin."

He wrapped himself in his mantle, crossed his arms on his chest and fell asleep.

❖　　　　　❖　　　　　❖

Twelve days later the *albarrada* was finished. It encircled the whole of the waterfront and so the whole of the city, which stretched behind the waterfront.

From the ship nothing stirred. The sails remained furled, the cannon silent. If not for the sailors walking on deck, she could have been a ghost ship. Not that Gonzalo expected any further communications with the Adelantado. Having sent out his refusal, the only thing left to be resolved was the test of wills between one man determined to land and another determined to keep him from landing.

During those twelve days Ah Dzan Chi was able to send a single discouraging message. The Castilàn had plenty of everything on board—food, water, gunpowder, and some incredibly smelly animals that they slaughtered and ate when the need arose. Since the ship had sailed directly to Chetemal, clearly she was prepared to make of Chetemal only the first stop in a long voyage.

But after the first discouragement Gonzalo dismissed the news as unimportant. How could even a ship as well provided as this one compare to the entire province he had at his disposal? He must simply stay put, wear out the Adelantado's patience before his own. If luck was with him, he wouldn't have to endanger the life of a single one of his warriors, even those warriors who grumbled at just having to stay put and kept vexing him with their calls for an attack on the ship.

There would be no such attack, he reminded them. It would be suicide, spears against cannon. But sometimes some of his warriors would sneak away and row out to the ship. There they would taunt the Castilàn, flourishing their weapons and shouting that they would cook them and eat them with tomatoes and peppers. The most hot-headed ones shot arrows up at the deck, to which the sailors responded by dumping bucketfuls of filth onto the canoes. Such confrontations afforded both sides nothing more than a venting out of hostility.

Inevitably Gonzalo found his men out and brought them back to order.

But soon the days began to stretch into weeks, and inactivity to make itself felt. The same heat on which Gonzalo counted to wear out the Adelantado also oppressed him and his men. Some missed their families, others had left cornfields and shops untended. He thought of Ix Na and the boys, and he became aware of yet one more disparity between the men he commanded and the ones he sought to repel.

Most Castilàn came to the New World as he himself had come, torn loose from home and kin. Often they had no home and no kin, no property, no trade, not even honor. Each man had to take care of no one but himself. But his warriors were tied to the warp and woof of family and clan obligations. Even those who made of war their profession went to war with their minds trailing back to the loved ones who stayed behind, who would have nowhere to go if the enemy invaded.

How could the father of small children, the newly-wed husband or the only son of an old mother compare to the Castilàn murderer who'd been given a choice between the gallows and duty overseas? The basic injustice, he thought, was that men who had everything to lose were forced to defend themselves against men who all too often had nothing to lose instead.

As time wore on, life behind the *albarrada* returned to its usual pace. The market was lively as always, the twin temples of Ah Cab and Ek Chuah smoked with their daily offerings. Gawkers who'd had their fill of looking at the ship went back to their villages. Nachancan had his duties to attend to, and went every day to the men's house to meet with his *batabs*. Gonzalo was left with the hardest task—keeping discipline among a full army that was under orders to remain alert but sometimes couldn't be blamed if it didn't.

He spent much time among his men, sharing their supper talk, keeping up their spirit. He wanted them to stay afraid, sharp to the danger; he wanted them to feel as though they were on a boat surrounded by sharks. If that gave them a better chance to survive, he was ready to swear to them that the Castilàn killed with a glance, like the monsters of his childhood's fairy stories.

Then one morning there was an unexpected arrival, a scout from the inland, the one place no one was worried about at the moment. The scout bore disconcerting news. Before coming to

Chetemal, the Adelantado had sent ashore a party led by his second-in-command, a man named Alonso Dávila who was an expert on gold mines.

Dávila and his party had landed about thirty leagues to the north, in a wilderness of swampland. That was why they hadn't been detected sooner; their landing place was too far from village or town. There Dávila and his men had been for the past thirty days or so, wandering about from a temporary camp with no one to show them the way but also no one to block it.

At first Gonzalo was chagrined by the news. Just by luck the Castilàn had managed to do what he'd been trying to keep them from doing with the *albarrada* and five companies of warriors—sheer blunderers' luck, the sort that directed children past a sleeping alligator. But then he took heart, ready to challenge the unforeseen complication. He ordered one of his men to row to the ship and recall Ah Dzan Chi ashore. The time had come to send to Dávila the interpreter and guide the gold seeker must be desperate for.

When he caught sight of the returning craft, for a moment he thought one of the Castilàn was coming. But it was Ah Dzan Chi, who as soon as the canoe landed tore off the linen shirt and velvet cap he was wearing. He tossed both into the sea and splashed sea water all over himself.

"Lord Itzamnà," he moaned in disgust, "will I ever be clean of the smell of that ship?"

Gonzalo wondered whether with the smell he might have also brought along lice. Luckily, however, among their countless medicinal remedies Ah Dzan Chi's people also had an excellent powder against lice, something he suspected the Castilàn would have sought almost as eagerly as they sought gold.

Quickly he filled his second *nacom* in on what had changed and on what must be done now. A short time later Ah Dzan Chi was on his way to Dávila's camp, with simple and absolute orders: keep the gold seekers away from the coast and the Adelantado's ship, mired in the swamps for as long as possible, until new orders.

Within a few days Ah Dzan Chi reported through his runners that he had found Dávila, had been fully taken into his confidence, and was now leading him further inland, into the worst part of the province. He added the Castilàn were so greedy for gold that they put up with every hardship. They were like monkeys after bait, he said, wild-eyed at the mere mention of the metal. But the best piece of information was the last. Dávila didn't know where the Adelantado was, and the Adelantado didn't know where Dávila was. After the gold seekers had landed, all contacts with the ship had been severed.

When Nachancan returned from the men's house Gonzalo gave him the news right away. Then the two of them sat together to eat. Their eyes were fixed on the ship, on that alien thing that day and night stood at the mouth of the harbor like an evil guardian.

Gonzalo laughed. "Ah Dzan Chi must be enjoying himself," he said. "'This way, kind lords, this way to the gold. Only two more days, only one more day and we'll be there!'" And he saw Dávila sweating and swatting mosquitoes, tramping industriously through the jungle after the God-sent savage who promised to make his hammock sag with yellow nuggets. "Like monkeys after bait," he sneered. "Well, we have the monkeys by the tail now!"

It took him a while to fall asleep that night, as he followed his thoughts while listening to the hushed noises of the men around him. He now had the Castilàn under control, and divided so they could sooner be conquered. But he must keep them divided and, most of all, ignorant of each other's fate.

This ignorance, he thought, could be his most precious ally.

What would happen for instance if Dávila were to think the Adelantado was dead, or vice-versa? Might not the loss of their companion persuade both men to abandon an unprofitable enterprise? Into the night that thought grew, took on the strength of a plan.

Hadn't it been too late, he would have put the plan in action right away.

In the morning he again summoned the runners. One would go to Ah Dzan Chi in the jungle of the north, the other to the ship. Both would bear the same message. It was a very simple plan, plain trickery in fact. If the trickery didn't work, he would lose nothing; but if it did work, he might win everything.

With the runners gone, again he settled down to wait for what the day would bring. The rain that had started before dawn stopped for a few hours, then came back with the same slow drip down the stiff branches of the palm trees. He paced the beach and stared anxiously at the ship, squinting for the sign of a canoe that might be bringing the runner back with the answer. What he wouldn't give to see the anchor being lifted, to order his warriors back to their villages, and he himself to start back for home.

But the day slipped into evening, then into night, and nothing happened. Gonzalo's strain became a tightness in his shoulders, as if he'd been carrying something heavy for many hours. Nachancan spoke little, and not of the Castilàn. It was his way of hiding the same strain. He too knew the men were beginning to blunt with homesickness and boredom. He knew they didn't understand this war of nerves. He'd never asked Gonzalo out loud, but the question had been there all the time, as oppressive as the heat: how long must they wait?

Late and in a bad humor Gonzalo resigned himself to going to sleep. Again, as he'd done so often lately, he thought of Ix Na and the boys, of the cool porches of Xul Ha where life was sweet and safe. He wondered when he would return to them, to that sweet life. He felt a stab of anguish at the prospect of waking up tomorrow to yet another endless day of uncertainty.

But in the middle of the night he got up from his hammock to relieve himself, and he became aware that something seemed to be different from all the other nights. His mind, still only half alert, told him something was missing. He looked toward the sea, toward the surf breaking over the reef: yes, the lights were missing, the lights from the lanterns that the Castilàn soldiers always lit at nightfall on the quarterdeck. Where for nights on end there had always been those distant bright dots, now there was only unbroken darkness.

His heart quickened, his whole being snapped to life. With his eyes he pinpointed the other lights, the signal fires along the bay. He couldn't rejoice yet. What if the ship was only hiding, not gone but only gone out of sight? For a moment he was at a loss. He could not wait until daylight, he thought, and daylight would take forever.

He hurried back to his hammock, waking up the men as he went. Soon the whole beach was astir with voices, torches, and the first shouts of victory. Could it be true? Gonzalo wondered as he shook Nachancan awake. Could it have been so easy? Gone at last, defeated without the shedding of a single drop of blood!

Nachancan nearly bolted from his hammock. When Gonzalo told him, he too had all sorts of questions. The fires ashore only made it harder to scan the sea. Within moments a whole flotilla of canoes set out, headed for the spot where the Castilàn ship had been fastened to the horizon like an evil charm to the door of its intended victim.

The canoe that bore Gonzalo and Nachancan was first to buck beyond the surf. The rowers began to cry out to the other men in the other canoes. The harbor was empty, the invaders had fled. An upsurge of relief swept everyone. The warriors started to dance in the bobbing craft, thrusting their spears at the empty space where the enemy had been, as if slaying their ghosts.

Dizzy with the bouncing of the craft and with his own joy, Gonzalo steadied himself against Nachancan. There was such comfort in that, he thought; the body of his brother was solid and strong to lean on. Nachancan laughed, struggled for balance and almost fell overboard. But who wanted to stop, even if they must all fall into the sea and wriggle about like fish!

With that celebration, daylight came quickly. And finally, at daylight, the runner Gonzalo had sent to the ship reached the waterfront. The Castilàn had put him ashore at some distance from it, to give themselves time to leave without being followed. Before the five companies of warriors, before the *batabs* and the people of Chetemal, the runner gave his account; and it was short and it was final, the public confirmation of Gonzalo's triumph.

Following Gonzalo's orders, he'd given the Adelantado the false news that Alonso Dávila, was dead along with everyone else who'd gone ashore looking for gold. The Adelantado had believed the news, no one knew why except the Gods, and may the Gods be praised for their wisdom everywhere they dwell, the runner said. So the Castilàn had left Chetemal, with no intention of returning.

Afterwards, no one could hear what his neighbor was saying, so loud were the joyful voices rising as one to the sky. Gonzalo was lifted on the shoulders of his warriors and carried from the shore to the temple above the crowd. He caught a glimpse of Nachancan, for whom the men were bringing a litter; but him, not Nachancan, they carried first into the temple, as the men jostled one another to share in the carrying.

It was like reviving after a long illness. There were still Castilàn ashore, in the inland with Ah Dzan Chi. But he was confident now that if one half of his plan had worked, the other half would work as well. Flush with pride, he allowed himself to think that this province alone, this province where he lived and was *nacom,* would escape the clutches of the Castilàn and remain the only free province in all of the mainland. Wouldn't that show the Castilàn something, he thought; if he hadbecome a thorn in their side, wouldn't that thorn sting deep.

The warriors carried him all the way to the great stone images of their protector Gods. The drums began, fast and thundering.

Around him all was a happy whirlwind. But all he was thinking about was Ix Na and the boys, and the cool porches of Xul Ha, where he would be tonight.

❖   ❖   ❖

Ah Dzan Chi's response came soon enough and, as Gonzalo hoped, sealed his expectations with success. As instructed, Ah Dzan Chi had given Alonso Dávila the false news that the Adelantado was dead, perished in a wreck along with the ship and crew. Dávila, tired and bedeviled as he was already, had believed the news and decided to return to the safety of the closest Castilàn settlement in the north, having found, of course, not an ounce of gold.

Fifteen days later Ah Dzan Chi too was back in Xul Ha. He was unkempt, footsore from the marches to nowhere he'd led the Castilàn on, but a very happy man. One fine morning he'd slipped away from Dávila's camp, and hadn't been followed, clearly because the Castilàn had no need for him anymore. By now Dávila and his men were on their way back to where they'd come from.

Gonzalo embraced warmly the young man who'd been such a valuable ally in his bloodless war. Tomorrow Ah Dzan Chi would stand between him and Nachancan when the priests would lead the formal ceremony of thanksgiving.

Then Ix Na came in, with food and drink for both men.

During the past fifteen days she'd been visiting Bird Woman often; now she was the first to give Ah Dzan Chi news of his family. She smiled quietly to herself while she poured *cacau* for the two men.

Gonzalo wondered whether she might be thinking about the two straight days and nights they had spent in their bed with the door cloth drawn against all comers, like a newlywed couple.

THIRTY-ONE

White Feather was in love, and miserable. During the ceremonies of the month of Paax the handsomest young warrior she'd ever seen had smiled to her while he danced the *holkan akot,* the Warriors' Dance; and from that moment the world for her had one more cardinal point to turn to.

Ix Lolkin had found out who the young man was: Tu Manìk, the son of a wealthy and respected priest in Chetemal. She approved of White Feather's choice, and would have done all that was in her power to see the match accomplished; but it was not in her power to persuade Nachancan that the time was ripe for White Feather to be a wife.

So the days passed and Nachancan wondered without a clue about the ill that had taken his daughter. The jade he bought for her didn't brighten her lovely face, the gowns he had made for her didn't bring back the happy little girl he loved more than anything in the world. He paid musicians and players who knew all the latest farces, from *The Cacau Vendor* to *The Maid With Seven Petticoats;* but after the players left, White Feather still brooded, Nachancan still wondered, Ix Lolkin still grumbled, and everybody was as miserable as before.

Finally it was White Feather herself who forced the bounds of convention and told her father, in tears, that no presents and no performers, nothing he would ever give her could heal her sorrow.

This time the healing must come not from him but from another man.

Nachancan was stunned, like someone who is betrayed without a reason. After White Feather ran back to her mother, still in tears, he went to Gonzalo's house and spent the rest of the day there—as if hiding out, Gonzalo thought, refusing to face something unpleasant.

Gonzalo had nothing to offer as consolation except the vague truths all parents must accept when their children outgrow them. Why, he said testily, only yesterday the twins, who were now sixteen, had beaten him for the first time during their daily swim in the lagoon, and had felt old and tired, like an old man with softening bones. He could tell, however, that Nachancan's mood was different. Nachancan behaved more like a spurned lover than like a father. But he shrugged that off as something he just couldn't understand because he didn't have a daughter.

After two days of sulking in Gonzalo's hammock, Nachancan at last accepted what he must, although not to White Feather's face.

Instead he told Ix Lolkin that he gave their daughter permission to marry Tu Manìk, then left to go hunting with the bow. When he returned he found his favorite porch crowded with women.

Surrounded by happy laughter, White Feather was choosing from among her gowns the one she would wear for her first meeting with Tu Manìk before the wedding. When she saw her father she ran to him, greeted him, thanked him all in one breath. Nachancan smiled only with his eyes;

then he added to her gowns a magnificent wedding cloak covered with the finest, silkiest white heron feathers.

The wedding was a sumptuous affair. Tu Manìk's gifts to the bride were things of great beauty. The house he built for himself and her, the third one now in Xul Ha, had furnishings to rival those in Nachancan's own quarters. His father performed the ceremony and tied together the couple's mantles. Ix Lolkin was especially happy that her daughter would now be under close heavenly protection, since Tu Manìk's father was a conscientious priest who never forgot to honor any of the Gods.

Gonzalo enjoyed himself very much during the four days of feasting. He loved these gatherings—the music, the dancing, the food, the good-natured chance to make Ix Na jealous if he let another woman fuss around him. He liked Tu Manìk, who'd manifested his wish to serve directly under him, and he was glad to see White Feather finally a contented bride.

Ah Dzan Chi brought his children, and Bird Woman again made every heart soar with her singing. The twins were now old enough to lust after some young lovely, and during the celebrations they wandered off to a quiet corner of the *cacau* grove. Even Temah, shy as he was, gave himself license to indulge and made his parents proud by behaving like any other fourteen-year-old boy.

Life was good once again, Gonzalo thought. The Castilàn had been beaten, the Adelantado and his ship were gone, so were Alonso Dávila and his gold seekers. His status had risen to its highest peak, not just in Chetemal but everywhere his name was known. His people thought of him as their sword and shield, almost as a charm against invasion. They seemed to think that as long as he was with them, though he was but one man, they would be able to hold off the enemy forever. If he wasn't careful, he reminded himself, he could almost begin to believe that.

Life didn't stay good for long. White Feather and Tu Manìk were still enjoying their honeymoon when everything changed again, and in the worst possible way.

At first it was rumors of something unusual stirring in the north. The Xiu had been quiet for years, so quiet that Nachancan had cut in half the number of men who guarded the border. Even the old fortifications seemed to have become unnecessary, and were left to fall into disrepair. But now Xiu scouts were sighted prowling around the least protected spots, as if sounding for an easy entry, and the villagers who came upon them on their way to the cornfields were very much alarmed by the strange doings of their untrustworthy neighbors.

Ekuneh, whose town was the closest to the northern border, rushed to Nachancan a fretful message saying he feared for his safety and wanted a company of warriors sent right away in case of attack. Nachancan thought Ekuneh was worrying for nothing, and delayed the sending of the warriors. But in the following days more and more sightings were reported from the border, until it became impossible to dismiss them. So Nachancan charged Gonzalo with selecting the company to be sent to Ekuneh. But by the time Gonzalo had his warriors ready, it was too late.

The last day of the month of Kayab Ekuneh appeared at the gate of Xul Ha looking like the bearer of the world's worst tidings. Gonzalo rushed to the council hall from the glade where he'd been training the twins with their first full-sized *hadzabs*. In his hurry he let the two boys follow him.

Ekuneh asked for a moment to compose himself, an anxious moment in which all sorts of disastrous possibilities seemed to hover in the room like carrion birds.

"Hun Halal," he began, "three years ago I was told the Castilàn had left our land... I was told the one named Dávila had gone back to the north." He ran his hand on his face. "But now Dávila has returned, with more Castilàn. At this very moment he's in my house, and holds my wife and sons as hostages!"

Nachancan made a gesture to calm his brother down, but he himself was shaken. As for Gonzalo, no one was more shaken than he. He realized what a mistake he'd made, and he was overwhelmed.

Three years ago he'd had Dávila in his hands, ready for the kill. Yet he'd let Dávila go, as though that were victory enough. But an enemy left alive is an enemy forever; the last of his warriors could have told him that. How could he, who was their captain, have forgotten that fundamental rule?

Ekuneh was far from finished with the bad news. "And I must still tell you just how the Castilàn have made it to my house, for surely they couldn't have stumbled onto it by accident. The ones we once tried to win over have led them to me... The ones with less honor than a monkey have brought ruin to our land!"

Nachancan traded a quick glance with Gonzalo. "The Xiu. All those reports..."

"Yes," Ekuneh confirmed, without trying to hide his loathing. "At this very moment two of them sit at my table and eat my food with the Castilàn. They flatter these strangers, they serve them and they even serve their horses, those horrible beasts... And Dávila promises them honors and rewards, while he turns my house upside down for gold and empties my corn pits for his meals!"

Gonzalo got up and started pacing around the room, one fist into the other, oblivious of everything but the exploding anger inside him. His thoughts came in clipped, obsessive bursts, like repeated cannon shots. Xelha all over again; another failure, another job half done; another miscalculation that would cost lives and grief.

But recriminations would not help. Even demanding that Ekuneh explain how he could just have let the Castilàn and their Xiu allies into the province would not help. Ekuneh had never been the bravest of men, and this time it might well have been impossible even for someone else to keep the unwanted visitors at bay.

The only thing to do was plan a new course of action, the course of action needed to fight the fire that this time was next door. He looked at Akil and Pa'ap, and for a moment his mind went blank with panic as he wondered what he would do if his sons were being held hostage by the Castilàn.

"What do the Castilàn want?" Nachancan asked.

Ekuneh's voice was terribly strained. "I was ordered to bring you a message. If I don't return with your answer by tomorrow, my wife and sons will be killed."

Nachancan took the names of several Gods in vain, something he'd never done before. "Out with this message," he said then.

Ekuneh tried to clear his dry throat. "In the name of his ruler and king, the Castilàn named Dávila summons you to go before him and to make him offer of peace. He wants a promise from you that you will become his ally. He wants a tribute of corn and fowls and other foodstuffs, and on pain of the greatest harm he commands you to —"

"Commands me!" Nachancan roared. "Commands *me*, the True Man of Chetemal, whose ancestors have lain buried in this land for nine thousand generations!"

He got up in a fury, and with his closed fist he hit the shield of woven cane that hung on the wall beside him. "We will have no peace with these strangers but war, and the tribute we'll send them will be spears in place of fowls, and arrows in place of corn!" he cried. He turned to Gonzalo. "Ah Holkan, what do you say? What words of answer are to be given to the Castilàn?"

Gonzalo's voice was cold and calm. "The very same words I just heard you say, my brother. Nothing more, nothing less." He addressed Ekuneh. "You will go back to your wife and sons, and you will give Dávila this answer from the True Man of Chetemal: the people of Chetemal do not want peace but war, and the tribute they will send will be spears in place of fowls, and arrows in place of corn. You can leave when you're ready."

Ekuneh demurred. "But how can I hope to live if I return with such an answer? Hun Halal, hear me out. Promise peace, promise friendship. Appease these invaders until a proper time and way can be found to get rid of them."

"No," Nachancan said angrily. "We are not the Xiu. We do not appease the enemy." His voice softened a little. "I am sure the Castilàn will not harm you. They could have done so already, and sent someone else as their messenger. It's me they want," he said. He looked at Gonzalo. "And my war captain."

Ekuneh appeared somewhat reassured. "That I can believe," he said. "The name of your war captain is constantly in Dávila's mouth. He was furious when he discovered that the town he'd come to was not the one where Ah Holkan lives. I think he wants to find him even more than he wants to find gold!" Then he nodded. "Very well. I'll set out in a while. I'm thirsty," he said apologetically. "I have traveled in a hurry..."

"Eat and drink with us," Nachancan told him. "We have much to talk about."

❖   ❖   ❖

It was hard to sleep knowing the enemy was so close and so strong.

As Ekuneh had made clear, this expedition wasn't for Dávila just a military campaign but first and foremost a personal quest for revenge. How they must have fumed, Dávila and the Adelantado, when they'd finally met and discovered how Gonzalo had deceived them. This minor masterpiece of trickery had become rather famous among the Castilàn, again according to Ekuneh who'd listened to their talk as an unwilling witness. From what Ekuneh had heard, the Castilàn's first order was to find the "vile and low traitor" and drag him in chains to the nearest stake—although Gonzalo didn't need to have this told.

The most important thing to do this time was decide where it was best for the True Man of Chetemal and his war captain to be when Dávila would come looking for them. As soon as Ekuneh left with his answer for the invaders, Nachancan and Gonzalo called a private war council. This time the circumstances demanded that the House of Can think of itself first and notify the *batabs* later; also that the House of Can hear the opinion not only of its men but of its women as well.

There wasn't much debate. The only reasonable place in which to make a stand was Xul Ha—men, women and children. If the House of Can must end, it would end within the same walls where it had endured for years beyond counting. Ah Dzan Chi and his family, who didn't live in Xul Ha, would move in with Tu Manìk and White Feather in their spacious new home with the nursery still empty.

Once that was settled, all that remained to do was fortify Xul Ha just as Chetemal had been fortified three years earlier against the Castilàn's ship.

Warriors would be called in, but no more than what Xul Ha could sustain by itself. Like long ago when the smallpox had struck, Xul Ha must become a closed stronghold, the last refuge in the midst of danger. Also this way, should the Castilàn try as they usually did to fragment the power of the True Man by pitting his *batabs* against him, the True Man would not be at the mercy of his own divided chieftains.

So the men and women of Xul Ha began the task of turning rooms and patios built for luxury and enjoyment into a military compound. What had once been the spare but clean servants' quarters became a barracks. Gonzalo and Nachancan put the warriors to building an *albarrada* of trunks, cactus and stones, and a ditch full of sharpened stakes. Ix Na and Ix Lolkin had the corn pits and storage rooms filled with the most food that would keep; the *dzonot*, the underground well that had served the needs of the place for centuries, would supply the water.

In the midst of all these preparations, Ix Na found time to think of something else. One night Gonzalo noticed beside their bed a large, unlocked mahogany box. He asked her what it was, and she opened it for him. The box was full of gold: every scrap of gold she owned and everything she had persuaded the other women to hand over was in there. On top of that small treasure he could see the necklace with the golden frogs that she'd worn in Tulum the first time they'd met. Now this was strange, he thought. He knew, since he'd done that himself, that the truly precious jade jewelry was safely buried in the *cacau* grove; but the yellow trinkets whose loss would mean little to all Ix Na had stored in the very first place a Castilàn would look.

Puzzled, he pointed at the box. "Why would you leave such a hoard so poorly protected? This is just an invitation to any Castilàn to take it."

Her answer was plain. There was no vain hope in it, but a deliberate calculation. "Once you told me the Castilàn think gold can even deliver one from the torments of the World Underneath. Perhaps this gold can deliver us from the Castilàn."

Gonzalo stopped undressing and looked at her with a smile. "Perhaps, yes," he said, approving of her idea. Then he placed his *hadzab* across the lid of the box, as if to seal it. "But they will have to get to it first."

About a week later, while the *albarrada* was still being built, more bad news came from Ekuneh's town. This time they were brought by Ekuneh's wife and sons. Upon Ekuneh's return the Castilàn had released them, but only because Ekuneh himself was now their hostage. Dávila had left the town, taking Ekuneh and four *batabs* along. Ekuneh's wife couldn't hold her tears as she told of how Dávila had forced the five hostages, hands tied, to set out on foot before his horse. Of course she and the two young, badly frightened boys were given shelter and lodged in Nachancan's house. Xul Ha was now bursting at the seams with people, its resources stretched to the limit.

As everyone could surmise, with Ekuneh as his unwilling guide Dávila wouldn't be long in finding the place he was looking for. Perhaps Ekuneh could detour him for a while, but certainly this time Dávila would make doubly sure he was being given the right directions. At most he would stop at Chetemal on his way to Xul Ha, and only because he must have been told three years ago by the Adelantado Montejo that it was a large and prosperous-looking city. It was only a matter of time before the guards gave the alarm. All that could be hoped was that the *albarrada* would be finished before that time.

By now the *batabs* in Chetemal had been given the news and put on the alert. The old fortifications around the waterfront were hastily patched up and manned anew with warriors. But the *batabs* were scared and of too many minds, and this forecast nothing but trouble.

Once again the scouts became Gonzalo's eyes and ears.

Scattered throughout the province, they kept him well appraised of Dávila's progress. Their reports came in almost daily, and almost daily got worse.

The first report said that Dávila had received Nachancan's defiant answer and accepted the challenge. He would crush the ruler of Chetemal with all speed and severity, as he would all rebels, and he would finally get his hands on the white traitor who helped him.

The next report said Dávila was searching for a land route to the south but his march was hampered by the difficult terrain, that maze of sounds, lagoons and swamps that became all but impassable during the rainy season. Gonzalo listened and in his heart he hoped

Dávila would never discover the truth. There was no land route, and the only way to get across was by means of canoes.

The next report said Dávila had found canoes, requisitioned from villagers through Ekuneh. Often the horsemen had to leave the canoes and move along the banks as best they could, for the animals were skittish and hard to transport by water. Gonzalo listened and in his heart he hoped the horsemen would get lost and the horses bolt from the canoes and drown.

The next report said the Castilàn had passed only three leagues away from Xul Ha, yet by some miracle hadn't spotted it beyond the *cacau* groves. Gonzalo listened, shuddered, and in his heart he hoped the Castilàn had all gone blind.

The report after that dealt the final blow to every hope anyone could still entertain. Dávila had arrived in Chetemal; worse, he had arrived without the slightest opposition from the *batabs,* who were too confused and too frightened to know what to do and had simply let him into the city, just as Ekuneh had let them into his town before. A few days after his arrival Dávila had begun to build a settlement. The scouts had learned its name: Villa Real.

The *requerimiento* had been read, and the population of the city had been divided into *encomiendas,* the name the Spaniards gave to their private holdings in the New World. Each encomienda must provide foodstuffs and manual labor to its new rulers. The *batabs* had carried out the division and had begun supplying the invaders with all that they demanded. The first thing they demanded was of course gold, of which there was very little in Chetemal. Even so, Dávila regularly sent out search parties in the city and the surrounding country. It wasn't at all clear how all this could have happened. The scouts gave jumbled accounts. All that could be said was that it had happened, and without resistance, which was even more astounding. The province was like a man paralyzed by the bite of a scorpion. Everyone in it seemed to have lost the power to think like a creature of reason. Confusion alone reigned.

Under the impact of such news, Xul Ha seemed also to have fallen under an evil spell. Gonzalo paced the bank of the lagoon along the still unfinished *albarrada* and repeated to himself the details of the catastrophe, as though by uttering them out loud he could finally make them sink into his mind. This was Chetemal, he had to tell himself, this was the place that had defeated two waves of invaders, the only place that had remained untouched while the rest of the mainland fell piecemeal into the hands of the Castilàn.... It was too much to believe.

Nachancan was no less numb. How could his own people have surrendered just like that, without striking a blow? How could his own chiefs have made offers of peace to the enemy, against his every order? It was as if they'd forgotten he was their ruler, and a good and fair ruler who never before had had cause to doubt the love of his subjects. Never had he imagined that his power could be so easily wiped out, like a footprint by the sweep of a wave.

The only sane man left in Chetemal seemed to be Tu Manìk's father, the old priest Ah Kin Mo, who had sent a messenger of his own. Ah Kin Mo said he'd first tried to rally the *batabs* against the invaders, reminding them the allegiance they owed to their lord and the danger their rash actions put him in; then, outnumbered, he'd spent four days and nights in the temple of Ah Cab, the Bee God, praying for deliverance and making offerings to heaven, whose wisdom he could no longer decipher.

But then Dávila had come with some of his men and had forced the old priest out at gunpoint. After looking in vain for gold among the temple's sacred objects, Dávila had removed the image of Ah Cab from its altar and put a wooden cross in its place. When Ah Kin Mo had tried to go back in, one of Dávila's men had struck him on the head with the butt of his gun, drawing blood; and as the Castilàn rode away, the old priest had smeared the door of the temple with his blood. If henceforth he would no longer be able to make any more offerings, Ah Cab would surely accept this last one from him.

Nachancan was especially distressed by this incident. Ah Cab was Chetemal's own Father, the most beloved of the Gods. The beehives were not only the staple of Chetemal's wealth but also the living symbol of peaceful and orderly life, a mirror of the ideal government. During the Festival of

Beehives Nachancan wore the mask of Ah Cab, as he became invested with the sacred power of the Protector. The Castilàn' desecration of the God's dwelling place meant the most grievous omens of disruption.

Fortunately the *batabs* had retained enough common sense not to reveal to Dávila the whereabouts of their territorial ruler and their war captain. The message from Ah Kin Mo concluded by saying that indeed Dávila didn't know about Xul Ha, and if common sense held, he might never find out. No *batab,* no matter how confused he might be, would willingly reveal to the Castilàn where Nachancan and Gonzalo were. In the meantime, Ah Kin Mo said, Nachancan and Gonzalo must stay put and keep all contacts with Chetemal well concealed from the Castilàn—Ah Kin Mo's messenger had left the city disguised as a water seller.

Finally the *albarrada* was completed. Every able-bodied male in Xul Ha was prepared. Gonzalo saw to it that even the servants and household retainers be taught some self-defense. The members of the House of Can had taken to eating together in Nachancan's main hall.

It wasn't only a show of solidarity but also a deep need to find strength in the bonding of the clan.

The talk around the meals was sober and to the point, almost a daily military report. The women, who'd never taken part in public affairs before, now had each a newly-found voice. Even Ekuneh's wife, who spoke seldom if at all in the presence of her husband, showed much courage in the face of a great upheaval. At the moment she was the one who stood to lose the most to the Castilàn, yet she never hinted that something should be done to rescue Ekuneh from Dávila's hands.

It was the men who yearned for action. Gonzalo especially had become exasperated with having to hide like a hunted rabbit, and his mood was always on edge. It wasn't just the desire to force a confrontation that vexed him, but also the need to see for himself what was happening outside. The scouts hadn't been able to find out the number of Castilàn who'd invaded. They said only that the Castilàn were everywhere, thick as ants in the grass.

About two months had passed since Dávila's arrival. The runners had been coming regularly all that time, one in the morning and one at night;

even if there wasn't anything new for them to report, they still came to report that there was nothing new. But one day, without warning, both runners stopped making their eagerly awaited entrance. After waiting for them almost in a frenzy for three days in a row, the men and women of the House of Can gathered together to decide what they should do next.

The air in Nachancan's main hall was heavy with worry. For the first time in these gatherings, the twins and Obsidian Blade sat with the men. They were of warrior age now, and wore the new *hadzabs* their fathers had given them in private, without the ceremony that accompanied this recognition of adulthood. Temah sat with Ix Na. Now he clung to her more than ever, as if he'd become her special protector. Tu Manìk and White Feather shared the same mat like on their wedding day. It was especially sad to see their handsome young faces so dark with fear.

"This disappearance of the runners means one thing only," Gonzalo began without preambles. "Dávila has found them out. And if Dávila has found out about the runners, he has also found out about Xul Ha."

It was the one thought that occupied everyone's mind. An anxious silence hung in the room.

"If the Castilàn come," Gonzalo added, "they will come from the lagoon."

There was a sound of agreement. It had never been a secret that, were Dávila to look for the easiest way to Xul Ha, he would find it in that smooth body of water that linked the inland with the coast. For that reason the men had given up their daily swim in the lagoon. Between them and it now rose the massed stones and sharpened poles of the *albarrada*. The silky blue water in which it was so good to dive on a hot day had become a dangerous emptiness, wide open and unprotected.

"Then if the Castilàn will come from the side of the water," Ah Dzan Chi said, "we must keep a way out for ourselves on the side of the land."

"There's the gate to the *cacau* grove," Ahau Can pointed out. "But a way out to where?" Nachancan said. "Into the jungle, under the bushes? Ekuneh's town is not to be considered. There are certainly Castilàn there."

All were silent again, and for the first time all were aware of the unnerving possibility that Xul Ha might have become a trap.

"And how many of us would be able to take that way out?" Nachancan said. "We are warriors. We are trained to march on a handful of corn and no more moisture that could be sucked from a root. But could the women follow us into the jungle? Could the children?"

This time Ix Na spoke, quietly and firmly. "Hun Halal. Even if you asked us, we would not follow you. We would not slow down your escape." She turned to Ix Lolkin, to White Feather and Bird Woman and Ekuneh's wife and the mother of Obsidian Blade. On each face she read the same resolve.

"We will stay here, with the children," she said. "I don't know how the Castilàn deal with the women of their enemies, but I want to think that they will spare us." Her eyes went from her brother to her husband. "You two are the ones they want. You two are the ones who must be safe before all else."

The thought of having to leave her behind drove horror into Gonzalo's heart. He could see the same thing in the eyes of every other man in the room, yet he could see also that Ix Na was right. But then he shook his head. "Enough. We talk as if the Castilàn had broken in already," he said briskly. "There is another way. Let's march on Chetemal tomorrow. Let's strike first. Enough of this waiting."

Nachancan balked, but the other men tipped the balance; and Ahau Can led them, Nachancan's firstborn. "I am with Ah Holkan.

The first strike is half the battle," he said, repeating every warrior's maxim.

"We are as ready today as we will ever be," Ah Dzan Chi said. "It makes no difference whether we meet the Castilàn here or in Chetemal."

"The people are asleep," Gonzalo said fiercely. "They must be made to wake up. In Xelha I saw old women going at the Castilàn with their grindstones... Surely we can do no less."

With that Nachancan gave up, nodding his assent. He looked at Gonzalo earnestly. "But please, Ah Holkan. Make also sure that everybody knows where the gate to the *cacau* grove is."

Gonzalo hurried out of the hall. Upon seeing him, his warriors clustered around him; and when he told them they broke into a shout that was eagerness to fight and hatred of the enemy bursting out all at once. They couldn't wait to go out tomorrow.

Then he made a round of the guards around the *albarrada*. It was almost sundown, and the lagoon looked beautiful in the soft smoky light. The guards too were glad to hear about the impending expedition, and called out the news to each other. Finally Gonzalo went by the gate to the *cacau* grove. There too everything was in order. But beyond the gate stretched a deserted countryside that was now no less threatening than the water—a way out to nowhere, as Nachancan had put it.

He thought with a shiver that the world all around him had become a wilderness of enemies. The only free land left was this one corner he had surrounded with wood and stone, this one corner that held within it everything he loved. How many Castilàn were out there? he wondered. How many cannons, how many muskets, how many horses? What would his warriors face tomorrow when they would leave the safety of Xul Ha? What if the odds were overwhelming? It was agony not to know, not to be able to gage the disparity. This was the most frightened he'd ever been, the most helpless.

Ah Dzan Chi's voice almost startled him. "Ah Holkan. All is done out here. Let's go back in."

The house seemed eerie with only the last of the sunlight to guide him through. Since three days, by his orders, no lights were lit in Xul Ha except those that couldn't be seen beyond the *albarrada*. That night he would have to sleep apart from Ix Na, as always before war; but first he must seek her out. He saw that she was waiting for him.

Certainly she knew already the first thing he had to tell her. "I'm taking Akil and Pa'ap with me."

She nodded, weary. Sixteen years ago when the twins were born the priests had predicted this day when they would pass from her world into the world of their father, a world of change and destruction. It seemed like such a short time, that was all. Obsidian Blade also would go with Nachancan. Earlier she'd been sharing her grief with the boy's mother, a grief she could share only with another woman. "I've packed for them too," she said simply. Then she clasped her hands together hard. "You will see that they understand your orders?" she asked tentatively, as if her question were an impropriety, a breach of men's rules.

Gonzalo took down his *hadzab* and ran his fingers on it. There was a small crack in one of the blades. He must have Ah Dzan Chi look at it.

"Of course I will," he said. Then he stopped fumbling with the blade and raised his face. She looked so alone, he thought. There was a bad feeling in his soul, like a premonition of disaster, and he had to struggle to conceal it. Even words were difficult in such misery.

Temah came in. He'd been standing just outside the doorway without his parents' noticing. His face, his parents noticed now, was set with a determination that had never been there before. Something had done for him what the new *hadzabs* had done for Akil and Pa'ap. Akil and Pa'ap would follow their father as warriors tomorrow, but Temah was as sure of his place as they were.

Gonzalo took him by the arm and smiled. "You will look after your mother, won't you Temah Can? You are the only man left in Xul Ha now... until we return," he added quickly.

Temah didn't smile back. "Yes, father, I know," he said calmly, almost coldly, as if his father were reminding him something he didn't have to be reminded.

There was another long, strained silence. "We leave early," Gonzalo said then. "You two sleep... no need to see us off," but he knew both would do otherwise.

Ix Na was on the verge of tears. She grasped Temah's hand and turned her face.

He must go, now while the silence held, like a scaffold under a heavy load that was about to crash. He gathered his things and got up. His eyes fell on the mahogany box that Ix Na kept by their bed, the box with all of Xul Ha's gold in it.

"Perhaps I should take some of that gold with me," he said, and he wanted it to be a joke, but it didn't come out like one.

THIRTY-TWO

It took him a while to fall asleep. It was always hard without Ix Na's comforting presence, and he wasn't used to the place, a covered patio by the warriors' quarters.

Akil and Pa'ap lay in hammocks beside him, Obsidian Blade on a mat. He could hear the three boys toss and turn in the dark. How much harder sleep must be for them, who were about to know war for the first time. Further away was Ah Dzan Chi, who slept well in all places and at all times, and half the men of his battle guard.

Nachancan, Ahau Can and Tu Manìk had taken mats along the other side of the patio, where the two guards kept a lookout.

His ears caught every small noise. A sigh from the twins, the grating of the guards' spears against the wall, the distant howl of a monkey. Everything came to him in the night, and far too many thoughts. The worst thought was that he was old enough to have grown sons, and that his sons were old enough to be killed in battle. If he let that sink in, he knew he would lose heart altogether.

There was only one way, the way of all soldiers—put his mind wholly to the task at hand, as calmly as if the task at hand were nothing more complicated than mending the straps of his sandals so he wouldn't have to go barefoot. Where to attack, when, how, what if; that he could handle, that was easy. It gave him a feeling of control, it made him the player instead of the pawn. Finally, slowly, he drifted off.

Just as day was breaking, the sound of a commotion woke him up, then Pa'ap's voice strangled with fear. In a moment he was wide awake. Everything around him was tumult, the ominous confusion of a camp caught by surprise. In the streaky, uncertain light of dawn the warriors were scrambling for their weapons, the guards were shouting, his battle guard milled around in disorder. Nachancan tried to make himself heard over the noise, while Ah Dzan Chi and Tu Manìk where nowhere to be seen.

Pa'ap was still calling him. "Father, they've landed! They're on the shore of the lagoon!"

Gonzalo's heart was racing, torn from the quiet of sleep into a hellish uproar. He reached for his *hadzab* and motioned Pa'ap to remain where he was. "Stay with your brother and Obsidian Blade. Stay with these men of the battle guard." Pa'ap nodded yes. Gonzalo ran over to Nachancan, shouting to know what was going on.

"Castilàn," Nachancan blurted out. "With guns and horses, from canoes... Just outside the wall by the main gate."

Gonzalo couldn't believe his ears. "And no one saw them coming across the water?" he roared. "No one heard them?"

Nachancan shook his head, his face mirroring the same dismay.

"Clever demons," Ahau Can said in his teeth. "Where is Ah Dzan Chi?" Gonzalo asked.

"To the wall, with Tu Manìk and his men," Nachancan answered.

"I'll go find him," Gonzalo said. "My brother, I need you here.

The Castilàn might try to break in two places at once. You and Ahau Can must see to that second place. Keep the boys with you," he added. "Let me find out how many guns first." Nachancan gestured that he understood. Quickly Gonzalo was on his way to the wall, accompanied by the other half of his battle guard.

Even before he reached the *albarrada* by the main gate he heard the muskets from the shore. They sounded very close, and he winced at the thought of Ah Dzan Chi and Tu Manìk who'd rushed to meet them without even the time to put on their quilted armor.

The warriors crowded along the palisade—cowered rather, crouching in a mass below the edge of the wall. Above the edge of the wall the musket balls fell in steady volleys; it was impossible even to raise one's head to see. Only the spearmen and the archers could venture up there, but they were hurling their weapons at targets they could barely make out in the smoke.

From the other side of the wall came the neighing of horses, the pounding of hooves. It was a sound most of the warriors had never heard before, so that to them it seemed like the sound of hell itself about to pour in, and they covered their ears to shut it out, bumping into each other in the dim light.

Ah Dzan Chi at one end, Tu Manìk at the other were trying to herd the men into something resembling a battle formation. But no sooner did they have the men together and facing the enemy that a new volley of fire whistled among them. Out of the crowd three, four warriors fell wounded or dead, and the others scattered in every direction once again. It was chaos. Gonzalo had come to see how strong the enemy was, and what he saw told him they were too strong for resistance.

"Form ranks," he shouted to the panicked warriors. "Hold your positions!" But no one seemed to hear him. Even more useless were the servants and retainers he'd spent so much time training. He could see them running around, not one of them armed even with a stick, shouting and managing only to get in the warriors' way.

As he started to plow through to Ah Dzan Chi and Tu Manìk, he caught an even more foreboding sound—that of something being pounded against the wall, certainly a tree trunk the Castilàn were using as a battering ram. He could hear the wall rattling, the poles groaning under the impact, yet not one warrior was at that spot to protect it. All his instructions had come to nothing, all his plans had unraveled. What he had so often decried in others was now happening to him, and he was powerless to stop it.

Ah Dzan Chi saw him. "Ah Holkan," he called out, "we can do nothing here. But we can buy some time... They must not find you!"

Gonzalo wasn't ready to run. Every nerve in his body refused to accept the very thought. How could he leave Xul Ha to the Castilàn? How could he desert his own home? In his rage he turned toward the cringing warriors and began to strike them with the handle of his *hadzab.*

"Fight, you cowards!" he damned them. "Have you forgotten everything I taught you?"

The warriors stumbled this way and that, their arms raised above their heads, their eyes wild. He dragged them toward the wall, turned them around to face the muskets' fire.

"You are my men," he shouted hoarsely. "My men don't run!" Right then another volley of bullets hissed through the air.

The man he was holding by the arm was torn from him; all that was left of his face was a bloody mask. The others began to wail, too terrified to run from their war captain but equally terrified to obey his orders. If Tu Manìk hadn't jumped at Gonzalo to bring him down, the next ball would have made of him nothing more recognizable than the mangled dead sprawled at his feet.

"Ah Holkan," Tu Manìk begged, "you must run. If this is to be a defeat, your capture will only make it a worse one."

"Take as many warriors as you can," Ah Dzan Chi pressed. "We will keep the Castilàn busy until you're safely out. But in the name of the Gods, hurry!"

Gonzalo was in torment. He turned in the direction he'd come from, then in the direction of his house. Ix Na, he thought, Ix Na and Temah... This was some nightmare, he told himself, these were his worst fears playing a trick upon his soul. In such a paralysis of indecision he was barely aware that Ah Dzan Chi was leading him away from the *albarrada,* and that the *albarrada* was splintering under the final thrusts from the outside, and that through the breach the soldiers were already pushing their muskets in.

Not until he found himself back in the patio where he'd left Nachancan and the others did he realize that he was running from the Castilàn, with nothing more than the clothes on his body and a weapon he'd never even had a chance to use.

"What is happening at the wall?" Nachancan asked him. "How many guns? Should we charge now?"

Gonzalo spoke as if in a daze. "No, my brother. Gather the battle guard. The gate to the *cacau* grove... we don't have much time." Then he turned to his sons. "Go first, and don't stop to wait for us."

"But you will follow, father, won't you?" Akil pleaded, looking as lost as a small boy.

"Yes, we will follow," he promised, and again he thought of Ix Na and Temah inside the house. Then he prodded the two boys and Obsidian Blade on their way, motioning the men of his battle guard to go with them.

Nachancan grasped his arm. "Ah Holkan, is there no other way?" he asked. "Must we run like prey from these dogs?"

Gonzalo looked at him, then looked away. He started to move, leaving Nachancan to give the order to those warriors who would go with them.

The gate to the *cacau* grove was open. Who knows, Gonzalo wondered bitterly, perhaps it had been open all night long. In silence the small group of men slipped out, while at the other end of Xul Ha the invaders swarmed in and everything was noise. A little outside the gate Gonzalo made out the slim shadows of Akil and Pa'ap and Obsidian Blade on the run. When they saw the men the boys slowed down, and the two groups became one.

The light of dawn steamed with the mist that exhaled from the ground, hanging in hazy palls from the ghostly shapes of the trees. It was like running into an endless void, an open grey maw where they would all disappear without a sound. He was a castaway again.

❖ ❖ ❖

No one knew how long they'd been running, then walking, or how far from Xul Ha they'd gone; but the sun had risen to the lowest branches of the trees and was already warm enough to make one sweat.

Gonzalo was in such a stupor that he felt nothing, beginning with his own exhaustion. There was only one thing left at the bottom of his heart, one dark dull thing that throbbed like a cut. At first it had been many things—fear, anger, shame, guilt—but now it had clotted into a single featureless pain. At first his mind's eye had envisioned all he was leaving behind, with the intolerable precision of some bad dreams more real than reality itself. Now everything had blurred into one murky glimpse of blood and smoke.

Ahau Can went ahead with a few warriors of the battle guard, not as a scout but only because he could go faster. Nachancan went with a deadly stiffness in his limbs, as if all his energy were aimed at keeping his body from collapsing. The three boys looked haggard. The men had slowed down several times to let them catch up, but even so they were out of breath.

Their path was shaped only by the features of the jungle—a smoother turn around a clump of vines, an easier jump over a fallen trunk. Not a word had been spoken all that time. Even the most rudimentary warnings had passed among them unuttered, by means of gestures. It was hard even to look at one another, and for some time it seemed that just walking in silence would be enough. But eventually the moment came when they had to stop.

Gonzalo took a last few steps, then put his shoulders against the trunk of a tree. One by one the others drew to a halt and sat or hunkered down around him. For the first time they were able to see what a small group they were, about twenty in all.

Suddenly they were all aware of their thirst, a thirst so overwhelming it blotted out everything else. It was the worst enemy in this land where every drop of water disappeared into the skin of the earth as if soaked through the mouths of countless sponges. From what they could tell, it might rain soon. The clouds had that patchy look that made them resemble the scales of a snake, as if a huge sky serpent were gliding above the earth. But it was too long to wait for just some rainwater caught in the hold of one's hands; so the warriors began to search for the one scanty salvation everyone relied on in times of direst need.

It was a thick vine hanging in long black ropes from the canopy of trees, and as the gods had decreed, it grew abundantly in this place, wherever this place might be. One warrior pulled the vine down, chopped it in half with his *hadzab.* It yielded enough clear liquid for a good draft, and never had Gonzalo been more thankful for such a draft.

The next sip was for the three boys, while the men found more of the vines for Nachancan, then for themselves. It was a while before this most pressing concern was taken care of. Precious time was wasted, but at least afterwards they could think of what must be done next.

"My brother, what now?" Gonzalo asked with a long sigh. "It's too soon to stop for good, we might have been followed. But it's no use to keep going if we don't know where we're going."

Nachancan was silent for a moment, his eyes vague as though lost in a reverie. "I came hunting once in this part of the forest," he said then. "This part of the forest is really good for nothing else but hunting..."

He pointed toward the north. "There is a cave further ahead. I remember I hoped it might be the den of a jaguar, but it was empty... I found no kill that day."

"I was with you that day, father," Ahau Can said. "I also remember the place. It seemed like a good shelter."

The faintest smile seemed to play around Nachancan's mouth. "For a wild beast, yes," he said. Then he shook himself back to the dismal present. "I think we should look for the cave."

Gonzalo leaned once more against the great buttressed tree, relishing the feeling of security given to his body by something that nothing could uproot. He nodded wearily, then started to walk, motioning Akil and Pa'ap to come along.

It was almost midday when they reached the cave. They had walked for what felt like endless hours of misery, growing more and more despairing with each step they had to take away from what they'd never wanted to leave in the first place. It seemed miraculous that Nachancan could locate the mouth of the cave, which was all but hidden by the jungle growth and barely above ground, more like the entrance to a sunken well.

Two warriors of the battle guard went in first, on hands and knees, and came back to say the cave was just as empty as the day Nachancan had discovered it. But there was a look of fear on the faces of the two men as they emerged from that lair.

"It's cold as death in there... May the gods guard us, "one of them whispered,touching his hands together in the gesture that warded off evil. And as Gonzalo went in himself, he was reminded of the ancient superstition that made of caves the gateways to Xibalba, the Land of the Dead.

It was cold indeed inside. At any other time they would have welcomed that refuge from the steamy heat of the jungle, but not today. The limestone walls were smooth and clammy to the touch, and made even the softest sound bounce around in long echoing whispers. Water percolated from the ceiling, dripped down into large pools; that clayey-tasting water they scooped up and drank, this time until their thirst was really quenched.

Some of the men started to make a fire with dry branches they had gathered outside. When the fire sputtered, then blazed in their midst, they saw that the cave was much larger than they'd imagined, and also that it had housed men before. Coaxed by the flames, drawings and script emerged from the twisting recesses of the walls, around the stout pillars that linked ceiling to floor.

Here a bat spread its sooty wings, to which were attached its own plucked-out eyes; there a dead man was carried away in the talons of a monstrous bird, while further off two snakes coiled around a dish full of human hearts. A shiver of terror went through the men crouched inside the flickering blackness. Those signs were tainted by the breath of evil that wafted up from the World Underneath. This was a place that must be left undisturbed, a place to which the living should never come.

Gonzalo averted his gaze from the walls, although he could find not much more cheer in the faces around him than he did in those painted nightmares. Exhausted, he sat down, almost collapsed, while Akil and Pa'ap curled on the ground at his sides, drawing close to their father for protection.

Now it was hunger, the other ancient enemy, which came to remind it-self with the same overpowering urgency. Yet no one spoke of looking for food. It was simply understood that for the moment the need to stay hidden must override even that vital imperative. For the moment, everything must be suffered—hunger and thirst, fear and discomfort and fatigue. And to think that only a short time ago food and drink, safety and comfort and rest were just within reach of their hands.

Around the fire, which wouldn't last much longer, time began to drip like that water that oozed from the ceiling. They were idle yet hard at work on all sorts of conjectures, wrestling with a thousand misgivings. Finally, however, all those thoughts were whittled down to just one question. It was Akil who voiced it for all.

"Father... how long will it be before we can go back home?"

It took Gonzalo a great effort to hold the boy's eyes, not to flinch from that look of sorrow and dread that made of Akil's dear face the face of a grown man. He had no answer to his question, but he didn't want to lie to him and Pa'ap, even if that might lighten their burden. What if the Castilàn decided to make of Xul Ha their permanent camp? What if they razed it down? It wasn't just a matter of how long before they could go back home, but also of whether there would still be a home.

"We'll have to send someone," he answered. "To see what is there, to tell us..." He broke off, and was silent. There was simply nothing more he could say.

Slowly, agonizingly, the afternoon crept into evening. The two warriors who'd stayed outside as guards were relieved by two others. They brought in armfuls of cut branches, with which they made pallets for Nachancan and Gonzalo where the floor of the cave was driest.

Whatever sliver of light could penetrate from outside went out along with the fire. There was nothing to do but lie down and hope for sleep, if the gods were merciful enough to send it.

Gonzalo curled up beside his sons, his body pressed against theirs. Eve-rything seemed to have been stripped down to this elementary contact, he thought, the warmth of living beings huddled together against the night.

There was a great emptiness inside him. His soul had become a place of echoes, like that cave.

❖   ❖   ❖

Two days later, when they could be reasonably sure they hadn't been followed, they ventured out in search of food. By then hunger had become their foremost preoccupation. Even in their dreams thoughts of full dishes shared the same obsession as thoughts of home and of loved ones.

They hunted for anything that could be eaten—not the lordly prizes the men of the House of Can were used to pursuing for sport but the easier, more modest quarries: rabbits and coati and wild turkeys, and lizards and snakes when nothing else could be found.

They couldn't range far from the cave, and often they had to wait for the prey to come to them, perhaps a startled young deer strayed away from the herd, a kill which under normal circumstances they would have found wasteful and therefore repugnant.

They cooked the meat inside the cave, choking on the lingering smoke. There was enough to keep them from starving, though never enough to satisfy their hunger. For water there was the one that constantly dripped from the ceiling of their shelter. Then there were some roots that could be dug up, the tender new shoots of palm trees, and maybe some berries worth climbing up a branch.

Seeing to the pitiless demands of the body took much time, but they were grateful for that. It was so much better to pass the hours setting snares or scraping for roots than to sit inside that awful cave under the staring eyes of the minions of hell.

The nights were the worst, those few unsettled intervals that seemed to tire them even more instead of refreshing them, and those interminable stretches of wakefulness with nothing to do but listen to one's own heartbeat in the dark. What could be held in check during the day came back with a vengeance at night.

The floodgates of despair gave just like that *albarrada* that should have protected Xul Ha, and the rout began all over again. The women raped, the children killed, the houses looted, the survivors enslaved, and for no other crime than living in one's own land and wanting to go on living in one's own land.

After six days Gonzalo could take no more. If everything else was lost, to save his own life seemed like the worst cowardice; and this wasn't life, but the bare survival of an animal. He looked at the twins and in his heart he prayed that they didn't despise him for leaving their mother and younger brother to the enemy. His hatred of the Castilàn had grown into an illness. If the Castilàn didn't kill him, that illness alone would. It was time to go back home. If home was now nothing more than a befouled stable for Dávila's horses, he must go back there and die there like a man.

Nachancan had to argue with him, because Gonzalo wouldn't even let some of the warriors go ahead as scouts. Gonzalo wanted no scouts. He wanted all of them to march back to Xul Ha and, if the Castilàn were still there, stop fighting only when the Castilàn killed them all.

Nachancan said this was no strategy, no war captain's plan, but just the desperate attempt of a desperate man. Gonzalo nodded in full agreement, and replied that he saw nothing wrong with desperate attempts. But finally Nachancan forced him to listen to reason.

Reluctantly, Gonzalo chose three of his best warriors to be sent to Xul Ha, not in an hour or two but right away, to make the most of the daylight. The argument abated only after the three warriors left.

Then the long wait started. Gonzalo could not be made to return to the cave. The very thought of having to crawl back into that damp hole revolted him, and he sat instead with the guards by the entrance. After a while, without a word Nachancan came to sit next to him; and after Nachancan, without a word everyone filed out of the cave and sat with him. Together they waited past midday, then past sunset. When daylight faded, they understood the scouts would not return today. But no matter, Gonzalo said, for this would be their last night in the jungle.

That night was the hardest one of all. The thought of dying was nothing to him. He'd been a soldier since he was twenty, death was just a part of the bargain. But the thought of his sons dying long before their time was too grievous to bear.

Yet if he had to choose he would choose for them to die rather than to live as slaves under the Castilàn. When he was in the islands, one of the most familiar sights to greet him and his erstwhile companions upon entering a village was that of small clusters of dead bodies in front of each hut. The man had clubbed his children first, then his wife, then he'd thrown himself on a sharpened stake set in the ground. So there they were now, all of them forever delivered from the hands of the invaders.

Often it took the islanders a bit more imagination, since some of these people didn't even have a word for weapon. So the newcomers would see one neighbor who'd strangled others with vines, some who'd drowned themselves in their own cooking vats, and yet others who'd hurled themselves from treetops. It was not uncommon, he remembered, for a captain to claim for the Spanish Crown an entire village populated only by corpses.

He could see himself in the place of those islanders, he thought. As much as one may love life—and he'd met few people who loved life more than the islanders—there was a boundary beyond which life stopped being a higher good than freedom. After those past days in the jungle, he had crossed that boundary. What mattered now for himself and his sons, and for Ix Na and Temah if they were still alive, was that they be delivered from their enemies like those families he'd seen huddled together in death in front of their homes. That night he couldn't sleep at all.

At long last morning came. They drank cold water scooped up from the floor of the cave, ate cold meat left over on sticks by the ashes of the fire. Then again they sat outside to wait. Just as they were about to give up again, the three who'd gone back as scouts appeared from the green backdrop of the jungle.

They were led by Ah Dzan Chi, and Gonzalo thought it such a good omen that he ran to his second *nacom* and clasped him in his arms, pouring out his relief at seeing him alive and unhurt. But Ah Dzan Chi's face bore a look that dashed all expectations. He began to answer questions even before anyone asked them. He spoke fast, almost glibly, as if he were trying to cover something.

"The Castilàn have left. They've taken some prisoners with them, retainers and servants. They've taken much booty, they've destroyed the beehives, but most of Xul Ha is still standing." He moved his hands too much, and he avoided their eyes.

"The Castilàn are gone," he repeated, as though that were the only important news. "They've gone back to Chetemal... Dávila questioned us about the True Man and our war captain. We told him they were both dead, and he believed us. We showed them two of the bodies from the battle, one of them was Seven Macaw... Do you remember Seven Macaw, who would never pluck the hair on his face? We told him it was Ah Holkan. That's what we told them, and they believed us, so they left. You will be safe now that they've left..." He stopped, and wouldn't go on.

The warriors prodded and urged him, wanting to know a hundred things he'd left out. But then Nachancan silenced them. "Where's Tu Manìk?" he asked. "Where is my daughter's husband?"

It seemed strange to Gonzalo that Nachancan should inquire after Tu Manìk, though he himself was curious to know. But when he saw Ah Dzan Chi cringe, he understood Nachancan's question.

"He is well," Ah Dzan Chi replied. "He is... well."

"If he is well," Nachancan said, "why isn't he here with you?"

Ah Dzan Chi's face was cast down. At that moment everybody realized that he had made no mention of the women.

"Are the women all right?" Nachancan asked. Ah Dzan Chi would not answer. Nachancan shook him hard.

"Are the women all right?" he shouted.

Finally Ah Dzan Chi looked up. "The Lady Ix Na is alive," he said, "and the Lady Ix Lolkin. The wife of lord Ekuneh is alive, and Bird Woman, and the mother of Obsidian Blade..."

One name was missing. Nachancan blanched. "White Feather...?"

Ah Dzan Chi fell down at Nachancan's feet, touching his forehead with the back of his hand in the gesture that signified death.

"Dávila tried to take her..." he said, and his voice choked. "She fought him off... He had her killed."

Nachancan took a small step backward, pulling away from the bringer of such news. Behind him Ahau Can gave a strangled sound of horror. Gonzalo stared at Ah Dzan Chi bent on the ground and for a moment he thought that when he'd stand up he would laugh and tell everyone he just wanted to play a prank.

For a while no one could speak. To look at Nachancan, one would have said he was a man mortally wounded. His arms lay flat against his body, his eyes were vacant, not a muscle moved. Ahau Can's face was etched with grief for his sister, but Nachancan seemed to have let go of his soul. Then he gathered the spear he had stood against a tree and motioned the others to follow him.

"We're going home," he said in a hoarse whisper.

If it was possible for men to be worse than beaten, such were the men who made the long trek back to Xul Ha. By the time they finally spotted first the blue of the lagoon, then the white of buildings and porches, what spirit remained in them had been crushed.

From a distance Xul Ha seemed the same, a blessed refuge they had so feared they would never see again. But as they walked in with the weary pace of many miles of jungle, each step began to reveal a new loss. The *albarrada* had burned down. Nothing was left but charred stumps, which the servants were gathering for firewood. The fire had spread to the *cacau* grove, although some trees in the farthest corner had been spared. What had once been the house built for newlyweds White Feather and Tu Manìk was now a burned-out shell, blackened debris heaped by its doors. The beehives were empty, not one left whole. Honey still dripped from the wooden frames into dirty puddles.

Out of this devastation Ix Na emerged, holding Temah by the hand. She wore a plain, dirty cotton gown, and her hair was just loosely braided down her back, so that she looked like one of her own servant women. Temah was barefoot and half naked, but he too seemed unhurt.

On seeing them both alive Gonzalo was overcome with the full force of all the emotions he'd kept in check for all those days. His eyes welled up, he couldn't stop it; when he took her in his arms the tears came out freely. She too was sobbing, reaching out to the twins even as she embraced him. Knowing what his first question would be, she looked at him and said, "They haven't touched me." Relief swept through him, new tears ran down his face. He was holding her so hard his arms ached.

"Oh gods," he whispered. "Oh gods..."

But to Nachancan Ix Na didn't know what to say. It was even harder because Nachancan remained silent, like one who'd lost his voice, and seemed content with catching whatever words came his way.

While the warriors scattered, each one in search of what was most important to him, Ix Na led her men into Nachancan's house. The main hall had clearly lodged the Castilàn for a time. She had cleaned and put back in order what she could, but what had once been the gathering place of the House of Can would bear forever the marks of the invaders.

Curtains and door hangings had been ripped off, benches and mats destroyed, weapons looted. The ancestors' altar was bare. The wooden statues that used to hold the ancestors' ashes lay broken underneath it, along with the shards of incense burners and offering bowls. The images of the Gods the Castilàn had smashed with particular relish.

The most visible traces, however, hadn't been left by the soldiers themselves. The horses' hooves had gouged holes in the tiles and the stucco, and everywhere were deep scratches and bite marks and the remnants of things that had been clawed or chewed off. The signs of some bestial fury were embedded in the walls of Xul Ha, something that went beyond the mere wantonness of men.

The rest of the women rushed to the hall, first among them the mother of Obsidian Blade, who couldn't hide her relief as she welcomed back her son. Ekuneh's wife brought mats, Bird Woman a vat of corn water. While the men slaked their thirst, a long piercing scream came from somewhere inside the house. After it another and another, in a strangely regular cadence, like repeated pleas to someone who would not listen.

Gonzalo started, almost letting go of his cup. He'd recognized Ix Lolkin's voice; yet Nachancan seemed to have heard nothing, and kept drinking absently. But Ahau Can was shaking. "Where is she?" he asked. "Where is my mother?" Ix Na pointed behind her, and Ahau Can strode out with a savage curse.

The telling fell to Ix Na. She alone seemed to have the strength for it. First she tried to coax Nachancan into giving some response. "Hun Halal... Do you want to know what happened?" she asked him gently.

Nachancan turned slowly toward her with a befuddled look. "My sister," he shrugged, "it looks as though I must."

Ix Na slid closer to Gonzalo, took his hand and began to speak.

"When we were told the palisade had yielded and was on fire, we gathered here with the children. We were wearing our sleeping shifts, and that I counted a good thing, because in that attire the Castilàn would not be able to tell our rank. Indeed I ordered everybody to say we were just serving women, just slaves with our slave children. Our greatest fears were not for ourselves but for you, since we didn't know you had escaped.

"Dávila came into this room sitting on his horse. There were four other horsemen, but the whole group was small, twenty-five men in all. I couldn't count the number of guns, but that too seemed small... nine or ten, I'm not sure."

Gonzalo's hand clenched hers. Twenty-five men, he thought, ten guns and five horses; and from such a mighty army had come such a defeat. Ix Na paused, feeling his anguish. Then he motioned her to continue.

"There were also some dogs. Not our sort, the small gentle ones that don't bark, but a breed such as I'd never seen in our land... Huge brutes, as heavy as men, with fangs like jaguars' and a bark that could make one die of fright. The Castilàn could manage them only by means of whips and chains, by means of the same cruelty as the beasts themselves showed..."

She shuddered. Gonzalo too remembered them well—war mastiffs of a temper to make their own masters afraid of them. He looked around again, and this time he recognized the strange bite marks left in the room.

Ix Na went on. "It was a while before Dávila took notice of us.

He was looking for gold, and destroying what he could in his search. When he could find nothing, he came to us. He spoke through one of our own, a man who said he was from Chetemal. I told him right away where the gold was, and I had the box brought down. When he saw the box, he was very pleased. He told us he would consider it a ransom for our lives, and he even laughed...

"At that point I imagine I hoped he would leave...Instead he began asking us about you and Hun Halal. He made the horses jump and the dogs lunge at us to frighten us... Right then I was very much afraid, because I didn't know what it was best to tell him. But then Ah Dzan Chi spoke. He told him you two were dead, and took him out to show him the two bodies. I thought Dávila wouldn't believe him, and would kill Ah Dzan Chi for lying. Instead Dávila didn't even recognize Ah Dzan Chi from three years ago... Instead it worked."

She let out a deep sigh. "That was all that mattered," she said, looking at her husband and her brother. "When I heard Dávila shout and curse before the two bodies, I was no longer afraid."

"So the gold is gone," Gonzalo said. "So now for the first time the greedy monkeys have what they came here for. Did they take everything?"

"Everything," Ix Na answered. "Even the turquoise masks of Itzamnà and Ix Chel... and my necklace with the little frogs." Then she looked at Nachancan. What she'd said so far was nothing compared to what she must say next, and everyone knew it. She squared her shoulders, steeling herself for it.

"After he took the gold, Dávila ordered us to leave the main hall. We were to serve food to him and his men when he asked, but we were not harmed. White Feather, though..."

Upon hearing his daughter's name, Nachancan was startled. But it was only a moment's awakening. Ix Na breathed in, then began to speak in slow, careful, clipped sentences. Her words were like the steps of a lone survivor who must clear the battlefield without pressing his foot on the bodies of his friends.

"Dávila ordered White Feather to remain with him. Ix Lolkin and I begged him to let her go. We had to speak to his interpreter, and the man couldn't talk very fast. Dávila began to beat the man to make him stop talking. He threatened us as well. He told us he would go back on his promise not to harm us. Then he ordered his soldiers to take us out of the room... We had no choice.

"What happened after that we were told by the servants. We did not see it with our own eyes. White Feather told Dávila she had recently been married. She told him she would be touched by no man but her husband. She tried to take the knife from his belt, to kill herself with it...

"Dávila ordered that her husband be brought before him. Tu Manìk was being held prisoner with the rest of the men, guarded by a soldier with a gun. So Tu Manìk was brought forth. Dávila mocked him. He gave him a spear and told him to try to kill him, for that was the only way he would ever have his bride back.

"They went outside. Tu Manìk was told where he must stand, which was too far for a good throw. So he only hit Dávila's horse and wounded it. Dávila became terribly angry. He had Tu Manìk tied to a tree and told his men that he must be left there to die of hunger and thirst. Then he spoke to White Feather for the last time. White Feather spat in his face. Dávila made a gesture to the men who were holding the dogs. The men let the dogs loose... They went for her throat, just as jaguars do, so she died quickly. We don't know what was done with her body."

Ix Na stopped talking and looked up at Gonzalo. Although he'd had time to take in the news of White Feather's death, the manner of her death was something he thought he would never take in. Not that he was unfamiliar with it; the Spaniards used it often in the islands, especially on runaway slaves. They had a word for it, a word he didn't remember from any other language except Spanish: *aperrear,* to give to the dogs.

What he would never understand was how such a thing could have taken place right there in his own home. White Feather was the loveliest treasure in Xul Ha; everything that was lovely the Castilàn had destroyed, and her they had destroyed in the most horrible way of all. Sickness rose in the pit of his stomach.

But from Nachancan, nothing. He stared out at some far point, running his fingers along the edge of his mat. Again Ix Na tried to bring about a reaction from him.

"Hun Halal, my brother... I must hear something from you."

Nachancan looked at her and gave a soft quiet laugh, as if he'd just heard something funny. Then he lapsed back into his distant silence. Ix Na let him be.

"And Tu Manìk?" Gonzalo asked.

"After two days, when the Castilàn were ready to leave, Dávila had forgotten all about him. He hadn't eaten or drunk in all that time, but even now he refuses to touch food. He sits in the ruins of his house, day and night."

Gonzalo had no more questions. Visibly relieved that her telling was done, Ix Na gently pulled her hand away from his and took a sip of corn water from his cup.

A sound of footsteps came from the door. Her braids undone and her dress torn, Ix Lolkin burst into the hall. Ahau Can behind her couldn't stop her. She went straight for Nachancan, and threw herself against him as if she wanted to stab him.

"Hun Halal Nachancan! Father of your people, Lord of the Four Corners of Heaven, Protector and Defender of the House of Can!" she screamed. "I woke up in the night and did not find you. I called you but you were not there. So our daughter became like the doe in the hunt, meat for the Castilàn's dogs!"

She was clutching a piece of cloth from which white feathers hung raggedly—White Feather's wedding cloak, Nachancan's gift. She shook the piece of cloth under Nachancan's face.

"Look, Hun Halal Nachancan. This is all we have left. Not even a handful of ashes that we might keep on the ancestors' altar....

What do you say to that? What do you say to our daughter who became meat for the Castilàn's dogs?"

Nachancan took the battering as if he were a hollow wooden statue. Ix Lolkin struck him across the face, sobbing and shrieking and shaking her white rag at him. He made no motion to protect himself. Only Ahau Can finally managed to pull her away.

Then, unexpectedly, Nachancan got up. He walked over to her and took her in his arms. She collapsed against him, blurting out words no one could catch—words without meaning, the ranting of a woman gone mad. Nachancan and Ahau Can led her to the door.

Together the three of them left, bent under the weight of their grief.

❖   ❖   ❖

In the year the Castilàn counted as 1531, an ill year, a year of great calamities, the House of Can came to know its most terrible hour.

Ix Lolkin cried and ranted and clutched her white rag for three more days. On the fourth day she went out to the *cacau* grove and chose a tree that had been spared by the fire. With her own sash looped around one of its branches she found the only peace she sought, the one which Ix Tab, Our Lady of the Rope, mercifully provided for those who could no longer bear the burden of life.

Tu Manìk chose instead to make of himself an offering to the gods. The ceremony had to be performed by a priest from an inland village, since Ah Kin Mo, although Tu Manìk had asked him, could not be persuaded to take the sacrificial knife to his own son. Before he lay down among the ruins of the house he'd once shared with White Feather, Tu Manìk asked only that her body, should it ever be recovered, be buried next to his.

The priest from the inland village was a skilled man. He sent Tu Manìk on his way quickly, and placed his still-beating heart in front of a small clay image of Itzamnà, the only sacred image the Castilàn hadn't found. Tu Manìk's heart was brave and true and full of his love for his bride, and it made a lovely offering. It burned in the brazier with a good clear flame, and for a few moments it made the night a little less dark.

THIRTY-THREE

Nachancan was never the same man again. What made his being quicken went with White Feather; what gave his life sweetness went with those beehives that would remain forever empty. For days, while Xul Ha struggled to regain some normality, Gonzalo stayed out of his brother's way, waiting for him to overcome the worst of his grief. The rest only time could begin to diminish, perhaps.

Yet time was a luxury Gonzalo couldn't afford. The Castilàn were back in their settlement of Villa Real, only a stone's throw from Chetemal, and every passing day meant a consolidation of their power. There was no way of predicting how their victory at Xul Ha would affect the *batabs*, though Gonzalo doubted it would renew the fighting spirit of men who'd surrender at first sight of the invaders. But whenever he approached Nachancan with such matters, he found no response. So at last he understood he would have to think of the next step on his own.

It seemed that even from such a crushing defeat he'd gained one very valuable thing, Dávila's conviction that he was dead. Three years ago it had been the Adelantado whose death Dávila had accepted, which he judged a most fortunate shortcoming. Let the Castilàn think they'd removed the threat, that they had the province under control now that both the True Man and his war captain were gone. Now that no one was looking for him anymore, he was free to move about as he pleased. If he thought out his actions, he would be able to organize his counterattack before the Castilàn realized that.

The first opportunity came to him from Ah Kin Mo. About a week after Gonzalo's return, the old priest came to Xul Ha in disguise, bearing very useful news. Dávila, he said, had dispatched a small group of Castilàn to the north, where the Adelantado Montejo was. The group was to inform Montejo of the victory at Xul Ha, and to bring him the gold and precious stones taken from Xul Ha. Since Dávila was sure that the territory through which his men must pass was entirely pacified, he'd sent only six soldiers, three crossbowmen and three horsemen.

Those six soldiers, Gonzalo vowed, would never reach Montejo in the north. Ahau Can volunteered to lead an expedition to intercept the group: unlike his father, he had been fired by his grief into an unquenchable desire for revenge, and he seized the chance eagerly. Recovering the stolen gold was surely not the goal of this first counterstrike; the goal this time was quite simply to kill as many Castilàn as could be killed.

There was one hurdle. The six Castilàn soldiers were now within the boundaries of Chetemal's other neighbors to the north, the province of Cochuah, which had long been a buffer between the Can and the Xiu. The True Man of Cochuah wasn't hostile to the Can, but neither was he a true ally. Would he now allow Can warriors to pursue the Castilàn in his territory?

"We will convince him," Gonzalo said. "Just as we once convinced Ah Kin Cutz. The True Man of Cochuah couldn't possibly be more stubborn than the True Man of Tulum." He turned to Ahau Can. "I will prepare a message for our neighbors. Assemble your warriors."

He then offered Ah Kin Mo the protection of his house; but Ah Kin Mo was full of hatred for the men who'd caused his son to die, and wanted to return where he would best help bring about their downfall, near them in Chetemal. Gonzalo gave the old priest the

most heartfelt thanks, and as a sign of honor escorted him personally to the gate.

The following morning Ahau Can left with thirty warriors, with Gonzalo's message and with instructions to relay back to Xul Ha all that transpired.

Nachancan came to see him off. He stood with Gonzalo at the edge of the lagoon, by the charred remnants of the *albarrada;* and as he watched Ahau Can climb aboard the canoe, he murmured a prayer of help to the Gods. It was the first thing he had uttered in days. Then he went to sit alone at the spot where Ix Lolkin and Tu Manìk were buried.

Gonzalo eyed him from a distance, and his heart sagged. Nachancan had already lost five loved ones to the Castilàn, and Ekuneh was still a hostage in their hands. To watch his firstborn set out against those same Castilàn must be the hardest thing to bear, he thought.

While he waited for the first runner from the north, Gonzalo pondered the other news that Ah Kin Mo sent him from Chetemal. The Castilàn' settlement at Villa Real was growing larger. Now there was a meeting house, a jail where Ekuneh and the other hostages were kept, one hut for every two soldiers and a small army of slaves to keep the soldiers fed, their horses scrubbed and their dogs sheltered.

But what most outraged the old priest was the church Dávila had begun to build in the shadow of the temple of Ah Cab, which he'd already desecrated by destroying the image of the Bee God. The wooden crosses that rose everywhere in the city were bad enough, but this ugly black box of a building seemed like the very banner of the invaders' gall.

What arrogance lived in the souls of these strangers, Ah Kin Mo marveled, that they should appoint themselves the sole owners of the truth! Many of Chetemal's people, prompted simply by curiosity, did go to the church to hear what the Castilàn priest had to say. But he was just an angry little man spewing out threats of divine punishment against the people who allowed him to do his ranting among them.

And those same people had also to endure the strangers' inexplicable rules. They were made to stand in the back of the church while the Castilàn sat on benches in the front, and the women who came bare-breasted as was their usual custom were turned away in horror as though they were whores.

The Castilàn had even a name of their own for the people of Chetemal—Flatheads, they called them. On the surface the name seemed innocent enough, an allusion to the native custom of flattening the forehead as a mark of beauty. But that word was unmistakably colored with mockery and contempt; on the lips of the Castilàn it became a nickname for a new breed of curious-looking animals. Ah Kin Mo himself, whose forehead was flattened from infancy, heard himself called that often enough, and he said that each time it was like being struck in the face.

Who knows where it came from, Gonzalo wondered, this deep-seated hatred for those of another race. It might be nothing more than the fear you felt as a small child whenever strangers came to your house, visitors from another town who didn't speak like you, didn't dress like you and didn't eat like you. It might be nothing more than distrust for those intruders who sent you hiding in the closet at the age of four because you didn't know what to make of their different ways. Perhaps it was nothing more than a little thing like that. Yet there was no end of grief coming to grown people from just a little thing as that. These days the ones among whom he'd been raised wanted him dead because he no longer spoke or dressed or ate like them.

Ahau Can's first runner returned late, but with news that was worth the wait. Not only had the True Man of Cochuah let him and his Can warriors cross into his territory, but he'd also managed to delay the six Castilàn soldiers until the Can caught up with them in the town of Hoya, thirteen leagues from the border. While the six were having their evening meal, Ahau Can and his men had fallen upon them and killed them all; they'd also killed the three horses.

Ahau Can had recovered the gold taken from Xul Ha, and he'd given the two turquoise masks to the ruler of Cochuah, in thanks for his help. The ruler of Cochuah had pledged to be Chetemal's ally and to wage war until the invaders were tossed from the mainland once and for all.

The news not only made Gonzalo glad, but brought new life also to Nachancan. On hearing of his son's masterstroke, some of the old warrior spirit of revenge was rekindled in him, and for the first time since White Feather's death he sat in council with the others. If they were indeed to wage all-out war against the Castilàn, Nachancan said, they could not hope for a better ally than Cochuah. It was a province rich both in men and supplies. Its very name, "Broad Bread," spoke of its wealth. The three men were again engrossed in battle plans. Hope was possible again. The first thing to do, Gonzalo decided, was travel to Hoya. There they would meet with the True Man of Cochuah and devise a united course of action.

Ix Na's life had become a life of welcomes and goodbyes. By now she could tell that Gonzalo was about to leave just by the way he walked into their room. But this time she looked neither downcast nor apprehensive; this time she looked as though she were ready to take up a weapon and follow him.

"I've heard about the six Castilàn killed at Hoya," she said, and nodded with satisfaction. "That was well done, Ah Holkan. You're going to Hoya, aren't you?" she asked. "That too is good. You must bring me something taken from the dead bodies of the Castilàn. A piece of their clothing, a strand of their hair. Something that might help give peace to the soul of White Feather."

Gonzalo looked at her with narrow eyes, startled by the coldness in her voice. Then he reached for the small marble box where he kept his red and black paint. "With the help of the gods," he told her, "I will bring you just that."

He too was leaving with a different heart this time. There was the sadness of the separation, and also the acknowledgment that this was going to be the longest separation ever. But at least this time he knew Ix Na and Temah would stay behind in what had become the safest place in all the province.

He touched her cheek. "And your necklace with the little frogs. I'll bring you back that too," he said, trying to smile. "Lord Itzamnà," he sighed. "So much has happened since that first day I saw you in Tulum... Who would have ever guessed?"

"I regret nothing," Ix Na said. "Nothing." She pulled away from him gently. "Please watch over Akil and Pa'ap," she begged him.

They couldn't march to Hoya with a whole army, for they would be detected by the Castilàn, so they took only one company of warriors. Canoes were scarce, since many had burned with the *albarrada* along which they were kept; half of the company would have to take the more difficult overland route. Weapons were also in short supply and would have to be made or borrowed in Cochuah. As Gonzalo turned back for a final look, a rainbow rose from the lagoon over the remaining two buildings of Xul Ha. It was the sign of Ix Chel, the Mother of Heaven, and it seemed like a good omen. Then the canoe glided past the banks and into the branching channels hidden by the growth of the jungle.

The first thing that greeted them in Hoya were the severed heads of the six Castilàn soldiers lined up on the skull rack in the town's main plaza, along with the severed heads of the three horses. Tired as he was by the journey, Gonzalo couldn't help but feel refreshed by that sight. It seemed to pay for some of the devastation he'd left behind at Xul Ha, for some of the pain. He peered at the twins, gauging their response to what was for them the first look into the face of war. They neither flinched nor averted their eyes, and he was proud.

Flint Knife, the True Man of Cochuah, came out to greet them accompanied by his war captain and Ahau Can. He was short, but of the perfect proportions for a warrior. What made his appearance remarkable were the countless scars on his body. They weren't all war wounds but self-inflicted, and lay close together in regular patterns like decoration. This man had offered much of his blood to the gods for the good of his people, and perhaps for this reason the gods rewarded him and his people with abundance.

The Can guests were welcomed with the greatest honor. Nachancan embraced his firstborn in public, paying homage to his success. The people of Hoya followed them through the streets cheering, then stayed to talk about the visitors while the visitors sat at a feast that had been prepared inside Flint Knife's spacious house.

The house was decorated with the three crossbows and the iron darts that had been taken from the Castilàn. Without the metal for more darts, the weapons were worthless to their new owners; but their presence alone seemed enough, a reminder that the mysterious powers of the invaders could be stripped from them and used as nothing more than curious pieces of furniture.

There was much to be said; the ceremonial recounting of Ahau Can's victorious raid, the first plans for war, and the usual questions about the white *nacom,* about whom Flint Knife had only vaguely heard some years before. While he spoke, however, Gonzalo became aware that his eyes kept straying from his hosts and toward one of the women who served their drinks. It irritated him deeply that in the midst of such important conversations he should be so distracted by her; then again he couldn't help but be distracted, because this woman was stunning.

There was nothing demure about her beauty, for hers was the sort of beauty that could only be flaunted. She moved like a young jaguar, as if comfortably oblivious of her own power. With each supple step a mane of straight black hair parted and then came back together around the full curves of her body. The cotton wrap was fastened too tightly over her breasts, so that it left a mark like that of leather bonds, something Gonzalo found disturbingly arousing. Her skin was darker than that of most women he knew, and with a luster to make one think of smoldering amber. A man would have to forget he was a man not to look at her, he thought.

And if there was nothing demure about her beauty, there was also nothing demure about the way she set aside her best attentions for him. She came back to him much more often than to the other men, she smiled to him much more often. Whenever she knelt beside him to pour him another cup of balchè her thigh lay almost flat against his on the cushioned mat, and her hair brushed his arm so scented with some heady jungle perfume that for a moment everything was blotted out except that scent and that closeness. Once he nearly let go of his cup, and in his mind he damned himself for being so flustered, his own blood for leaping so. When the meal was over and she left, he felt nothing less than relief.

Flint Knife brought him back to reality by making known something he'd left out before so as not to cast a shadow over the celebrations. While his guests were traveling to Hoya, he said, Dávila had found out about the killing of the six soldiers and was now marching to Hoya to exact punishment for the ambush.

"I don't know how soon," Flint Knife added with a look of concern, "but we will have to meet him in battle."

"How many men?" Gonzalo asked.

"Twenty-two, and three horses," Flint Knife replied. "I can put together as many as ten companies of warriors, but none of them would know what to do in a pitched battle against enemies the have never encountered."

Gonzalo shook his head. "No. We will never best the Castilàn in pitched battles. We must devise another sort of war, one of constant harassment, of small ambushes like the one we've just won. We must keep them on the alert day and night. There must be not a town or a village where they can take shelter or find food. I want them worn down into surrender."

Flint Knife's war captain motioned an enthusiastic assent. "Yes, that we can do. Even the fiercest boar stops fighting when too many hunters seek him from too many paths."

"Also," Gonzalo added, "every town that lies in Dávila's expected line of march must be fortified with barriers of wood and stones. Hoya too must have its palisade."

"It will be done," Flint Knife promised. "Anything else?"

Gonzalo couldn't think of anything else for now. After a last cup of *balchè,* the three Can got up and followed attendants to their rooms. The twins and Obsidian Blade had left already. As he was entering his room Gonzalo remembered something, and gestured to the man who accompanied him.

"My beard... I must get rid of it. I can't afford to be recognized." He laughed. "After all, to the Castilàn I am a dead man."

The servant told him he would send someone to see to this matter and left. While he waited for this someone, Gonzalo began to undress for bed. It had been a long day, and he was more than ready for rest. It felt good to free his body at last from all the pinching, rubbing insignia of his rank. Separated from his bed by a curtain was a carved stone tub shaped like a small canoe; he let drop his *esh* and lowered himself in the warm bath water sprinkled with fragrant red flowers.

He closed his eyes and gave a deep sigh of contentment as the water rippled around him. He ran his hand over his beard and fought back a hint of regret at having to sacrifice it. Then from the doorway he heard the steps of the man who was coming to shave him. He'd so readily assumed it would be a man that his eyes flew open when he caught her scent instead.

She pulled a stool by the tub and sat down. Since her long hair would get in the way of such a delicate operation, she'd tied it over one shoulder with a strip of brown rabbit fur. She lifted to his cheek a tough-looking leaf with sharp edges—quite an effective shaving tool, he judged with a bit of apprehension. Her eyes met his with what looked like deep-seated pleasure for being just where she wanted, since surely she hadn't come to his room just by chance. She draped a white cloth between his neck and the rim of the tub, so the hairs wouldn't fall into the water; then with the serrated edge of the leaf she began to cut carefully the copper-colored growth on his face.

It was less painful than he'd anticipated, just a quick repeated scraping a warrior could certainly endure. What seemed much harder to endure was that he was lying naked under her eyes, and that in such circumstances it would be quite difficult to hide the response of his body to her presence. It had been a very long time since he'd tried so hard not to blush.

She seemed all taken by her task. Her full lips pursed slightly as she ran the toothed edge of the leaf down another strip of skin. But then her hands paused and her eyes moved to what was stirring under the water. She sucked her breath in, looking very pleased both with him and with herself, and that look sent like a running of fire through him.

Nothing seemed to help. Not the thought of Ix Na or of the twins sleeping nearby, not the awareness that he would soon be at war. In fact, everything conspired to make him jump out of the water and spread her right there on the floor. He certainly would break no rule, commit no sin. This woman herself lived for nothing else. He would probably insult both her and his hosts if he didn't take her.

Her hand let go of the leaf and slid under the surface of the water, parting the floating buds. She was leaning over the rim of the tub, and he could hear her breath gathering in faster. He lay utterly still, as if just wanting to see how far he could let his desire go before he reined it in. Then there was a shudder of mixed pleasure and panic; in her touch was all the skill that came from having been taught precisely how a man wants to be touched. All he had to do, he thought, was give in.

But it was that thought that made him stop her. She had come to him unbidden, as if nothing could get in her way, as if he could do nothing but give in. She had started something she was sure to finish, but without asking. Perhaps it was simply pride; but whatever it was, it was uncomfortable enough to shake him back to his senses. He clamped his hand around hers and lifted it out of the warm water with some harshness that meant finality. But she showed neither disappointment nor anger; calmly, almost lazily, she picked up again her sharp-edged leaf and went back to the task of shaving him.

Good, he thought, settling down in the tub again. That should show her who chose what and when. Then he winced when the leaf nicked his cheek, drawing a few beads of blood.

When she was done, she looked at him to see the results. She handed him a mirror made of polished black obsidian and stood back to await his response, which was a stiff nod of the head and a noncommittal sound of approval.

"I liked you better before," she said with a little laugh. And in her eyes was the plain, sure promise that she would have him.

❖   ❖   ❖

He saw her again, in fact every day, but only when he sat down to his meals with the rest of the men. They exchanged no words beyond polite greetings; her fussing around him, however, remained as open as it had been the first day. The Can men kept from making any remarks about it, but not the Cochuah men. They had begun to build the *albarrada* around Hoya, a formidable double row of wooden palisades masked by trees and undergrowth, and when he walked out with his hosts to see how the building went, often enough Flint Knife or his *nacom* steered the conversation toward that subject.

She wasn't from Cochuah, but from a faraway country to the south, a country where people didn't make stone houses or temples but lived as simply as the first men and women the Makers had shaped out of corn flour at the dawning of time. She'd been brought to Cochuah as a captive and sold to Flint Knife's mother.

Because she was so good-looking, she'd never been made to work. She graced Flint Knife's banquet mats, pouring drinks for his guests, and she shared Flint Knife's bed, but her hands had never known grindstone or loom. Flint Knife's mother herself had supervised her training in the arts of love; the old lady had also taught her how to use a certain herb that prevented conception, so that her beauty would never have to be marred by childbearing. She was happy in Cochuah, and didn't miss her simple circle of huts in the midst of the southern jungles. Flint Knife treated her very well, and sent her to his guests only if she agreed to go to them.

"When she saw you, Ah Holkan," Flint Knife added with a sly smile, she did not only agree but almost begged me."

Fine and well, Gonzalo thought with annoyance after listening to such information, which he'd never requested. If she was happy in Cochuah, he was a happily married man in Chetemal. Ix Na had always been enough, Ix Na who knew him inside and out, who was the underpinning of his life. If anything, he would ask her only to share the secret of that herb that prevented conception, because Ix Na worried about getting pregnant now that she was past forty. So he listened to Flint Knife, signaled polite attention, and let the subject drop.

Once, however, it wasn't so easy. One evening the woman—whose foreign name no one could pronounce properly without offending her—came to the banquet mat wearing over her cotton wrap the skin of a white-tailed deer hanging loosely over her breasts. For some reason Gonzalo couldn't fathom, that attire stirred among guests and hosts alike the sort of commotion that he would have thought more seemly in his sixteen-year-old twins. Instead of concentrating on the enemy, who even as they spoke was marching toward Hoya to destroy them, the men behaved like drunken celebrants at a wedding, with the exception of Nachancan whose pain nothing could soothe.

Flint Knife's *nacom,* a coarse warrior used only to the battlefield and the whorehouse, squawked like a macaw on the perch.

"Ah Holkan, have some more meat," and he rested lewdly on the word *bak,* which meant meat but also one's private parts.

Or he would grab Gonzalo's elbow and slur, "Now, Ah Holkan, this stew is as hot as the sting of a scorpion," and again he underscored the one word *ach,* which meant sting but also penis.

The woman was deaf to such banter, blind to the glitter in the men's eyes. She did nothing to encourage them; nothing but be beautiful enough to turn grown men into boys. As she bent over to refill Gonzalo's cup, she made her white-tailed deerskin flick against his chest with the most naked provocation. Heat rose to Gonzalo's head. If right then someone had shouted that Dávila was at the gates, he would have thought it a blessing.

After the banquet, when the woman left as she always did, he had to lean onto the arm of the slave who walked him to his room. He had drunk more *balchè* than it was wise, and he let himself down heavily on his bed. But before drifting off he must have an explanation to that matter of the white-tailed deerskin. While the slave helped him to get undressed, he asked him about it. The slave, a handsome young man no older than the twins, stifled a chuckle and said he would return presently with a much better explanation than his words could convey.

Half asleep already, Gonzalo waited for the young man to come back. He had a headache, and was in no mood for surprises. When the slave came back he paid no attention to the book of folded bark he brought with him;

but when he put a certain page under his nose, he did. It was a book of nothing but pictures, and this one picture was certainly worth more words than the young slave could put together. It was a clutter of the most astounding images he'd ever seen, men and women and beasts copulating in every possible combination and convolution, a veritable riot of lust. At the center was the image of a beautiful young woman lying on the ground naked with her legs thrown open. A white-tailed deer was shown leaping between her thighs; and as he leapt he left in her flesh the imprint of his split hoof, which resembled exactly the shape of a woman's sex.

"This is how the private parts of women were made," the young man explained, "when the Lord Sun turned into a white-tailed deer to lie with the Lady Moon."

Gonzalo couldn't take his eyes off the painted bark page. The explanation sank in as arousing as her hand had touched him while he sat in the warm water some days before. The slave left with his extraordinary little book; but all night long in his unquiet sleep Gonzalo kept seeing the woman of Cochuah lying naked on the ground, waiting for him to leap between her thighs.

❖   ❖   ❖

The *albarrada* was finished just in time for the war to begin.

It began badly. As he marched toward Hoya, Dávila seemed unstoppable. The first town he attacked inside the Cochuah border fell to him even though it was defended by almost two thousand warriors. Before fleeing, however, the defenders carried out Gonzalo's orders and left to Dávila nothing he could use. The town and the surrounding cornfields were set on fire, and the wells were plugged with stones, so that when the Castilàn rode in they found just a charred desert. Wild with thirst, they spent days trying to reopen one of the wells. Finally they managed to lower two captive boys with straps made from the horses' harness; that way they got enough muddy water for both soldiers and mounts.

As they pushed deeper into the province, the people fled from some villages; others let them through without resistance. The *batab* of one town, fearing for his life, warned them about an ambush and so allowed them to put to flight the Cochuah warriors who'd set up that ambush. But when they reached Hoya, four months later, their luck took a turn.

It was a hard four months Gonzalo spent waiting for his second chance. His plan of defense was settled, everyone knew what to do. He'd seen what had become of his expectations at Xul Ha, and he'd learned from his mistakes. Even so, the news he heard was discouraging, and time passed much too slowly. His guests treated him lavishly, but Hoya was still a foreign town. It was too far from Xul Ha for runners. He knew nothing of what was happening there and in Chetemal. The twins missed their mother, and their unhappiness made his own only worse.

And then there was the constant presence of this woman he couldn't avoid, this woman who turned each day and each night into an ordeal by temptation. He shaved himself now, yet that simple task brought back the compelling memory of her hands. He thought about her almost as much as he thought about Dávila.

If he wondered what Dávila was doing out there in the jungle, he also wondered what she was doing in whatever corner of the house she had her quarters. He wanted to know all about her, and there, as he didn't need to remind himself, lay the greatest temptation. It was one thing to lust for her in his body; but to start lusting for her in his soul was like peering into a bottomless well. At times he paced restlessly along the *albarrada,* wishing Dávila would hurry.

Finally one day the scouts reported that they had seen the Castilàn's column only a few leagues away. By the afternoon of the same day the guards gave the alarm. Out of the jungle the enemy had appeared, poised to attack.

At the sound of the conch shell both Can and Cochuah warriors rushed to take up positions behind the *albarrada,* with their leaders covering each point along the circle. Flint Knife took the south side, his *nacom* the east, Nachancan and Ahau Can the north, Gonzalo and Ah Dzan Chi the west.

From a gap in the palisade Gonzalo got his first glimpse of Alonso Dávila. He found his nemesis to be a man of no special appearance, but with a look of guarded cruelty lying below the surface. He wore an odd mixture of

Spanish armor and native quilted covering, and he carried a fine steel pike. By now, Gonzalo knew, Dávila must be desperate to capture Hoya, and that put him in the stronger position. He pointed Dávila out to the twins: there was their foremost target. Today, he promised them, Dávila's march through Cochuah would turn into a rout.

Ah Dzan Chi motioned that he was ready. He was with the archers, who formed the first line of defense and the only ones capable of fighting from a distance. If the archers failed to stop the assault and let the Castilàn come up to the *albarrada,* the rest of the battle would have to be hand-to-hand combat. There, however, the numbers were overwhelmingly against the enemy, and this *albarrada* was too high for the horses to clear.

Dávila was desperate. Three times he charged against the wall, with all the ferocity that his situation demanded, and three times the archers stopped him. Can and Cochuah warriors stood their ground waiting, but the archers proved to be enough. Before the gunners could reload or the foot soldiers move forward, the sky between them and the palisade blackened again with arrows and they had to fall back, having gained not a yard of ground closer to their target.

It took all afternoon. In between charges the soldiers had to stop merely to catch their breath, since they had no water and who knows when they'd last had food. From behind the wall Gonzalo could hear them moan with thirst and call to their saints for help.

Dávila went among them on horseback, shouting to rally them. One could tell he was frightened even in his determination, and that made Gonzalo rejoice. He took another long draft from his gourd canteen and he thought of the hardship he'd had to endure after he'd been forced to flee from Xul Ha. Now his enemies were in the same hardship, he thought; now they were being made to pay.

The fourth time, Dávila tried to take the albarrada from the south side, where Flint Knife was, only to be pushed back by a barrage of arrows and spears. Half of his soldiers was now wounded; the other half was too weak to fight on. After trying to convince his diminished troops to make a fifth attempt, Dávila finally gave the order to retreat.

Gonzalo had already decided not to pursue. It was sundown now, and he didn't want the warriors to leave the safety of the *albarrada*. Besides, he knew Dávila had nowhere to hide around Hoya and would have to spend the night out in the open. He would have plenty of time to find him and his exhausted soldiers.

He signaled Ah Dzan Chi to stop fighting and to relay the order to Flint Knife and Nachancan. Then he climbed to the rim of the palisade for a better view of his defeated enemy. They were in honest flight, bloodied, heads down, dragging their muskets like brooms. Dávila had come down his horse so that two of the wounded could be carried on it. There on the ground the barbarian who'd ravaged Xul Ha looked no different from his soldiers, a beaten man trying to escape with his life.

Gonzalo shook his *hadzab* at the sky and joined in his warriors' cheers. Not a life had been lost. No other sign was left of the battle except the holes the musket balls had gouged in the palisade. He pulled his sons to him and hugged them. He could feel his heart and theirs beat together like victory drums. In their eyes he read pride and admiration that wiped out the memory of the terror and the shame they had endured with him in the cave.

Never had he thought revenge could make a man so happy.

That night even the twins drank *balchè*. Hoya was a circle of light and celebration, and Flint Knife's house was at the hub. As he helped himself to the rich meal and watched the dancers whirl around him, Gonzalo hoped that beyond the safe shelter of the wall Dávila and his starving soldiers could smell the food and hear the music. The banquet mats were so many they spilled from patio to patio. During the assault the people of Hoya had huddled together in the plaza, praying to the Gods. Now they'd come to celebrate; the whole town was there.

She too was there, and she'd never seemed so bewitching. She was wearing the dress common to the women of these parts, a long tunic split open along the sides and tied with a sash. But what was common in other women became extraordinary in her. The tunic was not the usual white but a deep mottled crimson resembling fresh blood; it came from a dye made from the crushed bodies of certain female beetles, and it was a color to snarl the senses.

The openings on the sides were wide enough for a glimpse of high round breasts that seemed to play with his eyes. The sash went around her hips low and loose, making him think that all he had to do was grasp one end and give it one good pull. Yet tonight she hardly paid any attention to him. She didn't come back to him or linger by his side on the mat. No one would have guessed from her behavior that she'd once begged her master to be sent to his bed. She didn't ignore him, but neither did she favor him. She just treated him like all the others, which seemed to him much worse than being ignored.

The contrast between her allure and her indifference dug into him like a pebble. It soured his victory, crippled his satisfaction. Worst of all, it made him angry at her—an anger he couldn't explain, since he was the one who'd turned her down first. He wanted to make her stop and look at him; he wanted to take hold of her arm and say something harsh, something hurtful.

By and by his enjoyment became vexation. The food seemed to make him full too quickly, the praise sounded tiresome. In a pique he started to empty cup after cup of *balchè,* just to make her attend his orders. She served him dutifully. A brush of crimson cloth, a peek of amber skin, then again she was with someone else, maddeningly obedient and maddeningly distant.

Soon he had drunk enough to smash all self-restraints. There had never been any other restraints except the ones he made for himself, and these he had kept for months. Now all barriers were down. Only one thought was left: he must have this woman.

He was sitting next to Flint Knife, so all he had to do was lean into his ear. Flint Knife seemed a bit startled by the bluntness of his request, but then he smiled. Gonzalo got up, glanced at the men with whom he would return to Xul Ha: at his second *nacom,* at his brother, at his sons. He could live with their knowing, he told himself, and with Ix Na's knowing as well. He wished them all a good night, waved away the slave who was about to go with him, and walked to his room alone.

Finally some silence, he thought, before he realized that there was no silence inside him but instead a rushing of hot, angry blood. He stripped himself right away, casting everything off, even the small adornments he usually didn't bother to remove. If he could have, he would have removed the tattoo of his name, the last reminder of who he was. Then naked he lay down on his bed, his arms under his head.

Tonight for once he would be like any other man with a concubine, careless and impatient, indulging in the power that was rightfully his.

She came in quietly and pulled down the door hanging. Her expression didn't change when she saw him. She sat at the foot of the bed and looked him blandly in the eyes, as if asking what next.

He motioned her curtly to lie down. "Now you mind me," he said hoarsely. "Now you pay attention to me."

She smiled a deep, secret smile. "No, Ah Holkan," she whispered. "Now you pay attention to me."

Now he understood that her coldness had been only a ruse.

This time again she was where she wanted, not where he wanted her to be. This was her final temptation, and he'd already given in. Just as he'd imagined, he took hold of the sash around her hips and tore it off in one pull. The two halves of the crimson tunic came apart like the skin from a fruit. One more tug and nothing was left but her body—the perfect breasts that would never be misshapen by suckling, the smooth place between her legs that would never be torn in pain by childbirth.

The time had come to give himself over to that flawless schooling that had fired him four months ago and obsessed him ever since. But first he would show her something that even her flawless schooling had never taught her, so that no matter to whose bed she would go next she would be sure to remember him forever.

Holding her down he pushed his thumb between her lips, then harder between her teeth. Not knowing what to expect, she fought him hard. He had to throw his weight on her twisting, struggling limbs. He saw genuine fear in her eyes, and that aroused him even more. She was too frightened to bite, but her neck arched and her face swayed, caught in his grasp. When he was convinced she would be still, he forced her mouth open with his hand, then kept it open as he thrust his tongue in.

At that invasion her efforts to pull away became almost frantic. He could hear her gasp in shock, as though he were trying to steal the breath of life from her. But then, as his tongue kept probing and reaching, she stopped her struggle and slowly, uncertainly, began to respond in kind.

Her gasps changed into moans of joy. Her face strained no longer away but toward his, and her lips parted willingly under his spreading fingers. Now he had taught her. Now he could allow her to take control. He let go of her and lay back on the bed. Freed from his hold, as fiercely aroused as he was, she began her exquisite work upon him.

Four months of constrained desire turned into a night of the most un-bridled pleasure he'd ever tasted. Although his body was no longer that of a young man, she had ways to make it respond as it had in its prime. She reveled in her skill with an innocent, playful eagerness; she was utterly wanton but never indecent. After he tried with her even the whims he'd only permit-ted himself in dreams, she opened his eyes to a few things he'd never thought of trying. Through the night a new discovery came after a new fulfillment. There seemed to be no end to what she could draw from him; all he had heard about her was wondrously true.

At dawn, when at last he was too spent for anything but sleep, he felt her gently stir away from him. He reached out to stop her, but she'd already left the bed. The memory of his duty came back to him, blunted by the delicious exhaustion that kept him comfortably stretched out. Dávila, yes, the Castilàn. But there was time for that.

And there was time to think about what he should do about her, because after a night like this he certainly must think of what he should do about her.

He heard a shuffling of bare feet, the rustle of the door hanging being lifted. Then he thought he heard her voice, he thought he heard her say goodbye—not with the word that meant until tomorrow but with the word that meant forever.

He settled his head on the pillow. In the morning, he told himself drowsily; in the morning. He drew the soft cotton robe over his body and fell asleep.

It wasn't morning when he woke up, but late afternoon. The memory of the night kept him company like a secret attendant while he put back on everything he'd taken off for her and then walked out to Flint Knife's council hall at a pleasantly slack pace.

He wondered what Ix Na would do when he would return home with her along as a concubine. Gods, he bristled, why should he even worry about that! Wasn't it understood that a noble of the House of Can could take as many women as he wished into his household? Ix Na would just have to accept her, he concluded, stifling the countless objections he could hear in his mind already. Rather, would Flint Knife refuse to give her up? Would he have to think of a suitable gift in return? These questions he too stifled for now, as his mood changed to anticipation of the next night he would spend with her.

In the council hall the men were all assembled and waiting for him, which made him feel uncomfortably at the center of attention.

He avoided their eyes and took his place on the mat. He also remembered that he was famished, but he should have thought of that before.

The men's somber faces told him right away something was wrong. He turned to Ah Dzan Chi. "Haven't the scouts come back yet? Do we have their report?"

"We do," Ah Dzan Chi said. "Dávila seems to have vanished. They've looked for him everywhere... He is nowhere around Hoya."

Before realizing that he had no one to blame except himself, Gonzalo was shouting. "Vanished? How does a man vanish? How do soldiers and guns and horses vanish? You sent out the wrong scouts!"

Flint Knife's *nacom* took that remark as a personal insult. "I did not send out the wrong scouts, my lord Ah Holkan," he said hotly. "My scouts are the best in Cochuah, and if they could not find the Castilàn it's because the Castilàn cannot be found! You gave the wrong order, rather," he blurted out. "Yesterday you said you would not pursue the Castilàn, and today you were too flattened out from lovemaking to—" He caught himself in time, but his coarse gesture was enough.

Only a great effort prevented Gonzalo from lunging at the man with his closed fist. Flint Knife had to throw out his arm to keep the two away from each other. It was a while before everyone was calm enough to resume the council in the proper manner of warriors.

"Do we know at least in which direction they're headed?" Gonzalo asked Ah Dzan Chi.

"South, we presume," Ah Dzan Chi said. "Toward Chetemal. Most certainly they intend to retreat to their settlement there. I know that's what I would do."

"Could someone be helping them?" Gonzalo wondered. "Could some *batab* we don't know be giving them shelter?"

"That is what we suspect," Flint Knife replied. "Either a renegade or a captive must be leading them by little-known paths, away from towns and villages."

Gonzalo addressed Nachancan. "My brother, we must go back to Chetemal. We must intercept Dávila along the way if we can, or wait for him at his settlement if we can't. We have not an hour to waste."

Nachancan was already leaving his mat, motioning agreement. But Flint Knife's *nacom* twisted his mouth. "*Now* we have not an hour to waste," he said scornfully.

Gonzalo threw the man a venomous look, but those words stung him to the quick just the same. While he was taking his pleasure Dávila had managed to elude him; while he was passing the hours in thoughtless abandon his enemy had regained the advantage. No matter how swiftly he responded now, he would still have to hope most earnestly that he could live down that upset.

"I didn't hear a word of disagreement from any of you yesterday," he reminded Cochuah's *nacom* harshly. "All of you thought it unwise to pursue the Castilàn after dark."

Flint Knife extended a conciliatory gesture toward him and a sharp glance toward his ill-mannered *nacom*. "It was unwise. Yours was the proper decision. The whole province is alerted to the Castilàn. They cannot hide forever."

"No, they cannot," Gonzalo replied, getting up; then he turned sharply on his heels and strode out of the hall, back to his room to get dressed for war once again.

His mind was in turmoil. He called for a slave to pack his things, then harried the man for not working fast enough and began to toss at him whatever came in his hands. He rooted for his box of paint, started to cover the upper half of his face with red, the lower half with black; but he was smudging the lines and smearing the paste everywhere, so he slammed the box shut and went to wipe the paint off his face, cursing under his breath. Soon the slave was done, and left with the bundle.

Alone, he sat on the bed. He thought of her who had been there only a short time ago, who had gone at dawn with that one word of farewell he had barely heard. That word rang all too clear now, and so did the reason for it. She knew that he would have to leave, that he had his war and his revenge to carry out. She knew it had to be now. She had known all along, and he'd been blind all along.

He put his face between his hands, shutting his eyes. War and revenge, he thought. Duty, command, and the inescapable pursuit of one's chosen obligations—all the things from which she had joyously freed him for one extraordinary night. They'd all better be worth the loss of her, he grieved. They'd all better be worth it.

THIRTY-FOUR

Within an hour the jungle was echoing with what sounded like a huge jaguar hunt, with the cries and the noise of hundreds of warriors scouring the land in search of the Castilàn.

The Cochuah war captain led two companies; Gonzalo and the other three Can leaders had their one company. Flint Knife had remained to guard Hoya. Before leaving, Gonzalo had made clear that he would take the most difficult route to the south, the one Dávila was presumed to be following. The Cochuah war captain had argued that he wanted that route himself, but Gonzalo had refused to budge. Then they had split, fanning out in all directions.

The route to the south was so hostile to human presence that only a man without alternatives could be convinced to take it. First it was swamps, where they sank to the waist in mud; then it was almost impenetrable bush, through which they had to cut their way with their own weapons, step by slow step. They forged ahead as best they could, but as time wore on they began to wonder whether they were on the right track after all.

It seemed strange that the Castilàn, especially the Castilàn's horses, could have passed through this jungle without leaving well more than one trace—trampled undergrowth, broken branches, the signs they themselves were leaving behind. Frustrated and angry, Gonzalo pushed on beyond the limits of his endurance. Eventually, however, they had to give up.

They camped in a bit of clearing and shared the dry rations they'd brought with them. Everyone was glum and disappointed.

Before going to sleep Gonzalo spent some time with the twins. He wanted to comfort them, but felt almost as despondent as they. There was also the newest sadness of knowing he would never see the woman of Cochuah again, and the bitter irony of this night when he thought he would be with her, not alone in the middle of the jungle.

Another day of fruitless chase followed. At one point they came across a great number of trees that had been felled by a recent storm; it took them hours to clear that welter of roots and branches. Then toward midday they reached a hamlet of about a dozen houses, where they rested for a while. The hamlet was abandoned, so there was no one to whom they could ask whether the Castilàn had passed that way. By now they had progressed much too far from their Cochuah allies. They were on their own: even if they did find the

Castilàn, they would have to think twice before attacking them with no one to back them up.

Three more days of exhausting march, three more nights in the open jungle, and still no sign of Dávila. Finally they sighted Chetemal's border, and the first town that flew the banner of the Can. There they were welcomed by the people, who crowded around them and escorted them to the men's house. And in the men's house, from the mouth of the town's *batab,* they learned such news as to repay them for every hour of their trek.

Yes, Dávila had beaten them to Chetemal and was back in his settlement of Villa Real since two days. Since two days, however, Dávila was also a man under siege. The people of Chetemal had finally roused themselves from their cowardly daze. Upon hearing of the victory at Hoya, they had followed Cochuah's example and had risen against the invaders. Two days ago, the *batab* added, when Dávila had reached Villa Real he had found nothing but Castilàn. The slaves had deserted them; food and supplies had been cut off.

First the Castilàn had sent out raiding parties to seize supplies in any place and in any way possible. Soldiers armed with guns had broken into corn pits and smokehouses, stealing all they could. Then, in desperation, they'd begun to plant corn in the open spaces between the huts of the settlement, scraping the dirt with the blades of their own weapons.

If it hadn't been too late in the day, Gonzalo would have resumed the march immediately. Instead he had to resign himself to spending the night in the town. The *batab's* slaves brought them their evening meal and strung hammocks for them in the men's house.

After so many days and nights in the jungle, those accommodations seemed luxurious. The food was good, Gonzalo noticed, and the *cacau* rich and hot. Suddenly he felt terribly homesick. He missed Ix Na from the bottom of his soul, and with an overwhelming feeling of guilt. He'd kept her too far from his thoughts, he told himself ruefully; he'd overlooked her too easily.

He got up and went to seek the *batab* just outside the men's house. "How far is this town from Xul Ha?" he asked him.

The old man drew smoke into his nostril from his rolled tobacco leaf and smiled. "Not too far for a runner, my lord Ah Holkan."

"Then please send one tomorrow," Gonzalo said. "Please let the Lady Ix Na know that we are all well, that we are all together...

That we have good hopes of prevailing and of coming home soon."

Afterwards he felt better. He stretched out in his hammock and mulled over the news he'd heard today. In his hasty flight from Hoya, Dávila had ended up putting himself in the worst possible position: isolated within a tiny settlement, surrounded by two provinces at war, squeezed between impervious land and empty sea. Nothing short of a miracle would save the Castilàn now.

He glanced at the hammock next to his and saw that Nachancan too was awake. He wanted to talk, to open his heart to someone dear.

"I sent a runner to Xul Ha," he said. "To let Ix Na know."

Nachancan turned his head. "That is good, Ah Holkan," he replied politely. "She will be happy to hear from you."

Then he tugged his mantle closely around his body, as if he were cold, and withdrew again into his own soul. When he'd heard about his people finally rebelling, there had come in his eyes a flash of pride that for a moment had brought back the man he'd once been.

But now, in the silence of the night, Gonzalo could discern no particular feeling.

If this war that he must fight, this war that he had not chosen to fight, had taken one woman from him, he thought, from Nachancan had taken everything. He hated the Castilàn, and his hatred gave his life purpose; but Nachancan had been pushed to the point where even hatred had no purpose. If tomorrow he brought him Dávila's head wrapped in a shawl, he knew Nachancan would remain as silent and as still as he was now.

Two days later, when they reached Chetemal, they were no longer on their own. As the news of their return spread, more and more runners came to them from everywhere. They were being sent, along with weapons and supplies, by the same *batabs* who'd let Dávila into their land and who now swore with words of shame and remorse that they would never again allow a handful of strangers sway them from their allegiance to the House of Can.

Gonzalo welcomed everybody without ill feelings, assured of their good faith and glad to see so many behind him. With each step he took toward Chetemal his confidence grew. By the time he was able to see Villa Real and to be seen from it, the one tired, ill-equipped company with which he'd left Hoya had become the vanguard of an army that should give the Castilàn good reasons to seek shelter within their crude wooden church.

A trumpet sounded the alarm from a platform high above the thatched roofs of the compound. The soldiers swarmed out of the huts, out of the stable and the meeting house. Gunners and crossbowmen positioned themselves. The horses were led forth and saddled. The dogs strained at the end of their chains, fangs bared.

But Gonzalo was in no hurry. Today he would only send a message to the inhabitants of Villa Real. At a safe distance he called a halt and signaled with a wide sweep of his hand. Keeping at a safe distance, his warriors spread out all around the settlement, locking it in a circle. Silently crouched, their faces painted for war, their spears aimed and their bows taut, they were warning enough. Nothing stirred from the compound, as a hush fell over the soldiers poised behind the palisade.

Let Dávila break out of this trap, Gonzalo told himself. He looked at the tattered Spanish flag that flew by the gate and couldn't hide a smirk. What a grand name: Villa Real, the Royal Town, an outpost of civilization amidst the savage hordes. And in this royal town the proud sons of Spain, who would rather lose both hands than soil them with manual labor, were reduced to the indignity of having to grow food by the sweat of their brows! Let's see how long their bellies would stay full for war, he scoffed. Let's see how arrogant they would remain now that they could no longer rob someone else's pantry for their meals.

Once it had been the Adelantado Montejo who'd stood surrounded, in his ship beyond the surf. And as that ship had been made to vanish from the sea, so would this settlement be wiped out from the land. Time was again on his side. Waiting was an art of war he had learned well.

At first the waiting seemed all too easy. One week of blockade became two, two weeks became three. The soldiers kept a sharp lookout from their high platform but made no provocations. They were too busy trying to grow corn and edible plants, a hopeless task in the thin red soil of the compound.

Every day they came back to those seedlings, to water them and to spread the horses' droppings around them. Food had been rationed since the first day. They quarreled over a chunk of salted fish or half a mildewed tortilla. When it rained they gathered what rain they could in whatever vessels they could. The animals seemed to suffer the most, the horses without hay and the dogs without meat.

This while Gonzalo and his warriors feasted every day under the Castilàn's eyes. Often, after they brought the warriors their meals, the people stayed to eat with them and to make of the eating a taunting display. Children pelted the walls of the compound with fruit peels, and women improvised lewd dances, laughing when the Castilàn shouted unintelligible insults.

Ah Kin Mo, who too came every day, found a special pleasure in defying the besieged enemies as he himself had once been defied.

After he tore down all the wooden crosses the Castilàn had erected in the temple of Ah Cab and elsewhere, he had them dragged in front of Villa Real's gate and set them on fire. Dávila came out to see, and he could only watch as the bonfire rose menacingly close to the gate.

In the third week of the siege things changed. The one thing the Castilàn had in plenty was canoes, which they kept with extreme care because in this part of the country they were the best means of transportation.

One night a small party of soldiers tried to slip down to the beach and take some of those canoes out to sea. The soldiers made it part of the way, until the guards saw them. Without waiting to hear from Gonzalo, the guards aimed their bows, killing one of the group. They would have killed more if the guns hadn't responded from the palisade, covering the retreat of the others back into the compound.

Gonzalo was told of this incident only in the morning, when the guards took him to see the body of the Castilàn soldier still lying on the beach. He wasn't upset by that delay. The guards had done what he would have ordered them to do, and in fact he praised them for their quick thinking. Then he hunkered down for a better look at the dead man. Young, he noticed, good-looking. Perhaps in Seville he'd been a good guitar player who charmed the ladies at their high windows; perhaps in Xul Ha he'd urged the dogs to go for White Feather's throat.

He remembered something Ix Na had asked him. He took his knife and looked for a token to bring her. A bit of shiny metal around the soldier's neck caught his attention. It was a brass medal of Santiago the protector saint of soldiers; he'd worn one himself so many years ago. Ix Na would like that, he thought, and he snapped the chain off. He handed it to Ah Dzan Chi. "Keep this for me," he said. Then he turned to the guards. "Bury him."

As he was making his way back, he heard a commotion inside the Castilàn's wall, followed by Akil's call. "Father, look!" He ran up the steps of nearby house, while Ah Dzan Chi and Ahau Can joined him.

At first nothing made sense. The Castilàn had gathered in front of the jail, in the clearing that passed for the town's square. There Dávila was waiting, protected by two gunners with cocked muskets. He stood next to a lighted fire and six odd-looking wooden stools set around the fire. Next to him was a soldier holding a smoking brand. Then out of the jail the soldiers dragged out six men—Ekuneh and the other hostages.

They forced the six down on the stools, pinioned their arms to the backrests and stretched their bare legs out, exposing the soles of their feet. One of the captives was a boy of about fifteen; Ahau Can recognized him as the son of one of Ekuneh's judges. Ekuneh looked gaunt and wild-eyed. None of the prisoners spoke a word. The boy was terrified as he looked at his father for help.

"Butchers," Gonzalo rasped under his breath. He looked around for Nachancan. Nachancan was alone by the trunk of a tall tree where the arrows were being kept in their bark quivers. He would see enough from there, Gonzalo thought. He would hear enough, too.

Dávila signaled to the man who held the smoking brand. The man went for Ekuneh first, as the hostage of highest rank. Then he went for Ekuneh's judges, and then for the boy. The smell of burning flesh rose from the clearing and was carried out of the enclosure along with the screams. Gonzalo turned his head, sat on the steps of the house and dug his nails in the handle of his *hadzab*. He could hear the twins beside him gasping in horror. Once he glanced at Nachancan: he hadn't moved from where he was, and he was looking at the six captives with an unflinching stare.

It went on all morning. The boy kept begging his father to make the soldiers stop. Dávila had taken a seat and lay back in it like a spectator at a play. When the brand was almost consumed the torturer lit another. The skin of the captives' feet blistered and peeled, turning black.

Finally Dávila got tired, and he ordered his soldiers to take the captives back to jail. The six men couldn't stand up and had to be carried. Ekuneh's face was a mask of tears. The boy had fainted. His father had nearly cut his own tongue in two to keep from crying out. Then Dávila spoke to the man who'd plied the hot brand. The man climbed atop the platform where the guards usually stood and waved his arms to call for attention.

"This is what all rebels will suffer," the man cried out in broken Mayathan. "This is just punishment for those who refuse us friendship. Let the warriors withdraw, and let us come out unharmed. If not, these six men will pay again for your stubbornness until you are convinced!"

His message delivered, the man started to come down from the platform. The twang of an arrow rent the silence. Shot cleanly through the throat, the man staggered and tumbled to the ground, dead. The people of Chetemal let out a sound like a massive breath being released. Their eyes all turned to the same spot, to Nachancan standing under the tall tree, the cord of his bow still quivering.

Startled, for an anxious moment Gonzalo didn't know what to do. For all he knew, the Castilàn were about to open fire on the crowd, and his warriors to surge toward the wall of the compound. Dávila's face showed how enraged he was. Yet he said nothing. He got up and walked back into his meeting house. The soldiers picked up the body of their dead comrade and carried it away. For the rest of the day the compound was quiet.

At nightfall Gonzalo doubled the number of guards and put the warriors on the alert. To Nachancan he had said nothing before and would say nothing now. Had he been in his place, he would have shot the arrow himself. Only time would tell what the killing of the soldier would bring—time as short as the hours until dawn.

At dawn the Castilàn made a gallows with some of the timbers left from buildings they'd never built. They set up two vertical beams, lashed them to-

441

gether with a horizontal one, and knotted up six nooses. The people of Chetemal watched and wondered what that thing was for. Gonzalo sat again on the steps of the house, his sons beside him, his heart too tight even to curse. Nachancan stood again by the tall tree where the arrows were kept, with his arms empty.

When the gallows was ready Dávila came out and again took his seat in the clearing. The soldiers led the six hostages out of the jail, holding them since they couldn't walk on their charred feet. They propped them under the six nooses and put the nooses around their necks. Ekuneh's eyes were closed; he'd come out of the jail like that, as if refusing to let in the sight of the Castilàn. But his judge was no longer silent. It was too far to hear what he was saying, but clearly he was pleading for the life of his son. Dávila lifted his hand and then dropped it.

Nachancan looked at the body of his brother dangling at the end of the noose, and Gonzalo looked at Nachancan. He knew what Nachancan was thinking. Ekuneh and the others had been dead since the first day they'd been taken hostages. They had borne the torture well, and they had died for a reason. But on the path to the World Underneath where they were now, they would find at least one Castilàn leading the way, with an arrow through his throat.

❖   ❖   ❖

The six bodies were left to hang from the ropes for three days. Certainly Dávila meant them to be both a lesson and an instrument of persuasion. But the only thing the people of Chetemal were persuaded to was to endure.

Ah Kin Mo made an animal sacrifice and chanted the appointed prayers for the six dead. On the fourth day the soldiers took the bodies down. They cut them up for the fat—it was a customary practice among the Castilàn to salve their wounds with fat taken from the bodies of dead Indians—and then they fed the rest to their hungry dogs. That day Gonzalo couldn't swallow a single morsel of food.

Then for another long month nothing happened. It was a mystery how Dávila and his men could go on for such a long time with the little food they had. It was an unusually dry summer. The corn and other plants they were trying to grow wilted and died. The horses were so thin their ribs showed under their skin. Only the canoes remained as well tended as ever.

At midsummer the New Year came, the new fire was lit atop the temples. Then summer began to give way to the days of autumn. Outside the palisade of Villa Real life went on as it always had. One would have hardly called this a land at war. Gonzalo waited. Long as the siege might be, he was prepared to bide his time.

Of the three other Can leaders who waited with him, Ahau Can was the most impatient. He'd always been hard to keep in line, and he hated being idle. Why wait? he argued. This was a strategy for old men; were it up to him, he would just gather the warriors and attack Villa Real, even if that meant losing ten men for every Castilàn soldier.

Ahau Can was also given to dwelling on things the other deemed unimportant. He thought every small movement of the Castilàn was worth watching, every departure from the usual warranted attention. Gonzalo found this trying, and even Nachancan was annoyed at times.

One autumn day, after a particularly uneventful stretch of time, Ahau Can came to Gonzalo with yet another one of his warnings. This time he'd noticed the Castilàn priest carrying out of the church pictures, candles and other objects of his religion.

"It's odd," Ahau Can said. "Why would he do such a thing? I say we should mind this sign."

Gonzalo, as always when he wanted a better view, climbed the steps of the house where he kept his hammock. Yes, he could see the priest shuttling between church and meeting house; this time he was carrying out his prayer book and the purple stole he wore to hear confessions.

Gonzalo told Ahau Can that he saw no reason to be concerned. A bustle from the soldiers would have concerned him, a taking out of weapons or a moving of the canoes; this was just one little man doing housecleaning. But Ahau Can stalked down the steps angrily and sulked all day. The priest made one more trip between church and meeting house, then was seen no more. At nightfall the compound was quiet as always.

At dawn the following morning it was even more quiet.

Gonzalo got up, breakfasted with his sons, made the usual round of the guards. As he retraced his steps back toward the house that was his observation point, he nearly ran into a warrior who was racing up from the beach. At the same moment he heard the sound of the conch shell.

Out of breath, the warrior was pointing behind him. "They're leaving! The Castilàn... they're out at sea!"

Astounded, Gonzalo wheeled around. There was no time now to have the guards punished, but by the gods he would see to that.

"My sons stay here, watch over them," he ordered the warrior. Then while the calls of the conch shell resounded all around, he started to run. The warriors were assembling on the beach. Nachancan came on the double, then Ah Dzan Chi, then Ahau Can, whose warning no one had heeded and whose face was dark with fury. Had he looked toward Villa Real, Gonzalo would have seen the gate open, the huts empty, the flagpole bare. Dávila must have the devil himself on his side, he raged in his mind, for he could not possibly have slipped out of that trap.

Without even waiting to see if anyone followed, he jumped into the first canoe he found ready. The beach shook with the warriors' yells, with the noise of their outrage. One after another the great cedar craft hit the surging waves; for each canoe forty paddles plunged in at once, stabbing at the water. A convoy of perhaps twelve formed, while the shore swarmed with people rushing to see.

Crouched at the prow, wet with spray, Gonzalo strained his eyes toward the horizon, where the sun had barely risen. His heart seemed driven by the same mad speed as the canoe, buffeted by the same waves. The thought of Dávila eluding him again, and again when he had him in his grasp, made him want to dash his head against the gunwale. For a moment all he could feel was despair, as if some laughing god were taunting him.

His warriors kept paddling with all their strength. The other craft followed at their own best pace, some slower some faster.

Sometimes they could barely see the shore, so far out they came in their pursuit. Then finally something appeared on the horizon, a ripple that grew closer and closer. Gonzalo grabbed a paddle from one of his men and started to row with them.

"Faster," he shouted. "There they are... Faster!"

With the sun up now, Gonzalo could see them well. Some of the canoes had makeshift sails. Others were fastened together with ropes, and these carried the horses and the heavy guns. He was dumbfounded. How long had the Castilàn been preparing for this?

And how had they managed to keep the preparations secret? Not a noise, not a hint for all those many months. Nothing except a priest dismantling his church.

And now they were going south, another puzzle. Why south? he wondered. The closest Castilàn settlement there was in the valley of Ulùa, but that was almost two hundred miles away. Did Dávila really think he could reach Ulùa by following the coast, that coast so armored with reefs and so treacherous with swamps? Yet that must be his plan, to take the route that was hardest for himself but also hardest for his pursuers, just as he'd done when he'd left Hoya. Were he not so enraged, Gonzalo would have had to admire his nemesis' daring.

The rowers were getting tired, their pace slacker. His own arms felt the effort; but giving up was out of the question. In the canoe behind him Ah Dzan Chi was shouting to him. "Ah Holkan, how long will we give chase?"

"All day long if we have to," was Gonzalo's reply.

And all day long they rowed, with nothing more than the water and the parched corn they'd hastily loaded aboard. At times the distance between them and the Castilàn was so short that they could make out the horses standing precariously in the unwieldy paired canoes, and the soldiers struggling to keep their muskets dry. At one point Gonzalo saw the gunner in the last canoe taking aim, and he could swear he was about to fire. Then again the distance grew, and the convoy seemed to merge with the harsh light that beat on the surface of the water.

The warriors were no longer shouting; all that could be heard was their labored breathing, along with the ceaseless dipping of the paddles. Yet no one spoke of resting. Too many months of waiting had been endured, too much hatred stored up. Dávila would have to go ashore for food and water sooner or later.

Gonzalo gestured to Ah Dzan Chi in the canoe that followed. "Send one of the canoes back to Chetemal," he told him. "Tell them to alert the people along the southern coast. I want signal fires and runners ready in every village when the Castilàn land."

Ah Dzan Chi motioned he understood. Right away one of the craft pulled away and headed back.

They followed on for about another hour. The sun began to arch down. The distance from their quarry remained steady. The sea was calm; there was no wind to swell the makeshift sails, and Dávila's soldiers must be even more tired than the warriors. What would Dávila do now? Gonzalo wondered. Almost as though Dávila had heard, the convoy turned westward, heading for the coast. The warriors saw that and shifted course after it.

"How far from Chetemal do you think we are?" Gonzalo shouted to Ah Dzan Chi. "Are you familiar with this stretch of shore?"

Ah Dzan Chi signaled no, then bent to hear what one of his men was saying. "I'm told it's just swamps, just land flooded by the mouths of rivers and streams."

"And the nearest town?"

"Some leagues inland. Only small villages, not towns."

They were nearing the foaming white crests that indicated the reef. Gonzalo had to shield his eyes with his hand; with the sun now shining straight ahead, it was harder to keep track of the convoy. Once in a while it vanished in the strong glare; then again the distant black ripple bobbed up from the ocean. But then the convoy passed through the reef, still heading toward the shore; and now the land that loomed behind it gathered it into its own dark mass, making it invisible.

Gonzalo's heart was racing, his eyes scanning every direction: nothing! Spitting out an oath, he waved his arm to call Ah Dzan Chi.

"If we let them slip into one of those streams you spoke of we will lose them for good," he shouted. "We must keep going."

Ah Dzan Chi looked concerned. "The men are at the end of their strength... And look how far the others are. We must let them catch up with us before nightfall, or else we will become separated."

Gonzalo's hands gripped the carved wood of the gunwale. The thought of having to quit was something he couldn't stomach. But Ah Dzan Chi was right. His men were bent over their paddles, worn out. They had given him all they had; he could ask no more of them for the time being.

"All right," he surrendered. "We'll wait for the others, then we'll go ashore for the night. In the morning —" He didn't finish.

He'd heard himself say those same words before, at Hoya. He stared at the darkening land where the sun had dipped, and in his heart he knew that nothing good would come in the morning.

After the others caught up with them at the reef, they made landfall on a small beach. The canoes had to be left in the shallow water, anchored by ropes to the trunks of palm trees that grew out of the sea. Their evening meal was more of the same parched corn they'd eaten at midday. Some of the men had taken with them a few gourds full of *posol,* while others caught fish and crabs. Many just took a sip of water before they lay down on the sand and fell asleep, exhausted.

In the morning they split into three groups, and each group searched for the Castilàn in different directions. Gonzalo and his men followed the course of a stream for some distance, and looked along both banks. But this second full day of pursuit brought nothing but more frustration.

The morning of the third day Gonzalo decided to return to Chetemal. Nachancan and Ah Dzan Chi agreed; Ahau Can was still too angry to speak to the others, and simply obeyed their orders.

Rowing back took them twice as much time and, it seemed, twice as much effort now that they were again defeated.

In Chetemal, Gonzalo was told that his order had been followed. The people who lived along the southern coast had been put on the alert. Wherever Dávila and his men might be now, they were alone and adrift between hostile land and hostile sea, with warriors waiting for them behind every bush and every sandbar. But it was only a few days later that the first runner form the southern coast came with real news.

The Castilàn had been spotted some distance away from the place where Gonzalo had lost them. They were in such a sorry state that the villagers who'd come upon them had decided they weren't worth wasting arrows. Nearly all their canoes were leaking; nearly all their weapons were lost, and they were armed with just knives tied to sticks.

They were so famished they ate even the peels of the wild fruit they found in the jungle. Many looked ill and could barely stand. When they'd seen the villagers they'd fled, leaving behind the carcass of one of the horses, which perhaps they were about to eat. They'd climbed back aboard their ruined canoes and they had desperately rowed out to sea.

On hearing this Gonzalo understood he needed not worry about having let the Castilàn escape. They had delivered themselves into the unforgiving arms of the country they'd come to conquer, and the country itself would deal the final blow for him. For all he knew, Dávila and his soldiers were already nothing more than skulls and bones bleaching in the jungle or at the bottom of the sea.

So he and the others made ready to return to Xul Ha. It was nearly a year since they'd left, but only now did it seem like a long time. Before setting out he cast a last look at what remained of Alonso Dávila's Royal Town, the burned-out church in which the Spaniards had tried to change the names of heaven. Soon even that battered remnant would be gone, eaten away by the rust and the rain. Nearly a year ago he had sworn to wipe this settlement from the face of the land, and this he had accomplished. This war was over.

Ahead of him were the two warriors who carried the mahogany box with Xul Ha's gold. On top of the hoard he could see Ix Na's necklace with the little frogs, and he smiled. Ah Dzan Chi handed him the latest treasure, the brass medal of Santiago taken from the young Castilàn killed on the beach. Gonzalo placed it next to the necklace, closed the lid of the box and started toward home.

THIRTY-FIVE

The day before his nineteenth birthday Temah announced his decision. He had thought about it long and hard, and he knew it was time to make it known: he would become a priest.

It was not at all an unexpected announcement, since he'd hinted often at such a choice. It was also a common choice among the second sons of lords. Ix Na was very pleased, and only concerned about the long and arduous training. A priest must become a treasure- house of the people's knowledge; he must learn to interpret the sacred books, to expound the needs of the people and prescribe remedies when they got ill in body or in spirit, to keep the genealogies, to compute the years, months and days, to observe the festivals and ceremonies. All this would take much time and much dedication, but Ix Na was sure of her son's vocation, and ready to help him in any way.

It was Gonzalo who took the news badly. He'd always known Temah was fond of studying, a thinker and not a doer. Still, he couldn't tell precisely what it was that so disturbed him. Perhaps it was the thought of his son performing sacrifices, although he knew that it was not the priest but another religious functionary who cut the breast of those chosen for sacrifice. Temah never did have the stomach for the shedding of other people's blood; but he did have the stomach for the shedding of his own blood, which was yet another priestly duty.

When he walked into his parents' bedroom to make known his decision, Temah's body was marked with the telltale signs of self- sacrifice. His cheeks, lips and arms had been pierced with the sharp thorns of the *maguey* plant. There was a spattering of red even on the front of his loincloth: blood from a man's member was a particularly precious offering. He'd jabbed and cut himself clumsily, as a novice, causing himself more pain than necessary. He was weak from ritual fasting, dirty and unkempt, but ecstatic. Bloodletting induced visions, answers to the quests that stirred the soul; and four days of it had yielded for him the discovery that the life of a priest was the only life he wanted.

The sight of his youngest son looking like the victim of a vicious beating put a deep anger in Gonzalo's heart. The words didn't come out easily, but the refusal did.

"I won't try to stop you," he told Temah curtly, "but don't ask for my approval. That I cannot give you." Then he walked out of the house so he could be alone with his turmoil.

For two days after that, father and son didn't speak to each other. Temah seemed to suffer terribly because of this, and their meals especially became a time of misery. On the third day Ix Na found out that Temah had left home in secret and no one knew where he was.

She was frantic, and mad at Gonzalo for causing Temah's disappearance. Gonzalo was no less upset. After combing all of Xul Ha with a small army of household servants, he decided to go to Chetemal. Quite certainly Ah Kin Mo had a hand in this; the old priest was a mentor to the boy, always encouraging him to learn more about the office he had held for most of his life.

To get through the crowded streets of the city faster he left his litter and walked instead to the temple of Ah Cab, where Ah Kin Mo went every day. He went from patio to patio, calling now the priest now his son. When he finally found them, he thought he would curse and shout even though he was within sacred walls.

Inside a dim cell framed by a steep arched entrance, the old man and the boy were huddled together over a book. Ah Kin Mo ran a stick under a certain line of writing, while Temah read character by character. When he pupil stumbled, he anxiously looked up at the master for help; and when he finished a line without errors, he beamed with joy and touched the master's wrist with a gesture of respectful gratitude. Even as he felt relief that the boy was all right, Gonzalo was hit by that sight with a new pain—jealousy, because Ah Kin Mo had taken his place in the guiding and the showing that was a father's task.

"My son," he called from the doorway.

Startled, Temah almost let go of the book. "Father, I..." He could say nothing more, and he looked away.

"You will not give your parents such grief again," Gonzalo sternly warned the boy. He addressed the old priest. "And you will not abet his foolishness behind our backs. Didn't I tell you I wouldn't stop you?" he reminded Temah. "So why run away, why hide like a thief?"

Ah Kin Mo seemed genuinely sorry, and was about to say something, perhaps an apology. But Temah cut him off. "I ran away because I could not bear the silence between the two of us. I beg you, father. We must talk about this."

Gonzalo made a motion of denial. "There is nothing to talk about. I haven't forbidden you to follow your choice, though you know well I could have. You should be happy with that."

Temah's face showed a great deal of anguish—a man's anguish, the equal of his father's. "Then should I also be happy to bear the silence for the rest of my life... to live with you as if with a stranger? No, father. I am not going back to the home of a stranger."

This time Gonzalo made no reply. The thought of losing his son scared him. He took a step toward the boy, as if to show that he was willing to make peace. But then he saw Temah put his hand flat on the book he'd been reading. The characters on the painted page were utterly incomprehensible to Gonzalo, and it was as though the boy were marking a boundary beyond which he could not trespass. Abruptly he turned on his heels and walked out.

That same evening he was back home. All he told Ix Na was that the boy was fine and living in the temple as Ah Kin Mo's apprentice. But Ix Na understood the rest anyway. She was crushed, and fearful for what this rift would do to her family. She'd never been separated from the boy. She'd seen Akil and Pa'ap go off to war with their father, but Temah had always been her special companion.

She wanted to know if the boy was going to be all right by himself, if she would be able to see him as often as she wished. Of course, Gonzalo replied testily; had he ever said she couldn't see him, or would he ever let the boy starve? What sort of a father did she think he was?

Eventually she accepted what she couldn't change. She packed Temah's clothes and his favorite foods and sent them to him by two of the servants. She also sent a boy a message, whose content Gonzalo never found out. Gonzalo too dug in. He knew how stubborn Temah could be, and how he never made an idle threat. For all he could tell, the boy was indeed determined to spend the rest of his life in Chetemal. It pained him to think about it, but his anger kept too strong a hold on his heart.

How could Temah do this to him, he wondered, how could he desert him like that? He felt challenged, betrayed. He turned to the twins for reassurance, but the easy, carefree time he spent with them only made the pain worse. Akil and Pa'ap listened to him and looked up to him. They were eager to follow in his footsteps, as all good sons should. He could train them for the hunt and for war, and they made him proud to be the one who taught them. But to Temah who was different, to Temah who'd run away from home to become another man's son, he had nothing to teach.

If not for what he considered the loss of Temah, Gonzalo would have been quite happy with the state of things now that he was almost fifty and the land was again free from the threat of invasion.

Since he'd fought Dávila back, four years ago, not a single sighting of white men had been reported anywhere in the land the white men called Yucatán. For a while after his latest victory he'd considered launching a punitive expedition against the Xiu who'd given Dávila their help. Ahau Can was especially in favor. He now ruled the town that had been Ekuneh's, and the closeness of that town to the border made him determined to exact revenge for the treason.

There had been clashes along the border, but eventually Gonzalo had chosen to avoid war, and he had convinced Ahau Can to follow his lead. The Xiu kept their distance, and so did the Can. As long as no Castilàn interfered, the balance of power within the land held fast.

But though he'd kicked them out of Yucatán, Gonzalo knew the invaders remained well established in the regions around it. Their strongest settlement was still the one Dávila and his soldiers had tried to reach four years ago: the valley of Ulùa, in the place the Castilàn called Honduras. It was rich and densely populated, especially near the mouth of the great Ulùa River. The soil was fertile and well-irrigated, the weather favorable. The Castilàn could not have hung onto a better foothold.

The valley's native inhabitants were those Miskito who for centuries had traded with Chetemal the feathers of the birds they hunted and the jade stones they gathered from their streams. Some time back Gonzalo had met in person a Miskito delegation led by the powerful chieftain Coxumba. Ties had been ceremonially renewed, gifts of friendship exchanged. Coxumba and his men were a plain lot, tribesmen instead of city dwellers, like the islanders had been once.

But they were also a fierce and shrewd people whom Gonzalo could hope would manage to resist subjugation, despite the advantages that drew the invaders to their land. It was a good thing indeed, he thought, to have allies who lived so close to the Castilàn and could report to him all that took place in Ulùa.

And it was from Coxumba that he got the news. As he stood facing the Miskito messenger who'd traveled almost two hundred miles to bring it to him, Gonzalo was too stunned to speak: Dávila was alive.

Not that Coxumba had ever been told to look for Dávila, since Gonzalo was sure he'd rid himself of his nemesis once and for all. The way the chieftain of Ulùa had found out was utterly fortuitous, the result of having to share his land with strangers. It was just that the people of Ulùa had noticed, after some time, that Gonzalo's name was the one most often mentioned among the Castilàn, and that each time it was mentioned it was followed, as surely as rain was followed by corn, by the name of someone named Dávila.

This had made Coxumba curious enough to investigate. The Castilàn had built a fort near the mouth of the river, a well-made stronghold from which they could control a good stretch of the valley. To the men and women the chieftain sent to work there he added scouts in disguise; and he'd thought worthy of reporting to his friend in the north what his scouts had discovered.

It seemed, Coxumba's messenger said, that the favorite argument among the Castilàn was about how much of the trouble they were having in pacifying Yucatán should be blamed on Gonzalo. Some said that the renegade sailor from Palos was just a hindrance that would soon be swept aside, but the majority openly attributed their misfortunes to Gonzalo's cunning and military talent.

One group of soldiers in particular had no doubts at all in this matter. If not for that bastard, they argued, they would not have been forced to abandon their settlement at Villa Real. Seven months it had taken them to reach safety, and before God they could swear that no human being had ever encountered hardships such as they had faced during those seven months.

They were starved, covered with sores, weak from fevers and wounds. They had no horses, no weapons or canoes. They'd eaten grasshoppers and snakes to stay alive. Every hour of the day and of night they'd been afraid to die, if not from hunger and disease from drowning or from an Indian's arrow. But from all these trials God had chosen to save them each time. May

God bless Captain Dávila who'd led them out of danger, the survivors said. May God keep Captain Dávila for a hundred years to come; and may God strike down to hell the traitor who'd caused them that terrible rout.

Coxumba's messenger had memorized every word of the soldiers' speech, down to the slight slurring of their Andalusian accent. It was like hearing a chorus of voices from one's faintest dreams, Gonzalo thought, voices underscored by the beating of his heart as if by an Andalusian goatskin drum.

"I see," he said with a dry throat. "And is Dávila still in Ulùa with his... survivors?" he asked.

"He was when I left," the Miskito replied. "Good," Gonzalo said simply.

As the shock slowly faded, nothing but a strange calm remained inside him. There was only one way to follow such a piece of news, only one thing to do. Choices would have brought about agitation, a clanging of inner debate. But as it was, the agitation was superfluous. He directed the messenger to where he could rest for the night, then headed straight for Nachancan's quarters.

Nachancan was, as he often was these days, alone. These days he was also in the habit of staying up late, sometimes pacing the shore of the lagoon in the dark. Gonzalo stopped away from him, away from the single torch that would reveal the look on his face.

"My brother," he said. "I came to tell you that in the morning I'm going to gather warriors and canoes. I'm going to Ulùa." Then briefly he explained why.

Nachancan stood up briskly, startled, but not by the news that Dávila was alive.

"Ah Holkan. Though you're not asking for my advice, still I must speak my mind. I have never questioned your judgment in matters of warfare, but this is a most unwise decision. I beg you to think about it before you do anything so rash."

But Gonzalo shook his head. "Twice already I left him alive.

How many times do you expect me to make the same damned mistake?" His voice was raspy with self-reproach.

"So you will not listen to reason?" Nachancan said passionately. "So you will go out of your way to seek war? We are not in danger from Dávila. He is hundreds of leagues away. If you want to fight the Castilàn, then why not in the islands? We can be attacked much sooner from the islands than from down there."

He paused for a moment, then looked at Gonzalo again. "But it's only one Castilàn you want to fight, isn't it? For that one Castilàn you would go not just to Ulùa but to the last corner of the world."

Gonzalo turned to leave. "You know me well, brother."

Nachancan raised his arm. "Ah Holkan," he warned, "you are a man obsessed. This time your obsession could get you killed." Gonzalo was already gone.

Telling Akil and Pa'ap was easy. At twenty-one, they had fulfilled all the prophecies given to them at birth and had become perfect warriors, swift as birds and skilled with every weapon. But so far they'd seen little of actual warfare, and their eagerness was like a twin flame blazing at the top of a temple. They asked to be the ones to gather the two companies he wanted, and to see that the canoes would be ready as well.

Anticipating Gonzalo's order, Akil also sent for Ah Dzan Chi. "Father," he said, "this time we won't come back without complete victory." His eyes bright with confidence gladdened Gonzalo's heart.

But Ix Na, much as she was shocked to hear that Dávila had managed to beat all the odds, repeated Nachancan's objections with almost the same words and twice the passion. Gonzalo must be mad, she said, to travel such a distance in search of his enemy.

"You seem to have forgotten what that enemy did in our own house," Gonzalo replied in his teeth.

Ix Na was outraged. "Forgotten!" she nearly shouted. "After I faced Dávila alone in my nightgown, with nothing but screaming women and cowering servants around me?"

"Then why so many doubts all of a sudden?" he nearly shouted back.

She was earnestly torn, earnestly worried. "It's just that it is so far... You will be walking into Dávila's own territory without protection. Who will back you up? On whom can you count in such a distant place?"

"Coxumba is our friend. He has men and resources. He will help."

Ix Na was silent for a while, pacing around. "I am afraid," she said then. "I am very much afraid."

He came up to her and took her in his arms. "You... afraid?" he wondered, knitting his eyebrows.

"For the first time in many years, yes." She searched his face, holding anxiously onto his arm. "Will you at least let this night pass before you make your final decision?"

He breathed out. "All right," he promised. "Because you asked. But it won't make a difference. Even as we speak Akil and Pa'ap are assembling my warriors."

"Your warriors can still be sent home," she countered. "And you can still come to your senses," she added tautly.

That night, as always before war, he slept badly. It bothered him to have heard so much hesitation when he himself had none. He felt let down, as if Ix Na and Nachancan were trying to sap his determination on purpose. He didn't want to go against them, but why were they so fainthearted? Then he cast those thoughts out of his mind and turned instead to the new task at hand, the task of making sure Dávila would never again come back to haunt his life.

Coxumba's messenger would make a good guide for the long voyage along a coast he'd never traveled, he thought. But two companies of warriors were too much, he decided. He needed only the best of his men: a thousand would be enough. In the morning he would pick the ones he knew to be the toughest and bravest.

But what about himself? he wondered a moment later. He was getting old. There were broad streaks of grey in his hair and in his beard, wrinkles in his skin; his joints ached sometimes after a swim, and after a practice session with the *hadzab* he was a little short of breath. Well, he shrugged then, if he was getting old so was Dávila. He would have to do, that was all. At most he would add one or two men to his battle guard, just to be on the safe side.

Ix Na woke up long before him. She hadn't packed his things, as always before war. She just sat waiting for him—stubbornly, he thought, since he'd already told her he wouldn't change his mind. But when he left their bed and reached for the *hadzab* hanging on the wall, she understood there was nothing more she could do or say. Quietly she began to pack, her face turned aside. The two of them went about the room picking things up, putting them down, handing them to one another in silence.

"Look," she finally let out, "you can't leave without seeing Temah first. Please stop by the temple, after all it's on your way."

He tossed his box of paint in with the rest of his things. "Wouldn't it be more fitting for the son to come see the father?" he rebutted. Then he remembered that Temah had no way of knowing he was leaving, and relented. "All right."

When it was time to go she followed him to the main gate, where Nachancan and the twins were. The goodbyes were short and awkward. Disagreement split the two who were staying from the three who were leaving, but everyone was trying hard to hide that from each other. War was bad enough without ill feelings adding to the hurt.

"Mother, please smile," Pa'ap asked.

Ix Na complied, her hands stroking affectionately the faces of her handsome grown sons. She was about to say something, but then kept her peace. Her hands went down, remained clutched together in front of her lap.

Gonzalo gave her a quick kiss on the cheek. "Make room for more than a brass medal this time," he told her gruffly. "This time I'll bring you Dávila's ears... See how *those* will look pinned to your loom."

She smiled as wanly to him as she'd smiled to the twins before. "We want news of you soon," Nachancan said, with some sharpness that betrayed his concern. "Do be careful, Ah Holkan."

Gonzalo clasped Nachancan's arm, then signaled the twins to get ahead of him in the canoe that would take them to Chetemal.

When the canoe began to glide on the smooth surface of the lagoon he cast a glance over his shoulder. Ix Na had drawn closer to Nachancan, as if seeking comfort while she was being left behind once again. She looked small under her brother's arm.

In Chetemal the two companies of warriors stood ready by the seashore, with Ah Dzan Chi watching them over. It took Gonzalo some time to pick from them the thousand men he wanted. He wanted only the strongest, the ones who could prove by their insignia that they'd killed the greatest number of enemies in battle. The others were sent back—the too young, the too old, the ones who'd recently been ill. Those who were chosen took their places in the canoes moored by the pier; fifty craft, also chosen among the sturdiest and best. Water and dry foodstuffs were loaded, weapons and paddles, and an image of the God of war was lashed to the prow of the canoe under the banner of the Can.

"Everything is in place," Ah Dzan Chi reported. "We need only your order."

"Well done," Gonzalo praised, his eyes scanning with satisfaction the finest army he'd ever led. "We leave as soon as I return."

On his way to the temple his humor soured again. What would he say to Temah? he wondered. What could he say to him now that he couldn't say to him before? It was nearly five months since Temah had left home, five months since he'd last seen him. Ix Na had gone to visit the boy every month, and Gonzalo had been content to let her bring him news of their youngest. Temah was learning much and quickly, she'd reported the last time, and Ah Kin Mo was very pleased with his pupil's progress. It had been a wise choice, the old priest said, because Temah possessed all the qualities of mind required to make a true custodian of the people's knowledge.

Good for Temah. What else did one need to know, Gonzalo grumbled to himself as he entered the courtyard of the temple of Ah Cab. A young man pointed him to where he could find Temah, to the communal room where all the temple's attendants slept. It was a dim hallway furnished simply with rows of sleeping mats lined up against the walls, vessels for the drinking water, and a few wooden stools. To think that his son had given up Xul Ha to live in this place.

At the far end of the room was someone sweeping the floor; he strode toward him.

"You!" he called loudly. "I'm looking for someone named Temah Can. They told me he was here."

Temah lifted his head, almost letting go of the broom. His eyes grew wide with surprise; Gonzalo thought he was blushing.

"Father!"

"So... there you are," Gonzalo said.

After a moment of acute embarrassment Temah put aside his broom and motioned his father to sit down.

Gonzalo groped for the nearest stool. He looked Temah up and down with a critical look. The boy seemed pale, thinner than when he'd last seen him: certainly he fasted regularly now and drew his blood regularly too—the fresh scars attested to that. He thought by contrast of the twins, of how tall and healthy they were, of what good muscles showed under their dark lustrous skin.

"Are you well?" Temah asked nervously. "Is mother well?" "We both are," Gonzalo nodded. "You could go home to see your mother, you know. She will be alone for a while. Your brothers and I are leaving."

Temah eyed his father's attire, the *hadzab* strapped to his thigh. "Leaving... for war?"

"For war," Gonzalo replied pointedly. "I am war captain of the Can. That is what I do."

Temah blushed again, but this time not with embarrassment. "And I am going to be a priest of the Can. That is what I am going to do," he said.

Gonzalo couldn't help twisting his mouth. Strong convictions were certainly a trait of character he desired in his son; but did that desirable trait have to be used against him? He glanced at the broom Temah had been plying, at the plain white robe that covered him from neck to ankles, at his uncombed hair.

"I imagine humility is to be commended in a priest," he said. "But why the abasement? Why the giving up of comfort, of one's appearance, of one's own blood? Why this constant bargaining? You give the gods something, they give you something in return... It's more like a thing of the marketplace, a deal among merchants," he scoffed.

Temah was quick to answer. "What you call a deal I call a covenant. Nothing in the world is done without a covenant. Even the jaguar must agree to be trapped by the hunter, and the deer to be chased by the jaguar, and the grass to be torn up by the deer."

His words came out in a rush of emotion, like water from a broken dam. Who knows how long he must have waited to say all this. "Everyone gives and takes, father. You give up your safety for victory. I give up my comfort for knowledge."

Gonzalo arched his eyebrows. He'd never thought about it that way. Temah had always spoken beyond his years. Could the son now be teaching the father?

"I know what you think of me," Temah went on. "I know you think I'm a coward because I'm no good with weapons, because I don't like to handle spear or bow like my brothers —"

"I never thought you a coward," Gonzalo interrupted. "But we are in danger. Each one of us must know how to fight, or we are powerless against those who want to wipe us out."

"There is more than one way to protect ourselves, father," Temah replied. "Our bodies may stay alive is we fight in war, but what of our spirit? How do we keep that alive? When the Castilàn make us forget who we are, who will make sure that we remember? When they try to force their one truth upon us, who will hold onto our truth?" His eyes welled up with passion. "You see, father, I too am a warrior."

Struck silent, Gonzalo looked at his youngest son as though seeing him for the very first time. Here was a lesson, he thought.

Everywhere the Castilàn conquered, he remembered, priests were the first they rounded up. They seemed to fear those frail old men even more than they feared warriors in the flower of their youth. They knew the power

461

that lay stored in the minds of those old men, the accumulated knowledge of a hundred centuries. On that knowledge the people fed hungrily in times of trouble, for it gave them the strength to defy cannon and sword.

He smiled, moved by the courage he was only now recognizing in his son. For a while neither one spoke. From somewhere out in the courtyard came the sound of chanting accompanied by the soft beat of a drum. Then Gonzalo reached out for Temah. Temah, who for more than five months had waited for this moment, responded eagerly to his father's embrace. The resentment that had hardened between them melted and was washed away. It was a most welcome feeling, Gonzalo thought, to finally see that the two of them had been on the same side all along.

"I will pray for you, father," Temah said then, pulling away. "For all of you, for your safety and your deliverance."

And the prayers, Gonzalo knew, would be accompanied by much shedding of blood, because Temah would make sure the Gods heard him. But now he understood. There was no difference between the blood he was about to shed in battle and the blood Temah was about to shed in the temple.

"Thank you," he said.

He stood up and with a last look at his son headed for the doorway. It was a good thing to have come to the temple, he told himself; it was a very good thing. Now he could leave. Now everything was really in place.

It was a long voyage, and not an easy one. Miles and miles of reef had to be negotiated, an underwater coral wall teeming with life, as beautiful as it was deadly. Hours were lost trying to find a breach before landing for the night, and they must land every night and set out again every morning. Squalls broke out often, churning up the waves and flooding the canoes.

Once they passed the boundaries of Chetemal, they had to deal not only with the elements but also with the disposition of the people along whose lands they traveled. No more comforting signal fires lit atop watchtowers, no more villagers welcoming them with fresh corn and fresh meat. If nothing else could be obtained from the inhabitants, a narrow strip of sand tufted with palm trees had to do for camp, and the sand and one's own mantle for bedding.

But to Gonzalo one thing only mattered, that with each day he came closer to the man he hated. With that thought in mind the endless hours in the canoe passed more quickly, the rain dried faster, dawn rose earlier. The twins shared in his high humor, and Ah Dzan Chi could be counted on to keep the warriors in line. The paddles held to a good steady rhythm, and the men's war songs rose strong above the ocean.

A few times it did occur to him that this was the longest voyage he'd ever made since he'd made the voyage to the New World. A few times he asked himself whether he was indeed going too far.

But it was too late for second thoughts, and looking back was the most barren thing he could do. He would not quit now for fear of the unknown, which he had faced so many times before. So instead whenever he felt any doubts he took up an oar and joined his men in the rowing, singing with them, drawing strength from the knowledge that none of these men had ever doubted him.

Nearly three weeks later, when his Miskito guide told him that tomorrow they would reach their destination, he called a halt and summoned the scouts. The Miskito volunteered to lead them to Coxumba and to bring back a detailed report; he was also to tell Coxumba that his Can allies had arrived and that they intended to attack the invaders.

After the guide and the scouts left in one canoe, the rest of the convoy found a safe landing place not far from a small village. Watched by curious villagers, Gonzalo and his warriors set up camp on the beach. He put the men through their paces and shared in the footrace. He'd been sitting too long, his body screamed for action. But when it came to running, no one could best Akil and Pa'ap; the Crane and the Jay seemed to grow wings and left all the others behind, their proud father first.

Spears and *hadzabs* were checked for cracks in the blades, arrows for balance. Some of the men cast lines for fish, others bartered with the villagers for corn and fruit. At night there were plenty of palm trees for the hammocks, and the beach was secluded enough for campfires. Now they just had to wait. The hours he spent waiting on the beach seemed to Gonzalo twice as long as the entire voyage. When the Miskito guide and the scouts returned, they brought nothing but bad news. Ulùa simply crawled with Castilàn. Their fort built of stones and logs was a massive fastness straddling the mouth of the river. Not a leaf could float by without being spotted.

Worse, Coxumba was no longer in a position to help. From what the guide had learned, a week earlier the chieftain, tired of the invaders' demands, had stopped sending all tribute of food and supplies. Dávila had had him arrested and now was holding him inside the fort, threatening to hang him if he didn't change his mind.

If he let all this discourage him, Gonzalo thought, all he could do was beat a hasty retreat home and let Ix Na decide when he should make war next. Or he could force the odds and seize the heady victory that luck granted only to those who dared.

He turned to Ah Dzan Chi. "Tomorrow we charge the fort," he said. "Surprise, if nothing else, should help us. Are you with me?"

Ah Dzan Chi nodded. "I am always with you, Ah Holkan." When he relayed the decision to the thousand who waited on the beach, not one man voiced the least hesitation.

While the sun dipped behind the coast Gonzalo ate with the twins, then sat with them by the fire. They didn't speak much, but the mood among them was quietly confident. After he told them he wanted a stronger battle guard, Akil and Pa'ap begged him to be chosen. He was reluctant, because that would put them at greater risk. But he could see how much that meant to them, how they yearned to be close to him. He agreed, touched by their devotion and pleased by their fighting spirit. Night fell. There was a cool breeze, and the voices of the men around him were comforting. He slept soundly.

The following day they came to Ulùa. From the canoes they could see the valley lush with *cacau* plantations and villages, the broad red river flowing past and then merging with the green of the ocean. Dávila's fort commanded all this from the best vantage point. It was impossible to enter or leave the valley without being seen. But the flat muddy delta made a good landing place. From there they could move on to the fort and, if they moved fast enough, reach it before the gunners had time to load.

This was the clear, simple order Gonzalo gave his warriors: land and make for the fort with all possible speed. Within moments the convoy spread out, fifty prows pointed toward the shore. The Miskito guide jumped off first, to meet those of his people who were crowding around in confusion, to give them the news that these warriors from Chetemal had come to free Coxumba. No one stopped to moor the canoes. The moment they touched the ground they were running toward the fort's gate.

Preceded by his battle guard, with Akil and Pa'ap flanking him, Gonzalo led the charge. He could feel his legs pumping hard on the clammy silt of the shore. He knew the guns would soon start—how soon was his greatest worry. But he heard nothing yet, and as he approached the fort he saw that it wasn't such a massive citadel after all. His thousand men could easily encircle it.

He shouted the order to surround the stronghold, and the warriors split in two like the tongue of a snake flicking out at the prey it wants to devour. Ah Dzan Chi went with the other half. A few more yards and he was gone from sight. If there was another gate in the back, it would be up to him to force an entry through that side.

Just then Gonzalo heard the first bursts of gunfire crackling from the top of the palisade. The first four or five of his warriors were hit. They fell in his path; he was forced to jump aside or he would have stumbled down with them. There was no cover between the landing place and the fort. He had noticed that and he had disregarded it.He'd never sought the safer, slower way to the gate. He'd reasoned that if enough of his men made it to it alive, the sheer push of them would break the gate down and let him in to where Dávila was. And they were almost there, so close that they could see the heads of the soldiers behind the wooden wall.

Again the muskets sounded from the fort. This time they shot into the thickest of the warriors, and bodies piled up in the smoke.

The massed warriors swayed, regrouped, stepped over the dead and wounded and ran on. Another volley was fired, another column of men was mowed down, one man upon the other; still Gonzalo's warriors charged forward, just as he'd asked them to do.

At that moment he understood that what he'd asked them to do was follow him to their deaths. He felt the weight of a great sadness pressing on his heart. He remembered Ix Na—her worried face, her somber eyes as she warned him of what might happen, of what was happening now. Everything seemed to him so very familiar, the rehearsal of a clash so many others had enacted before him and would keep enacting for years, perhaps for centuries to come.

Still, this was the death he had always wanted, and the one Ix Na wanted for him, and the one his warriors wanted for themselves. Everything was as it should be after all, he thought; and then his sadness was only because of her, because he would never see her again.

When he looked up at the main gate he saw the Castilàn soldier waiting for him, in fact for a moment he locked eyes with the man. He saw him take aim high and carefully, as if for an execution, and he understood that the soldier would not miss.

The ball took him squarely in the neck, threw him down with great force. Strangely there was no pain, only a fierce burning as he dropped his *hadzab* and fell. He wanted to speak, but there was just a hot wetness in his throat. He couldn't move, but he was aware that his hands were working against the ground, that he was struggling to get up.

The last thing he saw was Akil and Pa'ap bending toward him to shield him. They were crouched over him, holding his head, dragging him away from the gate. Good, he thought, good sons. They would not let Dávila have his body, and he was grateful.

He closed his eyes and leaned back in their arms.

BOOK FOUR

THE SURVIVORS

THIRTY-SIX

FEBRUARY 1548

Fray Lorenzo de Bienvenida woke up early that morning, as befitted a man with a mission. His mind was already at work as he left his narrow plank bed, then breakfasted on black bread and milk from the goat his Indian parishioners had given him last Christmas. Writing a letter to the Crown of Spain was no trifle, and he was only a poor friar versed in matters of the Gospel, not the technicalities of official reports. But his heart was full of sorrow, and his soul hungered for justice. For too many years this land of Yucatán, where he'd chosen to carry out his ministry, had been laid waste by hard and greedy men who called themselves Christians yet rivaled Caligula and Nero in their cruelty —

That was a good sentence, Fray Lorenzo thought. He must put that down before he forgot it, so he could use it in his letter. He reached for his quill, dipped it in the dry gourd he used as an inkwell and wrote the sentence in small cramped script on the yellowish sheet of paper. The sheet was another gift from those among his oldest parishioners who still knew the craft of turning into paper the bark of the strangler-fig tree.

Outside were the early morning noises of the *pueblo* he had under his spiritual care: Salamanca de Chetumal, near the Bay of the same name. Fifty households of Indians, all of them the personal property for life of the one Spaniard who ruled the *pueblo,* eight soldiers, a dozen donkeys, ten pigs and six sows, sundry chickens, turkeys, cats and dogs, one milk goat and a humble representative of the Order of Saint Francis of Assisi.

Fray Lorenzo remembered well what his little pueblo had looked like once, because the destruction that had been visited upon the province of Chetumal had all been accomplished within little more than a decade. It had been by far the worst campaign in the entire *Conquista.* He could liken it to something out of the pages of the Old Testament, only it had been wrought by the wantonness of men, not by the righteous anger of God.

It would be a miracle if the cornfields around Salamanca, the cornfields he blessed before each planting, would ever be able to feed more people than those they barely supported these days. Yet only a little over a decade earlier this had been a prosperous city of two thousand homes, with temples and warehouses and a market and a fleet of canoes that went to the four corners of the world.

True, the temples had been places of the wickedest worship, and the merchants had bought and sold slaves. All this had been changed, as it must be. The temples had been razed, a church had been erected, and the Indian practice of slavery had been eradicated, as had the other pernicious Indian sins of public drunkenness, polygamy and sodomy. But the pacification of Chetumal could have been accomplished, and on this Fray Lorenzo had not the slightest doubt, just as quickly without the crimes he was documenting for the Crown.

He sopped up the last of his milk with the last of his bread and put aside the bowl. He picked up his net bag and in it he packed the rolled-up piece of bark paper, the quill and the inkwell. He walked out, locked the door behind him—a simple cotton cloth hanging in the doorway no longer kept intruders out—then he slipped the key into the sleeve of his worn brown habit. His old leather sandals had long given out, but the ones the Indians made out of twisted rope were just as strong and comfortable, and he needed both strength and comfort with all the walking he had to do.

A boy driving a pig called out to him from the edge of the clearing. He waved back, recognizing Eusebio's oldest son: quick- witted for an Indian, one of his best catechism pupils. He now taught children and parents together, but for a time at first children had been taken away from their parents so they could be indoctrinated without interference from their elders.

This was a necessary thing, but not without its complications. There was for instance one girl whom he had personally taught and baptized, and to whom he'd told to inform about cases of idolatry she might find among her people. This she had done, as she was a sweet and obedient soul; only, the idolaters she'd found out were her own parents, and they got very angry at her, threatened and beat her.

Caught between her duty to God and her duty to her parents, the girl hanged herself. Well, Fray Lorenzo sighed, such were the difficulties that must be expected when bringing a new land into the fold of the one true faith.

He took the narrow footpath that led into the jungle. It wasn't really a jungle anymore, he thought with relief, or at least not the wilderness he'd had to brave a decade before. War had done much to tame it, along with the need to build proper roads where horses and carts could pass, on occasion even the coach that might bring a bishop or a *hidalgo* to these backwaters of civilization. The fire ants were still there, he noticed, skipping out of their way, and their sting was as bad as ever.

The visit he would pay today he had put off for months, in fact it was the last he needed to make. The two he wanted to see lived outside the *pueblo,* on a piece of land that nobody had ever claimed and on which they'd squatted for years.

The woman, Maria, was very old—sixty-four, or so he'd been told. He saw her often enough at Sunday Mass, although she only took Communion once a year, the strict minimum required by the Church. She had made her living weaving on her loom, until her eyesight had failed; but her memory had remained as keen as a girl's, so she would be valuable in recounting for him the events he sought to put down on paper for the Crown.

Her son, Juan, was thirty-one and a corn farmer. He was rumored to be a sorcerer or diviner, who practiced his arts on the sly. The people of the *pueblo* said he could cure diseases with his chanting and forecast lucky and unlucky days the way it had been done once, because Juan had once been a priest of his people. Those who sought his help paid him sometimes two, sometimes four Spanish coins, depending on how difficult was the cure or the forecast.

This bothered Fray Lorenzo very much; in fact the other reason why he was going to see Juan and his mother was to find out whether such rumors were true. Practicing the ancient superstition was a very serious offense, for which one could be burned at the stake, as so many had been. He knew these Indians were a tough, stubborn people who found it hard to let go of the old ways.

They could be quite deceitful, too. He himself when he was younger and more inexperienced had been duped often enough by their craftiness. Before he learned their language well, for instance, one of his flock would tell him right in church that he was praying to God in his own tongue, while all the time he was reciting instead the heathen incantations to the idols that his forefathers had taught him. One must be ever watchful of the Devil, Fray Lorenzo reminded himself, for the Devil too is ever watchful.

The footpath grew narrower as it went, and the heat of the morning more pronounced. Let's hope for rain soon, Fray Lorenzo prayed, since nothing could be accomplished in this land if the Lord didn't send down the rain.

Of course the most intriguing thing about the two people he was going to see was their past. To all the Indians he had baptized in Salamanca he'd had to give Christian names; but these two had come to him with their own family name already in place. So he had decided to let them keep it; it might be that of a traitor, but it was as proper a Spanish name as the one he himself bore. Maria and Juan Guerrero were a well-known pair, the widow and the only surviving son of the most notorious man in the New World.

What a strange man that had been, Fray Lorenzo mused as he trotted on the path through the jungle. Deluded by Satan, wholly seduced by his infernal lies, a lesson for all Christians to behold. The people of Chetumal held on to his memory as though he'd been a great warrior and a gallant man, but to the Spaniards the renegade sailor from Palos was an embarrassing chapter they'd just as soon forget.

When he'd finally died, down there in Honduras, it had been like the end of a nightmare, the friar recalled. Captain Alonso Dávila had been so relieved to learn the traitor was dead that he had taken down the day and the month and the manner of his death, something few captains ever bothered to do with fallen enemies. Many a nobleman of Spain had died in the New World in circumstances no one could remember; but everybody in Spain and in the New World knew when, where and how Gonzalo Guerrero had finally met his fate: on the first of August of the year of Our Lord 1536, in the Valley of Ulùa, of a musket ball that had nearly detached his head from his neck.

That day had also marked one of the most disastrous defeats for the Indians. After the guns had done their part, Dávila had led a charge of horsemen and pikemen out of his fort; of the thousand hand-picked warriors who'd attacked the fort, only about eighty managed to run back to the canoes left near the mouth of the river and survive.

Guerrero's painted, half-naked body had been positively identified by the beard he wore, right before it was spirited away from the battlefield, which had deprived Dávila of the pleasure of hanging it from the beam of his main gate until the rain and the birds did their work upon it. Nobody knew what had become of it after it had disappeared, but some said it had been buried in the native fashion, with a funeral worthy of a great Indian lord. Not that all this mattered; having been automatically excommunicated the moment he'd refused to return to Spain, Gonzalo Guerrero now burned forever in Hell with the rest of the damned.

With all these things occupying his mind, Fray Lorenzo got to his destination sooner than he'd expected. The thatched hut rose just off the path, yet the dense jungle made it nearly invisible from there. It was built in the same shape and of the same materials as the commoners' homes of old; that hadn't changed and probably never would, Fray Lorenzo mused, since the Indians weren't inclined to improving their lot, as demonstrated by the fact that they'd never even used the wheel. But the vegetable garden seemed well stocked with onions and cabbage and other foodstuffs from Spain, and there was even an orange tree fighting for sunshine next to the straggling avocado bush.

Juan was cutting firewood by the side of the hut. When he saw the friar he put down his machete reluctantly, with an air of displeasure. He was dressed in white cotton trousers, white cotton shirt and rope sandals. This was the common dress of corn farmers everywhere in Yucatán; nothing fancy for sure, but at least it was decent, unlike the loincloth of yore that barely covered a man's privates and buttocks.

Fray Lorenzo had expected Juan's cool welcome, and didn't let it bother him. He knew Juan and his mother kept to themselves and went to the *pueblo* only when they had no choice. They didn't like visitors, least of all white visitors. It must be because of their kinship to a man who had turned against his own people, he reasoned, and also because of their having belonged to the aristocracy, which had lost so much more than the common folk.

"Good morning, my son," he greeted Juan, coming up to the hut before Juan had invited him to do so.

"Good morning, Fray Lorenzo," Juan answered with the same cool, detached air. He spoke Spanish with nearly no accent, Fray Lorenzo noticed, and in the manner of a person of spirit; one would have said he had a natural intelligence for the language. Fray Lorenzo wondered how much like his father Juan looked. Certainly his blue eyes were his father's, but not his glossy black hair; from what the friar had been told, Gonzalo Guerrero had red hair, like Judas the Betrayer.

Juan would have been good-looking, he mused, if not for the scars. He found something sinister in all those large and small cuts noticeable in the flesh of his cheeks, of his arms and who knows where else under his clothes. This was another great delusion these people had once; they gave their blood to their gods thinking it would please them, when only Christ's precious blood was an offering worthy of the Father, the blood He had shed on the Cross for the redemption of all mankind.

"It's a fine day, isn't it?" Fray Lorenzo said awkwardly. "Is your mother home? I would like to talk to her."

Juan resigned himself to leaving the rest of his morning chores unfinished. He picked up what firewood he'd already chopped and headed for the hut's door. "Yes, she's home."

Maria was making tortillas, like every woman at that same hour everywhere in Yucatán. She sat by the three-stone hearth, patting the moist corn dough between her hands. Her hands shook with age and her back was bent. Her braids, almost entirely white, were pinned to the back of her head with a piece of bright red cotton—a strangely vain thing for an old woman, it seemed. She was slim and bony, though not frail. In fact the bones that showed under her wrinkled brown skin suggested not mortality but strength; a hundred years from now those bones, bleached in the earth, would be as whole as they were now, as enduring as stone.

On hearing someone come in, she turned her weak eyes toward the door. "Temah?" she called. "Is that you?" she asked in Mayathan.

Juan cleared his throat. "Yes, mother, it's Juan," he answered nervously in Spanish. "There's someone else... Fray Lorenzo is here. He wants to talk to you."

Maria patted a few more tortillas in silence, a silence as hostile as Juan's look before. She knew she'd been caught committing a serious infraction when she'd called her son by his old heathen name, but she seemed careless of that, defiant. She raised her head, her filmy eyes casting about for the dim shape of the visitor.

"Do sit down, Fray Lorenzo," she eventually said with a strained, formal courtesy. Her Spanish wasn't quite as clear as her son's, but she spoke with the good manners of the high-born lady she'd once been.

Fray Lorenzo took a stool and sat down, not as close to her as he wanted to sit. He dragged another stool in front of him, and on it he put the sheet of paper, the quill and the inkwell. These preparations made Maria and Juan even more nervous; when a Spaniard came to the house of an Indian carrying recording instruments, most of the time it was for the sort of inquisition no Indian ever found to his advantage.

"Why the pen and paper, Fray Lorenzo?" Juan asked.

Fray Lorenzo understood his hosts' uneasiness and tried to allay it with a smile. "Nothing to worry about, my son. Neither your name nor your mother's will appear on this paper."

"How can we know this?" Maria said, slapping another tortilla on the griddle. "We cannot read or write Spanish. Besides, names aren't that important these days. Many a confession of idolatry is signed with just a cross-like mark. Anyone can make a cross-like mark and send an innocent person to the *auto de fé.*"

She did have a sharp tongue, Fray Lorenzo thought. He hoped her memory was just as sharp, or he would have put himself through this vexation for nothing.

"I give you my word that no harm will come to you from what I am going to write," he swore, and as proof of his oath he held up the small crucifix he wore at his neck.

Juan seemed only a bit more convinced than his mother. "But what are you going to write, Fray Lorenzo?" he wanted to know. "What could we possibly say that's worth putting down on paper?"

"This is to be read only by our king and sovereign in Spain," Fray Lorenzo said, preparing to dip his quill in the inkwell. "I intend to document the way and the manner in which his subjects in this land are abused by the men he sends to rule it."

Maria squeezed her eyes toward the griddle, waiting for the tortilla to brown. "I see," she said. "And will this be the first time our king receives such a letter?"

Fray Lorenzo didn't catch the sarcasm in her voice. He shook his head with genuine grief. "Unfortunately not. Many members of the clergy have complained to him about the conditions in Yucatán."

"Then perhaps he should have the clergy rule Yucatán," Maria said, plucking the tortilla from the griddle between thumb and forefinger.

Again the friar didn't catch the mockery in her reply. "Then will you help me?" he said. "Will you tell me what you have witnessed?"

Maria grinned. "One piece of paper isn't enough for what I have witnessed, Fray Lorenzo. Maybe that is why my eyes have filmed over." She stacked the tortilla on top of the others she'd already cooked, set a bowl of chili sauce next to the stack. "Eat, Juan."

"Well," she said a while later, "where should I start then, Fray Lorenzo? What sort of abuses would you like to begin with? Murder? My brother Hun Halal Nachancan, who was the head of this province. He was captured in battle by the Xiu, who gave him to the Spaniards. The Spaniards promised to spare his life, then hanged him as a rebel. The Xiu would have given them also his son Ahau Can and my twins, Akil and Pa'ap. But Ahau Can had already died in that battle, and my twins had the good sense to kill each other instead."

She spoke in an animated way yet without any passion, as if just in a hurry to go over a long list.

"Rape? An everyday occurrence. Bird Woman—"

"Mother," Juan put in.

"Ah, yes, my son, you're right. She no longer sings like a lovely bird... I meant Catalina. You do know her, Fray Lorenzo. She lives in the *pueblo,* but comes to see us often. A Spanish soldier took her from her husband Ah Dzan Ch.... Diego, I mean. When he returned her, the soldier 'paid' for her with a cheese. He wanted their daughter, too, but Diego fought to keep the girl and was blinded in one eye by the Spaniard's knife."

While she spoke Fray Lorenzo wrote everything down in his small cramped script. He dipped his quill in, shook off the excess drops of ink, made the tip of the quill rustle and squeak on the sheet of bark paper. Maria's voice was relentless.

"When the Spaniards first came into Chetemal, some years after my husband died, they divided us among them as is their custom and used us as burden-bearers, men and women alike. We were made to follow them through the jungle where they wanted to go. We were tied together with a chain, so if one of us —"

She was interrupted by a fit of cough that convulsed her viciously, as Juan bent toward her to hold her. But she gestured to him that she was all right. She sucked her breath in and went on.

"If one of us became too weak to walk on, the soldiers just cut off the head of that person, so as not to waste time while traveling. And if the children couldn't walk as fast as their parents, they too were killed on the spot to avoid delays."

Fray Lorenzo kept writing fast. A look of great pain was on his face. It seemed as though he had to force himself to put down what he was hearing. When Maria mentioned the children, his hand stopped for a moment. His head sagged, then he nodded to Maria to go on. In all this Juan kept eating his morning meal; his eyes were distant and blank, as if he were hearing nothing, or as if he were past catching the meaning of what he heard.

"Because we had to work for the Spaniards," Maria continued, "no one was left to tend the cornfields or carry out trade, so there was famine and starvation. Obsidian Blade, who was my brother's son, became ill because of the lack of food and died of his illness. His mother... I don't know what became of his mother. She and her other son were separated from us, we never saw them again."

Another fit of cough forced her to stop for a moment. Fray Lorenzo wrote in a hurry, to keep up with her words.

"To amuse themselves the soldiers tied squashes around the feet of the women and threw them into the lagoon. They tied men and women to stakes, and cut the breasts off the women and hands, noses and ears off the men." The most violent fit of cough yet jarred her old body, forcing her to hold onto her son's arm for strength.

"Enough now, mother," Juan said, worried. "You've talked enough, you've remembered enough."

"No," she rasped. "One last thing. The names of the two who did all this, or who did nothing while others did."

Fray Lorenzo looked up, surprised. "You remember their names too? That is very good," he said. There was one small corner left on his sheet, but it was enough.

Maria gathered her breath in. "Gaspar and Alonso Pacheco. Uncle and nephew, the worst of the worst. They liked the *garrote* especially, and they liked to do their own killing with it."

Fray Lorenzo wrote down the two names. Then he stopped, looking at the full page before him. His eyes welled up, and he shook his head.

"Such is the justice rendered in this land," he murmured. "Thank you, Maria," he said then, rolling up his piece of paper and putting it back into his net bag. "I see you have suffered. But I promise you that this suffering will not be forgotten," and he reached out to touch her hand with heartfelt sympathy. Maria seemed startled by the touch. She was gasping for air.

"Rest now, mother," Juan begged her.

"Yes," she breathed. She let Juan help her to her hammock.

She lay down, looking very tired.

"You know, Fray Lorenzo," she said after a while, "even if the king never reads your letter, it was good just to have it all come out." She shut her eyes. After a while she seemed to be sleeping.

Fray Lorenzo got up and headed for the door. "Has she been ill for long?" he asked Juan who was coming behind him.

"The cough gets worse every day," Juan replied grimly. "And... don't you do anything for it?" Fray Lorenzo asked.

"They say you know certain ways of old..."

Juan understood all too well what the friar wanted. But he didn't blink; instead a strange glint came into his eyes.

"The old ways were wicked and evil. We are in Christendom now," he said with much conviction. "The only way I know is the one you taught me, to pray to the Holy Virgin Mary." He pointed at something on the wall of the hut. "There She is, Fray Lorenzo. We never forget to offer Her flowers and a candle."

Fray Lorenzo turned around. It was a small altar, and it did hold flowers and a candle. But the statue on it was like an eerie reflection seen through layers of deep water. Her smooth brown skin was Indian; her bare feet, her sensuous limbs were Indian. She was wrapped in a piece of beautiful cloth woven in designs of hummingbirds, butterflies and other Indian symbols; she wore a crown of twelve paper stars around her head and a paper half-moon curving under her feet. The thin wooden cross stuck in her fist seemed to have been tacked on as an afterthought. It was Ix Chel, dressed to look like the Mother of Heaven. Fray Lorenzo's mouth gaped open.

Juan was staring him right in the eyes. He brought his right hand to his forehead to cross himself. It was a slow and careful gesture, like that of a true believer; but as his arm went up Fray Lorenzo could see the scars in it, and he could swear that some of those scars were as fresh as the *plumeria* buds on the altar.

For a moment Fray Lorenzo didn't know what to do. Like Maria before when she'd called her son by his old heathen name, Juan seemed fearless and defiant, as if throwing down a challenge. He would still look that way if he were standing at the stake, the friar thought—and the stake was where Juan Guerrero belonged, because he had once been a priest of his people and he was still a priest of his people.

Then he looked again at Juan and tried to smile, knowing he had been beaten. So he would have to let this blatant defiance lie, he told himself; so he would be played for a fool after all. He knew that not even the shrewdest inquisitor would ever be able to prove a charge of idolatry against these two clever survivors; not unless he could lay bare their very minds, storm their last and most impregnable stronghold.

He walked out. "Goodbye, my son," he said. "Take care of your mother."

This time Juan smiled back, a wry little smile. "Goodbye, Fray Lorenzo."

Fray Lorenzo walked out of the hut and took the path that would take him back to his little *pueblo* of Salamanca de Chetumal. As he was walking he understood something he could never put in his letter to the Crown, something he would have to live with for the rest of his years without anyone else's knowing.

Yes, he thought, Spain may have conquered these people in their bodies. She may have seized their land, razed their cities, destroyed their temples. But after all that had been done to them, after the hangings, the rapes, the tortures, the starvation, even after their near extinction as a people, deep down in the secret of their souls they still remained unconquered.

AFTERWORD

With the exception of those characters listed as fictional, all the men and women in this story are real, and the events are reconstructed from eyewitness accounts. All Maya customs and beliefs of the historical times that I describe come from the best of all historical sources, the writings of Fray Diego de Landa. In the cases where de Landa gives no information I have adopted the anthropologist's method of "upstreaming"—tracing Maya customs and beliefs of the present time to the historical past, where it is reasonable to assume that they originated.

Throughout the story I have used entire sentences taken verbatim from the various sources. These include the words of Gonzalo's refusal to Jerónimo, the content of the letters sent to him by Cortez and by Montejo, the answer he wrote with charcoal on the back of Montejo's letter, and Nachancan's defiant response to Dávila's ultimatum to surrender.

The part of the story that I had to fill out with imagined but plausible facts, because the actual facts aren't mentioned in any chronicle, is how Gonzalo managed to escape from Ah Kin Cutz to Nachancan, and how he rose to become Nachancan's war captain. It is known, however, that the escape to Nachancan was engineered by Gonzalo and not by others.

Jerónimo's life story as Cortez's interpreter is well documented. The incident of the warriors threatening to use him as a practice target is taken from Jerónimo's autobiographical narrative, as is his temptation by the girl on the beach, his adventurous rescue by Cortez, and his crossing of the Yucatán Channel in the leaky canoe. Jerónimo, however, may have embellished facts to his advantage.

Gonzalo never wrote a personal narrative. Most historians of his time, however, mention his story; he was, after all, the most wanted man in the New World. The best account of his captivity is found in the most reliable of the chronicles of the conquest of Mexico, the *Historia Verdadera de la Conquista de la Nueva España* written by Bernal Díaz, who was there in person with Cortez, Aguilar and Malinche.

Malinche, also known as Doña Marina, was the Native woman who made the opposite choice, siding with the invaders and helping Cortez by translating Jerónimo's Mayathan into Spanish.

Historians have interpreted Gonzalo's refusal to return to the Spaniards in ways that are more or less sympathetic according to the historian's bent of mind. Bernal Díaz, who is only repeating verbatim Jerónimo's words, attributes the refusal to Gonzalo's shame of his appearance—tattoos, pierced ears, etc. That seems like a laughable reason for a man to put himself in the position of traitor to his people. Others have said that he was under the thumb of his Maya wife; again, quite a flimsy excuse for such a profoundly life-changing choice. To Robert Chamberlain he is a "strange and bizarre Spaniard"; to Walter Morris he is a "remarkable man"; to yet others his choice to defend his adopted people shows "gallantry."

The people of Mexico, however, have no doubts as to what Gonzalo Guerrero is to them: *"el Padre del Mestizaje,"* the Father of the Mestizo People. These are the people of mixed European and American ancestry (America as in American continent); the Mestizo are therefore all the people who now inhabit the Americas. A life-size statue near Tulum where Gonzalo lived depicts him in a heroic stance, bearded, wearing native garb, carrying a spear and surrounded by his Maya wife and the three beautiful children he refused to leave. The statue is dedicated to The First European-American Family. There were of course many Spaniards who had children by Native women before the American mainland was discovered; but these unions did not have the status recognized as an established family in an established society. The first Mexican was Gonzalo's first-born, not the son of Hernando Cortez the oppressor and of Malinche the collaborator. The Mexicans are not, as some have called themselves, *todos hijos de la chingada,* all children of a whore.

In the vicinity of Tulum archaeologists have discovered the grave of an adolescent male having mixed physical characteristics of European and Maya descent. The grave predates the arrival of the Spaniards. If we want to stretch the import of this discovery, there is no excluding that the dead adolescent might be the child of Gonzalo and a Maya woman (who would not be, however, my fictional character Kanalsin). The adolescent was not buried with the customary grave goods, but doesn't show indication of having died in sacrifice. In the main temple of Tulum there is also the mural depiction of an animal that has been identified as a horse. The mural depiction also predates the arrival of the Spaniards; again, there is no excluding that it was Gonzalo who described the horse to the Maya of Tulum before horses were brought in.

Fernando de Oviedo, who wrote his chronicle a century after the events, insists that Gonzalo must have been poorly indoctrinated in the Catholic faith, which led me briefly to think that perhaps he was one of the many persecuted Jews for whom the Inquisition was established. If so, however, his refusal to return to the Spaniards would indicate only and again that, whatever his faith may have been, his allegiance to his adopted people was stronger than his allegiance to his faith. Another point of debate is Gonzalo's literacy.

Jerónimo's literacy is explained by his holy orders, but Gonzalo was a common sailor. Historians have wondered, as I have, about his ability to read and write at a time when illiteracy was the norm not only among commoners but often among their high-born captains as well. If anything, it shows Gonzalo's departure from the norm in one more remarkable way.

No chronicler, however, has any doubts as to Gonzalo's free will in his choice to stay with the Maya. Although his answer to Montejo would seem to suggest that he's staying under duress, it is clearly a lie, laced with what historians have called a fine sense of irony—sarcasm, in fact. Earlier Gonzalo had said to Jerónimo that he was a "chief"; and indeed a slave, no matter how valuable, would have never been allowed to marry a woman of such high rank and great wealth.

Of this woman who helped operate Gonzalo's assimilation precious little is known, including her name, which some say was Zazil Ha. I gave her the name of a famous woman in the Maya Book of the Bacabs. I also chose to make her Nachancan's sister rather than his daughter, since the sources only speculate that she was his daughter. She comes to the fore only once in Bernal Díaz's *Historia*, and that is when she throws Jerónimo out of her house.

Her intervention was so memorable to Jerónimo and to Bernal Díaz that both men relate her precise words and actions. This told me that she knew who she was and could make herself heard in a decidedly male-oriented society; that she was fiercely attached to Gonzalo and afraid to lose him; and finally that she was not cowed by a white man, because when Jerónimo comes to her house he is no longer a slave, yet a slave she calls him contemptuously, as if to emphasize how Jerónimo could never rise among her people while her warrior husband had progressed from slave to the highest military rank in the land. This single intervention gave her to me as a formidable, unforgettable woman.

As for the letter sent to the Spanish Crown by Fray Lorenzo de Bienvenida, the text is also transcribed verbatim from Fray Lorenzo's own writing. The only advocates for the Indigenous peoples were the Franciscan and Dominican friars, who witnessed the atrocities first-hand and who had nothing to gain by fabricating lies. Some call the crimes against humanity committed by the Spaniards in the Americas *"la leyenda negra,"* a denigrating legend, but these crimes are no legend.

In the chronicles of the clash between the Europeans and the Natives of the North American continent, tales of white captives who sided with their captors abound. In the great majority of such cases the captives were children under sixteen, easily adapted by virtue of their age alone. For an adult male to survive first, and to be totally integrated second, was extremely rare; even more so to remain integrated to one's death. North American captives wavered all their lives between sides, often painfully so. Gonzalo made his choice as a grown man, of his own free will, and forever.

It's interesting to speculate what would have happened if Gonzalo had been captured forcibly by the Spaniards after he refused to return to them. Quite possibly he would have been tortured to reveal all he knew, in which case he would have either broken down and revealed all he knew or he would have died under torture refusing to reveal anything he knew. As it was, it's hard to downplay his role in the historical events. The places where he lived and fought were the ones that held out longest against the Spaniards, and the last to surrender; and while there are no longer people in Mexico who can call themselves Aztecs, there are still thousands of people who can call themselves Maya.

One of the fondest hopes of our age is that we might encounter beings from another world in the universe. If such an encounter would ever take place, it would duplicate on a global scale the first contact between Europeans and Indigenous peoples that began with the Age of Exploration. Should these beings from another world be technologically inferior to us, we would find ourselves in the position of 15th-century Europeans facing the Natives armed with steel and guns. On the other hand, should these beings be technologically superior to us, we would be the Natives confronting another civilization armed only with arrows and stone.

For my part, I would wish that I would never be forced to choose sides; and I would wish that in bringing two worlds together some other way could be found instead of repeating the past that was visited—and is being visited still—upon the Maya, the Aztecs, the Inca, the Taino, the Caribs, the

Yanomami, the Kayapó, the Aleut, the Inuit, the Iroquois, the Cheyenne, the Lakota, the Zulu, the Arapesh, the Koori, and too many other fellow human beings.

CHARACTERS

(in Yucatec Maya 'x' is pronounced 'sh' and all words are accented on the last syllable)

HISTORICAL

- ❖ Gonzalo Guerrero (Ah Holkan)
- ❖ Gonzalo's wife: Ix Ahau Na, Ix Na (Maria Guerrero)
- ❖ Gonzalo's sons: Akil, Pa'ap, Temah (Juan Guerrero)
- ❖ Jerónimo de Aguilar
- ❖ Captain Valdivia
- ❖ Captain Valdivia's crew

- ❖ Ah Kin Cutz, True Man of Tulum
- ❖ Nachancan, True Man of Chetemal
- ❖ Flint Knife, True Man of Cochuah
- ❖ Ah Yuntun, True Man of Ecab
- ❖ Mok Kouoh, True Man of Chanputun
- ❖ The Xiu, lords of Manì
- ❖ Coxumba, *cacique* of Ulùa
- ❖ Hatuey, *cacique* of Hispaniola
- ❖ Motecùzoma Xocoyotzìn (Montezuma)
- ❖ Hernando Cortez
- ❖ Melchor, Cortez's interpreter (Nakehya's son)
- ❖ Francisco de Montejo, Adelantado of Yucatán
- ❖ Alonso Dávila
- ❖ Alonso de Ojeda
- ❖ Fray Lorenzo de Bienvenida
- ❖ Gaspar and Alonso Pacheco
- ❖ An anonymous woman of Chetemal killed with the dogs by Alonso Dávila for resisting rape

FICTIONAL

- ❖ Kanalsin
- ❖ Citam
- ❖ Ix Chebel
- ❖ Ah Yax Ceh
- ❖ Paichè
- ❖ Ah Balam Tun
- ❖ Ahau Can
- ❖ Ix Sak Kukul (White Feather)
- ❖ Ix Lolkin
- ❖ Obsidian Blade
- ❖ Natohcan
- ❖ Ekuneh
- ❖ Nakehya
- ❖ Ah Dzan Chi
- ❖ Tu Manìk
- ❖ Ah Kin Mo

❖ The Woman of Cochuah

BIBLIOGRAPHY

* Arciniegas, Germán. Caribbean, Sea of the New World
* Blom, Franz. The Conquest of Yucatán
* Butterfields, Marvin Ellis. Jerónimo de Aguilar, Conquistador
* Chamberlain, Robert. Conquest and Colonization of Yucatán
* Clendinnen, Inga. Ambivalent Conquests: Maya and Spaniards in Yucatán
* Collis, Maurice. Cortez and Montezuma
* De Landa, Diego. Relación de las Cosas de Yucatán — Report on All Things Pertainingy to Yucatán

❖ De Las Casas, Bartolomé. La Devastación de las Indias — The Devastation of the Indies

❖ De Oviedo, Gonzalo Fernandez. Historia de las Indias — History of the Indies

❖ Del Castillo, Bernal Díaz. Historia Verdadera de la Conquista de la Nueva España — True Story of the Conquest of New Spain

❖ Dianond, Jared. Guns, Germs and Steel

❖ Galeano, Eduardo. *Memory of Fire*

❖ Heard, Norman. White Into Red: A Study of the Assimilation of White Persons Captured by Indians

❖ Johnson, William Weber. Cortez Conquering the New World

❖ La Fay, Howard. The Maya, Children of Time

❖ Mitchell, James. The Conquest of the Maya

❖ Morley, Sylvanus. *The Ancient Maya*

❖ Morris, Walter. *Living Maya*

❖ Neruda, Pablo. *Canto General*

❖ Tedlock, Dennis. Translation of the *Popol Vuh, The Maya Book of Counsel*

❖ Roys, Ralph. The Indian Background of Colonial Yucatán

❖ Stuart, George. The Mysterious Maya

❖ Todorov, Szvetan. The Conquest of America: The Problem of the Other

❖ Vaillant, George. *Aztecs of Mexico*

❖ Von Hagen, Victor. La Tierra Del Faisán y del Venado — The Land of the Wild Turkey and of the Deer

❖ Von Hagen, Victor. *World of the Maya*